"Wil   ghter of
                                              trilogy

"Brig   . It's a
fant   ntem-
por   Ages
12-   eview

"Br   iend-
shi   the
sin   de-
scr   the
no   here
jus   and
sus   t to
sp

                                      eries

"F

"Brignull develops story and characters slowly—long, luxurious sentences balancing the magic and the mundane expertly and building the world of the witches."   —*Kirkus Reviews*

"Irena Brignull's *The Hawkweed Prophecy* is a book of wicked, beautiful magic. Compulsively readable and delightfully gritty, one does not mess with these Hawkweed witches."
          —Kendare Blake, author of the *Anna Dressed in Blood* series and *Three Dark Crowns*

"Wise, weird, a touch evil, and totally charming, Irena Brignull's tale of magic in our time is as rich and complicated as sisterhood. From the first page, I felt drawn into a modern classic."
          —Anna Godbersen, author of *The Luxe* and *Bright Young Things* series

"*The Hawkweed Prophecy* is as beautiful inside as it is out . . . Irena Brignull's writing is seamless. . . . The atmosphere is dark, haunting, chilling with a dash of sunshine and fairytale magic."
          —Never Judge a Book by Its Cover

"I loved this book! Irena has created such a beautiful complete world—our world, and nestled within it, a simmering world of magic. *The Hawkweed Prophecy* has everything: friendship, desire, delicious earthy magic, secrets and spells, and at its center, the wonderful young Poppy, on a journey of self-discovery."
          —Karen Foxlee, author of *Ophelia and the Marvelous Boy* and *A Most Magical Girl*

The
Hawkweed
Legacy

Also by Irena Brignull:

The Hawkweed Prophecy

The Hawkweed Legacy

IRENA BRIGNULL

NEW YORK   BOSTON

Hachette Books
Hachette Book Group
1290 Avenue of the Americas, New York, NY 10104
hachettebooks.com
twitter.com/hachettebooks

Originally published in hardcover and ebook format by Perseus Books: August 2017
First Trade Paperback Edition: August 2018

Hachette Books is a division of Hachette Book Group, Inc. The Hachette Books name and logo are trademarks of Hachette Book Group, Inc.

The publisher is not responsible for websites (or their content) that are not owned by the publisher.

The Hachette Speakers Bureau provides a wide range of authors for speaking events. To find out more, go to www.hachettespeakersbureau.com or call (866) 376-6591.

Print book interior design by Jack Lenzo.

ISBNs: 978-1-60286-337-8 (trade paperback); 978-1-60286-314-9 (hardcover); 978-1-60286-315-6 (ebook)

Printed in the United States of America

LSC-C

10 9 8 7 6 5 4 3 2 1

FOR MY MOTHER AND FATHER,
VOULA AND TONY

PROLOGUE

S he had been sleeping for months now, stirring only rarely to nibble on nuts and seeds. During her hibernation, she'd hardly woken from the dreams that had drifted her so far from the darkness of the hole in which she lay. But today she felt a shift in the temperature and a warmth on her back. It was spring.

The woman uncurled her drowsy limbs and crawled out from the roots of the tree. The colors were so vivid they hurt her eyes. She blinked, struggling to adjust to the light of day. When she'd taken to her earthy bed, it had been winter, and nature had slumbered with her, suspending all production. But now she could see grasses growing green and tall, and yellow daffodils summoning the sun. The beginnings of blue bathed the sky. The blackthorns blossomed white and she knew the cherry trees would follow soon with their pinks. The woman stretched her arms up high, then wide, relishing the space, lifting herself up onto her tiptoes and tilting her face to the vast expanse above. She breathed in the fresh air, long and deep, exhaling the dank soil scent of the burrow that had entered her lungs and lodged there.

Betony was her name—this she could remember, though nothing else of her younger life. She sensed she had not been born here. She imagined some place far afield, another darker wood, but she could not picture any family there. Someone must have taught her the words that came to her lips and the knowledge that filled her mind. How to forage and plant, to store and cook, to survive. She hadn't always been alone, that was for sure. Yet, for seventeen years, she had lived this way. On the banks of rivers, in the thickets, pulling her barrow of seeds and clippings, avoiding the people who stared at her and kept their distance.

The lake was cold. Its water was refreshing to drink but bracing to wash with. Betony's skin prickled as she stepped into the shallows. A speckled fish slid silently around her, its scales slippery on her skin.

"Hello, old friend," she croaked, sounding like the toads who were leaping onto lily pads to watch through bulbous eyes.

Then, from the lake, appeared another familiar face, this one with black nose, long teeth, and whiskers. It rolled onto its back and waited for her to tickle its tummy.

"Otter." She smiled, reaching out a hand to stroke its silken fur. "Now let me bathe, for I must stink."

The otter flipped and dived under the water as she began to splash herself—her legs, her face, under her arms, her belly. Her hands lingered there. This was where she felt it most—the emptiness. Not in her heart or her mind but in her middle. She felt a tear upon her cheek. Then another. She didn't know why she was crying. She just knew she had good reason. For her tears refused to be forgotten. As they hit the water, they turned to stony beads of white that sank and glinted from the riverbed below.

1

POPPY

As a bird, there had been little thought, just instinct. No yes-terdays and no tomorrows. No prophecies from the past. No visions of the future. Just the present. And it was liberating—existing in the moment, this second and only this. Poppy Hawk-weed had transformed into a swallow to seek freedom and, up there, in the endless skies, she had found it.

Her tiny wings had carried her thousands of miles, so much farther than her human legs had ever taken her. No map—just the setting sun and the night stars and the earth's pull. No company—the other swallows had left in the autumn while the weather was still mild. Without her magic, speeding her on, protecting her, she would have failed. She was certain of that. First the bitter cold of winter, then the blistering heat of the desert to contend with, as well as the constant threat of hungry predators and thunderous storms. Poppy was amazed that, each year, so many birds survived. Their migration felt far more marvelous than anything she might conjure.

The farther she'd flown, the more the endeavor had taken over all her mind and body. The world was vast and she a mere puny ball of feathers, knocked by gusts and tossed by gales and yet still flying on. So many people below—chaffs or witches, she could not tell. They looked the same from up high. So many forests, rivers, mountains, fields, so many homes to stop and live in. But Poppy had kept on going to where the other swallows had finished their journey some weeks before.

Here, in Africa, beyond the smudge of cities and smatterings of smaller towns stretched a seemingly boundless area of sloping hills and plains where animals, large and small, roamed wild. This land was unscarred by fences or electricity towers, roads or railroad tracks. There was hardly any trace of man at all. Zebras were bending their necks to sun-bleached grass. Beyond them, a vast herd of wildebeest ran, dust rising from their hooves like smoke. And, in the distance, a river curved like a reel of ribbon dropped from above.

Weak with exhaustion, Poppy began her descent. For a moment she felt she might tumble. *I can't die now,* she thought. *I've come so far. And I don't know who I am yet.* Then a breeze, warm and welcoming, came to usher her in, carrying her downward to meet this new earth.

The African insects tasted rich and spicy, and Poppy feasted on them. Then she slept, and in her dreams she became human again, with ridiculously long limbs and stubby nails, and strangely bare skin with no feathers to adorn it. Poppy writhed with the pain of this transformation, her nerve endings screaming out their protest at the assault as every vein and sinew was twisted, ripped, and elongated out of all proportion.

As her body squirmed, her mind turned with it, back to the past, back to the memories she had flown miles to forget. She was Poppy Hooper again, the baby who'd been swapped for another, the child who had grown up in the wrong home with the wrong mother, the girl who'd never fit in. Then, in her delirium, she saw Ember, sweet Ember, who had grown up in her place, in the coven in the forest, part of the Northern clan. The sky above Ember turned black, the earth froze to white, and there stood their aunt, their enemy. Raven Hawkweed had cast the spell to swap them. Her pointed face became a beak, above it beady eyes.

Poppy cried out in her sleep and Raven's body crumpled to the snow, a corpse that couldn't hurt them anymore. Into the forest Poppy drifted, through the trees, until the ground sloped sharply downward to a dell. There was Ember smiling at her, welcoming her in. At her side was Leo, his eyes dark with desire, his skin like gold. He didn't know that he had witch blood in his veins. He didn't know that Poppy loved him back. She had left him with Ember, to have a better life, away from witchcraft, away from her.

Poppy's body curled into a ball. The witches said she was a queen, but she didn't know how to be one. And she wasn't a chaff anymore. Nor a daughter, or a girlfriend, or a friend. *Who am I?* thundered the question in her head.

When Poppy awoke, she saw a boy squatting down on the red earth. He was staring at her, the whites of his eyes and his teeth shining like stars from the night of his skin. She tried to speak, but no voice emerged. The boy reached out and she flinched away from him, but it was the feathers scattered around her that he was after. He grabbed a handful and ran. Poppy watched him disappear through the yellow grasses into the haze where the light shimmered in the heat. It was only after he was gone that she realized she was naked. Too tired to care, she closed her eyes and hoped that rest might ease her aching bones.

"*Dumela.*" The word rumbled low in Poppy's ears. "*Dumela.*" It came again.

Something prodded her gently in her side. She lifted her lids just a fraction to glance at it. A dark, gnarled stick, held by a withered, crooked hand. She raised her eyes further. Above her stood a tiny woman with a white nest of hair upon a head kept aloft by a neck coiled with wooden beads. The woman smiled so wide that it filled her whole face.

"*Dumela,*" she said. Poppy blinked, and the woman translated for her in stilted English. "He-llo."

Next to her the boy, her visitor from earlier, nodded in greeting. "You are bird girl, yes?" encouraged the boy. "You are shaman?"

"I . . . I don't know."

"Witch?" asked the old lady, the smile remaining just as broad.

Poppy blinked. She didn't want to answer this. She didn't want to think of it.

Luckily, the boy spoke again. "You must come with us."

He handed Poppy a piece of cloth and her cheeks burned as she once again realized her nakedness. Awkward and slow in her cumbersomely human form, Poppy got to her knees and tried to dress herself. It was then that she noticed the stone wrapped tightly to her ankle. So long had it been tied there, through all weather, across whole continents, that she no longer felt its touch. The stone had become a part of her, just as Leo had.

"It's the heart stone," he had told her, and for a moment, Poppy let herself remember how his voice had turned soft and shy and how his cheeks had flushed as he watched for her reaction to his gift.

Poppy pulled the tunic down to cover herself.

"Thank you," she muttered to the boy without looking at him.

"You must come with us," the boy repeated. "We must keep you safe."

"From whom?" she asked instantly, her eyes scanning the landscape.

In the distance, she saw a herd of zebras grazing and a group of giraffes nibbling at treetops. There was not another human being in sight.

"You are witch." The woman smiled, holding out her hand, helping Poppy to her feet. "We wait many days for you." Then she handed Poppy her stick, and Poppy leaned on it gratefully. "You feel better soon."

Their dwelling was circular, like a clay anthill rounding out of the earth itself. On the top was a small chimney; beneath it, in the center of the room, a fire. For Poppy, it was like sitting in an oven, her flesh slowly baking. The sweat dribbled from her hair down the sides of her cheeks like warm rain and ran in sticky rivulets from under her arms. The boy gave her cup after cup of an acrid tea to drink. The liquid flowed in and out of her. The air was smoky and she was desperate to make a dash for the door and the freshness of outside, but the ache in her muscles and joints was easing and the old lady simply kept nodding for her to drink some more.

It was only in the evening, when the sun was sinking, that Poppy was allowed out. As she got up, she realized with a sudden surge of joy that she no longer felt any pain from her transformation. She was as light on her feet as the impalas springing through the bush beyond. The boy brought her an earthenware bowl of stew. Poppy ate ravenously, unaware until now of quite how hungry she was.

"Slowly," the boy told her, gesturing with his hand, and Poppy began to chew each mouthful, savoring the flavors.

"What's your name?" she asked him between bites.

"Teko," he told her.

"I'm Poppy." She scraped the last of the gravy from her bowl, then put it down next to her. Ants, bigger than any she'd seen before, immediately started scaling the sides.

"Your grandmother—is she . . . what did you call it . . . a shaman?"

Teko gestured with his hands. "Hmnn, she is more medicine-maker. And she is my mother's grandmother."

Poppy felt her eyes widen. "Your great-grandmother?"

"Yes, she is great." Teko smiled. "She is a hundred years old."

"Where's your mother?"

"She is in the city. My father, too. Where is yours?"

Poppy drew a circle in the dust with her toe. She tried hard not to picture Charlock's face and the worry that she knew would feature there. She quickly rubbed out the circle with toes streaked brown. "She's far. Across the seas."

"You have run away from home?" Teko asked.

Poppy stared into the setting sun, liking how it made everything blur. "I don't really have a home."

In the glimmering light, she saw the shape of Ember and missed her friend so badly that she had to take a breath to steady herself. Teko looked at her, then offered her a fruit she didn't recognize.

"You are here now," he said, and Poppy nodded, feeling the relief radiate out of her and mingle with the sun's rays.

"I'm here," she echoed, and the shape of Ember faded.

Poppy bit into the fruit and the juices ran down her arms.

"Mma says you are great too," Teko told her. "A great shaman. A queen."

Poppy felt the smile leave her face. "She said that?"

"She said we must look after you."

"Keep me safe?" Poppy remembered. Teko nodded. "Safe from whom?"

"We do not know. Mma can only feel the danger."

Poppy shrugged. "Well, I'm used to danger. And I'm not a queen. Not anymore."

A sour taste filled her mouth. The taste of a lie, she realized, and she took another bite of the fruit, hoping the sweetness might soften it.

The next morning, Poppy walked with Teko to fetch water from the lake. They passed a herd of antelope, their horns rising so elegantly from their pointed heads. She stopped to take in the view, relishing how utterly different it was from any of the towns she'd lived in, with their thousands of inhabitants, and from the darkness of the forest where the coven were.

"I love it here," she said, noting how unlike her it was to keep her feelings so unchecked.

"That's good," said Teko, his face lighting up with pleasure.

When they bent down at the water's edge, Teko showed her how to tilt the jugs to fill them. Farther in some elephants were wading and she could feel the weight of them in the ripple of the water against her hands.

"Leo," said Teko suddenly. "Does this mean lion?"

Poppy paused for a second, then carried on filling the jug. "It can," she replied.

"You spoke of this lion in your sleep."

"Did I?" Poppy winced. "I'm sorry."

Teko took the water jug from her and placed it next to his. "Come with me," he said, grabbing her hand so she couldn't refuse.

They walked for some time through grasses that came to their waists and then up a steep hillside. After a while Teko's hand became a comfort. There was none of the sensation or sparks she'd had with Leo, just warmth.

Suddenly Teko crouched, pulling Poppy down with him. Keeping low, they crawled up the lip of the hill until they reached the top. Poppy stared out in amazement across a valley that seemed to hold all of creation within it. There were too many different animals and birds to count. Teko pointed to a baobab tree. Beneath it, a huge lion, crowned with a sunflower mane, sat surveying his domain. The carcass of a zebra was laid out before him like an offering to a king. Poppy gasped, and Teko put a finger to his lips. The lion turned his head in their direction, his eyes searching, before he became bored and yawned lazily with a gaping jaw and giant tongue. Teko looked at Poppy and grinned.

"Leo," he said. And Poppy smiled back, the tears pricking behind her eyes.

"Thank you," she mouthed.

The lion dipped his head to his meal, and Teko tugged at Poppy's arm to leave, but she shook her head. Riveted, she watched the lion feed. If she really concentrated, she could hear its teeth crunching into bone, masticating muscle. Then she glimpsed the zebra's expressionless eye staring back at her, and into her mind another image stole. Another eye, green this time, with a black dot above the pupil. It was her own eye, blank and lifeless within her own pale face, her hair splayed out on a bed of blue. Not blue, bluebells, Poppy realized. And then the vision vanished. The face she had seen wasn't old and wrinkled. It was young. It was her face now.

"Poppy?" came Teko's voice. "We should go, yes?"

"Just a second," Poppy mumbled, unable to look at him.

She closed her eyes and took a deep breath. It was just an imagining, nothing more. A morbid, teenage notion. But she had experienced a vision once before—a glimpse into the future—and that had come true. Ember and Leo hand in hand. A couple. Even now it hurt to think of it. But this . . . surely this must be different?

"I'm sorry," Teko whispered, breaking the silence. "I thought you will like him."

"I did." Poppy turned to look at him. "I do." She tried to smile. "I don't know what came over me. It's silly."

"You were frightened," Teko told her innocently.

As she remembered the danger that he and Mma had warned of, her body started shaking and nothing could stop it. Not the walk back, not Mma's tea, not even sleep.

Poppy woke the next morning to Mma's ancient hand on her shoulder. She knew from Mma's expression that something had happened. She moved fast, hurrying outside. There, golden against the reds of the sunrise, were the cats. Lions, cheetahs, leopards, and caracals, padding back and forth, their heavy paws soft upon the dusty dirt, come in their prides—come to visit her. *Cats,* she thought, like the ones she'd left back home. The same shaped head, soft fur, triangular nose, and whiskers. The same striking eyes and padded paws and nails. Only, these creatures were so much greater and more magnificent. Poppy felt like dropping to her knees at such an awesome sight. Instead, she nodded slowly, formally, in acknowledgment. All at once, her trembling stopped. She felt the magic flutter within her, then fly through her body and out through her fingers and toes. She turned to Teko and Mma.

"Witch." She smiled proudly and held up her hands to show them the power sparkling from them.

"You are a queen," Teko whispered.

"I'm just me," she said, but for the first time the word "queen" didn't scare her.

"Still we must protect you," Mma cautioned, glancing at Teko.

Poppy shook her head. "There's no need. I can look after myself. I always have."

2

CHARLOCK

Charlock had felt Poppy's departure like the pricking of a needle on her fingertip. When she held up her hand, a drop of blood sat there, red for danger. She wiped it on her skirt before any of the sisters could see. Quietly she slipped away to search for her daughter, past the caravans, through the vegetable patches, out between the gray stone boulders, and into the vastness of the forest.

Scouring the gaps between the trees, Charlock headed for the dell where Poppy used to meet with Ember. She knew this was a special place for Poppy and hoped that she had gone to seek some comfort there. Since returning to the coven and leaving Leo with Ember, Poppy had withdrawn from her.

"You lied," she'd accused. "You knew Leo was a witch, but you made me believe I couldn't love him." Charlock had not been able to deny it. She argued that she'd been acting out of love, to protect Poppy and secure the throne for her. But Poppy would not be persuaded. "Not love," she corrected. "Ambition"—as though the two were irreconcilable.

Charlock had thought that Poppy just needed time—to adjust, to understand. She never once imagined she would run away.

Quickly, not caring whether she fell, Charlock clambered down the hill that dipped so steeply in the forest floor. She could see why Ember and Poppy loved it here. It felt like an enchanted place. A strange union of two different worlds, with old, unwanted furniture and machines becoming home to so many plants and creatures. But Charlock had no time to appreciate the curious sight of a robin sheltering on a velvet chair or mice hibernating inside a cracked and broken oven. Her eyes could only see what was missing from the scene—her child. Sinking to her knees, Charlock began to conjure a spell. There was little prospect of it working. Poppy was a queen, and if she didn't want finding, even magic might fail to locate her. But Charlock had to try.

She ripped a piece of material from her sleeve and doused it with oil from a vial that she took from her pocket. Then she gathered some sticks and hastily arranged them in a stack. Grabbing two stones, she struck one hard against the other, letting the spark ignite the cloth. With the fire lit, she put her finger inside her mouth and scratched the soft flesh there, then spat the blood onto the flames. Immediately, there was a crackle, and a twist of greenish smoke appeared. Closing her eyes, Charlock uttered a spell:

> *Blood burn, smoke rise*
> *Bracken, fern, smoke flies*
> *From the soil, to the skies*
> *Smoke coil, be mine eyes.*

The smoke spiraled upward, lifting into the air and traveling up and over the trees. The waiting was a kind of torture. Charlock tried to keep her mind focused on a sign, anything that might prove to be a clue to Poppy's location, but there was nothing but the bitter chill of the winter air and the cold dampness spreading from the earth to her knees. Then, all of a sudden but with an unmistakable force, came a wind, stinging and tangy with salt. Charlock leapt to her feet and ran.

Why hadn't she thought to look there—on the battleground by the clifftops where Poppy had celebrated her victory against the clans? Her daughter wasn't fleeing inland but out to sea. Charlock sobbed with grief and frustration all the long way back through the forest to the cliffs. By the time she reached there, she was crippled with exhaustion and gasping for breath. But only when she spied the clothes, so neatly folded by the cliff edge, did she stop. Poppy had flown the coop. She had become a bird and Charlock could never catch her now. The power of transformation was one that belonged only to the most powerful of witches. Charlock's sister, Raven, possessed that skill and, not for the first time, Charlock cursed her luck at being the weaker sibling. Her eyes scanned the skies, her hands holding back the hair that was whipped around her face by the violent gusts of air.

"Come back!" she cried, over and over, out across the ocean, knowing Poppy's wings would have already carried her too far to hear. Crouching down, she touched the clothes reverently. This was all she had left of her girl. She longed to take them with her and sleep with them beside her, but she left them there . . . just in case . . . just in case Poppy returned to that spot and needed them.

Charlock began her slow retreat home and, with every painful step, agonized over how she would explain Poppy's disappearance to the coven. How could she tell them that their queen had left them? It was unthinkable. And if the other clans found out? Charlock's breath caught in her throat. Only days before, the clans had attacked to prevent Poppy, an unknown, untrained witch, from taking the throne. Lives had been lost on both sides. Without Poppy's magic, the Northern witches could not defend themselves if the other clans sought vengeance.

When Charlock returned to the camp, she went straight to her caravan and tried everything to locate her daughter, scouring every book for every spell, searching every divination and sign. Nothing worked, not a glimmer or an inkling. Her tears tasted bitter with regret and sour with self-pity, before finally turning sweet with sorrow. At that, Charlock wiped her eyes and contrived a story to tell the sisters. She rehearsed it several times, trying different intonations and gestures to invoke sincerity. It was the tale of a young girl, exhausted by battle, who needed time to recover and prepare, to be schooled in their ways, to hone her skills so that she could be a queen truly worthy of them. For a moment, Charlock was carried away by her rhetoric and found comfort in this narrative. Having believed her own lies, Charlock knew then that the coven would believe her too, so great was the want and the need of it.

For four months, Charlock told this story and stuck to it with all her might. With every passing week, the words felt weaker. The coven's patience was wearing thin. Disappointment had turned to anger, and now suspicion was creeping in. And other clans were demanding answers, too. The witches needed a queen, not just as a figurehead but for their survival. *Like the bumblebees*, thought Charlock, as she spotted her first of that spring. The queen was the peacekeeper, the most powerful and respected witch of all, who ensured that their ways would live on for generations to come. With so many different covens scattered across the lands, she was the one who kept them united. She could sense when magic was used unwisely, when danger from chaff detection was drawing near, when enmity between the clans was escalating. Without a queen, the covens could have easily become extinct centuries ago.

Charlock summoned the coven for a meeting. When the sisters arrived, she stepped onto a stool to address them. All had come, even the mothers with babies on their hips, even the old and infirm, filling the grassy plot at the center of their camp. But now that they were gathered, most were engrossed in conversation.

"Quiet!" Charlock called. "Please, it is time to listen."

Her voice was small despite her effort and became lost in the noise of their chatter.

"Quiet!" she demanded once more, with all the volume she could muster.

Still there were murmurs from the clan. With Raven, their silence would have been instant. No one would have dared flout her sister's authority. Charlock tried to summon the withering look that Raven had so successfully adopted, but she felt only as if she were squinting.

"Listen to me!" she cried. Her voice sounded hoarse with desperation, but thankfully they hushed. "Your queen has asked for more time."

The babble bubbled up again like a broth on the boil.

"How much more time?" exclaimed one of the witches; Charlock wasn't sure who.

"We must be patient. My daughter was not brought up as one of us. She is ignorant of our customs and our ways. She must prepare herself so she can govern wisely. Surely we can give her a few more weeks?" Charlock pleaded.

One of the young witches, Kyra, stood up. This girl was strong and brave but outspoken for her years. "The other clans are getting restless," she declared loudly. "They are demanding an audience with their queen. There are troubles in the west that need her attention. Yesterday I heard a report of a feud brewing there. Could the queen not show herself, or at least receive visitors?" Kyra immediately sat down again, as was the practice for a clan gathering.

"And what about us? We need our queen too!" called out another witch.

"Stand and show yourselves before you speak," reprimanded Sister Ada.

As the oldest of the clan, Sister Ada was respected by all, and Charlock was grateful for her help, although she sensed that even her sympathy was dwindling. The chastened witch rose slowly. It was Sister Frey, her head lowered, her cheeks flushed with both shame and anger, but she spoke more softly this time.

"The longer Sister Poppy stays away, the more vulnerable we become to an attack." Immediately a murmur rose up from the crowd, but Sister Frey pressed on.

"Many are still unhappy with having an outsider rule them. They call her 'the chaff queen.' An excuse is all they need to try and take the throne for one of their own."

Charlock saw the fear spread like a sickness across the coven. Sister Frey, now sagging back down like a sack, had only said what all of them had been thinking, but still it came as a shock and caused alarm.

"They would not dare attack," Charlock declared, hoping to transmit a confidence that she did not feel. And then she lied. "In any case, our queen would return as soon as she sensed any invasion." Charlock waited to see if anyone could tell her falsehood, but, truth or not, it was what they wanted to hear, so none objected. "We have the stone, do we not?" she said, pointing to a smooth, oval stone that lay in the center of the wide, ringed plane of a tree stump. Carved into its polished gray surface were the letters that appeared by magic as one queen died and the title passed to another. "Poppy Hawkweed—that is the name written there," Charlock reminded them. "No one can dispute that."

Sister Martha was the next to stand and speak. "But Poppy is not here, Charlock," she stated simply. "The new queen should have been the one to collect the stone from the old queen's coven, to bring it home, to put it in the center of the tree, to say the spell, to make her vows. Instead, she let her mother fetch it and it lies there waiting for her—just as we do."

"She will come home. And soon," promised Charlock. "And when she does the tree will grow back around the stone until it towers over all the others, with the queen's name at its heart." The sisters gazed at the stump, letting themselves imagine this glorious sight. Charlock grasped the moment while they were open to persuasion. "Please," she urged. "Many of you are mothers, so I know you understand. My daughter may be powerful but she is young. She will return soon. I promise."

Sister Morgan got slowly to her feet. Looking all around for the clan's unspoken approval, she then answered on their behalf. "We will wait, Charlock. But tell your child to hurry home. A barren throne is a fecund curse."

After the clan dispersed, Charlock caught up with Kyra and beckoned her to her caravan.

"How is my niece?" she asked. Out of all the clan, Kyra cared for Sorrel the most.

"She is still far from her old self. Since she awoke from her long sleep, she has become soft. And she is so . . . so joyful all the time," Kyra said, as if this were a failing. "I think the potion that harmed her has left its mark upon her mind."

"She still thinks it was the Eastern clan who poisoned her?"

"She does."

Charlock let her eyes close for a moment. It was she who had given Sorrel the potion. She could hardly believe she had committed such a wicked act. She hadn't devised the potion. Nor had she brewed it. That had been Raven's doing, intending it for Poppy. But Charlock had dealt it. She had discovered Raven's treachery—that she had taken Poppy away from her at birth—and her fury had possessed her. She had lost all sense of self, of love, of decency and she had hurt her own niece. If that wasn't dreadful enough, the knowledge of this had killed Raven. And now Charlock wore her guilt like a corset, the strings ever tightening, making it hard for her to breathe.

She opened her eyes. "When Poppy's back, I will tell Sorrel everything. But not before." Kyra nodded, but Charlock sensed the girl's reluctance. "It is for all our sakes. Sorrel is happy now. Recovered. The story of what led to her mother's death could break her. And if the clans sense more trouble . . . "

Charlock didn't have to finish. Kyra was nodding and getting to her feet. "You are right, Sister Charlock, and I will do as you say. But we have had enough of secrets here."

Charlock held Kyra's gaze until the girl blinked and looked away. Charlock could not allow some young upstart to challenge her so. The sisters were suspicious of Poppy's whereabouts, but none had yet confronted her with their misgivings. She would dearly love to confide in one of the elders, but how? If it was inconceivable four months ago, it was impossible now after all her pretense.

Kyra picked up her pail as she left and Charlock followed her out. The sisters were all at work, but there was a somber mood in the air. Charlock had hoped the arrival of spring would lift their spirits. It was not to be. There had been little celebration at the changing of the seasons—no feasts or entertainment this year. Today, the sky was the bluest it had been since last summer and the trees were green with bud, yet inside their stoned encampment, it still felt like winter. Only Sorrel had tossed the shawl from her shoulders and wore a warm expression on her face.

Charlock turned her eyes to the sky and looked for birds. The wheaters had arrived first, then the warblers and the sand martins. The swallows should be only a few weeks behind. Charlock hoped that Poppy would be with them, but hope was not enough.

She had to act. She had to find a way, however risky, however forbidden, to bring Poppy home. All she lived for was to see her daughter again. But Poppy wouldn't come back for her. And she wouldn't come back for the coven. There was only one for whom she might return—the boy. And for that to happen, Charlock would have to make amends for other wrongs. She'd have to revisit her past, dig up old secrets, and undo the damage done.

Late that night, when all the lamps were dimmed and the candles snuffed, Charlock put a cloak around her shoulders and, hood over hair, she glided through the darkness, out into the throng of trees. She trod as light as the muntjac deer that roamed nearby. When she emerged from the forest and on to the heather, she looked up at the sliver of moon. She thought of Poppy looking up at that very same moon and it gave her some solace. Leo, too, standing beneath its low light. And then she thought of Betony. Her friend of old. The friend whom she had tried so hard to forget but now was traveling in search of. And Charlock's step quickened and her skirts swished as she hastened on her way.

3

LEO

Leo didn't even check whether the coast was clear before he took them. His hand just slipped from his pocket to the shelves and back again, so casual, so relaxed. Only when he reached the door did he act the thief and run. He did this for the thrill that came from fear—the fear of being chased and being caught. And even when he ran, he didn't look back. He just charged through the streets until he felt the pain of his heart and lungs battering his chest and his muscles burning. It didn't matter that there was never anyone after him. It still felt like an escape.

He knew the area well enough by now to slip down alleyways, around the back of people's yards, avoiding the high street with its gift shops, boutiques, and cafés. It was a smaller and far prettier version of the northern towns he'd come from. Everything a little too neat and pretty, all in proportion and well maintained, with freshly painted fences and window frames, clean pavements and old brick walls that were bare of any graffiti. It even had a town square, which was where he found Ember setting up their new market stall.

"Oh! Thank you," she gushed when he handed her the supplies.

He felt terrible for it, but even her gratitude had begun to grate on him. Ember had been thanking him for one thing or another for weeks now and Leo wished she'd stop. For a moment, he considered telling her about the shoplifting, but somehow he couldn't face her disappointment either. Instead, he started to lug the boxes of soap that she'd made to the stall.

"This is it. Our first day!" Ember announced as she opened them.

Leo envied her excitement. He always felt empty when she seemed full.

She had loved the marketplace from the very first time he'd taken her to it. Every Saturday, in the center of town, sellers would arrive and put out their wares, usually fruit and veg, oils and condiments, jams and marmalades, pies and cakes, all home-made, organic, and overpriced. It was Ember's idea to have a stall of their own. He'd just helped arrange it, finding out who to talk to, who to pay. In the boxes were the bars of soap that she had spent the last few weeks toiling over. Early that morning, he had pushed those boxes all the way from home in a shopping cart he'd stolen from the supermarket. His legs and arms were tired, but he liked that.

Life had been too comfortable for too long now. Ember's mother dished up meal after meal, never even letting Leo clear his plate from the table. She never mentioned school or work but just seemed happy to provide a home for them with the money she received each month from Ember's father. Having lived on the streets for so long, Leo found his bed too soft and the duvet too warm. Most nights, he took to the floor and lay there without any cover at all. The central heating stifled him, especially now that spring was on the way. But Melanie was used to the warmth of the hospital, so he and Ember walked around the house in T-shirts while she kept herself cocooned in a knitted cardigan that she wrapped around her like a survivor in an emergency blanket.

Leo knew that Ember felt as smothered as he did. She just would never admit it. These little luxuries were a world away from the wooden caravan in the forest that she'd described to him. Sometimes she joined him on the floor of his room before creeping back to her bed before dawn. And she kept clippings from magazines of faraway places—Paris, mostly—hidden away in a drawer in her room, away from Melanie's view.

"I'll get there one day," she told him once, when he found her staring so intently at a photograph of the Eiffel Tower. "I just always thought . . . "

"What?" he prompted gently.

"Never mind," she mumbled, but he knew she was thinking of Poppy and how she'd planned for them to go there together.

Not for the first time, Leo wanted to comfort Ember and tell her he understood, that he missed Poppy too. But he dared not. That truth might be too much for their fragile relationship to bear. He wondered if Poppy realized that when she left, she took with her their ability to speak of her. Could she know her absence might be larger than her presence; her silence louder than her voice?

Mr. Hooper hadn't heard from Poppy, either. He called once in a while, and they told him she'd gone traveling. Only a half-lie, Ember had reasoned. Even Poppy's real mother, Charlock, had no knowledge of her whereabouts. She had visited a while back,

assuming Poppy would be with them. Her body had crumpled
into a chair when she learned they hadn't seen her. Her hands
had covered her face, her fingers rubbing at her scalp. When she
stood, her face was calm once more. But Leo knew she was simply doing what they did—pretending.

The town square was growing louder with voices and scrapes and
clatter as other stalls were set up. Leo began to unpack the boxes
of soap. The air was heady with the scent of them and it made him
feel a pang for Ember. She was the girl who wanted him, the girl
who hadn't run away. Poppy was a witch, but Ember had her own
magic. She was an alchemist, transforming Melanie, changing
him, turning oil and lye, herbs and flowers into perfect, oblong,
rainbow bars of sweet-smelling soap. He felt as though Ember
was laundering them all, washing away the past, cleaning up the
hurt. But Leo had glimpsed her pressing the hardened soap from
the molds and lifting the bars to her nose, closing her eyes and
inhaling. And for those few seconds, Leo knew she was back in
the woods where the witches walked. Back with Charlock, the
mother she'd always love. Back home.

Ember's arms came around his waist and her cheek rested
warm against his shoulder blade. He turned and she kissed him
and he let himself relax.

"Thank you," she whispered again and, for a moment, Leo
thought she was thanking him for the kiss, not for the boxes.

Ember always kissed him first, never the other way around.
Often when she was close by, so close that he could smell her,

that he could spot the different shades of gold in her hair and hear her gentle breathing, he thought about it—reaching out a hand, lowering his head, putting his lips on hers. It would be so easy. But always Leo hesitated and, before long, it was she who reached out to him and she who stretched up to press her mouth to his.

"I hope people like them," she was telling him. "Do you really think they'll buy some?"

"Of course they will." He smiled.

She kissed him again and, feeling guilty, Leo kissed her back more deeply this time so that she closed her eyes and softened in his arms. He realized in that moment she'd do anything for him, and that felt wrong. He pulled away and she looked up at him with glistening lips and shining eyes.

"I love you," she whispered.

"Me too," he replied, as he always did. Then he turned to open another box. Together, they laid out the soaps, decorating the stall with a flowerbed of colors.

It was the prettiest stall in the market and Ember the prettiest girl. Leo knew he should be happy at his good luck, but it felt like forcing a smile. He might be able to fool Ember, but he couldn't fool himself. Deep down, never to be spoken of, Leo wished his luck would change.

4

EMBER

The bills felt crisp between Ember's fingers. The change jangled in the box. *I'll have to make more soap*, she thought. *A lot more.* The joy swelled in her chest and traveled upward, making her cheeks flush and her lips smile. She caught Leo's eye and raised her palm high in the air like she had seen on the television. He tilted his head and gave her one of his wry looks but then clapped her hand with his own.

"Amazing," he congratulated. "Look what you've done."

But for once, Ember didn't hang on Leo's words. In fact, she heard them only faintly through the excitement that hummed inside her head. She didn't need Leo's recognition for this. She was already proud enough. She would tell Melanie, of course, but she knew her mother's pleasure would be tempered with worry— worry that she wouldn't need her anymore, worry that she'd leave her all alone. The people who she'd really like to share in her success were Charlock and Poppy. But they were far, far away and that made Ember long to tell them all the more. Instead, she put her arm around Leo's waist.

"We did it together."

"No," he disagreed. "This is all you."

He was good at that. Saying the right thing, giving her hope when the rest of the time he was distant and sad. He thought she didn't notice. He thought she was naive. But she knew what he was thinking and whom he was thinking of. It will fade, Ember told herself. Just as winter turned to spring. It would be her season soon.

The woods were different down south where Melanie lived. Less wild and dark than the northern forests that Ember was used to. She'd gotten lost, though, that time she'd gone walking. She'd been distracted, looking out for signs of a coven. A boulder, a bird, a stone like an arrow pointing the way. She'd even called out in the faint hope that any witches might respond.

"Hello!" she called. "It's me. I was once of the Northern clan. I lived in a coven all my life. Until now." Her words bounced off the bark and faded through the treetops. "My name was Hawkweed. Ember Hawkweed. Maybe you've heard of the Hawkweeds? My mother was Charlock and my aunt—she was the great Raven Hawkweed." There was a rustle in the undergrowth and a crack from the snapping of a twig. Ember started and her eyes searched through the tree trunks for any glimpse of life. But no one emerged, not even a squirrel. Ember strained her ears, but the only sound was the whisper of wind through the branches like waves on a leafy sea. She made one last attempt. "I know your queen," she said. "Poppy Hawkweed. Poppy is my friend and . . . "

Ember's eyes were suddenly full of tears, her voice hoarse. "And I love her," she finally managed in a small, wobbly voice. "More than anyone."

Ember walked through those woods all afternoon, but if there were witches present, they didn't show themselves that day. Not to her or any of the other ramblers she passed, maps in hand, jackets over their shoulders, knapsacks on their backs. *Go away,* she wanted to urge. *They'll never come out if you're here.* But they would nod and greet her, and she would smile back, a chaff, like them, only without a map and with little sense of direction.

"Where's home?" one queried when she asked for help, and it had taken her a few moments to think of the answer. Not up north but in a cottage on Merton Lane. This was home now. Not within the trees, lined like armies protecting the magic that lay hidden deep behind their ranks.

Ember never told Leo about her walk in the woods. She had her secrets too. Instead she'd described the food aisles in the supermarket. Each apple, pear, plum identical to the next. Strawberries in January and other fruits she'd never even seen before. No sore shoulders and fingers from the picking. The meat already cut and packaged. No slaughter or blood. Then she'd talked of the smells from the bakery and the bread that hardly had a crust and that was as light as sponge within. And Leo had listened and his arm had felt heavy on her shoulders as she buried her face into his chest and heard his heart drumming its slow rhythm to her voice, so steady and familiar.

❧

Tonight, Leo wasn't in the listening mood. He had gone out into the garden, into the dusky light, and started tearing down the broken fence. Ember went to the back door and tried to call him in, but he wouldn't come. She stood there a minute, watching him fling the rotten wood into a heap, his hands scratched and bleeding from the thorny hedgerow. The breeze was cool and fresh on her face and the air was filled with birdsong. Clusters of daffodils had burst through the lawn, disrupting the sensible green with their outlandish yellows. It should be good, this scene, this new life of hers, but there he was ripping away at the edges of it.

Ember retreated into the stuffy warmth of the house. Voices were chattering on the television, keeping her muted mother company.

"We sold all the soap today," Ember told her.

"That's lovely, petal."

It had taken a while for Ember to notice that her mother never called her by name, only by endearments. She understood why. It was not the name Melanie had chosen for her baby girl. Poppy Hooper was. Ember had tried saying it, writing it, claiming it as her own. It was too late, though. She would always be Ember Hawkweed, at least in name. She wondered if Poppy felt it too—that they could never be one thing, or the other. In truth, it was only when they were together that their lives, their names, themselves, made any sense.

"One day, when I've saved enough money, I thought we could go to Paris."

"Oh." Melanie blinked.

"Would you like that?" Ember asked hopefully. "We could see all the sights, sit in cafés, go shopping."

Melanie nodded slowly. "That sounds nice, my love. But expensive."

"I'll just have to sell a lot of soap, that's all."

Ember sat down next to her mother and stroked her hand. She knew she was trying, just like they all were. They watched the television together for a while, neither one of them speaking. A man was trying to cross a pool of water by balancing on strange plastic shapes that made him topple and fall. Ember had learned most of what she knew of the chaff world from this screen that sat in the corner of the room. She had spent her first few days transfixed by it. But this, she couldn't comprehend.

"Once," Melanie spoke suddenly, "me and your father, we took in a stray." Her eyes didn't turn from the screen. "A scrawny excuse for a dog really. Sad eyes, ribs jutting out of its sides, starving hungry. Never seen anything eat so much. I fed him, cleaned him up, kept him warm, but the next morning, he sat by the door and whined. I couldn't understand it. He'd have had such a better life with us. But when I opened the door, he ran."

Melanie gave Ember's hand a quick squeeze. She never glanced outside at Leo, but Ember knew what her mother was trying to tell her.

"Did he ever come back?" Ember asked.

"I made your father go out looking for him. But truthfully, I don't think that dog wanted to be found."

Ember thought of Leo, her stray, and felt relieved he was still here. He had more sense than that dog. He knew she'd take care of him. Her mother was wrong. And the more Ember thought about it, the clearer it became. Leo wasn't knocking down the fence, he was rebuilding it. If she looked outside again, Ember was sure that's what she'd see.

5

YOUNG CHARLOCK

Every year, the coming of spring was greeted by a celebration from the coven. On the last day of winter, the sisters wished for night to fall quickly, for then the preparations would be over and the merriment could begin. As if mindful of its unpopularity, the sun hardly bothered to show itself through the clouds, and day stitched to darkness almost seamlessly. Immediately, circle upon circle of candles was lit in readiness for the night's festivities. For this eve was not for sleeping. The coven had taken to their beds that afternoon in order to remain awake the whole night through. Fires were burning and hogs roasting. Cider was being poured. Young witches were practicing spells for their displays.

Charlock and her friend Betony were responsible for lighting the candles.

"We're lucky there's no breeze tonight," murmured Charlock as she admired the tiny flames.

"Your sister has made certain of that, most likely," joked Betony. "It is not just us she bosses but the weather too." Charlock smiled, then looked around guiltily to see if Raven might be watching. "Don't fear her so," whispered Betony. "You are a Hawkweed too."

Charlock shrugged. "Not the one that matters," she said simply, without complaint.

It was true. She was the younger, softer sister, a witch with only moderate magic. Raven, on the other hand, was already the most powerful witch their clan had ever known. As if able to hear these thoughts, her sister turned her head and peered at Charlock from across the camp. Charlock waved in nervous greeting, but Raven only narrowed her eyes before returning her attention to her young daughter, Sorrel. Betony moved closer to Charlock in a show of solidarity. The pressure and warmth of her friend's side against her own were comforting, as were Betony's words.

"Come on," she said. "These candles, this celebration, are for us. We have turned seventeen this winter. Not her. It is us who will be yoking for the first time tomorrow."

"It is our night," Charlock admitted, gazing out at the candles they had lit. She felt a sudden shiver of nerves, and the flames seemed to flicker in response. "Do you ever doubt it, though?" she whispered. "That we are ready?"

Betony didn't hesitate. "I want an adventure. I want to see something new."

"But what of making a daughter?" Charlock reminded.

Betony took her hand. "We have many years for that," she said, pulling Charlock toward a small throng of sisters by the storeroom. "Besides, look at Sisters Caraway, Mildred, and Ivy. They are keen enough for all of us."

Each seventeen-year-old was collecting a garland for her hair—snowdrops, irises, and crocuses. Normally, flowers were not for picking, but this celebration was different. For many of these girls, it was to be their first foray into town; for all, their first encounter with a male. As Charlock bent her head and felt the delicate petals caress her hair, she reminded herself of all that she'd been taught. Yoking was a part of life. It was natural and not to be feared. To bring a daughter into the world was the greatest achievement of any witch's life—greater than any spell or magical gift. Charlock inhaled the sweet scent of the flowers and felt soothed. She didn't have to go tomorrow. She knew that. It was only for those who wanted and there were many sisters who chose to remain childless. This was her choice. Besides, she had promised Betony and would not let her down.

She squeezed Betony's hand. "I think I smell cake."

"Sister Clover's honey cake!" And they both laughed with delight as they ran to fetch some.

That night they danced until their feet were sore and feasted till their bellies were full. Sister Wynne read their horoscopes and told their fortunes. Sister Ada produced her usual falconry display. Sister Starling, Charlock's mother, told them stories of times long since passed, of witches strong and true who suffered for their craft. The youngest of the group put on their own displays—one magicked mice from her sleeves. Another turned water into juice. One bent a spoon by staring at it. A small group recited healing spells in high and lilting voices. Everyone oohed and aahed and clapped as the children took a bow.

Charlock and Betony were the last to sleep and the last to awake. None minded, though. The first day of spring was for the mothers in the clan and all those trying to become one. By the time Charlock rose from her bed, her mother had already received gifts from the other sisters, praising her achievement of bringing a daughter into the world and raising her in the ways of the craft. The Hawkweed table was laden with jars of nuts and dried fruits, hocks of ham, and pots of pickles. Charlock gave her mother a hug when she saw them and thanked her as she always did on this day.

"Thank you, Mother, for all you have done and do for me."

Her mother put her hands on Charlock's cheeks, rough skin against smooth. "It is your turn now, my sweet. It makes me very proud to know you will join the others for the yoking this evening." Then she plucked a fragment of a flower from Charlock's hair and handed it to her. It lay in Charlock's palm, crushed and damp, and Charlock felt a second's sorrow at its loss.

After picking the rest of the garland from her hair, Charlock placed the dying flowers between the pages of her book of spells. Then she changed from her nightgown to her clothes. Her belly hardly curved and it was difficult to picture a baby curled up within it. Instead, she imagined how proud her mother would be if tonight she proved successful. Her reverie was broken by Raven's strident tones.

"Charlock, stop dawdling!" came the call from outside the caravan. Charlock leaned out the window and saw her sister holding a little lamb. "Chop chop," Raven said without a smile.

As the lamb roasted on a spit, Charlock and Betony took turns sitting before it, winding the crank around and around, the smoke stinging their eyes, the smell seeping into their skin. It was tiring work, but Charlock knew Betony was simply glad to be involved on this mothers' day, having lost her own when she was young. The kestrel that had been Betony's companion these last few years gave a shrill cry and Charlock watched him circle overhead, drawn to the smell of the meat. It did smell good. Charlock picked a crispy morsel that was about to fall and popped it in her mouth.

"Charlock!" exclaimed Raven, making Charlock almost choke before she could savor the taste. "Mother, first."

As always, Raven noticed everything. Charlock chided herself for not checking her sister's whereabouts, as she'd been training herself to do. It hadn't always been like this between them. She remembered how, as a child, she used to feel so lucky to have a sister such as Raven—famed for her talent and her skill. For a while, Raven had welcomed her adoration until gradually it had become an irritant. Before long, Raven had no words to offer her little sister anymore. Instead she craved solitude and silence. Charlock remembered weeping into her mother's lap and being told to "let her sister be." When her tears finally dried, she found consolation with the other young sisters and made her first true friend.

Betony could not be more different from Raven. It wasn't just her looks, though she was tall and strong, not small and skinny like Raven, red-headed and freckled, not drab and wan, husky, not shrill; it was every facet of her character, her ability to laugh at herself as well as others, to use magic for entertainment's sake, to make mistakes in order to lighten a mood. Raven was always so serious; Betony irreverent and carefree. And it was such a relief for Charlock to be on an even footing, sometimes actually to do better. But most of all, Charlock had an ally in Betony. Someone who would be on her side no matter the rights and wrongs;

someone ready to take the blame on her behalf, to make the good times as well as the bad times better.

Everyone had always presumed that Charlock and Betony would partner together for the yoking, so it came as no surprise when they asked to do so. For support, the witches went and returned in groups of two or three. Most would never have had more than the briefest encounter with a chaff, and now they must go into the heart of that world and flow through its veins and arteries as though they were made of the same blood. No young witch wished to brave this alone. Also, the groupings allowed the elders to keep track of any blunders or betrayals. Come what may, on pain of death, the coven must be protected and their secret kept. So each girl's partner was both defender and informant.

Not in Charlock and Betony's case, though. For months they'd been whispering their assurances over wood chips and potato peelings, over potions and dirty pots. Their pledge of loyalty was to each other and not to the coven, scandalous as that might sound. Friends first. A thrill leapt up inside Charlock like salmon in a river when she first uttered these rebellious words. They were out where the silver birches grew, but still she looked around to see if anyone had heard or, worse, if Raven was lurking near.

Unperturbed, Betony took a small knife from her pocket and cut into her palm. Charlock's heart was pounding and it seemed to stop beating altogether when she took the knife and cut into her own. Then, as she and Betony clasped hands, their blood blending, her heart beat strong and steady and she felt secure in a way she'd never experienced before.

"Friends first," Charlock vowed, and Betony's green eyes locked with her own amber ones.

Then, to their surprise, a kaleidoscope of butterflies fluttered forward and settled in their hair, as if to show approval of their pact.

"Twins." Betony grinned, lifting up her bleeding hand and licking the blood from it. And Charlock had burst out laughing, happy and excited about the yoking day to come.

After the lunch, there were speeches to the mothers and toasts to the young witches who were yoking that evening. Betony tickled Charlock's side, making her snort with laughter, which she then had to disguise as a cough. Just like the mothers in the coven, those who were yoking were excused from clearing up the plates. They were allowed to sit and drink their tea while the others around them worked. As the afternoon drew to a close, the girls readied themselves to leave. They needed to make their journey as the sun began to set so that by the time they neared the town, darkness would be ready to shield them. Their departures were staggered. Sisters Caraway, Mildred, and Ivy were the first to depart; Betony and Charlock, the last. The waiting was hard, the nerves mounting despite the deep breaths and the mantra of spells. In the end, it was a relief to get going and have their journey begun.

Charlock's jitters settled as her legs started walking and she felt the soft earth underfoot and Betony's cool hand in hers. She could hear the well wishes of the coven even after they'd slipped past the towering rocks that circled their encampment. She felt the sisters' magic on her skin protecting her. Her mother had placed an amulet around her neck and Charlock felt it cool against her chest, calming her pounding heart.

"All will be fine," she said more to herself than to Betony, but suddenly her friend stopped and looked back toward home.

"What's wrong?" asked Charlock. She took her friend's hand. "Do you want to go back?"

"Do you?" Betony asked, her face a ghostly white.

Charlock considered this idea for a moment, then shook her head. "You called it an adventure, Bet. And you were right."

Betony's eyes flicked up to meet hers and the color returned to her cheeks. "Well, what are we waiting for?" she said with a smile.

After that, they didn't look back and their feet hurried across the forest floor, swishing through ferns and jumping over fallen branches until they reached the fields beyond. There they strode out into the open, covering the miles of grassy moors at just as fast a pace. As they reached the top of the last hill, Charlock caught sight of Betony's kestrel hovering high above them, pointed wings and fanned tail outstretched. Never had she felt so glad to have his watchful eye on them.

"Look." Betony pointed to the valley, but she needn't have. Charlock had seen them too—the lights of the town glimmering in the distance. Thousands of them, like fallen stars, caught and caged in glass.

"It is a sight, is it not?" murmured Betony.

"It is, sister," Charlock agreed.

"Do you think there's a chaff for every light that shines?"

"More. We are more than our candles," Charlock reasoned. "How are we to choose one out of so many? Oh, I wish we were allowed to use our magic!"

"Charlock Hawkweed," Betony mocked.

Magic on chaffs is a last resort,
When all other avenues have been sought.

Charlock continued the rule that they'd been taught since childhood.

For spells may detection cause,
Break not this most sacred of our laws.

She and Betony smiled at each other. "So where do we start?" asked Charlock.

"Let us do as the rabbits. They mate enough." Charlock looked confused, and Betony smiled. "We'll follow our noses."

In the end, it was their ears they followed. The music had been impossible to miss. It had bounced through the walls of the house, out into the open air, and down the street, and the girls had taken it as a sign and let it carry them forward. Now they stood outside, the music was so thunderously loud that the building seemed to shake with its beat. Through the windows, Charlock and Betony could see chaffs of a similar age to themselves.

"Perhaps they too celebrate the coming of the spring?" whispered Charlock.

"They do not look as I expected," stated Betony, and Charlock knew her meaning, for this flock were feathered so peculiarly, like different breeds all congregating upon the same perch.

"We will be outnumbered," she replied, suddenly unsure. "Look at us." Charlock lifted Betony's long, muddy skirt.

"I don't think they'll notice," muttered Betony, her eyes fixed on the scene inside. The chaffs were dancing, lifting bottles to their lips and swigging at them. "Come on," Betony said, pulling Charlock toward the door.

It was ajar and they slipped inside unannounced. There was no one there to greet them. No one even looked in their direction. Betony had been right about that. The house was full of chaffs chatting, dancing, kissing. Charlock glimpsed a couple, then quickly looked away. But they were everywhere, limbs entwined, lips locked, on chairs, stairs, simply standing, leaning on one another in the middle of the room, swaying to their music. Charlock wondered how they managed to breathe, for they never seemed to come up for air.

"It is a den of depravity," she said out loud.

"I know!" shouted Betony, raising her voice to be heard above the music. They looked at each other in shock and then at once both broke into laughter, the nerves bolting from their mouths. "Do you think Sister Ada ever came upon such a scene?" asked Betony, doubling over with mirth.

"She would turn these chaffs to stone," sniggered Charlock.

"Or summon a plague of toads."

"There is a reason she is childless."

"Sister Wynne!" they both said at once, collapsing into further fits at the idea of waddling Wynnie wading among these waifs with their painted faces and their wiggling hips.

"What's with the costumes?" The boy's voice shocked them into silence. Charlock and Betony looked over at him, neither able to speak. His eyes were glazed and his hair stood up on end like he was shocked. "It's not a costume party," he slurred. Betony and Charlock stared down at their clothes. The boy took a drink from the bottle he'd been holding at his side and then passed it to them. "Here."

Betony took it and looked at Charlock, her eyes wide. Then she shrugged and, to Charlock's horror, she gulped the liquid down. She went rigid for a moment, then a hand went to her throat and she staggered and swayed as if poisoned.

"Bet!" cried Charlock in alarm.

"Your turn, sister." Betony stood up grinning, holding out the bottle. "I dare you!"

"You two are weird," the boy said, though not insultingly and, in response, Charlock took a drink.

It tasted sour but not nearly as bad as she'd been expecting. Making a playful face at Betony, she drank again. Suddenly this evening that she had been fretting about for so many weeks had become merry. Without letting consideration figure first, Charlock took the boy by the arm. Betony gawped, emboldening Charlock further.

"Is this your home?" she asked the boy. "Why don't you show me where you sleep?"

The boy blinked with surprise, then looked pleased. Charlock felt quite gratified. He led her away quickly, as if worried she might change her mind.

It hadn't taken any magic at all, thought Charlock as she followed him.

6

YOUNG BETONY

All merriment departed with Charlock up stairs as tall as the fir trees in the forest. Betony watched her friend squeeze past the throngs who loitered along those steps and she felt her spirits dim. She looked around at these youngsters who seemed to be celebrating like animals, high from a hunt, with no sense of self. She had seen a skulk of fox cubs behave so, rolling and tumbling until they were yelping in pain and limping. And she'd witnessed plenty of rutting between the many forest creatures. Yet none of that had ever disturbed her like this present scene of wild abandon. Suddenly Betony had to get out. The place was too loud, too odorous, and sticky with the fermented grapes and hops that had spilled on the floor. The door at the back was wide open and seemed the easiest route of escape to avoid the hallway jammed with swaying bodies and grinning faces.

Outside, the music was dulled slightly and became bearable to her ears. The air cooled her heated skin and she felt the flush fade from her cheeks. A few of the chaffs sat at a table smoking from white sticks that glowed at their tips like tiny fires. The fumes puffed from their mouths and nostrils like they had burning hot coals in their bellies. Betony walked away from them toward the end of the garden. She took off her boots and the cool grass felt soothing beneath her feet. When she reached the oak tree in the corner, she took shelter under its wide branches and sat down at its roots, leaning back upon its trunk. The bark against her head was a comforting reminder of home. Up above perched her kestrel, ever guarding her.

"Hello, my friend," she whispered.

The bird gave a flap and a ruffle of feathers in response.

Then before them, a boy appeared, lifting a ball from foot to knee to shoulder to head and back to foot again. Over and over he did this dance, lithe and limber, like a juggler or a magician, until the ball spilled and rolled toward her feet. The boy looked over to her and Betony picked up the ball. It was made of leather, stitched and brightly painted, and she liked the feel of it in her hands. The boy nodded and Betony threw it back to him. Catching it on his foot, he cradled it there before flicking it high up into the air and then rolling it along his outstretched arm, past the back of his neck and down to the opposite hand.

"Ninety-nine used to be my record," he announced, "when I was a kid. I practiced all the time."

"It's a good trick," she told him warily.

"You like soccer?" he asked. She shrugged, not knowing how to answer. "Not a fan, huh?" He came and sat right next to her, though uninvited. Betony felt his arm against hers, but it didn't seem to bother her, she noticed, for she didn't flinch or move away. "It used to be my whole life." He handed her a silver oblong from a packet. "Gum?" he offered.

There was something about the warmth in his dark eyes that made her take it, although she had no notion of what it might be. She watched him unwrap it and chew, over and over, without swallowing. Betony put her piece in her pocket, not wanting to remove it from its shiny casing.

"Danny," he announced. Betony wasn't sure if he meant the gum or himself. Then he asked, "You?"

"Betony," she replied, realizing too late she should have said Bee, the alias she had picked for the yoking. Charlock had chosen Clara, both of them liking the idea that their initial would remain the same.

Danny picked up the ball and spun it on his fingertip.

"How do you do that?" Betony asked.

"Practice," he told her. "D'you want to try?"

Betony shrugged. She didn't really, but he was already passing her the ball and telling her to roll it across her wrist and keep her hands soft. The ball dropped immediately.

"Try again," Danny instructed, but, each time, the ball hardly spun for a fraction of a second before it fell. "You need to focus," he said.

Annoyed, Betony chanted a spell inside her head and, this time, the ball turned and turned. Danny looked overjoyed.

"What did I tell you? Practice!" Betony felt guilty for using magic when it was so strictly forbidden. She had gained nothing from it and no harm had been done, but still she gave a nervous shiver. Danny took off his jacket and put it around her shoulders.

"Oh, no," she exclaimed, trying to shrug it off, "you mustn't." But Danny put it back over her arms.

"I never get cold," he told her. "Italian blood, my mom says. That's where they are. In Italy with my grandmother. They're not going to be happy when they find out about this." He gestured toward the house. "I'm supposed to be studying." He smiled.

Betony nodded like she understood. "Do they have to find out?" she asked with concern.

Danny grinned. "That depends on the damage. I'll clean it up, but my parents—it's hard to bullshit them."

Betony thought hard. "You mean lie? . . . But if it's all cleaned up, then it's only a white lie—not hurting anyone."

"Not even a white lie. An omission. I plan to keep my mouth shut and hope for the best."

Betony nodded. "That's a good plan. You don't seem like you'd be gifted at lying."

"What about you? You gifted at lying, Betony?"

For a second, Betony thought of telling him the truth, but she was too skilled a liar. "Only white lies," she said. "And omitting." She smiled.

"Well, that's okay then," he said as he bent his head to pick up his ball again. As he straightened, a lock of silky black hair fell across his eye, and Betony felt the urge to brush it back.

"So this is your home?" She asked, staring up at the back of the building, its bricks and glass, so much glass revealing so many people moving inside like puppets in a show. Danny nodded and Betony thought of Charlock and wondered which window she lay behind.

She looked away, not wanting to imagine any more. "And these people are all your guests?"

"Well, some of them are." Betony heard the hint of a joke, but it was only when Danny looked at her that she knew she was its target.

"I'm sorry," she mumbled. "We heard the music from the street. The door—it was open." She couldn't look at him, suddenly fearful of his reaction.

"Hey, it's all right." Danny nudged her with his elbow. "I'm glad you're here."

She knew immediately he meant it and felt a glow light up within her. She lowered her head to hide it from him, but this made her catch his scent from his jacket. She put her nose to her shoulder to smell closer.

The night bristled and hummed with life. Betony heard the padding of a nearby fox's paws and the hoot of a distant owl. She felt the twitching of a nervous mouse and the flutter of the moths around the garden lights. She was alert to every movement and every sound but most of all to him, his breathing, his pulse, his arm against her arm, his thigh against her thigh.

"Do you want to yoke with me?" she blurted out of nowhere, not thinking first, not lifting her head from his jacket.

"What?"

Betony glanced up at him. He seemed confused, but his lips were still upturned in half a smile. "Nothing," she lied.

"Did you say 'yoke'?"

"No."

"You did. What does it even mean?"

"I didn't." Betony could feel her cheeks burning and her freckles frying upon them.

"You're a terrible liar!"

"I'm excellent at it, actually."

"I'd better watch out then," he beamed, eyes shining with a mischief that enticed, then unnerved her.

"Yes, you'd better," she retorted as she stood up and roughly pushed her feet back inside her boots.

"You can't just ask me to . . . to, I dunno . . . yoke with you . . . and then go."

"Goodbye, Danny."

Betony had never thought about walking before. She'd just done it. Now her brain had to tell her legs to move, as if learning a new skill for the first time. She could hear Danny's voice calling after her, but she needed all her senses on the task ahead—to get to the house, to get Charlock, to get away.

Thankfully she didn't have to look hard. Charlock was waiting for her by the front door, seeming no different from before. There was no crease to her clothes, no blush upon her cheeks, no new glint of experience in her eye. In fact, her wide face and far-set, oval eyes had become impossible to interpret, still and unchanging as a painting.

It was only once they had reached the meadow that Betony realized she still had Danny's jacket wrapped around her, keeping her warm, reminding her that this night was real. She opened her mouth to share this with Charlock but stopped herself. The silence felt too hard a coating to crack. For Charlock had been so reticent on their return, eyes fixed on the horizon, answering Betony's questions with monosyllables.

"Are you well?"

"Yes."

"Do you feel different?"

"No."

"Are you happy that it's done?"

"Yes."

Silently, Betony slipped the jacket from her shoulders and into her bag, trying to ignore how cold she felt without it. As the woods finally appeared in the distance, the tops of them pointing sharp as blackened arrows into the smoky sky, it came into Betony's mind how strange it was that Charlock had not asked her anything about her night. Was she so wrapped up in her own yoking that she thought nothing of anyone else's? And then Danny's words came to her. Not lying but omitting. Betony reached for Charlock's hand.

"Charlock," she appealed. "Tell me. Why are you so silent? What happened?"

"I—," her friend started but couldn't finish.

"You can tell me."

And then Charlock's still waters of a face rippled with emotion and tears sprang to her eyes. "Oh, Bet," she wailed. "It was awful."

"What did he do to you?" Betony whispered, desperate to know and yet wanting to block her ears from Charlock's answer.

"Nothing!" Charlock sobbed. "That's just it—we kissed and then we lay down and then . . . he . . . he fell asleep."

Blinking away the shock from her eyes, Betony put her arms around her friend and let her cry until the damp spread into a patch that she could feel through her vest. "Oh, Charlock. Don't cry so."

"I tried to rouse him, but he didn't move. He just lay there snoring! What did I do wrong, Bet?"

Betony couldn't help but smile and Charlock must have felt it, for a laugh broke through her tears. "It's not funny." She sniffed. "What am I going to tell the elders?"

"We'll tell them we tried."

Charlock suddenly pulled away and looked at Betony. "You neither?" Betony shook her head. Charlock gasped guiltily. "I never even asked. I'm sorry."

Betony knew this was the time to tell Charlock about the boy with the ball, but for some reason she didn't. She found that she wanted to keep it to herself for a little while longer. Her time with Danny felt delicate as the dew now forming on the leaves, and to speak of it might burst it.

"Look at us pair of ninnies." Charlock smiled, wiping her eyes and taking Betony's arm once more. "Next time," she said, "we will succeed."

"You'd go back?" Betony asked in surprise.

"I want a daughter, Bet," Charlock admitted shyly. "I didn't know how much until tonight." Betony felt a prickle of apprehension at why she did not feel the same. Perhaps it was the lack of a mother of her own? "Will you come with me to try again?" she heard Charlock ask.

"To that same place?"

"It seemed as good as any, but we can try elsewhere if you prefer."

"No," Betony said hurriedly. "You're right. That place will do."

Charlock pulled Betony back into a hug. "You are a true sister."

The jacket felt heavy in Betony's bag. She knew she should speak of it and tell her friend. Now, this moment, before it was gone. But she didn't know how to say she'd met a boy but hadn't mated, just talked and played and laughed; that when she was with him she'd thought only of him and not once of any daughter. It was too strange, even to her, who had lived it. Yoking was for one purpose only. She had never heard any of the sisters speak of companionship or harmony. Quite the opposite. Betony wondered again what it was about her that caused these different feelings in her heart. She looked into Charlock's eyes and made a silent promise to tell her about Danny at another, better time.

The two girls reached the forest as the sun was rising, and they stopped and stared at the brightening sky.

"We must hurry," Charlock said, but Betony found it hard to leave the hints of peach and apricot behind and step into the cool darkness of the woods.

Charlock moved in front so they could fit between the trees. Walking behind her and out of sight, Betony's hand went to her pocket. In the depths of it, her fingers felt the gum in its shiny silver cover. The secret of it made her feel warm despite the early-morning chill and, looking up, she saw the sunlight dappling through the leaves.

7

SORREL

A cloud the shape of a ship was passing the moon when Sorrel noticed her aunt leave. Sorrel didn't call out to her. She just sat still on her caravan steps looking at Charlock doing up the laces on her boots and putting the bag across her shoulders before disappearing into the night's shadows. Her aunt had been quiet as a ghost. And Sorrel knew all about ghosts.

She had glimpsed into that world which was neither life nor death. She had walked in its plains. It was a colorless, timeless place and the others who wandered there seemed blind and deaf to anything but their own unfinished business. Never could Sorrel have imagined such a land of loneliness and loss.

But she was home now and nothing and no one could ever change the bliss of her return. Everything was a pleasure to her now. A graze to the knee or a burn to the hand was just as gratifying as the first bite of a crisp apple or the solidity of a friend's embrace. Both meant she was alive. The cold of winter and the freshness of spring; the warmth of a newly laid egg and the chill of the river; the silk of a horse's neck, the ache of a sore throat;

the sound of the cockerel's crow and a lamb's bleat; Sister Juni-per's snoring and Sister Jay's giggle—all were equally as joyful to Sorrel now. She was living. Though her mother was not.

Sorrel had seen her there in the place beyond. She was a raven like her name, black and blue, hard-eyed and beaked, long-clawed and wide-winged. And Sorrel had called for her, but, just like the others, her mother couldn't hear her. She was too busy searching for something.

"I'm right here!" Sorrel cried, knowing it was she her mother sought. But the bird had kept on pecking at the ground and at the trees and Sorrel had stopped calling, realizing then and there that she didn't want to be found. Not by her mother.

There had been no sense of time in that lifeless land, and Sor-rel had no notion of how many days she had spent there. There was no sun or moon, only an impenetrable mist, but somehow the light had found her. It had surrounded her, warming up her senses one by one and pulling her back into the world. She had felt buoyant, floating on the balmiest breeze. Then she had opened her eyes and seen their faces.

"What's wrong?" she had asked.

Charlock had wept when telling Sorrel the terrible news of her mother's passing. The tears and the snot had fallen in droplets, darkening the blanket on the bed with wet, uneven splotches that spread and merged into one. Kyra had been there too, her face a bloodless white. Ember was nowhere to be seen. Gone, Sorrel later discovered, to find her rightful place in the world. Poppy, the girl who had brought her back to life, her true cousin, she was told, had gone too. No one knew where. Something in the act of saving had given Sorrel a connection to this girl she once hated. She now felt a bond that traveled time and space and gave her the knowledge that Poppy was headed somewhere far, somewhere hot, and that she also did not wish to be found. So Sorrel had said nothing. She was good at keeping secrets. She had simply lifted a hand to her aunt's face and wiped away her tears.

"I'm hungry," she'd said, and they had jumped from their seats and busied themselves preparing her favorite elderflower tea and bean soup.

Later that evening, longing to see outside and check that all was as she remembered, Sorrel had lifted herself out of bed, her toes caressing the silky wooden boards before she trod. When she opened the door, she let the chill nip at her skin and the frost pinch her feet. The thrill she felt at being home would thaw her. She walked around, inspecting all she saw, making mental notes of all that she held dear—the three-wheeled caravan held level by blocks of wood; the hazel tree that bore her favorite nuts; the storeroom with all its glinting jars; the smell of baking from the bread oven; and her place at the dining table, so long and weather-beaten, where she had carved her initials into the wood.

As Sorrel moved past the water barrels, she noticed they were frozen over. She brushed the frost from one to reveal its icy lid. With no mirrors in the coven, it was rare to catch a sighting of one's own reflection, so Sorrel stopped and stared. She rubbed the ice until it gleamed just to make sure. But there it was. A red scar lined her cheek and suddenly Sorrel recalled the pain of its arrival—the fear and the desperation, her legs scrambling as she fled, her heart hammering as she ran, the panic that nearly choked her.

Sorrel's hand went to her face; her fingers touched her scar. Even this, she thought, makes me glad. She had survived. And, recognizing that, Sorrel saw how her features had softened. Still the same hooked nose and thin lips, but now her head was held high and her shoulders open. Her eyes sparkled after their long sleep and her cheeks glowed. Her bones were sharp, but there was a grace in their construction that she had never seen before. Despite all that had happened—no, because of all that had happened—Sorrel was content.

She wished the others in the camp might feel the same. After the delight of her awakening had come the alarm at their queen's departure. They argued about the cause . . . that Poppy must have been possessed . . . cursed . . . captured. But Charlock told the coven that Poppy had left of her own free will. That much was true. She said Poppy would return soon. That much was false. But Sorrel kept her silence and, when she saw how the sisters dipped into despondency, she understood why her aunt pretended so.

On seeing Kyra so glum and dejected, Sorrel had tried to point out the simple pleasures of the day. Kyra looked at her like she was a stranger, a mad one at that, and later, she overheard her worried whispers to the others. She knew they thought her affected by the poison, her mind mushed, her keenness blunted. It did not matter. Only the air she breathed, into her lungs and out, and her heart beating in time with the world.

On her departure, Charlock had left a letter informing the clan that she had gone to visit Poppy. Sister Morgan found it pinned to Charlock's door and read it aloud to the coven. Some of the witches were consoled by this, some angry to be kept so in the dark, others quietly skeptical about the veracity of Charlock's message. To escape their bickering, Sorrel headed out of the camp and through the trees.

The woodland flowers beckoned her—their brilliance more magical than any trick that Sorrel had ever witnessed. She stroked their petals with her fingertips and knelt to pick some for her table. She remembered Ember doing the same and scorning her for it. And with that memory, Sorrel missed her cousin that was, and realized that Ember had only wanted to be appreciated, just as she had appreciated the prettiness and fragrance of the flowers.

Sorrel felt a sting of regret at how she'd treated Ember. She had considered her cousin an outsider who had nothing in common with her or her friends. But now she saw all that they'd shared. They were family. They had grown up together. They had even both been rejected by that boy. Sorrel cringed at the memory of how obsessed she'd been. She could see now the boy's love had nothing to do with appearances, with fair or dark, with chaff or witch. His heart had belonged to another, that was all, and Sorrel found a sense of peace in that. It felt so good to be free. Free of him, free of her mother.

Sorrel stood up and admired the flowers she had collected. She was about to leave when she heard it.

"Charlock killed her," came the whisper on the breeze.

Sorrel looked around the forest fearfully. All she could see were the lines of trees. She tossed her head as if to shake out her ears.

"Charlock killed you," it came again.

The nettles covering the forest floor seemed to shiver in the sudden chill. Sorrel gazed upward to find the branches trembling above her. She turned and turned, her eyes searching all the spaces between the tall trunks.

"Who are you?" she called.

"She killed you both." It was louder this time, echoing before it faded.

Then they emerged. It was as though the trees had shaken themselves free of their roots and were moving across the ground toward her. Brown like earth, these witches were, both skin and clothing.

"What clan are you?" Sorrel asked them.

"We have come to tell you the truth," one of them said, her face cracked and lined like bark.

"Which truth?" asked Sorrel, and half of the witch's papery face smiled and creased further while the other stayed stern.

"You are wise, for one so young," another commented.

"Did my mother send you?"

"We hold no allegiance to your mother. It is not on her behalf we come."

"Then, mine? You come to help me?" Sorrel scoffed and she felt a hint of her old self return. She quieted it though.

"We offer truth and we want truth in return," said the first.

"One of the Hawkweed sisters will be queen. So tells the prophecy," declared the second. "But the throne lies empty. Where is she?"

Sorrel breathed. In and out. Her heart beat steadily. "My aunt has told you—my cousin is preparing herself and she will return when she is ready."

"You trust your Aunt Charlock?" a third asked. "For we were there, on the battlefield, when your mother died. We heard Charlock's confession that she poisoned you. We saw how her words killed Raven."

Sorrel's eyes closed though she did not mean them to. In the darkness, she could hear her heart racing, too fast, too loud.

"Without a queen, there will be more bloodshed, worse fighting, more witches lost. Every clan will claim the crown as their own."

Sorrel forced her eyelids open though they seemed stuck. The wood witches stared back at her; even the whites of their eyes were muddy.

"The stone has my cousin's name writ upon it. No one can deny that," she told them.

"If the chaff queen doesn't want the role, surely another must take it? And better a Hawkweed, than another ambitious clan's contender," the first of these wood witches argued.

"At least let it be someone we can work with. Who will listen. Someone like you," added another.

"I am not that person anymore," Sorrel said with certainty, and she turned and walked away. Not ran—she had done that once before, from another clan. Just walked, calmly and slowly, banishing all thoughts of her aunt and her mother, for with anger darkness lay.

"Think on it," the wood witches called after her.

"Think on it when you look into your aunt's face."

"When you think of the poison that killed you."

"When you think of your mother."

Her mother was there when Sorrel entered her caravan. Not in flesh but in spirit. Raven's ghost had finally found her. She had pecked her way through the film between this world and that. Perhaps the wood witches' words had made her able. The truth was out and she was in. Sorrel felt her presence as soon as she walked through the door. Raven's aura was too powerful to ignore.

She had already moved things around, reversing all the small changes that Sorrel had made to the caravan. An old, itchy blanket that Sorrel had thrown out now lay on the bed as it had always done. The trinkets that Sorrel had put on display—a fossil, a shell, a feather, a rabbit's foot, a mouse's skull—were stuffed back into the jar where she used to hide them. The cracked mug that Sorrel had hidden was out on the shelf. The hat that she hated was back on the peg.

"What do you want?" Sorrel whispered.

There was no answer. Then the shutters banged shut and, in the silence that followed, Sorrel heard one word. It sounded in her head. It came in her own voice, but Sorrel knew it was not her own thought but her mother placing it there.

Granddaughter.

8

POPPY

oppy was crushing berries on a stone when the bird appeared. In juices, dark and crimson, she saw first its wings, then its beak and talons, staining the stone like blood. Poppy knew at once. She smashed its image with a rock, grinding it away, but still it stayed, so she spat and her saliva sizzled there until all that was left was char. Then she threw the rock down and ran for an hour under the high sun until she reached the lake. The flamingos flapped upward to make way for her, patterning the sky with their pinks and whites.

When the water stilled, Poppy stared into it. First she looked for Ember. Slowly her friend appeared upon the water's surface. She was sitting on a bed, counting money from a tin, her head bent, her white-blonde hair hanging around a face that was focused and serious yet still just as lovely. Poppy could sense Ember's satisfaction with her task. All was well. Then came Charlock, who was on a path beside a wheat field. She looked tired from walking, feet sore, a bag weighing heavy on her arm. Poppy wondered where she might be going but could tell from her mother's eyes that she knew both her route and the reason for it. There was no danger lurking, no sign of Raven anywhere.

So Poppy went to Sorrel and found her on the clifftop, standing on the very spot where her mother had died. She was chanting a spell, throwing herbs to the wind, and Poppy understood that she was trying to send Raven away, back into the abyss. Poppy closed her eyes and whispered words to try to help her. In unison their lips moved, urging, pushing, shoving. Together, their power grew and revved like an engine. And then, just like that, Raven slipped out of their hands.

Sorrel turned around, searching for her, and Poppy, too, reached for Raven with her magic, hunting for her everywhere. In the lake's waters, Sorrel's reflection gazed directly at Poppy, her eyes full of hope of their success. But Poppy shook her head. Wherever Raven had gone, it was not to the other side of life where she belonged. She was out there in this world, watching, waiting, threatening. Sorrel looked at Poppy in despair.

"Help me," she mouthed, and Poppy nodded back. Then the waters rippled and Sorrel was gone.

The water returned to its bluey-brown. It was time to leave. Yet Poppy couldn't bring herself to go, not without one last look, not without seeing Leo. Just for a moment, she told herself as she focused her eyes on the lake and let the pictures form once more. She held her breath as the shape of him came into view. He was with Melanie, holding on to her arm, carrying her shopping. They were walking down the street and he was talking and she was smiling.

"Leo," Poppy whispered, and the tears welled and she felt that she might drown with longing.

She let herself look for far longer than she had promised herself. It was too hard to turn away. She stayed with them as they walked all the way home, stopping on a bench, popping into a corner store for a newspaper and a bottle of water. It felt so odd to see such everyday sights of home, like they were foreign to her now. Not him, though. He still felt a part of her, wherever she might be. Leo handed the drink to Melanie and she sipped first before letting him gulp down the rest. Poppy watched as his chin tipped up and his neck stretched as he drank. She noticed how his hair had grown long again and fell across his head. Poppy reached out a hand as if to touch it, then let her arm fall at the hopelessness of such a gesture. Instead, she searched for other differences. His face was a little fuller than before. He was wearing new clothes and he looked bigger, stronger, with broader shoulders and limbs less scrawny than she remembered. Yet there was no hint of magic about him, no trace of enchantment, and Poppy wondered if he had inherited anything of this witch mother of his at all.

She watched until Leo and Melanie reached the door, until his hand turned the key and opened it, until he had waited for Melanie to enter first before he followed. The door closed. Poppy would not cross that threshold. For inside, Ember lay. It would be unbearable to see her greet Leo and hold him and kiss him, or to watch as he kissed her back and put his arms around her waist, one hand on her shoulder blade, the other in her hair. Poppy reached into the lake and splashed the surface suddenly. Drops arced up, catching the light of the sun, dazzling her so she had to turn her head away.

She should look for her coven. She just couldn't face seeing their disappointment. She felt their presence sometimes when she slept. Other clans, too. But the rest of the time, she blocked them off, barring their way into her mind. She glanced back at the water guiltily and saw a feather floating toward her, long and black like death. She knew immediately who had sent it. It reached the shore and lay there at her feet, waiting to be retrieved. She shuddered as she picked it up. Then, holding it between two fingers, dreading its touch against her skin, she ran to find Mma.

"I have to go!" Poppy cried urgently as she burst inside the hut. "I have to go back."

She was flushed and panting and Mma went to the pot and scooped her a ladle of water.

Poppy held the feather out for Mma to see. Mma grasped it in her palm so fearlessly that Poppy almost flinched.

"Drink," Mma said, and Poppy gulped down the water quickly so she could speak again. "You want to leave us because of this?" Mma asked, stroking the feather with her fingers. Now that it was dry, it had a strange blue sheen to it.

"It's from a ghost," Poppy replied. "Raven. My aunt. A great shaman. Greater than me, probably."

Mma shook her head. "She has purpose. This is all you lack."

"My cousin, she needs me. We tried to send this ghost away, but maybe if I'm with her . . . "

But Mma was shaking her head. "This ghost only wants the worst for you. You must stay here."

With those words, Mma stripped the feather's spine of its softness, then snapped it into pieces.

"What are you doing?" Poppy asked.

"Wait," was all Mma said, and she put the broken bits of the feather into a pot with some molasses and oil and heated it over the fire. The mixture bubbled and caramelized. Then she handed the hardening, sticky substance to Poppy.

"Eat," she instructed.

Poppy looked at her in surprise, but Mma simply smiled. "The ghost will pass through you and be gone."

Poppy gave a laugh. "Well, that's one way to get rid of her," and she bit into the sweet and felt it crunch and melt inside her mouth. It felt too easy. Raven, the great witch, simply chewed and digested.

"What about Sorrel?" Poppy asked as the thought struck her. "Will the ghost leave Sorrel too?"

"This Sorrel," Mma asked. "She is the witch's purpose?" Poppy nodded. Sorrel, she realized, had always been Raven's purpose. "Then only she can find a way to send her home."

"Can't she do this?" said Poppy, taking another bite of the feather mixture.

"You know the answer."

Poppy sighed. "The sangoma. It's Sorrel's mother."

Mma tutted her disapproval. "Some cannot stop trying to control their young. Even after death." She reached for the pot and then got to her feet slowly. "Your Sorrel must cut the cord that binds her. Only then can she be free." Mma pointed to her belly button. "One cord cut when a newborn." Then she tapped her head. "The other when full grown."

Poppy winced as the feather mixture hit her stomach. "It hurts," she groaned as a sharp pain stabbed through her middle.

"Ghosts are always painful," Mma said.

9

LEO

Leo unpacked the groceries, putting the cans in the cupboard, fruit in the bowl, meat and cheese in the fridge, just as he'd been taught. Everything had its place in Melanie's home. It was only he that didn't fit. He slept in the spare room and his belongings had a drawer and hangers and were neatly put away, out of view. But his physical presence wasn't so easily contained and seemed to jar with the rest of the house. Everything matched—cushions with curtains, duvets with pillow cases, napkins with tablecloth, and even Ember with Melanie, both fair and blue-eyed and dimpled. Then there was him, too tall, too rough, too dark, like an odd piece of furniture that they'd inherited but didn't know quite know what to do with.

Leo thought of his home with Jocelyn, his adopted mom. Their apartment above the shop had been so higgledy-piggledy, such a hodgepodge of things scattered around, crammed to the brim with crystals and joss sticks and tiny bottles of aromatic oils. Nothing had matched there—not even the table with the chairs, or either side of the curtains at the window, not a single plate or knife or fork. Jocelyn had gathered what she could from second-hand stores and garage sales, and Leo remembered the times he'd gone with her, her hands rifling through boxes of knick-knacks until she'd pull out a girl made of china carrying a basket of flowers or a chipped cup with an L on it.

"Especially for you," she'd said, handing him the mug, and he had used it from that day on, putting his lip to the groove of the chip as though that was especially for him too.

It was only when Ember came into the kitchen that Leo realized he hadn't thought to greet her when he first arrived, nor she him. She must have heard him come into the house. Had she been waiting for him to come upstairs and see her?

"Hi," she said, and Leo knew from that one word he was right.

"Hey," he said. "How was your morning?"

Ember shrugged. Leo closed the fridge door. He knew what she wanted—some acknowledgment, some affection, for him to coordinate with her, for the two of them to match, or at least for him to make the effort to fit in. He felt a flash of anger that it wasn't enough that he had mowed the lawn and fixed the fence and persuaded her mother to come with him to the shops and put away the groceries and slept in that too-hot room in that too soft bed. Sensing his annoyance, Ember put a hand on his arm. He stared at it there, wishing he could shake it off.

"I missed you," she said.

He wanted to run for the hills.

"Me too," he said.

Leo woke that night sensing he was not alone. Ember's hair shone even in the darkness of the room, but he had to squint to see her face. She was sitting cross-legged on the floor next to him.

"You really should try the bed," she said, as though her being there was not worth remarking on. "It's comfy once you get used to it."

Leo pushed himself up on an elbow. "How long have you been here?"

"Only a little while. I'm just worried about you." Leo felt himself scowl. "Don't be cross," she said. "I only wish we could talk . . . tell each other anything . . . everything. You know, like a proper couple."

Leo's jaw clenched and he had to force his arms to stay by his side and his legs not to spring to standing. "A proper couple," he repeated. "Who do you know who's a proper couple?" He saw Ember flinch, but he couldn't stop now. "Did you see it on TV? Or read it in one of your books?"

"I'm doing my best to learn about this place. Become a part of it. You should try it sometime."

She sounded so different from the girl he'd met last autumn in the dell. He missed that Ember—so unusual and unrefined. "That's the difference between you and me," he said in a low voice. "I don't want to be a part of it."

"Well, what do you want to be a part of?"

As soon as Ember asked the question, Leo could see her find the answer for herself. He got to his feet so as not to witness her reaction, but she rose too and took him by the arms.

"Poppy's gone," she said through gritted teeth. "When are you going to get it through your head? She left us. She left you."

Leo pulled himself away, but Ember threw her arms around his neck and clung on so tightly that he felt he couldn't breathe. "I'm sorry . . . I'm sorry," she cried in between kisses to his chest.

"What is it you want from me?" Leo whispered loudly, pushing her up against the wardrobe.

"You. I just want you."

So Leo kissed her, with all the guilt and anger that was raging inside of him. He felt her body tense and then her hands trying to push him back. She began to talk, but he wouldn't let her. He couldn't bear to hear it, so he pressed his mouth to hers again.

"Stop," he heard her say. It came to him as if from a distance. "Stop," he heard again and he pulled back suddenly and saw the fear in her eyes. "Not like this," she said, and he could tell she was crying.

"I'm sorry." Leo groaned, shocked at the anguish that came out of him. He banged his hand against the wardrobe door.

"Leo!" she cried.

"I'm sorry," he said to the wood, his lips against the glossy paint. And then his fist was through the panel, pieces splintering and cutting into him.

Ember screamed, and Leo stared at his hand with a detached, scientific interest as the blood streamed from the multitude of cuts. Ember grabbed the sheet from the bed and tried to wrap it around the wounds.

"Come and sit down." Her voice was shaking.

He shook his head. "Leave me."

"Let me help you. It looks so painful."

The pain, in fact, felt good; a relief to have something so physical and exact to feel instead of such a swirling torrent of emotion.

"I'm no good without her," he confessed. "Can't you see that?"

Ember's chin trembled as she fought off the tears. "She's a witch, Leo. We're . . . we're just chaffs. And there's nothing we can do about it."

"I know," he admitted, and she didn't say any more. She did as he'd asked and left him there, left him staring at the hole he'd made, not knowing how to mend it.

10

BETONY

Betony was threading flowers through her hair when the chaff approached. Cowslips and blue-eyed Mary, stitchwort and red campion. The chaff was waving a stick and his features looked contorted, his eyes tiny brown dots, his mouth a huge red hole. He was shouting at her, but she didn't comprehend what he was saying until he drew nearer.

"Get off my land! Get off my land!" he repeated.

Betony looked around the square field, fenced and hedged on each side, a stable at one end, a trough at the other. His land. It still seemed strange to her that chaffs thought earth and water, grass and stone, trees and plants could belong to them. Did they think they owned the sky too? Betony raised her hand and let her fingers trail through the air. One of the horses whickered and ambled over to her. This was the palomino, bronze and gold, her favorite of the two. The other was a silver gray, more wary than its companion. Their hooves were lined with metal hoops, nailed in to keep them locked there. The gray wore straps around its face, which made him look imprisoned. Clearly the chaffs thought they owned these creatures, too.

"Didn't you hear what I said?" the chaff shouted. Betony stared at him. His cheeks hung mottled and heavy beneath his jaw; his neck rippled in rolls to his chest. "Do I need to call the police?"

"Shoo," she translated to herself. "Shoo."

Betony remembered making that sound as a girl, often to the chickens that had pecked around her feet and once to a stray dog with matted fur. How strange that she could remember these tiny details yet had no bigger context in which to place them.

The chaff was looking at Betony as though she were mad. He fetched a shiny, slim box from his pocket. Betony had seen chaffs speak into them and thought they had looked mad. While the man tapped at it with his finger, she picked up her barrow and pushed it away, out of this square field and into another larger one. When she looked back, the man had put the tiny box away but was still watching her. *He's scared,* Betony thought. *That big, jowled beast is scared of me.*

Later, when he was gone, she returned to that field and took the palomino horse. She wasn't sure why. It was an idea that had buzzed around her brain and then flown inside her ear and settled there. It had pressed against her mind and wouldn't be dislodged. So she beckoned the horse to her side and it came with her willingly, out of the gate, down the trail, and into the woods. She sat upon it, skirts hitched, her torso laid along its mane as she threaded its pale hair with flowers too. Corydalis, speedwell, and sow thistle.

"Sister," she whispered into its silken ear. "My sister."

The horse grunted and nodded, and Betony stroked its neck with her hand. It kept on moving, taking her where it willed, stopping from time to time to chomp at the grass. Betony idled away the day with her new companion, traveling from woods to pastures, down narrow paths and tarmac roads. It was on one of these that the car with the spinning lights stopped and blocked their way. Two chaffs got out, a man and a woman dressed in matching material. They called her madam, but that was not her name.

"Does this horse belong to you, madam?"

Betony felt it wisest not to answer. She squinted at the flashing lights that rested on the car's roof. They made her dizzy.

The woman checked a notebook. "We've had a report of a stolen pony—Princess Buttercup. A palomino—just like this one."

Betony wrinkled her nose. A princess. What fools these chaffs were.

"Dismount the pony, madam," ordered the male. "Dismount or we will have to remove you by force."

Betony cocked her head and pondered her situation. In the end, the horse decided for her. It reared up and, neighing its objection, it turned and galloped away. Betony clung on tightly as its hooves clattered and clanged upon the road. The car with the lights roared and screamed an awful wail behind them. The horse took to the air and leapt over a fence. Its sides were slick with sweat and Betony clasped her hands into its mane and her thighs around its body. The car's engine stopped and the sirens became less ear-splitting, but still the horse thundered on. Her body began to move in time with that of the horse, like they had become one.

"Sister," Betony whispered. "My sister."

11

CHARLOCK

Charlock's journey had been long but mostly pleasant. Many days she had traveled, through rain and sun, day and night. She had hidden in the back of trucks that had taken her for miles on roads so wide and full that Charlock could scarcely believe it possible this many people could be moving this fast in the same direction. She had walked so far that both her boots had holes that she had tried to plug with pieces of trash. She had eaten what she could—sucking from raw eggs that she stole from nests like a magpie, crouching beneath a cow and squeezing milk from its udder into her mouth, eating from the scraps thrown into hedgerows and marveling at what the chaffs discarded. While on foot, she had avoided the roads where she could, sticking to paths through fields and forests, noticing how the climate changed the farther south she traveled and how even the apple trees were already in bloom and the magnolia petals were fallen to the ground, soft and slippery underfoot.

On one road, a chaff stopped his car and offered her a lift.

"Where you headed?" He smiled at her with teeth so white and straight they looked unused.

"South," she told him.

"Hop in if you want."

His car was silver and cool to touch, but inside it was warm and had an unnatural, sickly smell.

"I'm Simon," he told her. Charlock didn't reply. She had never given her real name to any chaff. "What's down south?" he asked. Again Charlock didn't answer. He sighed. "You don't have to be scared, you know. I'm not going to hurt you."

"Nor I you," Charlock said quietly.

Simon raised his eyebrows, then turned a knob on a panel in front of him. Music started to sound from holes in the sides of the car and a lady sang sadly of love and magic and moonlight. Then the song changed and became a happy dance and on it went, from melody to melody, voice to voice, until Charlock couldn't recall the ones that she'd heard first.

After a few hours, they stopped to feed the car and themselves. Simon bought Charlock a meal in a restaurant with sticky seats and air redolent of frying fat. Her food arrived in a box. Inside, a brown disc lay between two discs of white—a burger in a bun, the menu read. It didn't taste like any meat Charlock knew and the potatoes were just as unrecognizable, cut into the thinnest of lines, all the same size, but seeming like they'd never touched the earth.

As Charlock reached for her water, Simon touched her hand. Charlock felt the hairs prickle on her arms. She looked him in the eye and held his gaze, readying herself for a battle. She'd use her magic if she had to.

"Perhaps we can see each other again?" he asked. "Somewhere a bit fancier next time."

Slowly, Charlock withdrew her hand. "No," she said softly. "We won't be seeing each other again." He seemed surprised, hurt even. "That does not mean I am not grateful," she added. "For the food and the transportation."

She waited for Simon to get angry or violent, but he just looked defeated, and Charlock felt a twist of guilt at presuming the worst of him.

"You can't blame a guy for trying," he muttered.

"No, I can't," she replied and, in her head, she chanted a good luck charm that she hoped might help him on another day.

As he sank back in his seat, Charlock got up and walked out of the doors that opened of their own accord. There, she turned away from the bright lights and constant buzzing of the road toward the quietness of the countryside.

For two more days, Charlock journeyed southward. Spring showers fell all the way. At first, she sought shelter beneath trees, in barns, or under shop awnings, but, when she realized the rain wouldn't pass, she walked on through it. Before long, her hair stuck to her head in strips and her sodden clothes clung to her skin. Her boots squelched with water and Charlock felt her feet wrinkle and rub inside them. A woman, older than her by two score years at least, stopped her van and asked if she could drop her anywhere.

"I'm not going far, mind," she warned.

This chaff had a gentle face and small but unguarded eyes that looked straight at her. Two dogs sat in the seat behind, their pink tongues sticking out of their grinning mouths. After Simon, Charlock had decided to keep to herself. No more mingling with chaffs. But her skirts were heavy with the rain no matter how many times she had tried to wring them out and her skin was shivery cold.

"They won't bite," said the woman.

Comforted by the fact this woman believed it was the dogs that made her hesitate, Charlock quickly opened the door and climbed in. The van was full of stuff and Charlock sat upon a pile of papers, her feet nestled in some bags.

"You can take off those wet boots, if you'd like. Let 'em dry."

When Charlock did so, she saw that her feet were red and blistered, but it felt so good to have them free. The woman put up the heat and it came gushing out through tiny vents. Charlock held her boots to them.

"There's some biscuits down there someplace. If the dogs haven't got to them."

Charlock felt one of the dogs panting on her neck. The van smelled of their breath and hair, but it was not unpleasant. She found the biscuits and offered them to the woman before munching on them hungrily.

"I'm Diana," the woman said.

Charlock looked into the chaff's open, honest face. "I'm Charlock," she replied.

As they drove, Charlock learned that Diana was a widow. Her two children had married and moved abroad. Diana was, as she described herself, an "empty nester." Charlock felt a pang at these words.

"I, too," she said.

"You need to get yourself some dogs," Diana advised. "Better company than any feller and loyal to boot."

Charlock smiled at that and thought to herself that Diana might like the coven life. Perhaps, in another age, she might have been a sister.

"So who do you come looking for then?" asked Diana, and Charlock looked at her in surprise. "Traveling folk are either looking or lost, in my book. And you don't look lost."

Charlock wasn't sure why she answered, just as she hadn't understood why she had told Diana her name. She knew it was wrong, going against everything that she'd been taught, but her intuition was pushing her to respond and so she did and found it felt surprisingly right.

"I'm looking for a friend. Betony's her name. I haven't seen her for a long time now. Sixteen years or so."

"And you figure she's still living in these parts?"

"I think she'll be close to the village of Fairwood. But she'll be lost. Her memory . . . " Charlock wasn't sure how to explain this, but Diana seemed to understand.

"Oh, poor pigeon. My Henry got the Alzheimer's. Couldn't recognize me in the end. But he was old at least. It's a dreadful curse, to forget."

Charlock looked down at her lap and closed her eyes. For Betony, it was a curse indeed. Diana reached over and patted her knee.

"Don't look so guilty about it. It's nobody's fault."

Oh, but it was, Charlock thought. "I let her down," she whispered, and she felt her shoulders drop and her neck ease as she confessed.

"Whatever's in the past, you come looking for her now," Diana comforted. "That's what counts. Now what does this girl look like? Maybe I seen her. I've lived around here my whole life."

As Charlock described Betony's auburn hair and freckled face, the length of her legs and the rasp to her voice, a tingle spread across her scalp and she knew her friend was near. She could predict before Diana spoke what she would say.

"I know the one! We call her the barrow girl. Keeps to the woods mostly."

"Can you take me there?"

"You're looking at them." Diana pointed across the fields to a distant line of trees.

Charlock's hand went to the door and Diana stopped the van. "I can drop you closer." But Charlock had already jumped out. "Thank you! Thank you!" she told her.

"Good luck," Diana cried, and Charlock waved, then ran, her feet bare, her boots swinging from her hand.

Charlock crossed the land swiftly. The slopes were gentle here, none of the dramatic highs and lows of home. The fields were smaller, too, separated by neat hedgerows and fences, rather than the tumbling rocky walls that Charlock was accustomed to. Little signposts guided the way, along well-worn paths, and there were kissing gates and stiles with steps. Charlock lifted herself over these with ease, jumping down from them and landing softly on supple, bended knees. After so many days of traveling, she had finally arrived. The woods were only a few minutes further, so close that Charlock could make out the different types of trees and see the shape of the leaves upon them. Betony was near. She could feel it.

As if to concur, a cuckoo called, the first Charlock had heard that spring. Then, in the distance, a horse neighed, loud and urgent, and Charlock knew it was a message sent for her ears. She stopped and turned to look across the horizon. A violent, screaming blare sounded. There was trouble. Charlock closed her eyes. The horse was being chased and she could feel its hooves knocking against the earth, heading fast in her direction. She waited and watched for what felt like several minutes. At last, the horse appeared, a tawny, titian blur of coat and mane and hair. And Charlock knew that hair so well. It belonged to the tiny figure of a woman crouched low upon the horse's back.

The horse slowed to a trot when it saw her, and Betony raised her face from its mane so that Charlock could see her features. Thinner now, fine lines around the eyes, but the same smattering of dots on the same nose and cheeks. There were flowers in her hair, drooped and tangled. Charlock felt like reaching up for her old friend and pulling her down into an embrace. But then Betony looked directly at her and that's when Charlock saw the biggest difference. The eyes were not those of her friend. No spark of Betony's character, her humor or vitality. They were a stranger's eyes and they sent a chill down Charlock's spine.

"Betony," Charlock tried. Still nothing of her friend in Betony's face. Charlock went to the horse and stroked its nose, letting it nudge her hand. "Thank you," she whispered. "For bringing her to me." Then she looked up at Betony and held up her palm. "See this scar. You have one too." Betony blinked, but otherwise her face showed little reaction. Charlock tried again. "I've come to help you remember."

Betony seemed to consider Charlock's scar for many moments, but then she reached out her own arm and took hold of Charlock's to dismount. Betony's hand felt dry and calloused in Charlock's, but her grip was firm. Her touch lasted only a moment as then she went to wipe the white slick of sweat from the horse's neck, before rubbing the animal affectionately between its ears.

"Go on home now," Betony told it, looking deep into its eyes. The horse shook its head unsurely. "Go on now. They'll be looking for you." She watched as the horse seemed to nod before trotting away.

"So, you know who I am?" Betony asked, with her eyes still fixed on the horse.

"Yes," said Charlock, not expecting such directness from someone so confused.

Betony suddenly turned her gaze to Charlock. It felt unsettling and Charlock had to hush the anxiety building within her.

"And you have come to tell me?" This was more a statement than a question.

"I have."

Then, before Charlock had time to flinch, Betony raised her hand and slapped her. Charlock's hand went to her stinging cheek. "Something tells me you deserve that," Betony said sedately.

Charlock bowed her head. "I do."

12

POPPY

The pain from the feather only faded in the early hours of the morning. At last, as the sun was rising, Poppy's mind fell into a deep and dreamless sleep. When she awoke, she felt well again with not even a hint of tenderness in her stomach. Poppy sensed immediately that Raven had left her. The relief was fleeting. Poppy knew where the ghost would have gone and she worried for Sorrel. Mma, of course, was right. No one could rid Sorrel of Raven but Sorrel herself. Yet it troubled Poppy; the idea that Raven was still so powerful, still beyond her reach. She might have driven away Raven's ghost, but that didn't stop her feeling haunted.

"You look better," Teko told her when she stepped outside the hut.

"It was a rough night," Poppy admitted.

"You know, you start to look more from this place," Teko said. "More like the sun."

Poppy glanced at her arms. Her skin was a golden brown. *Like Leo's,* she thought and, in that second, she yearned to see him.

"Teko, would you say you have a purpose?" Poppy asked, steering her thoughts in another direction.

"A purpose?" he questioned.

"You know . . . in life?"

"What I want?"

"Yes."

"I want to buy my mother and father a house so we can be together." Poppy almost wept, she felt so humbled. "And I want to run faster than anyone else in the world. And win a trophy for my speed."

Poppy smiled, and Teko tossed her some bread that she caught.

"Eat," said Mma as she approached with a big bag hanging from her shoulder. "You come with me today."

"Where to?" Poppy asked.

"You'll see," said Mma.

They walked for many miles until Poppy's throat was sore from the dust and her feet and calves hurt more with every step she took. She dared not complain, though, as Mma, so many decades older, kept a steady pace throughout, despite her hobbling steps and heavy bag. Poppy kept on offering to carry it, but Mma always refused. Occasionally, she handed Poppy some water from a small calf-belly sack. On one of these stops, Poppy heard the jarring sound of running engines. Concerned, Poppy looked to Mma, but she just gestured for her to drink. A minute later, a convoy of jeeps sped past carrying tourists with giant lenses around their necks.

"Maybe from your land," Mma mused.

"You don't mind them seeing you?" Poppy asked.

"Mind?"

"I mean, you live in the middle of nowhere . . . I thought you might be hiding?" Mma looked even more puzzled. "You know . . . because you're a witch." Mma gave a throaty chuckle that became a cough that turned into a full-blown burst of laughter. Poppy felt her cheeks redden. "Where I come from, witches live in a coven," she tried to explain. "Away from everyone else. Especially men. Even boys like Teko." Mma was laughing so much that she had to hold on to her sides to support herself. "They're really serious about it," Poppy stressed, beginning to feel defensive.

Mma took the water from her and had a gulp, then wiped her mouth with her hand. "No men," she said, "no fun."

An hour later, they finally approached a small village. The houses stood like a herd of buffalo in the empty landscape, dark against the sunburned earth. A man with a goat was walking up ahead and a small child saw them and began running toward them. It had been so long since Poppy had been in the company of people other than Mma and Teko that the nerves prickled like a rash along her skin. The child threw himself against Mma's legs and she rubbed the coiled hair on his head and squished his chubby cheek. The smile, so genuine, seemed to burst from his face, and he was dressed in a T-shirt and shorts two sizes too small so his body was bursting out of those too, the seams splitting under the force. The boy said something that Poppy couldn't understand. Then, without waiting for Mma's answer, out darted a finger to touch Poppy's arm.

"He asks who stole the color from your skin," Mma explained.

Poppy smiled. Perhaps she wasn't as tanned as she thought. She held out her palms, showing the child the milkier insides of her arms. He traced a finger along one of them and it tickled, making Poppy laugh.

"Come," said Mma, leading her into the village.

They held their clinic in a hut that belonged to an old man with no hair on his head but a long white beard that reached his chest. He greeted Mma with an affectionate hug.

"My husband," Mma told Poppy, and Poppy felt her mouth drop open.

"I didn't know you were married," she whispered to Mma as they emptied the medicines from the bag and laid them out in rows on the floor. "Why don't you live together?"

"We do and we don't," said Mma. Poppy turned the words over in her mind looking for their meaning. "We have lived long enough to do what suits," added Mma as if that clarified things.

That afternoon, they saw a man whose back hurt him so much that he could hardly remain upright; a young woman who could not get pregnant; a child with fits who broke into one as if on cue, his little body jerking and twitching on the ground and his eye-balls rolling in his head like he was being electrocuted; and an old lady whose hands were so gnarled and twisted that she could no longer open them. Each one, Mma listened to and examined, her words as gentle as her touch. With some, she prescribed medicine and dispensed small bags of herbs or bottles of lotion. With others, she laid on hands or massaged muscle and cracked joints back into place. With all, she said words that Poppy took to be a charm of some kind. Out of all the remedies, this was the one for which the patients seemed most grateful.

"Most often," Mma told Poppy, "it is the mind that holds the cure. The most powerful medicine is belief."

"Belief in you?"

Mma wagged her finger. "Not in me. No, no. In themselves. In their recovery."

Their last patient entered; a teenage girl with buck teeth and an awkward gait who wouldn't look at them. Her father led the way, the girl shuffling behind as if she were being pulled, though in fact the father wasn't touching her. He and Mma spoke while the girl stayed silent, her eyes staring at the floor. Mma turned to Poppy.

"Her father says she cries all the time. She won't speak. He says her stepmother thinks she has a demon in her." Poppy looked perplexed. "You help her," said Mma.

Poppy hesitated, but Mma nodded for her to begin. Stepping forward, she addressed the girl directly. "Can I take your hand?" she asked. "Is that okay?"

Mma translated and the girl lifted up her arm, offering her hand. Poppy took it in her own and the pictures swam into her mind, savage as sharks. A woman—the girl's stepmother—beating her. The girl curled up, her eyes squeezed shut, her mouth open in a silent scream as the blows rained down. Poppy blinked; the images were too harsh to bear witness to. Panicked, she looked to Mma for advice but none was offered, only a dip of the head telling her to continue.

The father spoke urgently, his hands jabbing the air. Mma looked at Poppy. "He wants to know about the demon."

Poppy took one of the father's hands and, before he could protest, she linked it to his daughter's, putting her own hand on top. The father tried to pull away, but Poppy clasped it there, and then, after a few seconds, she felt the father flinch and knew he'd seen it too. When the father tried to pull away again, Poppy released him. With an anguished cry, he hurried outside.

Poppy fetched a bag of herbs and gave them to the girl, who, for the first time, looked at her. "For your voice," Poppy told her.

The girl waited, saying nothing, but her eyes spoke for her—fear, relief, and expectation shining from them. Poppy tried to think what more she could do for her.

"The charm," explained Mma.

Immediately, Poppy began repeating the strange words she'd heard Mma use with each of her patients. When she finished, the girl bent and put her forehead to Poppy's hand.

At first, Poppy wished the girl would stand, but the longer the head lay bowed, the weighty skull heavy on her slender bones, the more Poppy surrendered to the moment. And then she felt a serenity wash over her like water, cool and calming. Poppy had felt this perfect peace only twice before—when she revived Sorrel from her coma and when she gave strength to Mrs. Silva's baby. And now she felt it again. *My purpose,* came the thought inside her head.

13

BETONY

Betony traced the silver scar that lined her palm. It matched the one the woman had shown her. "Friends first." The words hopped into her mind like a hare. She searched for images to accompany them, but there were none.

This woman didn't feel like a friend. She said her name was Charlock. Betony mouthed the syllables, emphasizing the way her tongue moved upon them. Still the name did not chime.

Charlock said a lot of things on the walk to the woods. She said that they were both witches from a coven far from here on the furthest reaches of the land. That they had lived as girls in a forest much greater than these small woods and thickets. When Betony tried to picture the size of this she found it dark and frightening, not like her home of trees where she knew every trunk and pathway, where the rabbits burrowed and the birds and squirrels nested. They had lived, Charlock told her, far from the others who for centuries had persecuted and murdered them. They kept their magic to themselves and the coven was for women only. It was forbidden for men to cross their boundaries. At this, Charlock stopped so she could look at her.

"You must understand, Bet. It is for our protection. Our coven would not exist if men could breach it. They are like the knotweed or the gray squirrel, invading and soon conquering. Our ways would die out. These men would trail our secrets behind them, scattering them like dust. We witches are sisters, all. Just like you and I. Males can only separate us, weaken our affections, dissolve our trust, our loyalty, split us one from the other. We cannot be our true selves with them amongst us."

Betony found her teeth grinding at this.

"What kind of sister were you to me, I wonder?" she said.

Charlock glanced away. "I did my best. You made it hard for me. You don't remember, but wait to judge me until you know it all." Looking back, she held up her palm once more, tears forming in her eyes like dew. "But this—this was your idea. So we could be like true sisters sharing the same blood."

Her idea. Betony looked down at her palm. So many times she had wondered how that faint snail's trail had gotten there. Now that she knew the answer, it felt even more bewildering.

"So what went wrong?" she asked, severing Charlock's sentiment.

Charlock sighed and shifted from one foot to the other. "You met a boy."

Betony looked at her with incredulity. "A man?!"

"A boy," Charlock corrected.

"So they threw me out? This coven of yours?" Betony assumed angrily.

"You wished to go."

Betony shook her head. It didn't feel right. This life had not been one that she had chosen.

"You . . . you have a son, Betony." Betony's hand moved to her belly and she knew it was true. "You wanted to keep him . . . no matter . . . "

"No matter the consequences."

She had to sit. Her legs had given up on her. Even her brain was in a spiral. She was all heart now, beating too loud and too strong so it was all she could hear and feel. A son. She had a son.

"And did I?" The thought was so huge, but these little words were all she could manage.

"Did you what?" Charlock sat opposite her, surveying her with worried, wide-set eyes.

"Did I keep him?"

"You kept him alive, if that's your meaning." Betony's head fell to her knees, so heavy was the relief.

"Where is he?" she said to the ferny floor beneath her legs.

"Close, I think."

"Have you seen him?"

"Once." Betony raised her head at that.

"How did he seem?"

"Oh, Bet. He has your eyes. Not the color, but the very same shape and expression. I knew who he was immediately. The rest is his father, dark skin and hair. I saw him in a train station and I sat with him a while. He seemed a good person. Caring. Wild and hurting, I think. But good at heart." Betony tried to paint a picture of him in her mind. "You would be proud of him," Charlock reassured.

"What did you speak of? What did he say?" Betony asked, and Charlock blanched like she had slapped her other cheek. "You did tell him about me, didn't you?"

Charlock paused and Betony wanted to reach out and shake the confession from her. "I asked his name," Charlock finally said. "He's called Leo. I . . . I thought you would be pleased at that. A strong name."

"Leo." Betony did not feel pleased. "Did I choose that? But what did you tell him about me?" she said again, flinging the words like stones.

Charlock closed her eyes. "Nothing." Then she cringed as if expecting a blow. When nothing came, she opened her eyes. "I was not permitted, Betony. Like I told you, it is not the witches' way. He is a male and he is a chaff."

"Chaff?" Betony spat.

"He is one of them. Not like us."

"But he is my son."

Charlock got to her feet defensively. "That's even worse. If the clans knew . . . "

"He is my son!" Betony could hear her voice shrill and sharp in her ears. "A son who knows nothing of his mother. And you call yourself my friend!"

Charlock's cheeks flushed and she flung her arms in the air. "You do not understand. You have forgotten our ways."

Anger surged through Betony's legs and she jumped to her feet, pushing Charlock up against the tree and putting her face close so she could smell her.

"And why is that? Why is that, Charlock the witch?"

Charlock didn't answer. "I want to help you," she said instead.

A magpie fluttered down from a tree, treading audaciously close, like he wanted to hear what would happen next. The women looked at him and Betony let Charlock go, as if the bird had caught her in a crime. They both looked around them to see if there was another.

"One for sorrow," Betony said, and Charlock nodded.

Simultaneously, they spat three times on the ground. As Charlock met her eye, Betony knew that they had done this together many times before. Charlock smiled, and the magpie flapped into the air and was gone. A silence settled and the breeze dropped so all was still for a moment.

"I don't remember you," Betony said softly. "I remember about magpies, but I don't remember about you or about a boy or about a baby."

Charlock reached out and took Betony's hands, but it didn't stop them shaking. "It is the magic," she explained. "A spell of oblivion. Please, Bet. Let me help you."

14

YOUNG BETONY

Betony hid the jacket under the caravan, where her aunt would never find it. In truth, Betony's aunt was half-blind, so it was the smell that Betony feared would betray her. As soon as she arrived back that dawn, she wrapped Danny's jacket twice over in old sacks that she took from the storeroom. Even so, Sister Sage's nostrils twitched at her appearance.

"Come hither, child." She beckoned Betony to come closer.

Reluctantly, Betony shuffled forward until her aunt reached out a bony hand and pulled her nearer. Then she brought her nose to Betony's skin and clothes and sniffed around them like a dog.

"No yoking," she stated.

"No," Betony replied, marveling at how her aunt's nose could detect this truth.

"Yet I smell a chaff. A male. Young." Her aunt's nose had started dripping and she wiped it on her sleeve.

"We met several," Betony prevaricated.

"I only smell one."

"I talked with one but . . . nothing more."

Sister Sage put her fingertips, rough as a cat's tongue, on Betony's face, feeling for her eyes. "You should sleep." Then she put her fingers to her mouth and tasted. "More than talk, methinks."

To Betony's relief, her aunt turned away and started hobbling out of the caravan. Betony took off her boots and slipped gratefully into bed. As she closed her eyes, she thought of the jacket and the gum lying under the boards beneath her. It felt good to have a secret to protect. It made her feel lucky.

Luck had not been a feature of Betony's life so far. Her mother had passed when she was three. A branch from the beech tree on the ridge had fallen while her mother had sat there. It hit her on the head, crushing her skull like it was made of shell. Apparently, the young Betony had run all the way home by herself and taken her Great Aunt Sage's hand and led her to the spot where her mother lay. Betony had tried many times to imagine this journey—wondering how her tiny self could have been so practical at such a time of shock—but she could not say that she really recalled it. Nor did she remember how the coven tried all their craft to revive her mother, though they swore this was the case. What was still fresh in Betony's mind was how she'd hidden her tears. For when her aunt tried to console her, her failing eyes rolled around their sockets so that only the whites were to be seen. And her nose, as if puffed up by its importance, seemed grotesquely large and fearsome.

Even at such a young age, Betony felt ashamed of being so repelled by her aunt's appearance. The coven clearly taught that value lay within, like a nut within its husk, or a fossil in a stone. Yet, to Betony's dismay, her aunt's looks scared her and she dreaded having to be in her company. So when she heard her aunt calling for her, she would wriggle like a worm beneath the caravan and hide there in the damp darkness with the woodlice and the beetles until finally it was safe to reappear. For Aunt Sage always gave up her search and turned to other tasks. This, Betony came to understand, was the difference between an aunt and a mother. And this was when Betony missed her mother the most, when the calling stopped, when no one noticed. To be motherless was a curse that Betony would wish on no one.

Sister Mildred was with child. Her group had come across some campers by the river. Older men, there for the fishing. Betony and Charlock grimaced at each other, then giggled when they heard. It was hard to keep their laughter within during the ring ceremony, a most serious affair. All the coven stood in silence as Mildred lay beneath the golden ring that was dangled above her stomach. All eyes were on the ring, waiting to see which way it turned. It spun in circles rather than back and forth. The sigh of relief was audible. The baby was a girl.

There was much jubilation in the camp at Mildred's achievement and Mildred made sure to milk this for all she could. Over the coming days, she made a show of running to the lavatories to be sick, her puking so loud and dramatic, it had to be exaggerated. Betony tried not to roll her eyes, but she did glimpse Raven clench her jaw and scoop little Sorrel into her arms, muttering, "You'd think she was the only witch to ever be with child." It reminded Betony that Raven's yoking experience had not been a happy one. Charlock had trusted Betony with this confidence. Apparently,

Raven never spoke of it, but the day after was the one and only time that Charlock had ever seen her mighty sister shaken.

Irritating as Sister Mildred was, she served to focus the girls' minds before their next yoking. But Betony had no need of Mildred to inspire her. Already she was counting down the days until she might see Danny again. Some flitted by fast, while others lagged so lethargically that she wanted to scream with frustration. Sister Sage noticed Betony's restlessness and tried to treat it with her special tonic. The medicine tasted foul, but Betony took it, hoping for a remedy even though she knew the cause to be incurable. Her kestrel began visiting more often, bringing her dead mice as gifts, and Charlock seemed worried, too.

"You're like a squirrel," she complained. "One minute up, the next down. Jumping from one mood to the next."

Betony longed to tell her friend the truth, but too much time had passed and she no longer knew how. Besides, the jacket lay there under the caravan—her buried treasure. Sharing it felt tantamount to losing it. For from it, sprouting like mushrooms in the darkness, spread the promise of finding Danny again.

"Don't be nervous," Charlock told her. "We will be together. I will make sure of it this time."

"It is not that," Betony tried to explain. "I want to go. It's just . . . "

Charlock looked skeptical. "You don't have to lie. There is no shame in being afraid."

"Perhaps we can set out earlier this time? Give ourselves more of a chance to settle, make a plan?" suggested Betony.

Charlock's eyebrows rippled in thought. "I can try and ask my mother," she said unsurely.

"We could go back to the same place, like we said. At least we are accustomed to it there."

"Are you sure?" Charlock looked at her with such concern that Betony couldn't meet her gaze. "It was not a happy hunting ground for you, I know that. We can try someplace else if you prefer?"

"And catch ourselves an old angler by the river?" Betony looked over to Sister Mildred, who already wore a smock although, as yet, she had no belly to speak of.

Charlock smiled. "We can go back to that street, that very house, if it makes you feel better."

In this way, when the eve finally arrived, Betony was prepared. She had stuffed the jacket into her bag and held on to it tightly, knowing it was her way back into Danny's life. The young sisters had gathered to watch Betony and Charlock set out. Their plan to leave before dusk had been approved and all seemed to be going smoothly. Then, just as they were about to depart, Raven spoke out. Betony winced as she heard that unmistakable voice, knowing from the first syllable it could only mean trouble.

"Sister Charlock. Sister Betony," Raven announced. "I have decided to accompany you this evening and help you find success." Betony could feel Charlock's body stiffen next to her, and her mind scrambled for an excuse. Not finding one soon enough, she looked to Charlock, who had frozen with an expression of open-mouthed shock upon her face. "It is agreed then," Raven declared.

Betony knew she must speak now or lose her chance with Danny. "It would be a great help to have you, Raven. And all your experience. Would it not, Charlock?" She gave her friend a sharp nudge and Charlock nodded, at last closing her lips. Then,

Betony latched desperately on to the only idea she could muster. "Come, Raven. We must find you a disguise too."

"Disguise?" Raven asked suspiciously.

"Oh, Charlock and I, we thought we might fare better if we dressed as the chaffs do."

Charlock looked at Betony in surprise, and Betony put her foot on Charlock's and pressed down hard. Then she held up her bag as if proof, praying no one would call her bluff.

"Yes," said Charlock, finally coming to her senses. "Like camouflage."

"Exactly," confirmed Betony.

"I will not don their costume," Raven muttered with a look of disgust. "And nor should you if you have any sense or self-respect."

"We will not try and persuade you, sister," Betony replied. "Would you join us all the same?"

Raven shook her head disdainfully. "I'll have no part in it."

As Raven hurried back to her child, Betony seized the moment, grabbing Charlock's hand and pulling her away. They walked as quickly as they could, wishing they could run, holding in their nervous giggles until they were well beyond earshot. Then, they stopped and laughed out their relief until their bellies hurt and Charlock had to pee. All would be well, Betony told herself. Luck was on their side tonight.

Once in town, Betony spied a clothesline with laundry hanging from it. She crept into the garden and returned with armfuls. Charlock looked aghast.

"I thought you were jesting . . . for Raven's benefit."

"I was . . . but then it struck me we could use a little help this time."

Charlock was shaking her head. "I cannot touch them."

Crouching down behind a hedge, Betony began to disrobe. "Don't be silly. They are material, just as ours." She pulled on a top and felt it smooth against her skin. "Only softer." She held another shirt out to Charlock. "Another dare?" she challenged.

Charlock waited for a moment, then yanked it from her. "You are so bad, Betony Swift."

Betony grinned as she took another garment, put each leg into the long blue pillars and pulled up the waistband. Charlock gasped.

"You look like a man! I'll not wear those."

"Here's a skirt."

Charlock held it up. "It's so short," she wailed.

"That's what the bucks like."

"And how would you know?"

"I saw it. I saw them in the house looking at those does' legs like they wanted to devour them."

Charlock's eyes widened with fear. "This is trickery, us dressing up like this," she said as she pulled up the skirt, then tugged it down as far as it would go.

"Trickery, maybe. But not magic. Trickery we're allowed," and Betony looked down and marveled at how long her legs seemed, encased in their blue covers.

Betony made Charlock wait at the corner while she went to knock at Danny's door. She rapped with her knuckles, then spied a little button. It rang like a tiny bell when she pressed it. At last, Betony heard footsteps and the door opened. It wasn't Danny who stood there but a young girl with black rings drawn around her eyes, a jewel in her nose, and a bored expression on her face.

"Yeah?" said the girl. Betony wanted to turn and run, but then the girl spoke again. "You looking for Danny?" She nodded. "He's at the playing fields, up at the park." Betony looked confused and the girl pointed. "Go up Dawson Street and hang a right. You'll see the gates." She nodded again and the girl looked her up and down critically. "You know your top's on inside out?"

Betony stared at its hem as the door shut with a thud.

The playing fields were easy enough to find, but it was harder to locate Danny. So many boys were gathered there of so many ages and appearances. Charlock gawped while Betony's eyes searched.

"There's herds of them."

"There are."

"Hundreds." Charlock took Betony's hand.

They stood there for a few long minutes and Betony's eyes began to hurt from staring. In the end, Danny spotted her.

"Betony," his voice called from afar, and Betony started like a cat, her muscles taut and hairs on end. "Betony!"

When she found him, she smiled and saw that he was smiling too and running, so fast, to meet her. When he approached, he was panting, mouth open, his cheeks red from racing.

"I've been looking everywhere for you," he said. "Where you been?"

"Away," she told him. "But I'm here now."

"You are." He grinned. "You look different."

"It's the clothes," said Betony, looking down at herself anxiously, but Danny had turned his attention to Charlock.

"Hey," he said.

Charlock stared at him, and Betony could feel her friend's thoughts scurrying, trying to scout the story behind this surprise.

"This is Clara," Betony quickly answered. "My friend." Then she turned to Charlock and spoke with purpose, hoping Charlock would catch the apology in her voice. "I met Danny while I was waiting for you last time." Charlock's eyes were wet with hurt. "I wasn't sure I'd ever see him again," Betony tried to explain.

"He knows your name," Charlock spluttered.

Betony glanced at Danny and saw a bewildered expression on his face. Quickly, she took Charlock's arm and leaned her head against her shoulder. "I should have told you," she whispered. "Forgive me." Then she turned to Danny. "Show Clara your tricks with that ball, will you?"

Danny seemed uncertain, but Betony entreated him with her eyes. Rather unsurely, he picked up a nearby ball and started to kick it from limb to limb, not letting it fall to the ground. Charlock looked unimpressed.

"Danny, you coming or what?" a voice yelled, and Danny caught the ball and turned to the group of chaffs heading farther up the fields. He looked back at Betony and Charlock.

"You want to hang out?"

Betony peered at Charlock, awaiting her approval. Finally, Charlock sighed and gave a half-hearted nod.

They sat on the grass in a ring around the bottles. So many bottles for so few mouths. Music played at a great volume from only a tiny box, but no one seemed to hear it, they were talking and drinking and laughing so loud. Danny kept close to Betony, pulling her hand onto his thigh and holding it there. Overwhelmed by this contact, Betony kept her head lowered and her eyes fixed on the patch of mud encrusted on his knee, itching to pick it off and see the olive skin beneath. She could feel the heat of Charlock's disapproving glare upon their hands and wished she was back in Danny's yard where they could be alone and she could say and do as she dared. She gave Charlock a gentle dig with her elbow.

"What?" Charlock muttered.

"See to your right?" Charlock looked confused. "That boy—I think he likes you."

Charlock's almond eyes grew even larger in her face. "He does?"

Betony nodded. "Why don't you talk to him?" Charlock shook her head in fear. "Just talk to him. The yoking, remember."

Making a face, Charlock slowly turned her attention to the boy and, after a minute, Betony felt her friend slightly shift away from her and closer to him. She couldn't hear Charlock's words but soon she saw the boy's arm reaching for a bottle and handing it to her. With Betony's guilt somewhat alleviated, she peeked back at Danny but found a girl sitting on his other side, legs crossed, her hand on his arm. She was a different breed to the females Betony was used to, her features soft and squishy as dough. Her nose hardly protruded from her face and even that seemed rounded. But when the girl looked at Betony, her eyes were sharp as nails. She got up and, swaying on her feet, tried to pull Danny up with her.

"Come on," she slurred. "You said you'd go with me."

The girl's top covered her breasts but then stopped, leaving her midriff bare despite the spring night's chill. Betony glanced at Danny to see if he was looking there, but his eyes were turned up toward the girl's face.

"I can't," he was saying. "Get Jake to go with you."

"I don't want Jake. I want you," the girl whined, pulling harder on Danny's arm.

Danny yanked himself free from the girl's grip. "I'm staying here," he said firmly.

"What? With her?"

"Her name's Betony. Betony, this is Emmy."

The girl didn't even bother to look at her. Instead, she knelt down and put her cheek to Danny's to plead into his ear. "But you said you weren't seeing anyone."

Danny turned to Betony with embarrassment. "Sorry about this."

The girl grabbed Danny's face in her fingers and turned it back toward her. "Hey, I'm talking to you."

"You're drunk, Emmy. Leave us alone."

"Who is this bitch, anyway?" The girl straightened and loomed over them. "Where'd she suddenly turn up from?"

"Betony's my friend." Danny spoke calmly, but Betony could feel the pressure of his hand as it squeezed hers.

Emmy snorted with laughter like a pig. Then, she snorted again and again, even more loudly as though she couldn't stop herself. Everyone stopped talking and looked at her. Emmy's hand flew to her nose, covering it up. Then she doubled over and turned yellow.

"I feel sick," she exclaimed.

Out of her mouth spewed a torrent of liquid that splashed and fizzed upon the ground. The others leapt to their feet, crying out in disgust.

Betony immediately looked to Charlock, who shrugged in response. With a gasp, Betony shook her head, but Charlock just winked at her. Then she looked back at the girl and muttered some words so the sickness stopped. As for Danny, he was on his feet and hurrying to Emmy's aid, putting an arm around her. She was weeping now and he held her tenderly so she could shelter her face in his chest. Betony felt her hopes drain away. It left her feeling hollow, as though she might be picked up by the night air and carried away on its breeze. So she planted herself there, in that spot, waiting for Danny to remember her, to look around and acknowledge her existence. It was Charlock who pulled her to standing, uprooting her like a turnip.

"Bet, let's go," she said.

Danny had been joined by other girls, all of them preoccupied with Emmy's well-being. He hadn't remembered her. He hadn't looked over or acknowledged her.

"Leave him," came Charlock's advice, and Betony nodded.

Walking away on clumsy legs, hating the material that rubbed on her thighs and got under her feet, Betony still hoped to hear Danny's voice calling after her. It didn't come, though.

"Here," said Charlock, handing her the bag with their clothes and Danny's jacket still inside. It wasn't supposed to have gone like this, Betony grieved. She'd never even given him the jacket. Betony felt the sob rise like a bubble inside of her and she tried to press it down.

"So much for yoking," Charlock tried to jest. And out the sob came, letting loose Betony's tears that rolled like rain along her cheeks.

"Oh, Bet. Don't be sad. I know I shouldn't have used the spell, but that chaff was poisonous and nasty and she deserved it so." Betony could only cry harder and Charlock took her hands, then gasped as she felt her friend's emotions seeping through her pores. "You like him! Oh, Bet, no! It cannot be. You cannot!"

"It is done," Betony wept. "I am a fool, Charlock. I am sorry."

Then Danny's voice came hollering down the hillside. *Too late,* Betony thought. *Too late.*

"Don't answer him," whispered Charlock, and she took Betony's arm and they rushed away.

Danny ran fast, faster than they ever could in their odd, ill-fitting clothes.

"I can stop him, if you let me," Charlock offered through jagged breaths.

"No!" Betony exclaimed in horror. Then she stopped moving and Charlock halted too and looked at her aghast. "No more magic," Betony said.

"We must go," Charlock urged.

Betony glanced behind them at Danny's approaching figure. "We can't outrun him."

"Don't talk to him," Charlock warned.

"Let me just listen," Betony pleaded, but Charlock was shaking her head.

"No, no, no," she kept saying, but then Danny was there beside them. "You're too late," Charlock said, echoing Betony's thoughts. "We're going, aren't we, Betony?"

But Danny ignored her, looking only at Betony, his eyes begging her to stay. "I'm sorry about Emmy."

Betony willed her eyes not to water. "You should go back to her," she replied. "You two have a bond."

"There's nothing between us," he protested.

Betony stepped toward Danny and put her lips to his ear for a moment. "Don't lie," she said. Danny blinked but couldn't seem to find a way to answer. "Don't omit," she told him. At that, he released the truth.

"I didn't think I would ever see you again. We were drunk. I hooked up with her once but that was it. I swear it."

Betony closed her eyes as she felt her body recoil from his. "I shouldn't have come back," she muttered, taking a step back.

But Danny reached out for her. "No, no. You should," he said, taking hold of her shoulders. Then he pulled her close. "Please don't go," he whispered. "Not again."

"All those days, I thought of you. But you . . . you were with her."

"I don't even like her."

Betony gave a bitter laugh that became a cry, and Charlock took her arm, tugging her free. "Let's go," she urged.

All Danny's energy seemed to desert him. "I looked for you. I looked everywhere," he said. "I'm sorry I hurt you."

The apology was Betony's undoing and so she made her own. "I made too much of it," she confessed. "An accident was all it was. Us meeting. Talking. You had no ties to me."

"I did, though. I felt them." He said this so plainly and quietly that it felt utterly true.

"Bet," Charlock cautioned. But Betony did not heed her.

"I won't go back there," she told him.

Surprised, Danny's body sprang out of its slump. "Just walk with me. That's all I ask."

Betony twisted her head around to face Charlock. Her friend had turned ashen with dismay. "I'm going home," Charlock said. "You should come with me."

"Don't tell them," Betony begged.

Charlock hung her head. "You know I won't." Betony wrapped her arms around her friend and hugged her close. "Be careful," Charlock whispered into the thicket of Betony's hair. And then she was gone, walking away, leaving Betony behind.

15

YOUNG BETONY

Charlock was waiting for her by the brook beyond the crag. The moon was a fraction from full and the stars shone sharp in the sky so that Betony saw her from afar, sitting so still and patiently on the rocks beside the trickling stream. Betony raised her arm in a wide overhead wave, her heart bursting with gratitude as she hurried toward her. The two of them embraced, holding on to each other as though they had been parted for years, not hours.

"I've been so worried," Charlock cried. "Tell me you are well and that he did not hurt you."

"He wouldn't, Charlock. He is kind and gentle, I swear it. He didn't even . . . " Charlock pulled back in surprise as if needing to see Betony's face to check her meaning. "I swear it," Betony promised. "He wouldn't. I asked him why, but he said that he should know me first. That I should know him."

"Did he not even touch you?"

"He kissed me, once, when we said goodbye. Oh, Charlock, I was shaking, it was so sweet and full of wanting. I wished it would never end."

Charlock's eyes were enormous in her face and her mouth had dropped open.

"Oh, Bet," she said. "This cannot be good, what you are feeling."

"Why?" demanded Betony. "Because the elders say so?"

"Because we are different from him. Because we live apart, with our own ways. Because we have magic and he and his kind do not!"

Betony hung her head as the truth of this weighed on her heavily.

"You are right. I know you're right," she whispered.

Looking up, she saw that Charlock's face was rumpled with another emotion, she knew not which. "What is it?"

"I want us to tell each other everything. To not leave anything out."

"I did!"

"Not you, this time. But I." Charlock looked away to where the water was running from the stones. "I may be with child."

Betony gasped. "You mean? . . ."

Charlock scrunched her eyes tight before she spoke. "After I left you, I met the boy. The one you spotted liking me. We did it, Bet. But it was not as you describe. It was quick. This boy and I, we were joined together and yet we felt so far apart." Betony sat down next to her and Charlock looked up at her pleadingly. "Say something," she implored.

Betony took Charlock's hand and turned it over so she could see her palm and the scar that marked it. Then she got her own hand, her own scar and pressed it there so they joined.

"Friends first," she said.

Charlock's eyes shone with tears. "Always," she replied.

In her bed that night, Betony tried hard to banish the memories of Danny. Instead, she went over her day's errands, recited charms that she had yet to know by heart, and promised herself that she would become the best witch in all the clan. But still she could not sleep for thinking of him. The touch of his lips and the taste of his mouth. His arms strong around her. Her hips melted into his. His voice had shaken as he said goodbye and his hands had shaken as he let her go. He made her promise to return, and she had sworn to come and find him as soon as she was able.

All through the evening, they had walked and sat, then walked some more. Always he had a hand upon her or an arm around her. Never did he let her go. Sometimes, he would stop and hold her and she would put her lips against his neck, only softly but enough that she could feel him stiffen and pull her closer. Every second was spent in expectation of a kiss. The waiting for it made everything that night extraordinary, every routine word, every self-conscious laugh, every tentative touch. Each blade of grass, each insect, each twinkling light from town seemed to exist just for them. Because this was the night they would kiss. Neither of them spoke of it—that might break the spell that cloaked them in a web so delicately fashioned, and so easily torn. Instead, they trod carefully, talking of anything else other than what lay at the end of their walk. Danny's life was so dissimilar to hers that it seemed to Betony as though they inhabited two different worlds. But the promise of the kiss—that they had in common.

Betony told Danny little of her life, conscious that she was guilty of omission but not knowing what she could say that wouldn't endanger the both of them. So she told him she was staying with her great aunt out in the hills. He assumed she was taking a year off and she let him believe it, not knowing what he meant. He'd be starting college in the autumn; as yet, he knew not where. It depended on the "dreaded results." And Betony nodded like she understood.

He told her, too, about the girl Emmy, though Betony didn't want to hear it. His words about going out and finishing it and getting back together were mysterious to Betony, but it was a code she could crack. She had one question, though, and she couldn't help but ask it.

"So you yoke with this Emmy, but not I?" Danny looked confused and Betony realized her language was hard to decipher also. "I asked you to lie with me," she said more shyly, wishing she hadn't been so impetuous as to raise this question. "That night in the garden."

"Oh," he said. "That." And she saw his cheeks blush. "You want to know why I slept with her and not you?"

"Not sleep exactly," Betony corrected, and he smiled.

"It's because I like you," he said simply, and Betony wrinkled her nose with puzzlement.

"That doesn't make any sense."

"It does to me. You're different. . . . It should be different."

Betony felt a heat in her tummy that spread to her core. She stretched up and touched her nose to his, their lips so close. "It will be," she whispered, letting each letter of her words caress him.

When it was time for them to part, she realized she still hadn't returned his jacket. He shook his head when she offered it back.

"I liked you having it, thinking of you wearing it."

Unable to admit she could never wear it once she reached home, Betony put it on. Danny reached out a finger and touched the collar and traced it down to where the jacket fell open, sliding his hand underneath and around her waist.

"It suits you," he said, and Betony's cheeks warmed.

She heard an owl hoot and then saw it fly silently over the field, pale against the night. It had a mouse in its sights, Betony could tell, and sure enough it plunged to fetch it, then rose again with it dangling in its beak.

"I must go," she whispered, heeding nature's warning.

And then he kissed her and her legs went limp so that he had to hold her up, though she wished they could fall to the ground and lie together.

"Come soon," he said when she departed.

"I will," she promised.

16

POPPY

The swallows were leaving. Out of the reeds and the trees they appeared and up they flew. Poppy stood on the plain watching them fill the sky, setting off on their mass exodus.

"You say goodbye?"

Poppy turned to find Mma, her long neck stretched up to the sky.

"They are so tiny," Poppy remarked.

"They will fly faster this time. To make their nests," Mma told her.

"Why don't they just stay?"

"It is safer for their babies there. They are good parents," Mma explained. "Putting themselves at such risk for the sake of their little ones."

"Maybe it's a sign? That I should follow them?" Poppy questioned.

Mma's hands quivered up and down on either side of her in agitation. "No, no, no. You stay here. You let me help you, yes?"

Poppy looked into Mma's old, dark eyes, still bright pools within the deep furrows of her face. What she glimpsed there made her shiver. "What do you see for me if I return?" she whispered. "Is it danger? Is it Raven?"

"I see what you see," Mma said somberly.

Poppy's heart skipped a beat. The image of her lifeless eyes against the bed of blue flashed into her mind. "That's why you want me to stay?"

Mma took Poppy's arm. "Help me home, child," she said, holding on to her so dearly that Poppy began to wonder if she'd ever let her go.

In the next few days, all the swallows left. After the last black dot disappeared over the horizon, Poppy hung Leo's crystal around her neck so that it lay against her chest, close to her heart, her only connection with her previous life, her only connection to him. It had felt so right to leave last winter, but now that the birds were returning without her, Poppy felt a tugging at her heart that not even her work with Mma could quash. There was nothing for her to return to. She knew that. Not a boy, not a friend, not a mother. There was no nest to go and build. Only a crown awaited and that might be the end of her. Still, Poppy felt the urge to fly home.

Mma and Teko sensed her disquiet. Poppy heard their hushed voices and saw how they glanced in her direction and how they stopped their conversation when she drew near. The next afternoon, Teko caught a snake, especially for her. He came home with it hanging round his neck and tied in a knot at his chest, its head like a medal on a thick metallic chain. That night, Mma cooked it on a spit over the fire.

"To make you stay," Teko said, gnawing the meat straight from the stick. Poppy took a nibble. "It tastes good, yes?" Poppy nodded as she chewed, though she could detect little flavor. "So you stay?" Poppy nodded again. "That means you say yes?" he asked, pressing her further.

"Yes." Poppy grinned. "If you'll have me." Mma tutted. "You've been so good to me," Poppy told them. "I don't want to outstay my welcome."

Mma reached over and stroked Poppy's face, baring her toothless gums in a celestial smile.

"Trust me, sangoma. You must not leave us."

Poppy nodded and tried to look happy. And then the words came blurting out. "I'm not scared," she said, and the defiant tone in her voice took them all by surprise. Teko looked to Mma and Poppy saw their distress. She softened her voice. "I'm not staying because I'm afraid. I'm staying because I want to."

The bird's feet were tiny and light and, in her sleep, Poppy hardly registered them, treading so softly up her arm and in her hair. Then she felt a peck and a tap, tap, tap upon her head, and she shifted and opened her eyes. The bird's pupils glinted in the darkness and, when it hopped in front of her, Poppy caught a flash of its white underbelly.

"You came back for me?" Poppy whispered.

The swallow took off from the bed and swooped through the hut to the door. There was no doubt in Poppy's mind she should get to her feet and follow it. It was a cloudless night and, out on the plain, Poppy could see her swallow friend clearly now—the stripe across its tail, the red beneath its neck, and the white beneath its fanned wings. Poppy took the heart stone from her neck and tied it to her ankle just as she had on her outward journey. Then she crouched down low and, as she waited, she thought of Mma and Teko and whispered a sorry and then a thank you, for they had been so good to her. A second later, the shock of transformation rippled through her, then a surge of energy and a sudden burst of change.

She opened her wings and tottered for a moment at the width and weight of them on either side of her tiny body before balancing herself. Then she opened her beak and trilled and the other swallow answered her, urging her upward, swooping through the air and waiting for her there, suspended in the heights above. Poppy rose and felt the earth leave her feet. Her wings beat the air. So light and agile she felt, until, with a whack, she was down, her eyes in the dirt and her feathers thrashing against a net. Poppy turned her head and saw Teko looming high above her, wielding the net, forcing it down, keeping her trapped. Desperate, Poppy tried to call out to him, but no human voice came from her, only a bird's chirping.

"You said you'd stay." He wept.

Poppy's thoughts turned to magic, but her bird's form made this slow and arduous. Then, just as her brain began a spell, came the smoke. It was Mma who waved the glowing sticks and spread the scented mist that caused Poppy's mind to mellow and her eyes to close. She fought to keep her eyelids open, but down they came, slowly slipping, losing light, bringing blackness.

When Poppy's lids cracked open, they saw lines—one, two, three, four, fuzzy at first but getting straighter, harder, and all around her. A cage.

"Sleep, little bird," came a voice; Mma or Teko's, she couldn't tell, nor did she try to.

The smoke was circling around the bars. *Another cage,* she thought vaguely. A cloud cage.

"We'll keep you safe."

Poppy felt so very tired. She would open her eyes again soon. In a while. Until then, she'd just let herself forget. Forget about the cage. Forget about going home.

17

BETONY

Betony was sweating, the effort of remembering was so great. "Relax," Charlock kept telling her. "Be loose and let it come."

Betony felt her shoulders tighten even further. She grabbed her scalp and dug her fingers in hard.

"I can't! This isn't working. Nothing is working." She shook her head in desperation, trying to rattle her brain.

She had listened to Charlock's droning chants and drank her foul-tasting potions. She'd levitated, meditated, and hallucinated but all for naught. At the start, she had felt so hopeful. At the first spell, she had thought the memories would blossom in her brain like flowers. Even at the fifth . . . the tenth . . . she still believed that the recollections would trickle back inside, seeping into the roots, watering her withered mind until it became green and fresh once more.

"We must go and find him," Charlock muttered, pacing back and forth.

"Not until I remember," Betony snapped. "How can I meet my son without knowing where he came from?"

"I have told you! I have told you about his father and how you met. I can try and tell you more if you'd like me to."

"It's my life—I don't want it told to me like a bedtime story. And that's what it is without the memories—a story about a stranger living in a distant land. A house, a boy, the chaff clothes, the nasty girl—I can't recall a single one of them. I can't even imagine them. Don't you see? I need it to be my story! I need to remember!" Betony stood up and kicked out at the tree trunk that she'd been sitting on. The pain seemed to calm her, directing the feeling away from her chest. "How can I let my son see me like this?" she put to Charlock. "Who would even want a mother such as I?"

"He will. You loved him then and you love him now and that will be enough."

"I am no mother. I am not even myself."

"Your magic is returning," Charlock encouraged. "I can feel it." Betony waved a hand dismissively. "You always had a gift with animals."

Betony made a scoffing sound. "That never left me. Besides, what good is any gift if it can't bring back my memory?"

"I do not know what else to try!" Charlock admitted through teeth clenched and grinding.

Betony sat back down heavily on the fallen tree. "I thought you were a witch."

"I did not cast the spell that took your memory, so I cannot break it."

"Then who did?"

"A far greater witch than I," Charlock said bitterly.

"Then let's find her."

"She is dead."

With that, Charlock got up and walked away. Realizing she wasn't going to stop, Betony got up and called after her.

"Where are you going?"

"To find your son."

Betony watched Charlock until she disappeared. *I should stay here,* she told herself. This was where she belonged, here in these woods that were her home. Everything would continue as it had before. But Betony knew this was a lie. She had the knowledge now and there was no forgetting that. So she ran, jumping over the nettles and creeping ivy, leaping broken branches and thorny shrubs until she saw Charlock's departing figure in the pasture.

"Wait," she cried, then stopped so she could shout louder still. "Wait for me!"

18

EMBER

Ember noticed the boy from afar. His hair was even blonder than hers, so pale it was almost white, but the deep blue of their eyes was a match. Looking at him felt strangely unnerving. Ember wasn't sure why. Perhaps it was because he resembled her so closely—like they both belonged to the same long-lost tribe. And maybe because he was older than her, only by a few years but enough to make him a man, not a boy as she first thought. As he neared, Ember didn't give him her usual friendly smile or chirpy greeting. Instead, she pretended that she hadn't seen him and purposely looked the other direction. She could feel him there though, flicking through the old vinyl records in the next stall, and it made her feel uneasy and distracted.

Ember tried to focus all of her attention on a customer, serving the person with exaggerated enthusiasm, hearing her own voice amplified in her ears. When she was finished, she surreptitiously glanced over at the record stall out the corners of her eyes. The man was gone. With the disappointment came relief, and it meant that Ember could now bend down and fold up the empty boxes at her feet.

It was Leo she should be looking for. He had left in the early morning after their fight. He hadn't waited to say goodbye. At first, she thought he'd come back when he was ready. Besides, she felt angry with him and refused to go out searching. As the days passed, it had proved hard to keep her eyes from seeking him out down every street, in every doorway, on every bench. Then the idea occurred to her that Leo might have gone for good. Immediately, she had thought of Poppy. Ember had promised her that she would make Leo happy. And it was the breaking of this promise, rather than her own feelings for Leo, that made her scour the nearby towns for him. She would look again tomorrow, she pledged, but for now it was market day and she had soap to sell.

"Did you make these yourself?"

It took Ember a second to stand up because a part of her wanted to hide. When she straightened, as she knew she must, she saw the fair-haired man across from her. He was holding one of her soaps to his nose.

"I did," she said, begging her cheeks not to blush. "Would you like to buy one?"

"I will if you let me buy you coffee."

Ember blinked twice. "I can't."

"Not now. After you're done. I could help you pack up? . . ."

Ember took the soap back from him. "You don't have to buy it if you don't need it."

"I want to."

He held out a ten and Ember hesitated before taking it. Willing her hand to stop trembling, she gave him his change. It took her a few moments to wonder why he was still standing there.

"My soap?" he asked.

Ember wanted to slither back down under the stall. "Sorry," she muttered, quickly putting the soap into a paper bag and handing it back to him.

"I'll see you later," he said confidently, and Ember felt her mouth drop open. "For that coffee."

"But . . . ," she tried to argue, but he was walking away, lifting his hand in a wave, wiping the sky with her soap.

Ember didn't like coffee but felt she couldn't say so. Particularly to him. He was so sure of himself. Nick was his name. He told her that, though little else. The rest were questions, fired at her so that she hardly had time to answer one before another question came. What was her name? Where did she come from? How long had she had the stall? How many soaps did she sell? How long did they take to make? How did she source her ingredients? How were the other stall owners? How were the customers? Ember's ears began to hurt.

"Do you mind if I write this down?" he asked, picking up his pen and beginning to write without waiting for her agreement. "I forget if I don't take notes," he went on. "I'm a reporter, you see. Trainee reporter for the Herald. Doing a piece on the market." Ember sipped her coffee. It was bitter and only made her feel more jittery. "So, Ember—that's an unusual name."

"Not to me," Ember replied, adding another spoonful of sugar to her coffee.

Nick gave an abrupt laugh that didn't sound amused. "Have you been in town long?"

"No. Have you?"

"So where are you from originally?"

"Up north. You wouldn't know it."

"Try me."

"Where are you from originally?"

"Hey, who's the reporter here?"

Ember looked at his notebook and saw tiny squiggles and dashes instead of letters. "What's that?"

"Shorthand. They made us learn it in college."

"It's like a spell," she said wistfully.

"What?"

"Nothing. It's like another language, that's all."

Nick peered at her, as though suddenly interested. "What's your story, Ember Hawkweed?"

Ember put her coffee down too quickly and it spilled on the white countertop. "Oh gosh. I'm sorry," she said, reaching for a paper napkin to wipe it up.

"Don't worry. It's not as though you liked it." Ember's eyes darted up at Nick, but he was smiling again. "Let's go for a drink," he said, more as a demand than a suggestion.

"We're having a drink."

"A real drink." Ember's brows furrowed as she tried to deduce his meaning, and Nick cocked his head to look at her so curiously that she made her face go blank. "Anyway, this is work," he said. "I'd like to see you off duty."

Ember twisted the wet napkin around her finger. "Why?" she asked.

"Why wouldn't I? You're beautiful. And sweet. And you sell soap. And hate coffee but are too shy to say."

"Beautiful?" Ember whispered.

"You do know that, don't you?" Nick leaned forward as though telling her a secret. "Every guy in here has been checking you out."

Ember quickly looked around. All the males she could see were on their phones or talking to their friends or simply drinking their coffee.

She smiled at Nick. "I don't think so."

Nick stood up and waited for her. "Come on, let's get out of here." Ember hesitated. His eyes were as blue as a speedwell flower. She wondered if hers seemed as startling as his. "Unless you have a boyfriend? I never asked you that."

Ember got to her feet. "No. I mean, I did. But he's gone."

Nick ushered her out, his hand on her back. "His loss," she heard him say.

People did look as they walked, but not just at her. It was the two of them together that caught people's attention. A matching pair. She wondered if Nick noticed. He was talking about his job so proudly, as though it were a prize that he had won in a competition. He was dismissive of the work he did now though—having to cover weddings, funerals, market stalls.

"No offense," he added.

It was only then that Ember realized Nick had been rude. Her work was boring to him, she could see that. But, strangely, Ember didn't feel offended. She liked walking beside Nick even though she didn't much like his personality. His company was so refreshingly different from Leo's, even his faults. Nick was sure of himself and where he was going. He wasn't sensitive, but he was bold and determined. He was selfish, that was very clear, but he wasn't confused or damaged. Above all, she was a different Ember with him. She didn't once reach for him or touch him, hoping he'd touch her back. Nick was the one who put his hand on her back to usher her out of the café, who touched her arm to emphasize a point he was making, who took her hand to cross the busy road, and it felt so good to be the one holding back, keeping her feelings in reserve and out of harm's way.

"What I need is a real crime. One that I can get to first. Not some petty theft or antisocial behavior. A murder or a car crash— that's what I need to cut my teeth on." Nick caught Ember's expression and stopped.

"Have you ever seen a dead person?" Ember asked flatly.

"Not yet," he said with an air of disappointment.

"I'd be careful what you wish for," Ember told him, echoing Charlock's motherly refrain, and at that moment a cat, black as coal, crossed her path.

Ember froze. Straight in front of her it slunk, appearing from nowhere and looking eerily out of place on this busy street.

"What is it?" Nick followed her gaze to the cat, who sat and stared at her with amber eyes.

"Charlock!" Ember whispered.

She spun around, searching for another sign, but found none. The cat opened its mouth in a wide yawn as if to show that it was already fed up with waiting for her.

"I have to go," Ember said.

"Where?" Nick asked.

"I'm sorry!" The cat was on the move and already Ember struggled to keep it in her sights between the marching legs of the pedestrians.

"What about our drink?" Nick complained.

"I have to go." There was no explanation that Ember could offer him and she could wait no longer.

Rushing down the street, Ember found the cat sitting on the roof of a parked car. As soon as it saw her, it leapt down gracefully, then carried on its way. At the top of the street, the cat turned the corner and Ember glanced over her shoulder before following. Nick was still standing there, in the spot she had left him, head bent and hand scribbling into that notebook of his.

Charlock was waiting for Ember beyond the parking lot. She was sitting with another woman among the sparse trees on the far edge, both of them blending into the background. The cat led Ember right to them. Ember gulped down a sob when she saw Charlock's face and rushed headlong into her embrace. Charlock might not be her real mother as Melanie was, but it still felt like a mother's arms enveloping her and holding her close, the same arms that had cradled her as a baby, carried her as a toddler, comforted her as a child. This hug was like home.

"I've missed you," Ember mouthed into Charlock's bosom.

"I, too," said Charlock, hearing her silent words.

Then she held Ember's face in her hands and put her cheek to hers, pressing her lips to her hair.

"This is the girl?" came a terse voice that Ember didn't recognize.

Ember pulled back to look at the woman beside Charlock. She had a face that Ember didn't remember from the coven. It was both young and old, colored like autumn with a scattering of freckles and framed by abundant, gleaming hair. She made no move to greet Ember, just waited impatiently for an answer.

"Who's this?" Ember asked warily.

"It is a long and winding story," Charlock warned. "But this is Sister Betony."

The woman nodded and her bright orange curls bobbed as though on springs. "Ember?" Charlock said in a manner that Ember knew so well, one laden with expectation and demanding of attention. No one else called her name like that. So Ember did as she was bid and looked up at Charlock dutifully. "We have come in search of Leo. Can you take us to him?"

"Why?" asked Ember sharply.

"We went to Melanie's house, but he wasn't there," Charlock continued, choosing to ignore Ember's tone.

"Why?" Ember challenged again, surprised at how possessive she suddenly felt about a boy who had abandoned her. Leo had hurt her and left her and still, like a fool, she felt this unbreakable attachment to him.

Charlock took Ember's hands and rubbed them gently. "You look thin, child. Are you eating well?"

"Please," said Ember sadly. "Just tell me the truth."

"You are right to feel protective about the boy, but we mean him no harm."

"Who is she?" Ember whispered. Charlock looked to Betony as if for permission. In response, the woman took a step forward and something in the tilt of her chin and jut of her jaw reminded Ember of Leo. "Who are you?" Ember asked directly, looking straight into the woman's wildly freckled face.

"I'm his mother," she said.

19

LEO

Leo was carrying a tray of glasses when he first felt it. His head spun and his vision blurred so that he had to put the tray down and hold on to the bar. The music from the band filled his ears, the instruments splitting apart so they no longer blended as one but each blared out their very different and individual song. Suddenly, he could make out every syllable that the singer sang. He could even hear the breaths between each phrase, up close, as though they came from his own mouth and not through the microphone and speakers on the tiny stage. The smells from the bar were so strong, they seared his nostrils. Alcohol, sweat, perfume. It was an overwhelming mix.

"Are you all right, man?" said one of the barmen.

Leo tried to straighten.

"Hey, Leo. No slacking, remember!" yelled Dave, the boss.

"Sorry," Leo mumbled, picking up the tray and making his way to the table.

It took all his effort and willpower to walk without tripping. It was as if the filters had been removed from his brain so now he noticed everything—every distorted face, every raucous laugh, every drunken burp—and it was impossible to block anything out. Focusing on a path through the crammed tables and heaving bodies, Leo somehow made it to his destination. He put the drinks down slowly, aware his hand was shaking, praying that they wouldn't spill.

One of the customers held his beer up to the light. "Hey! You call this full?" he jeered. Leo peered at the glass. He could see a thousand golden bubbles rising upward, bursting and turning into foam. "Hey, moron! I'm talking to you, man. You trying to rip me off or what?"

"What?" said Leo, so disorientated that his voice echoed in his ears.

The man stood up, his chest twice the width and breadth of Leo's. "What kind of retards do they employ in this place?" He thrust the beer glass into Leo's face so that it slopped over the sides and he spoke slowly as if Leo were deaf. "Get . . . me . . . a new . . . beer."

Leo looked into the man's eyes, saw the stupidity and aggression there, and felt a piercing contempt for this long-faced, muscle-bound creature. The man swore and, no sooner had the words left his lips, the glass shattered. The yellow liquid seemed to fall in slow motion; perfect globes of liquid hanging in the air, reflecting in the tiny shards of glass, then bouncing on the wood and flying upward in a spray all over the man's crotch.

"What the—?" the man yelled, and time sped up as the rest of the table jumped from their seats. They all looked at Leo with a collective fury. Leo took two paces back, then ran for the exit.

In the alley, Leo leaned against the wall. His heart was pounding and his breath came in ragged, shaking gasps as he tried to suck in the air. The back door opened and Dave stuck his head out.

"What's going on with you tonight?"

"Nothing. I dunno," Leo stammered.

He came over and took Leo's chin in his hand and stared into his eyes. "You on anything?"

"No!" Leo said adamantly. "I swear it."

"I gave you a chance. Don't you forget that."

"I won't," Leo promised, for it was true. Unlike the other shops and bars, building sites and cleaning companies that he had gone to in search of work, only this man with his dyed hair and golden chains and shiny suit had given him a job.

"Been on the streets?" he'd asked him in the interview. "Trouble at home?"

Worried it was a trick, Leo hadn't confirmed or denied it.

"Me too," Dave had said. "But it's no excuse for crappy work, okay?"

He had given Leo a new set of clothes and ordered him to keep them clean. Leo had started straight away, washing up, wiping tables, being at the beck and call of all the other waifs and strays the boss had taken in. Last week, he'd been given the nod. When the bar was at its busiest, Leo could start waiting tables.

Leo closed his eyes for a moment, feeling sick. The disappointment was churning inside of him. He was sure he'd blown it. When he opened his eyes again, Dave was rubbing the stubble on his chin thoughtfully. Leo tried to think what he could do or say to save himself. Suddenly, Dave clapped him on the shoulder decisively.

"When you feel up to it, you come back in. Stick to the kitchen. There's a ton of glasses need washing."

Leo nodded. A reprieve. The door slammed. As if objecting to the sound, the street light flickered and crackled. Leo stared down the alley, his body tensing with anticipation, his mind fearing what could happen next. He wondered whether Poppy might appear; whether all this weirdness was simply heralding her arrival. The electrical charge in the air reminded him of her. That other-worldliness she embodied; that strange power she always emitted.

Nothing happened though. Poppy didn't appear. Leo put a hand to his brow to feel if he had a fever. Then he shook his head as if to jog the pieces back into position. When he looked around again, he saw that it was just another drab and ordinary night and he was a lowly waiter who needed to get back to work.

It was three in the morning before Leo finished; he was last to leave. The bar looked unrecognizable now that it was empty; so sad and shabby, like it had served its purpose and been discarded. Leo had mopped the sticky floor, the wetness slip-slopping on the wooden boards. This humble sound came as a relief after the earlier assault on all his senses. It occurred to him that his drink might have been spiked and it had all been a drug-induced hallucination. The thought of it was grim, but at least it made sense.

He switched off the lights and headed into the kitchen. He froze, and the doors swung into his back with a thump. There, from the shadows, shone eyes, pairs of them glinting in the darkness like a starlit sky. Leo felt all the hairs across his body tingle and rise. Strangely, it wasn't fear that he felt, but anticipation. Leo blinked and let his eyes adjust. They were dogs. Five of them. Different breeds but all unkempt and matted, much like him.

"Get out of here," Leo told them. "Go on." They studied him as though in understanding, but none of them moved. "You're going to get me in trouble," Leo said as he walked to the back door and held it open. One of the dogs barked. "For God's sake," Leo said. "You've got to go." He pointed outside while staring at them meaningfully. "Now!" he ordered.

Leo could scarcely believe it but, one by one, the dogs loped out in straggly single file. Leo sighed. It was too late and he was too tired to deal with them. He locked the door and headed home to the rundown building where he'd managed to find a spot, the dogs following like a disheveled band of mongrel brothers.

All day, they slept around him, their hearts pumping collectively, their warmth serving as Leo's radiator. And Leo slept the best he'd done in weeks, not dreaming of the joy of seeing Poppy, not waking with the dread of seeing Ember. All the guilt disappeared that night, rising out of him like the bubbles in that beer spilling out of the broken glass.

20

BETONY

D espite Charlock's protestations, the girl had insisted on coming with them. She had been no use, this Ember. She was a flower of a girl—pretty to look at but no good to eat. Betony tried to imagine her boy drawn to such a one and couldn't help but feel disappointed. Charlock seemed to care for the child, though, and deeply, too. She let the girl talk her around and agreed to her demands to join them.

So here they were, three women in search of one boy. Ember used questions, Charlock spells to track Leo down. Betony felt redundant, her magic too undisciplined and unpracticed to be of use, and it gnawed at her, to be so superfluous when the mission was in fact hers. Not that Charlock's or Ember's leads had proved successful. All were dead ends and it was by chance rather than by design that they found themselves in the next town.

As they walked down the main street, an image flashed in Betony's brain, too fast for her to take in, too fleeting for her to recall. There it was again. A baby. Blood on its forehead, a slick of black hair on its head, a cord from its belly, the weight of it, of him, on her chest. Her baby.

"Bet?" Charlock was saying. Betony could see Charlock touching her arm, but she couldn't feel it. "Betony, what is it?"

"What's wrong with her?" That squeaking was the girl.

The image had gone and Betony's mind scrambled to retrieve it. *Don't go,* she told it. *Don't leave me.*

"Betony?" Charlock said again. "Tell me."

Betony looked up into Charlock's wide-set eyes. "He's here."

"You're sure?" Charlock glanced at Ember, whose mouth had dropped open dumbly like a fish's.

Betony nodded.

Later that day, they reached a building with boarded-up windows and crumbling walls. To the girl's credit, it was she who opened the door to the old house and stepped inside. Entering the first room, she put a hand to her mouth and nose. *The smell was bad,* thought Betony, *but the girl liked to exaggerate.* Inside the room, there were unconscious bodies. They were pale as corpses, but Betony knew they weren't dead, just sickening. They lay on tattered sofas, their arms hanging down limply, or sprawled out on the stained carpet with legs askew. Bowls of ash dotted the room, spilling over and onto one girl's head.

Betony scanned their faces. Her boy wasn't here. She was sure of that, and the relief made her head spin. With trepidation though, she followed Ember to the next room, a kitchen, where the flies had settled on moldy food and the trashcan overflowed with cans and bottles. All the other rooms were empty, upstairs and down, save for the clothes and bottles scattered on every floor like carrion and the dust that drifted above them in the gloom.

"Where is he?" Ember whispered, and Charlock looked across to Betony, her eyes asking the same question.

Betony walked to the window at the rear and peeled back the newspaper that was covering the glass.

"He's there," she said.

Outside was a boy, tall and thin and dark. He was surrounded by a mangy pack of dogs and he was throwing a ball for them. He bounced the ball and kicked it from one foot to the other, then to his knee and back. Betony's hands flew to her head and pressed against her temples. The picture was scaldingly vivid and primary. Another boy, olive skin, black hair, black eyes. Another ball moving at his command, still moving as he looked straight at her, smiling. Danny. The name blazed across her brain. Danny.

Betony's legs gave way, but Charlock caught her.

"Help her," she instructed Ember. Together they assisted her down the stairs and out into the garden.

"I can't," she groaned.

"You can," said Charlock firmly.

After the obscurity indoors, the light outside sparkled like crystals.

"Leo!" Ember called.

The boy looked up at them. *Danny,* Betony thought. And then she howled, the pain was so sharp.

Ember was walking over to him and he hung his head as if in shame. *Put your head up,* Betony wanted to tell him. *Let me see you.* Ember took Leo's arm, but gently he removed her hand. He was shaking his head, and the girl's soft features became edged with anger. And then Ember pointed to them. And he looked over to where they were. Straight at her. *My boy,* Betony wanted to cry. But she was weeping too much to speak.

Charlock had her arm tight around her, and Betony was grateful for her grip. "It's him, Bet," she was saying. "It's your son."

Betony wondered why he wouldn't come to her, why he was still standing there, so far away. But then Ember took his arm again and this time he let her lead him. She walked toward them, smiling, and he followed, and Betony felt a surge of love for this girl that, until now, she'd so dismissed.

"Leo," Ember said calmly, like it was any simple introduction, "this is Betony."

He was so close now. She could reach out and touch him, only she didn't. She couldn't, though she wanted to. Instead, she looked him over, absorbing every detail, trying to remember, and then she saw his hand and the recollection of his fingers flitted into her mind, not long as they were now but tiny and curling with such surprising strength around just one of hers. His body had been so small that he could lie along her forearm. And then she remembered the sweet smell of his skin and its softness like no other.

One of the dogs gave a bark, urging her to speak. Betony swallowed. Her tongue was thick in her mouth and her throat narrow and dry.

"I remember you," she croaked, wiping the tears from her cheeks. "Do you know who I am?"

"You're my mother," he said, his eyes wide and wet with wonder, and she began to bawl in earnest now, big heaving, noisy sobs.

"I'm sorry," she spluttered, but he reached for her and held her in his arms like she was the child and he the parent.

"My mother," she heard him whisper.

21

Young Charlock

Charlock's mother almost broke into a dance when she heard the news.

"A baby, a baby," she cried and then she started whispering good luck charms that it might be a girl.

Charlock looked to Raven. Not a word had yet left her sister's mouth. To her surprise, she saw that Raven's eyes were filled with tears.

"You're not crying, sister?" Charlock pleaded.

"With child?" Raven asked, as if to check that it was not a dream but fact.

Charlock nodded nervously. Raven did not seem herself at all. She was ushering Charlock to the chair and then set about waiting on her, offering her food and tea, saying she'd do her chores.

"Little Charlock with child," she kept on murmuring in a tender voice that Charlock hadn't heard from her in years. "You must let me take care of you now."

Over the following days, Raven was true to her word. She scurried across the camp, doing Charlock's work as well as her own, ignoring Charlock's claims that it was not necessary. Several times Betony raised an eyebrow at Raven's uncharacteristic response, but Charlock shrugged.

"Don't be like that, Bet," she told her. "Raven's happy for me. This baby has brought my sister back to me."

Betony opened her mouth with a sour retort but then swallowed the bitterness back down again. Charlock could see Raven's presence made her friend feel lost in some new darkness. For Charlock, though, it had the opposite effect. She was under the full glow of her sister's love, a light shining down just on her. Charlock only hoped that it would never wane but last a lifetime.

Between tasks, Raven would check on Charlock, bringing her treats and tidings of the day's events. She also made a tea to give the baby strength and fortune. It was the sweetest, most fragrant brew Charlock had ever tasted, and she sipped it now as she waited for the ring ceremony to begin.

"It will be a girl, won't it?" Charlock asked Raven anxiously.

Raven crouched down low to look Charlock in the face. Oh so gently, she swept her hand across Charlock's brow, tucking a stray strand of hair behind her sister's ear. "I'm sure of it," she told her. "Now drink your tea. The clan is waiting."

Charlock had caught Betony's eye as she walked to discover the fate of her child. If a girl, triumph. If a boy, disaster. *Make it a girl, make it a girl,* Charlock prayed to Mother Nature. Betony nodded to her as she approached, and Charlock could see she was willing the same thing. Charlock reached out a hand for her friend, and Betony began to step forward when Charlock felt another's hand in hers. Raven's. Her sister by her side. Her sister—the greatest witch there ever was—walking with her to know her fate. Charlock's confidence soared. It must be a girl. How could it not be with Raven there, shepherding her into the hut, laying her down on the wooden planks, lifting the shirt from her stomach, squeezing her hand and smiling?

It was not a girl. If it was not a girl, it was not a baby. Not her baby. Not a part of her. The ring had told her so. It hadn't moved at all at first. Lowered on a string above her belly, it had stayed utterly still. Not a breeze, not a breath had touched it. Then Charlock had heard the gasp from all the witches encircling her and she had known. She had strained her eyes to see, but, from where she was lying, she had only been able to make out the string. The string had been moving. Backward and forward like a pendulum. A straight line, back and forth. No spinning. No circles. No girl.

Charlock heard Betony's voice asking for her as they crossed back to her caravan. But she couldn't look up. She couldn't look at anyone. Again, she heard Betony calling her name as she climbed the steps, but then the door closed behind her and she was being helped onto the bed and covered with a blanket.

"Be strong, Charlock," her mother told her with a hint of reprimand in her tone.

Charlock tried her best to gulp down her sobs, but, when she lifted her head from her hands at last, she saw Raven looking at her with such concern and care that it made her weep all the more just to have her sister's arms around her.

"Now, there. Your time will come," Raven comforted.

"Will it?"

"Of course it will. Look how quickly this one took hold. You are so young. There are so many years ahead of you."

"I so wanted a daughter, like Sorrel. To make you and Mother proud."

"I know," Raven whispered so quietly that Charlock looked up. "You need to rest," Raven told her quickly, getting to her feet and turning away.

Charlock missed her at once. She glanced at her stomach. "I cannot carry it," she said. The sisters had many ways to still the life within them, some more quick than others. "Will you help me?" she asked, peering into her sister's slate gray eyes and seeing a grief there that made her vow never to doubt her sister's love again.

"I will," vowed Raven. "Always."

Life soon returned to normal but felt emptier for it. Raven, though still kind, was slipping further away. Charlock could feel the distance spreading between them like butter in a hot pan. She wished she could face the prospect of yoking again just to bind her sister back to her. Instead, the ingredients of daily existence were added in. Lessons, chores, meals—mixed and stirred. The crust of life. Even Charlock's time with Betony felt a little dry and flavorless, without their usual spice and zest. And then, one day, their first real argument broke out.

The two girls were planting vegetables when it happened. Never before had they lost their tempers or raised their voices at each other—Betony too comical and Charlock too calm for such eruptions. Both girls had been concentrating on their work, pushing seeds of beans and broccoli, beets and sprouts into their earthy homes, so neither saw the argument coming. In truth, the conversation had been boringly benign until Betony asked, "If your baby had been a girl, did you ever think she might be queen?"

Charlock's hands stopped working as her mind retraced the question. She didn't raise her head, just stayed there bent over her task, ready to resume.

"Don't be daft, Bet," was all she said and then her fingers started up again.

"Not even for a moment?" This time, Charlock did not answer. She wasn't sure why the question rankled so. "Three hundred and three years hence, the Hawkweed sisters will deliver a queen," Betony was saying. Words that Charlock knew so well, that every witch was able to recite. Then came words she'd never heard spoken before. "But it doesn't say which sister, does it?"

Charlock sat back on her haunches to direct her displeasure at Betony. "I know what the prophecy says," she told her.

"So?" challenged Betony.

"So?" Charlock fired back.

"So why would you never think it might be you—that you could be the mother of a queen?"

"Because it's clear as day. You know that. Everyone does. Raven is the one. Not I. Why do you raise such things now?"

"Because you belittle yourself, Charlock. I bet Raven isn't so certain. I bet she was relieved it was a boy you carried and not a girl."

Charlock felt the color leave her cheeks. "How dare you?" she hissed. "That is my sister you speak of."

"Exactly," Betony cried. "And she has a daughter to put first. But I am your friend and I have nothing to gain by speaking so."

Charlock sprang to her feet. "You say no more of this, you hear me! Not another word! My sister loves me. Look how she cared for me these last few days."

Betony's face was red beneath her freckles, the color clashing violently with her hair. "You know the saying. Keep your friends close and your enemies . . . "

Charlock didn't let her finish. She flung the seeds at Betony and saw her flinch as they hit their target.

"Keep away from me!" she shouted as she strode away.

"You are blind, Charlock Hawkweed. Open your eyes!" Betony's angry voice came yelling after her.

But Charlock didn't look back. She didn't want to hear. She didn't want to see.

22

YOUNG BETONY

When Charlock's pregnancy was announced to the clan, Betony had assumed she would be the one to look after her friend. She expected to laugh about baby names and motherhood; to hear about the changes Charlock might be going through; to gossip about the envy of the other sisters and about Raven twisting under the torture of having her little sister be the center of attention.

But Betony found she wasn't needed. To her surprise, Raven had taken on that role. Her first deed had been to confine Charlock to the Hawkweed caravan. When Betony tried to visit, she was gently but firmly turned away. On the few occasions she was allowed in, Raven listened to every word, making it impossible for Betony and Charlock to speak freely. Betony wished her friend would protest, but she never did. She never even gave a sideways look or secret gesture to show she minded. So Betony backed away and watched and waited, hoping that Charlock, in all her excitement, would remember her again.

Unused to having so much time alone, Betony found herself missing Danny all the more. She had only her kestrel for company, but he had mating of his own to do and was often at his nest. So Betony whiled away the days, plotting constantly how she might get away to see Danny again. She decided to set out after Charlock's ring ceremony, when all attention, whether good or bad, would be on her friend. Raven would be fully occupied and was bound to keep Charlock by her side.

The plan had seemed a sound and simple one. Betony stood dutifully outside the hut with all the other sisters, waiting for Charlock to arrive. In her head, she was counting down the minutes before she could leave. But then she saw Charlock's face as she approached. She was far paler than usual and her cat eyes even wider with anxiety. Betony had meant to stay back, to fade into the throng, but she couldn't help herself. She pushed to the front of the crowd and reached out a hand to Charlock. The relief crossed Charlock's face when she spotted her, but then there was Raven, stepping between them, cutting Betony off, blocking her view.

Betony followed the others inside and she joined in the chanting as the ring was lowered on the string. "A girl, a girl," she called along with the rest, but, in her mind, she was already on her way, sneaking out of the camp and running through the forest and over the hills to find Danny.

Then came the gasp, and Betony was flung back to the here and now—the circle of sisters, her friend lying prostrate on the floor, her belly bare, the glinting gold of the ring hanging from a thread that had begun to move. *A boy,* Betony thought, and then she realized she was the last to know it and the disappointment was already covering the room just like the blanket being spread over Charlock's stomach.

She had meant to keep quiet, whatever the outcome, but again she couldn't stop herself. She called out Charlock's name and tried to elbow her way forward. Again, though, she was thwarted. For Charlock was being huddled away by Raven and her mother. Now was the time to go, when thoughts were elsewhere and no one would notice her departure. But Betony knew she could not leave. For in the hut, when all were sad for Charlock, she had spied a look on Raven's face that had made her hairs stand on end. It had lasted less than a second, but it was one of triumph. Betony was sure of it. Just as she was sure Charlock needed her after all.

Never before had Betony thought to question the prophecy. She'd never heard anyone doubt it. Sorrel would become queen. Everyone took it as a given. Everyone, Betony now realized, apart from Raven. These thoughts seemed so treacherous that Betony hardly dared think them, let alone raise them with Charlock. Besides, Charlock seemed so sad these days that Betony couldn't bear to hurt her further. Then, one afternoon, when they were planting seeds together, she took her chance. Their conversation lasted all of a minute and ended terribly. If there was a crack between them before, now there was a canyon.

The very next evening, Betony pretended to her aunt that she wished to study the baby owls that had hatched in the tree hollow by the stream. Sister Sage seemed delighted Betony was taking such an interest in a species that she herself had so long admired. "You may experience their first flight," her aunt expressed.

"I hope so, Aunt," Betony told her, accepting the package of food her aunt had made and putting the cloak she offered around her shoulders.

She hung the cloak from the branch of the last beech tree as it smelled too much of home. And she ate the food as soon as she stepped out of the forest, hardly able to taste the cheese, the bread dry as sand in her mouth. As Betony headed down the valley, the trees felt like giant gates closing behind her and, for the first time since planning her escape, she felt fearful.

Betony looked down on Danny's yard, picking out the spot where she'd first seen him. She had climbed to the roof of the house, clambering from trellis to brick to tile, from one level to the next, hoping to spot him in one of the many panes of glass grooved into the walls. It was much like climbing the ancient yew tree that overhung the camp. Get a good grip, check your foothold, don't look down. Betony had taught this to the younger sisters many times.

None of the windows revealed Danny. She had seen his sister first, staring at an oblong on her desk that was magically lit with words and pictures. Betony had watched her for a while, entranced, until the novelty had worn off. Through another piece of glass, she had seen the family's elders, a woman and a man. His parents, Betony reasoned. She searched for signs of Danny in their features. He resembled his father most and Betony looked to see how Danny might become, years from now, a father with children of his own. The couple talked, but they didn't touch. They smiled, but they didn't laugh.

Only when she reached the roof did Betony realize how hard it would be to climb back down. Only then did it occur to her that, though setting out might seem easy, returning might prove harder. An owl gave a long, vibrating cry from the tree at the back of the yard and Betony saw that it had nested there. She wondered if its eggs had hatched. Perhaps she might get to do her studying after all. But then a light came up through the slanting windows that lay within the roof. Gripping hold of tiles, some looser than others, Betony tentatively made her way over to one of these windows and glanced inside. It was him. She pushed her face against the glass to get a better look, then suddenly it tilted, sliding her forward so her head shot into the room and her body balanced precariously on the glass.

Danny yelped like a dog when he saw her and backed into a chair.

"It's me," she called, and then she let her body slither further through, holding out her arms so he could catch her.

"Betony?"

He reached for her and caught her as she flew, her weight knocking both of them to the ground. He was laughing, but she, normally the first to see the funny side of life, could not. She tried to sit up and tug down her clothes, which had lifted upward. Pulling her back down, he kissed her and she could feel his teeth knock against her own as he laughed.

"Are you crazy?" he said between kisses.

"I must be to risk my neck for the likes of you," Betony retorted.

"Why didn't you just ring the doorbell?"

"I don't know," she said and then at last she smiled. "I didn't think of it."

She felt his hands touch the skin where her shirt had come loose from her skirt. She gave a shiver and he slid them round and up her back.

"I've never met anyone like you," he told her.

"Nor I you," she replied, knowing this was truer than he realized.

He kissed her just below her ear, then down her neck and all along her collarbone.

"Don't risk it again," he said.

"What?" she murmured, luxuriating in the sensations tingling along her skin.

"This," he said and he kissed her neck again.

And then she laughed and felt herself again but more so, bigger, brighter, more alive than ever before.

"First flight," she said to herself, and he looked puzzled. "Just something my aunt told me. You have an owl's nest in your garden."

"Good to know," he said.

"It is! If we go back up there," she told him, pointing at the window, "we can see if the eggs have hatched. We may even see the chicks fly."

"Later," he said, biting gently at her neck before kissing her. "Tomorrow."

"We might miss them," she said, no longer caring.

"But I've missed you," he declared earnestly, bringing his hands up to her hair, looking her in the eye.

"I, too," she said, suddenly shy of all she felt. "Too much." And then they didn't talk again for a great while longer.

The next time Betony visited Danny, she rang the doorbell. The high tone of the bell startled her and immediately she felt like running for the hills. She was wearing the small skirt she'd taken from the clothesline for Charlock. Her legs looked very pale protruding from it. As she tried to pull the skirt down and somehow lengthen it, she remembered Charlock's hands doing the same thing. Betony felt a belated stab of guilt for forcing her reluctant friend into such attire and then a stab of grief as she remembered how close they had been that night. For so long, she and Charlock had known the tiniest details of each other's lives—from what they ate to what they thought, every new idea, every old resentment. Since their fight, Charlock had hardly looked in her direction, as though she was a stranger.

It was Danny's sister who opened the door again.

"Oh, it's you," she said with the same disinterest and then she turned around and yelled into the empty space behind her. "Danny! Your girlfriend is here."

But still it wasn't Danny who appeared but his mother.

"Hello," she exclaimed. "Come in, come in. Betony, isn't it? What a lovely name! I've never come across it before."

It took Betony a moment to realize an explanation was expected. "It's a plant. An herb, actually," she said.

"How unusual." Betony felt the woman's gaze flick from her face to her body and back again. Suddenly, the skirt felt even shorter. "And are you in Danny's year at school?"

"Erm, no," mumbled Betony, debating whether or not to step inside.

To her relief, Danny chose that moment to arrive, jumping down the stairs and grabbing his coat.

"We're going out," he said, taking Betony's hand, his fingers gripping hers tightly.

"But we've hardly said hello," complained his mother.

Betony smiled at her apologetically.

"Next time," Danny told her, pulling Betony down the path so that she almost tripped after him.

"Remember your studying!" his mother called.

"Yeah, yeah," he replied, but his mother didn't seem to mind his impudent tone. She didn't run after him and pull his ear or whack him on the back of the legs with the broom handle like the elders in the coven would have. She simply rolled her eyes in good humor and closed the door, letting them go on their way.

Once they were on the street Danny muttered an apology. "Sorry about that," he said.

"About what?" she asked, feeling her nerves bristle with an unexpected tension. "Are you embarrassed of me? Do I shame you?"

"No!" he answered immediately. "I was trying to spare you. If we stayed, they'd be interrogating you all night." Betony thought of the witches questioned and tortured for their craft and then felt glad he had dragged her away. What could she possibly tell them about her life? "So what do you want to do?" Danny asked. "Grab some food? See a movie?"

Betony had no idea what to reply. "I just want to be alone somewhere." As she caught the surprise in Danny's stare, Betony worried she had answered incorrectly. "Don't you want that? Are you hungry?" she added nervously.

Danny gave a short laugh, then pulled her into a hug. "Of course I want that," he said into her hair. "I was trying to be a gentleman."

Betony tried to think what that word might mean, but then he took her hand and she felt a glow as though the center of her being was in her palm. It stayed with her, that feeling, as they walked, never dimming. On their way, they saw another couple walking hand in hand and Betony wondered if they felt it too. She studied the girl's face as she passed, looking for signs of breathlessness, or flushed cheeks, or any other symptom that she knew herself to be afflicted with. But this girl seemed calm. The boy also. Suddenly Betony feared she might be the only one to feel these things, and she glanced at Danny. His eyes met hers and she recognized the passion there. Without a word, their feet began to hurry as they left the town behind them.

She picked the spot, beyond the playing fields, out of sight, beneath a broad elm. Danny spread out his coat and they sat with hands still joined. He asked the questions that his family might have asked, but from him it didn't feel like an interrogation. Betony answered truthfully, telling as much as she could and leaving out as little as possible. She wanted him to know her. To know that her mother had died and that her Aunt Sage had cared for her since she was small. That she liked taking care of the garden and watching things grow, particularly potatoes—those were her favorite, the feeling of burying your hands in the earth and finding that cool, hard treasure. That she hated darning and mending. That she enjoyed drawing, especially faces, and that her favorite month was September when she could climb to the tallest branches to get the apples that no one else could reach. That her aunt was almost blind but had a nose to make up for it. Danny found a piece of paper and a stub of a pencil in his pocket and she sketched it for him.

"God, that's some nose. She looks like a witch." Betony blinked, then scrunched the paper in her hand. "Hey! Stop!" Danny cried as he tried to take the drawing from her.

Betony hid it in her fist and put her arm behind her back. He reached for it, but she refused to let him have it, swapping it from one hand to the other as he struggled to grab it. Unable to pry open her fingers, he then tried to tickle it from her. Soon she was laughing and writhing and his body was on top of hers, legs pinning her down, arms all around her. But still she wouldn't surrender.

"Okay, okay," he said finally. "You win." And he lay back, breathless, pulling her to him so her head lay on his chest.

Betony could hear Danny's heart beating fast. They lay like that for a few minutes, neither speaking, Danny's heart slowing to a steady beat.

"Does she know you're here? Your aunt?" Danny said in a quiet voice.

Betony looked up at him. She couldn't lie and so shook her head, hoping he would ask no more.

"Can I meet her one day?"

She made a face. "It's difficult."

"Are you embarrassed of me, Betony?" he asked so seriously that she had to search his face to see if she'd offended him.

Then he burst into more laughter and kissed her and she kissed him back so hard that he rolled them over so he was above her. Betony curled her legs around him to keep him there this time.

"Don't do that," he said.

"Why not?" she asked, though she knew full well the answer.

It had been nothing like Charlock or Raven or the other girls had said it would be. They had felt nothing, but she . . . she had felt everything, in every single part of her, in every single moment.

"Do we need protection?" Danny had asked her gruffly, hesitating, pulling his body back.

Betony hadn't understood his meaning, but she sensed her answer could end this moment when it had only just begun.

"We're safe," she had answered because she felt they were. They were in no danger. There was nothing near that might harm them. But she said a charm under her breath to protect them, just in case.

"I could stay here all night," he whispered, when they finally lay back, out of breath, their chests rising and falling in time with each other's, their eyes staring up to the dusky sky.

She smiled, wide and joyful, and said, "Let's."

When at last they fell asleep in each other's arms, it was she that woke first. The moon was high and the stars shining. Betony felt like they were blessing her, what she had done and all the rules she'd broken.

She woke Danny with two kisses, one on each corner of his mouth. He stirred and reached for her. "We have to go. It is late," she told him. Then he sat up suddenly and cursed. "Will you be in trouble?" she asked.

"Will you?" He looked even more alarmed at that.

"Not if they don't find out." She grinned and that made him smile.

They walked across the wet grass and Betony hung on to him, like ivy to a wall, feeling like she wouldn't be able to stand without him.

"I can't just leave you here. Let me walk you home? I won't come in. No one will see me," he begged.

A gentleman, Betony remembered, and now she comprehended a little of its meaning.

"It is far," Betony told him. "And you will never find your way back. You needn't worry. I promise you."

She tried to kiss the worry from his face, but he resisted this time.

"Come back."

He made her swear it. And only after did he let her kiss him goodbye.

23

LEO

His mother and Poppy's mother were arguing. Arguing about where they should go, what they should do, how to keep him a secret, and never agreeing on any of it. He had so many questions he wanted to ask, but whenever he tried, another round of quarreling ensued. For a minute, Leo just watched them, studying his mother. He liked to say those words, "his mother," over and over to himself as he tried to commit every detail of Betony's face to memory, replacing all the portraits of her that he'd pictured over the years. None of them had looked like her. None had hair that shockingly red, or that many thousands of freckles, or dimples when they smiled, or angry lines that appeared so suddenly, like an earthquake, ravaging the contours of their faces. And he never once thought she'd be smaller than him—in his mind, he had only ever been the child and she the adult.

For all his life, Leo had imagined different versions of his mother, never believing he'd be proven right or wrong in his depiction. Yet, here she was, promising to stay, swearing they'd never be apart again. His mother. But still, Leo stored every detail of her in his mind. For people didn't stay in Leo's life for long. He'd learned that the hard way.

Now, as the women's voices rose with anger, something inside him snapped. "Stop!" he said. "Talk to me. Not each other. Me!"

Betony and Charlock stared at him as if surprised by his request.

"We need to keep you safe," his mother insisted.

"Why?" he asked. "Am I in danger?"

No and yes, came the answers. Betony glared at Charlock, who gave a sigh.

"You are a witch," Charlock said, and Leo nodded. "A male witch." She paused again, and Leo gestured with his hands for her to continue. "There are only very few of you."

"We think," interjected Betony.

"If they exist, they keep their existence secret from the covens. Your mother had to run away to have you. She had to hide you."

"I still have to hide you," Betony cried. "The witches will hate you and fear you as they do all males—but worse because you share their power. They will come for you."

"Your mother's memory is not yet returned to her. I have never seen or heard of any clan hunting down a male witch."

Betony was shaking her head angrily. "Only because they don't know where they are. I feel the danger, Charlock. In my bones. And it is my job to protect him."

"Poppy will do that," Charlock soothed. "Don't you see? Now that you are reunited and Leo's magic has awoken, Poppy will return. And she will keep us safe."

"Poppy!" Betony's hand swept through the air. "So now our lives depend on some runaway girl. You don't even know where she is!"

Betony rose to her feet and stormed off, slamming the door and leaving a strange silence behind her. Leo wondered if he should go after her, but Charlock had spoken Poppy's name and suddenly all his other questions could wait.

"What makes you think Poppy will come back?" he asked quietly.

"The magic that's inside you—she will feel it and it will give her hope," replied Charlock.

"Hope for what?" Leo hardly dared ask.

"That you can be together."

Charlock went to find Betony and, after a few moments, he heard their bickering resume. He walked over to the window and stared into the darkness beyond. His mind was whirling with expectation and doubt. Poppy might come back. He might see her again. And soon. But what if his magic wasn't strong enough? Would she still come? Would she still want him? His breath made a cloud on the pane of glass and, in it, a shape began to emerge. It was a bird with pointed wings and a long forked tail.

"A swallow," came Ember's voice, startling him. "It's her, isn't it?"

"I think so," he said and then he turned around.

Ember stood there, staring at him intently, her chin set with a defiance he'd never seen in her before.

"What does it mean?" she asked him.

"I don't know," he replied helplessly. He might have magic inside him, but he had no comprehension of it yet. No control.

"I never stood a chance, did I?" Ember said, almost to herself, leaving Leo unsure whether or not she expected an answer. After a moment of watching the swallow's shape fading from the glass, Ember blinked, then spoke again. "Me and you," she said. "I thought we were the same. All of them magic apart from us. But now you're one of them too."

Her voice was low with bitterness, as though these feelings had been dug from deep inside.

"I'm sorry," was all Leo could think to say.

"You should be," she told him. "It's a curse, you know." Ember went to the window and, with the heel of her hand, rubbed away the last of the swallow. Leo grabbed her wrist to stop her. She looked down at it, his hand holding hers. "She wouldn't have wanted this for you. Why do you think she went? Why do you think she left us together?" Then Ember looked up at him, the light of her beaming into the dark of him. "She wanted us to have what she couldn't."

"We tried," Leo said roughly, his hand opening, letting go of Ember's arm.

She looked down at the red mark he'd left on her skin, then shook her head.

When she left, she took her lightness with her, and all around seemed murky and Leo knew Ember was right about Poppy's reasons. At last, he understood them. But he was used to living in the shadows. It was where he felt at home. Comforted, Leo looked back to the window. It was turning cloudy once more and there, in the mist, was the swallow.

❦

Leo and Betony started at the top and worked their way down, cleaning the house where he'd been squatting, opening the windows, scrubbing the floors, and dusting the surfaces. It was a strange way to get to know his mother, the two of them on their hands and knees, rinsing out cloths black with dirt, but Leo liked to be close to her. She was relentless, never pausing for rest, the energy crackling through her body, electrifying the curls in her hair that sprang from her head at all angles.

"Isn't there magic for this?" he asked, and she smiled.

Wiping a cloth across a filthy baseboard, she held it up to show him. "Magic," she replied, raising an eyebrow.

As they worked, she told him the little she knew of her past. To him, every detail was brimful of meaning. But to her, most were only facts, not memories, and she told them without feeling, unable to describe or elaborate, unable to answer his whys or whens or hows.

"Your memory will come back," he told her. "It's already started."

She broke off from her work to look at him. "It might. Now that I'm with you." She closed her eyes for a second as though it was hard for her to see through the haze of this new hope. When she spoke again, her voice became full of feeling. "I think I'm scared to know it all because of how it ends—me, in a faraway wood, without memories, without you. But, at the same time, my past is a part of me that's lost and I feel broken without it, like a ship with a crack in its hull or a bird with a broken wing."

Leo put his arms around her, and she held him so tightly that he could feel the love in the strength of her grip.

"I thought you didn't want me," he whispered.

Immediately, she pulled back to look at him. "Never," she said, "never think that." She looked deep into his eyes for several seconds until, content with what she saw there, she finally let him go. "Back to work?" she asked, walking over to the door of the front room where the squatters congregated.

"Not in there," he tried to tell her, but she was pushing open the door and striding inside, ripping down the moth-eaten curtains, tearing the newspaper from the windows.

The bodies flinched and writhed under the light like bugs.

"Out!" Betony ordered them, her voice cracking like a whip that got them up and on their feet.

Like zombies, they shuffled to the door.

"Are they awake?" Leo murmured.

Their eyes were open, but it was like they were sleepwalking.

"They are alive," Betony told him, leaving Leo just as uncertain.

She was picking up a dusty blanket when one of them attacked. In his hand, an ashtray. Leo thought he called out but couldn't be sure if any word left his lips, for what he saw amazed him. The guy froze, his arms mid-swing, the cigarette butts hanging in the air as though gravity had deserted them. Betony looked first at this statue, his teeth bared in a snarl, and then at Leo.

"That was you? Right?" he said.

"Be careful," she warned. "These chaffs are fragile and your magic is clumsy."

"I did this?" he asked, a wave of excitement rippling through him.

But Betony looked dismissive. She snapped her fingers and the ashtray and its contents fell and the guy trundled meekly away. When he was gone, she came over to Leo and took his hands and kissed them both.

"Keep it inside," she whispered. "They'll feel it otherwise." Leo felt a sudden chill and his smile froze. "That's right," Betony said. "Be afraid."

"But Charlock said . . . "

Betony stopped him. "Charlock is one of them. You and I are not. They'll not hurt her." Then she turned and picked up the blanket from the floor and shook it so that he coughed from the dust that floated from it. "Get some air," Betony told him. "It's foul in here. You'd have been better off living outside."

"I've done that too," he said. "It's just as hard."

Betony shook her head, then reached out a hand to touch his cheek. He wanted to grab it and press it there.

"Oh, my boy," she said. "I'm sorry for that. You too without a home."

When she took her hand away, his cheek felt warm and her touch stayed with him through the rest of the day.

Charlock found him outside, leaning against the wall, watching the zombies and the dogs laid out on the grass. She handed him a mug of hot liquid, which he took, not knowing what it was, but drinking it all the same. Charlock seemed to be waiting for something and it unnerved him.

"Ember's gone," he said to fill the void.

"I know," she said plainly, adding nothing further, just standing there in quiet expectation.

"What?" he said after another wordless interval, not caring if he sounded rude.

He'd had enough of Charlock's and Betony's cryptic silences. Suddenly, he missed Ember with her happy chatter, speaking lots but saying nothing, and he wished that he'd run after her and stopped her from leaving.

"You used your magic," was all Charlock said in reply.

"It was by accident," Leo explained quickly.

"Don't be sorry. It is a part of you."

"Betony said . . . " But Charlock cut him off just as his mother had.

"Remember—Poppy will feel it now that you feel it."

He wanted so badly to believe her. He had so much now—a mother, an identity, magic—that it felt greedy to still want more. But it wasn't enough. Nothing would ever be enough without Poppy. Then he thought of Betony and the love in her arms as she hugged him and the fear in her eyes as she warned him.

"Leo?" he heard Charlock say.

"Poppy doesn't love me," he muttered gruffly, without looking up. "She told me."

"The letter," Charlock said, and Leo's mind flashed to the words Poppy had written to end things between them. He felt the pain cut into him all over again. "I made her write it," Charlock confessed. "To separate you."

Leo swallowed. His heart had started thumping so forcefully against his ribs that he found he couldn't speak.

"Why?" he managed to gasp.

Charlock shook her head and closed her eyes for a moment. She took a deep breath and then spoke again. "Keep practicing your magic and she will come."

That night, Leo slipped away from Betony's watchful eye and sat with his back against the door and tried to summon a spell. He wondered if he should say something, some hocus-pocus abracadabra type of nonsense. He focused his mind, wondering if the power would come to him, but the more he thought, the tighter and smaller his brain became. He pointed his fingers at himself and let them flicker in front of his face, half-hoping that sparks might fly or magic dust sprinkle the air like glitter. There was nothing, not even a tingle.

Leo slumped back. He allowed himself to think of her, Poppy, her dark hair cropped and spiky like thorns around her face, her eyes clashing with the symmetry of the rest of her features, one eye blue, one eye green, both shining. He remembered how they looked when she reached up to kiss him, how her lips felt on his. Suddenly, Leo felt his hand fold onto something in his palm. It was soft and bright and red. His fingers opened and the petal curled and withered, drying brown, then black, then falling silently to powder.

Something was wrong. Leo could see it in his hand and he could feel it in his chest. Poppy was in trouble.

24

SORREL

S orrel woke suddenly from her nightmare, flying out of bed as though released from a catapult. She stood there panting, her fists still clenched around imaginary bars, encircling her, trapping her inside. Sorrel stretched out her fingers and waited for the panic to subside. Her breathing slowed, but the terrible sensation of being imprisoned, powerless to escape, remained with her. This was no dream. It was a message.

Sorrel went to her window and saw the candles in other caravans light up one by one, like fireflies grouping and glowing in the darkness. She was not the only one to receive this warning. She reached for a taper and held it against the dying embers of the fire. Cupping her palm around the little flame to protect it, she moved through the shadows toward the candle on the table. The draft from under the door chilled her feet, but the puff of breath that Sorrel heard was something different. It was a breath exhaled, no draft or unexpected flurry of air. The taper's flame vanished, leaving a tiny trail of smoke. Once again, she lit the taper, but again came the puff and out it went. With a shiver, Sorrel looked all around her.

"Mother?" she called softly.

"Leave her be," came the whisper, quieter than a breeze but clearly audible.

"She's our queen," Sorrel protested. "And she's a captive."

"Leave her," hissed the voice, and the candle suddenly flickered alight.

"Why can't you let me be happy?" Sorrel cried.

She felt a sudden pain in her belly that made her bend.

"A baby." The words whistled past her.

"Then you'll go?" Sorrel asked.

A cold gust of wind whipped around her, and the candle went out, leaving Sorrel in darkness, leaving her alone.

Outside, the elders were wrapping shawls around their shoulders as they huddled in the gathering circle, their faces taut with worry. Sorrel joined them, standing on the periphery next to Kyra, who threaded an arm through hers for the first time in weeks. Sorrel welcomed the contact and took Kyra's hand, squeezing it gratefully. The sisters were talking all at once and the noise of their mutterings began to rise like the hum from a hive.

"Hush!" Sister Ada cried. "How can we think with all this chattering?"

"Thinking won't help us," snapped Sister Morgan. "If we can sense it, the others will too."

"She is their queen also!" exclaimed Sister Martha.

"But they have yet to know her," wailed Sister Ivy. "What do they care for her authority?"

"If we try to reach her, all of us together?" suggested Sister Ada.

"It is all we can do," agreed Sister Wynne.

Sister Ada fetched the sacred stone from its place on the tree trunk. On gnarled and spotted hands, she held it out into the center of the circle. Carved into the stone's sleek curve was Poppy's name.

"I hold the stone with the queen's name. Only destiny can change it," spoke Sister Ada.

The nearest witches peered at it; the others strained their necks and stood on tiptoes to see. The letters were etched just as deep and clear as before.

POPPY HAWKWEED.

Nothing had yet changed. Poppy was still queen. Sister Ada held the stone aloft, then passed it to Sister Morgan, who handed it to Sister Wynne, who gave it to Sister Martha. On and on it went. Round and round in a circle. As it traveled, Sister Ada struck a note and held it, Sister Morgan another, until all were singing and each note blended into a wild and eerie call that carried through the air and through the trees, out across the moors beyond. This strange siren entered the earth, wending through weeds and trees, into the water that filled every living thing, down the river, and out into the sea. It traveled for miles and miles, but only those attuned to it could hear it, only the witches and the fish and fowl and the beasts that walked the land.

The stone reached Sorrel and its cool smoothness felt soothing in her hands. She wondered that she'd ever expected to see her own name written there. It seemed such a distant belief—the arrogant ambition of another girl in another lifetime—and not her own assumption. Sorrel passed the stone to Kyra and took up a note, high and sure, that added to the growing chorus.

Until dawn, the witches sang. The birds stayed quiet for them as did the lambs and the calves in the fields beyond the forest. Anxiously, the sisters waited for a sign that their call had been heard and answered. But none came.

"She is too far for us to reach her," Sister Morgan said, breaking off from the music as the night's blackness gave way to dawn.

One by one, the other sisters stopped their notes. Only Sorrel continued, until Kyra tugged her arm, then hugged her.

"She needs us," said Sorrel in despair.

"She never should have left," replied Kyra so sharply that Sorrel pulled back at the sting of it.

"My mother cast her out as she was born," she told Kyra. "She had no chance to know our ways."

Kyra shook her head. "Charlock lied to us . . . to the clans. And now they will know it and they will want answers. And what will we tell them? That we don't know where the queen is? And if they attack—how can we defend ourselves?" She took a breath. "If only . . . ," she started to say, but then her eyes darted away from Sorrel's.

"What?" whispered Sorrel.

"If only your mother were here."

"Don't," Sorrel muttered. "Don't wish for that."

She started to walk away, suddenly desperate to reach her caravan, but Kyra chased after her.

"It could have been you," she called. "Like we always thought. You would have stayed, not run away and left us to their mercy."

"Enough, Kyra. I had a whole childhood of that. The throne was not meant for me. It was hers. Even my mother knew it, that's why she banished her."

"But the prophecy said 'the Hawkweed sisters will deliver a queen.' It could still be you. The year is not out." Kyra's eyes were so feverish with feeling that Sorrel took a step back as if fearful of infection.

"The prophecy killed my mother," she replied as she backed away. "And if it wasn't for Poppy, it would have killed me. She saved me, Kyra. She saved me."

Sorrel turned and hurried away, but it was too late. Kyra's words felt like tiny eggs hatching inside her, unleashing worms, hidden but hungry, eating away at her happiness.

"You fool," called Kyra. "It was not the prophecy that killed your mother and nearly killed you. It was your aunt. She did it. She poisoned you."

Sorrel spun around, the anger spewing out of her. "You think I don't know? You think I don't care? I choose not to. I choose not to let it destroy me. You are the one who knows nothing. Not I! You know only life and that is but a fraction of what lies beyond. When you have died and been returned, then come to me with your petty aspirations. Then call me the fool."

With that, Sorrel strode away, but not before she saw her friend's face fade to white and her features fall into desolation. Inside the caravan, Sorrel splashed water on her head and neck to try and douse the fire of her fury. Where was her calm, her cheer, her clemency?

"I will not," she said suddenly. Then she turned around to face the room, to make her vow to her home as well as to herself. "I will not go back. I am different now."

She half expected her mother's spirit to rise up and slap her across the face, but her announcement was met only with a silence. Wearily, Sorrel lay back down upon her bed, knowing that peril was impending but not having the strength to care. She lay there for many hours, watching as the light shone through the cracks in the shutters, feeling how her stomach rumbled at its emptiness and how her throat became dry from lack of liquid. She ignored her body's complaints, even the straining of her bladder, and just lay there resting for the onslaught that was to come.

Even when it arrived, Sorrel was slow to rise and reach for the door handle and step out into the fight beyond. And even at the sight of the other clans, filling their camp, darkening their space with their enmity, Sorrel took a moment to appreciate the loveliness of the day. The spring warmth stroked her skin, the fruit blossoms sweetened the air, the lush green revived her tired eyes. Sorrel let the pleasure envelop her, but the feeling was tinged with sadness, touched by a sense of goodbye.

"There she is!" came a shout, and rows of arms reached up and fingers pointed toward her like spears.

Sorrel recognized the wood clan that had found her out among the trees that day, but there were other faces from other clans before her too, all of them staring at her now.

"Leave her be," called Sister Ada, stepping forward.

Another witch, dressed in white with silver hair, though young of face, reached up a hand and guided a cloud across the sun, pitching them all in gray. Then she gestured at Sorrel, who had to stop herself from flinching. But no spell came to wound her, only words. "So, here you are. The other Hawkweed," she announced. "The wood clan think you should be queen. That the prophecy may be for you after all."

Sorrel walked toward them. "My cousin is the rightful queen. Not I."

One of the wood clan responded. "For the first time in our history, our queen has forsaken us."

"Our queen needs us!" cried Sister Martha.

"She is not worthy," spat the winter witch. "All the clans agree we need a new queen. One ready to serve. The question is, who?" She nodded at one of her fellow witches and Sorrel watched nervously as this young witch moved toward the tree trunk where the stone lay.

"That is not yours to take," called Sister Ada, echoing Sorrel's thoughts.

"Why should the Northern clan keep it when their queen is nowhere to be found?" asked the winter witch.

"It holds her name!" cried Sister Morgan.

"The name of a traitor," retorted one of the wood witches.

Sister Wynne spoke now, but her voice was shaking. "You cannot place another's name upon it. Only when one queen dies will her successor's name appear of its own accord."

"Poppy Hawkweed has abdicated. There are no rules now. We will carve a new name ourselves if we have to."

The young witch was by the tree trunk, her hands reaching for the stone. Sorrel couldn't breathe, and all those around her seemed rooted to the spot, unable to move or speak. Only Sister Ada still had her wits about her.

"Stop!" she demanded fiercely.

The authority in her voice was enough to make the young witch obey. The girl looked to her leader, who nodded for her to continue. As the girl's fingers touched the stone, Sister Ada raised her arm and sent a bolt of fire that knocked the young witch back. She lay on the ground, writhing.

"I told you to stop," the old witch chided regretfully.

The retaliation was immediate. It came from the leader of the winter witches, a beam that severed Sister Ada's legs at the knees. A collective and almighty gasp flew through the camp like a flock of startled birds as Sister Ada fell back, slow and straight as a toppled tree.

"Whom shall it be next?" challenged the winter witch.

Sister Morgan stepped forward. Sorrel covered her eyes.

"You are the traitors, every one of you," Sister Morgan accused, and she flung out a blast of blue light from her palm that the winter witch deflected.

From the waist of a wood witch slithered a ropey vine that snaked swiftly across the ground, twisting around Sister Morgan, tightening with every turn despite her hands pulling so desperately at it. The others looked on in shock as it wrapped around her throat and squeezed the breath from her. Kyra ran to Sister Morgan's aid, chanting spells, and grabbing at the vine to loosen it. When she failed, she turned around and faced the other clans that so outnumbered them.

"Take us, then. Take us all!"

"No!" screamed Sorrel, so loud and piercingly high that all turned to look at her once more.

"I will be your queen," she said. "Until my cousin returns to us."

"If she returns," barked a witch so dark and squat she seemed more reptile than human.

"She is a Hawkweed," spoke the wood witch in Sorrel's defense.

"We have had one Hawkweed. Why another? Prove to us you are worthier than your cousin," ordered the winter witch.

The witch nodded at her clan and a group of them grabbed Kyra and dragged her before Sorrel.

"Save your northern sister and we will have you," declared the winter witch.

And with that, she showered a spell upon Kyra that chilled the very air they stood in. Kyra held up her hands and stared at her fingers, the tips of which were turning blue and icy. The frost traveled up her hands, through her veins and arteries, and Kyra cried out with the agony of it.

"Help me!" she begged Sorrel, her eyes full of terror.

Sorrel searched desperately through her mind for some magic that might save her friend, but all that came to her were paltry and pathetic hexes and charms that could do nothing to thaw such witchery. Kyra was frozen to her middle now and weeping with fear and pain.

"Sorrel!" she screamed.

"I'm sorry," Sorrel sobbed. "I know not how." Then she turned to the winter witch and went down on her knees. "Kill me instead. I beg of you."

The witch came to her and grabbed her hair, pulling her head back to show the crowd.

"Another Hawkweed!" she said, and the crowd cackled and roared with laughter.

With her face tilted to the sky, Sorrel could see the tops of the trees, and she blinked at what she spied there. At the highest point of the tallest pine perched a bird with black feathers and hooded beak, with hunched and mammoth wings. It gave an ugly caw.

Let me in, Sorrel heard, and then the bird was dust. *Let me in,* came the caw again, hurting Sorrel's ears.

Writhing under the winter witch's grasp, Sorrel caught Kyra's eye, the friend that she had played with, learned with, fought with, laughed with. Would she die with her too? *Not like this,* Sorrel pledged. And she let herself be pliant once more, lifting her head to the skies and opening her mouth to inhale. In flew the dust, filling her lungs, entering her bloodstream. Sorrel felt her body stretch and fill. She felt her mind expand and double. Rising effortlessly out of the winter witch's hand and standing tall, Sorrel realized she was towering over all the other witches. She heard them gasp and saw them pale. Sorrel closed her eyes and let the perfect spell come to her, the words bursting out of her, as Raven took her tongue, her lips, her mouth, her voice.

Immediately the spell was done, Kyra slid to the ground and started rubbing her arms over herself, trying to bring the warmth back to her once frozen limbs. Then she looked at Sorrel, startled and with another shade of fear in her eyes. Sorrel looked out at the clans, feeling the power surge and crackle within her.

"How dare you?" she accused in a voice at once strange and familiar. It was her mother's commanding tone. "How dare you come into my camp and make war with us?"

The winter witch, so small beneath her, was backing away.

"Oh no!" Sorrel told her, and she fixed her eyes on Sister Morgan's body and Sister Ada's wounds. As she looked, the vine slithered free and shot toward the winter witch, strangling her. And the silver blast that had severed Sister Ada's legs lit up once more and formed a shining arrow that flew through the air and pierced the winter witch straight through the heart.

The rest of the winter clan turned and fled, the wood witches lumbering after them. All the others scurried away like spiders. The Northern clan looked to Sorrel in awe. Part of her relished it. The other part rejected it. Sorrel felt her mind tugging and straining in both directions. Her hands went to her head to press her temples in an effort to contain it.

"Look to Sister Ada," she told them. "Her legs are gone but she can be saved. And prepare the fire for Sister Morgan. We will say farewell to her tonight."

Like obedient children, they did as they were told, but Sorrel found no pleasure in it, nor in the day, the sunshine, the fresh spring smell of the blossoms. Her mother lived within her now, pecking away at all her hope and joy, unfurling her dark wings around her heart.

25

CHARLOCK

It was close to bliss, this feeling of atonement. *If only she could distill just a few drops and bottle it to give to others,* Charlock thought to herself. Betony was found, she was reunited with her son, and her memory was slowly returning. Charlock felt a lightness in her chest that she hadn't experienced for years, not since she was a child. Before long, Poppy would be with her and she could redeem herself there too. The boy's magic would reach her daughter. Charlock was sure of it. Poppy would feel it and come home, if not to her, then to him. All Charlock's digging and planting was coming to fruition. Shoots of hope were sprouting and soon she would see the flowers of her success. It never crossed her mind that a blight might come and wither them so suddenly.

When Charlock felt the danger to her daughter, she was in the town gathering supplies under the cover of darkness for their long journey north. The instant she felt it, she dropped the food and ran to find the boy. He must have located Poppy. He might know more of her plight. As she flew through the streets, Charlock heard the song of her clan, the notes ringing in her ears.

For the first time since her departure, she wished she was with them and she sent silent thanks for their help. Their call would not reach Poppy's ears, though, Charlock knew. It was up to her to save her daughter.

At last, Charlock reached the house and burst inside, heading straight to where Leo usually slept. His dogs were there, but he was not. Instantly, the panic began to paw more frantically in Charlock's mind. She rushed from room to room, ripping open doors, then slamming them in desperate search of him. Each time, she was left more frightened than the last. The boy was nowhere to be found. Charlock blinked back her tears, but the tight leash she held on her hysteria suddenly snapped and she felt it bounding through her. The tears began to flood down her face and a scream curled in the back of her throat. Charlock refused to open her lips and let it out.

Covering her mouth with her hand, she grabbed the nearest dog from the slumbering mound of fur and yanked it toward her. Bending down, she looked it directly in the eyes. For a long moment, it stared back. Charlock could not be the first to blink. The dog succumbed, turning its head from her glare. When Charlock let it go, it leapt into the hallway, scratching to be released. Confident the creature understood its task, Charlock opened the front door. The dog sprang down the steps and, with head lowered to the pavement, its nose began to twitch and sniff. A minute later, the other dogs were after him and Charlock had to hurry to catch up.

She had hoped for one of these animals to aid her, not the noisy fanfare of the entire pack. But they worked well together. When one would lose the scent, another picked it up and barked for the rest of them to follow. They couldn't be far behind the boy,

Charlock comforted herself. His magic was raw and untrained and he would not know how to cover his tracks. She wondered where he might think to go and, as she tried to second-guess this boy she had only just met and hardly yet knew, Charlock's thoughts belatedly turned to Betony. Betony! Charlock wanted to pull at her own hair, so stupid had she been. Engrossed utterly in the boy's disappearance, Charlock had not thought to look for his mother. In her mind, she retraced her steps back through the house, room by room, and confirmed what she already knew to be true—Betony had been in none. She had taken her boy away and she would not want Charlock to find them.

Breaking into a run, Charlock urged the dogs on. They were on the edge of the town now and the dogs sniffed around a stream. A couple of them barked furiously at something they had found. Charlock waded into the reeds, her feet squelching on the slimy riverbed as she reached into the water. Dragging her hands through the plants, she finally made contact with something more solid. Lifting it up, she saw it was a shoe, rubber for running. Leo's shoe. Charlock looked across to the other side, then along the river to where the water disappeared around a turn. Charlock muttered a spell and closed her eyes. When she opened them, she pointed.

"This way!" she told the dogs.

It was several hours before Charlock was to find them. Betony had left clues as diversions, bits of hair, scraps of clothing, which had sent them down the wrong path and from which they had to backtrack, losing precious time. She and Leo had covered an amazing distance, returning all the way to the woods that were Betony's home. Often, on this journey, Charlock came close to despair. What hope had she of finding them in these foreign fields and copses?

Only thoughts of Poppy kept Charlock's aching legs moving forward. She knew not what trouble Poppy was in or who had caused it. She only knew it must be serious. Probably without even realizing it, Leo had located Poppy and, at that moment, the threat to their queen had been transmitted. As a mother, Charlock had experienced it as a tremor that shook the very ground beneath her feet and made her heart shudder against her chest. But even Betony had sensed something of it too, enough to take her son and run. Betony—a witch with no memory. Leo—a witch with no knowledge. Charlock shook her head at the farce of it.

There was more though. If Betony and the Northern clan had felt it, then all the witches must have. Charlock's worries wheeled around to her sisters in the coven and the dangers they must be facing from their enemies. But she could not help them now. She must focus on her child and no one else. Poppy was alive—Charlock felt this just as surely as she felt the jeopardy. Her daughter could be saved. Not by her, or the clan, but by Leo.

The sun was rising, transforming the night's chill to morning dew, the drops balanced on each blade of grass, waiting to rise up and join the clouds above. The nocturnal creatures had taken to their beds while the day's had not yet stirred. A perfect peace lay across the land until the dogs began their yelping. Charlock picked up her pace and followed their howls through the damp mist, for she could not see them, only hear their dreadful din. They had stopped beneath a large beech tree and their noses were pointed upward, sniffing the air, their front legs scratching at the bark in their excitement.

Charlock hurried to their side and peered up with them in search of anything or anyone above. There was little to see. The mist was ascending and most of the tree was lost within it. Stretching for the lowest branch and feeling for a foothold on the gnarled trunk, Charlock began to climb. It had been many years since she had climbed a tree. As girls, she and Betony had prided themselves on reaching higher than all the other young sisters. The sensation of choosing which hold, which crevice, grabbing hard and pulling up was a familiar one. The knack of it quickly came back to Charlock and she made swift progress despite the mist.

"Leo?" she called as she climbed from level to level, higher and higher. "Betony? Are you there?"

No answer came. Charlock looked down but could not find her feet. She reached up and her hand disappeared into the vapor. Suddenly unnerved, Charlock snatched her hand down. Grateful to have it back, she now longed to be on firm ground. Then the thought crept up on her, making the skin on the back of her neck tingle with trepidation. *How? How would she get down?* She was stuck, just as Betony wanted her to be.

"Betony!" she suddenly screamed. "Betony!"

A voice reached her through the mist, a voice from far below.

"Leave him be, Charlock. Whatever it is you want with him. Leave him be."

"My daughter. She needs him, Bet. You felt it. I know you did."

"I know I do not trust you. I know you say you came to help me but it is yourself you came to help, isn't it?"

"No!"

"Stop lying, Charlock. For once, stop lying to me."

Charlock sighed deeply. There was truth to Betony's words. Her reasons had been selfish first, altruistic second.

"Not just myself," she replied to Betony. "I wanted to make amends, truly I did. I wanted your forgiveness. But is it so wrong that by helping you and your child, I would help my own child also? My daughter is our queen. She didn't ask for it. It has caused her only pain so far and now she is in terrible danger." Charlock stared into the mist, wishing she could read the emotions on Betony's face below, wishing Betony could read her own and be convinced by them. She put all her feeling into her voice so it became thick and sticky and she could taste the tang of terror on her tongue. "Please, Betony. I beg you. I gave you your son. All I ask is that you help give me my daughter."

"You gave him to me?" Charlock could feel Betony's anger reverberate through the wood of the tree, shaking the leaves upon the twigs. Charlock had chosen her words badly, but it was too late to retract them. She braced herself for Betony's onslaught, clutching hold of the branch even more tightly. "You took him from me!" came Betony's accusation. "Didn't you? I don't know how or why. I only know you were my friend, closer to me than any sister, so you must have betrayed me. And I have been without my child a lifetime because of it."

Charlock felt her own fury flare at this last sentence.

"As have I!" she shrieked. "Raven took my baby from me just as she took your son from you. I should have tried harder to protect you. I know that. But I was weak. I was young and scared. And you had left me! You left me!" Charlock was sobbing now and only when her tears subsided did she realize that Betony hadn't responded. "Bet?" she whimpered. "Are you still there?"

When Betony spoke, her voice was soft with sadness. "I cannot risk losing him again."

"You won't," Charlock swore. "I will protect you both this time. I promise it."

There was a long and heavy pause. "I believe you mean it. I do. But you have not the power, Charlock. He is their worst fear—a male witch. He needs to come with me."

Charlock felt the strength seep out of her and her shoulders slump. She let herself lie along the branch, becoming part of it: a piece of wood, no thoughts, no feelings, just one small piece of a greater being. In that moment, her worries left her, her anger departed. There was only her cheek soft against the rough bark, her arms hanging loose and limp in the cool morning air. For many minutes, she let herself just be. She didn't count the seconds. Time was nothing to her now. After a while, she felt a breeze caress her skin, carrying away small patches of fog, revealing gaps of light. A stronger gust followed and more of the mist dispersed.

"Charlock?" came the voice.

She lowered her head and saw him far below, looking up at her, and her mind began to stir once more.

"You think I can help her?" he asked.

"I do," she said.

"Why me, if you can't?"

"Because she loves you," Charlock said, the truth of it lifting her up, before she lowered herself down, branch by branch.

When she jumped at the end, she stumbled and he caught her.

"Thank you," she said, looking deep into his dark, dark eyes.

Then she turned and saw Betony sitting not far off, hugging her knees, shaking her head.

"Betony?" she called. "We are in pieces, but we can put ourselves back together, bit by bit, until we are all united. I know we can. The past does not have to be our present."

"You are a fool," Betony said and bent her head to her knees as though she couldn't bear to watch.

Charlock led Leo to a stream where the water ran clear over silvery stones.

"You reached her last night. You must find her again," she said.

"How?" he asked, and she wondered how to instruct someone so ignorant of their talent.

"Look into the water," she told him. "Not just with your eyes but with your all."

Leo tried, to be sure. She could see him staring, squinting, glaring, until his eyes began to water and he had to stop and rub them.

"Relax," she instructed. She covered his eyes with her palm. "Look again but from inside you. Don't think. Feel. Just as you did with the mist in the tree."

"I hardly meant to do that," he said gruffly.

"Exactly. Stop trying so hard," she told him gently, trying to let her words be soothing to him. "Just think of Poppy. Think of her face, her voice, her eyes looking back at you."

Then Charlock took her hand from Leo's face and he looked into the water once more. He blinked and Charlock held her breath until he turned his head away angrily.

"It's only me. Only my face that I see."

Charlock sighed to calm herself so she could, in turn, calm him.

"Is there any detail?" she asked. "Any one thing or moment that you can focus on? Just that. No more." Leo closed his eyes. "Can you do that?" He nodded. "Can you see it clearly in your mind?"

"I can."

"Then open your eyes and look."

26

POPPY

The black of Poppy's slumber was darker than any night. It contained no stars or moon, no shadow or glimmer, just the pitch black of an empty cave with no cracks to let in even a pinprick of light. There were no dreams in this cavern, so far underground, no flickers of imagination or colors drawn from her subconscious. Which was why the sudden glow was shock enough to penetrate this deepest of sleeps.

The warmth behind Poppy's eyelids began to paint oily rainbows in her mind that made her shift her small bird body, then stretch her tiny limbs. It was then she felt the heat against her leg, urging her to wake, making her curious, giving her the energy to unfurl her feathers and unglue her eyes. Through the mist, Poppy saw it. A rose-tinted light that shone from her leg, lighting up her cage, offering her hope. *The heart stone,* Poppy thought. And she knew Leo had found her. The crystal shone even more brightly, as if it were spurring her on. It was not her magic but his, Poppy realized. Leo had found his power.

The warmth rushed to Poppy's chest. The need to see Leo was suddenly stronger than any of Mma's drugs. It was pulling her out of her haze, onto her feet, steadying her as she tottered. She felt Leo's magic holding her up and filling her lungs. By the light of the crystal, Poppy could now make out the room beyond the cage. There was no sight of Mma or Teko. She was alone and she knew that she must take her chance to save herself. Poppy tapped her beak against the metal bars, then turned and pressed the crystal tied to her leg against one of them. In the furthest reaches of her mind, she found a spell. Slowly, the bar softened so that Poppy could bend it. Only a small gap, but if she twisted her body and sucked in her breath, it was just enough to squeeze through.

"No!" came Teko's voice and his hands were hard and rough as they scooped her up and held her tight.

Poppy struggled and pecked at him, but he held her up to face him.

"Why, Poppy?" he cried. "Don't you know we are trying to save you!"

Poppy tried to find her voice but only a whistle emerged, high and fraught.

I love him, she wanted to say. *I thought we didn't belong together. I thought his destiny was with Ember. But we are meant to be.*

"What shall I do?" Teko said, and Poppy understood he was no longer talking to her.

She strained to see and found Mma standing in the doorway, shaking her head so the beads around her neck shimmered and clinked.

"Break her wing," Mma told Teko, shutting the door behind her with a bang.

Teko looked into Poppy's eyes and she saw her swallow's face reflected in his pupils.

Let me go, she begged him. "Let me go," she said.

She saw his eyelids blink with surprise and then she realized she had found her voice.

"Teko," she spoke again. "Please," she implored. "If you care for me at all, release me."

"Break it, now!" she heard Mma command. "For her own good. The wing will mend but you know what will happen to her if she flies home."

Poppy felt Teko's large fingers clasp her tiny wing, the bone so thin and fragile in his fingers. She closed her eyes and waited for the pain.

"I can't!" Teko blurted. Poppy felt a drop of water splash upon her head and looked up to see that tears were rolling down Teko's face.

"Give her to me, I'll do it," Mma snapped and she grabbed Poppy from his grasp.

"No!" screamed Poppy, and the crystal on her leg sparked with a white heat that made Mma howl in agony and drop her hands to her sides, releasing Poppy to the air. The old woman ran to the water pail and plunged her hands into it.

Poppy spread her wings and swooped to the door. But Teko was there first, his hand upon the latch. Poppy hovered in the air before him, the heart stone glowing at her leg like a beacon.

"I must keep you safe," Teko wept.

"I don't want to be safe. I don't choose safe anymore."

Teko reached out a finger and touched the crystal at her ankle.

"Leo," he said.

"Yes." Poppy nodded. "Leo."

Then Teko turned away, but, as he did so, his arm pulled the door, opening it wide. Out Poppy flew, into the light, up toward the sun, and on toward home.

27

EMBER

The house was dark apart from the glow of the television in the downstairs window. *Melanie must be up,* thought Ember, and, for the first time in hours, she felt glad. She had a home where a mother sat waiting up for her. She pictured Melanie wringing her hands in despair, constantly looking at the clock, panicked at her long absence. Hurrying inside, Ember couldn't wait to be enveloped in a hug, to be fussed over, even to be reprimanded.

"I'm home!" she called as she stepped into the warm.

There was no response.

In the living room, Ember found Melanie stretched out asleep on the sofa, her hand still clutching the remote. With a sigh, Ember took it gently from her, then picked up the blanket from the floor and covered her with it. Kneeling down, she studied Melanie's sleeping face and tried to imagine herself in twenty-five years' time. Perhaps she would be alone, too, just as she was now, without a friend in the world and without the boy she loved.

With a click, Ember turned off the television and plunged them into darkness. In the quiet, Ember could hear the faint breathing of her mother, and she lay down on the carpet next to her and closed her eyes. She pictured the moment she'd left Leo—how she willed him to call out her name, to reach out a hand and stop her. But, even in her imagination, he just stood there and watched her go. She pictured Poppy, smiling like she'd never seen her do. So carefree. So in love. Running into Leo's arms, putting her arms around him, pressing her lips to his.

Ember's eyes blinked open. The screen seemed to stare at her from its throne in the corner of the room, mocking her attempts to sleep. With another click, it flickered back to life and she watched another girl with another boy, until finally her eyes fell shut.

The next day, Ember went to the café where Nick had taken her and ordered a coffee. She would learn to like it, she told herself, especially if she planned to make it to Paris one day. It tasted just as foul, but she sat at a table and made herself drink it. It was a medicine of sorts, making her nerves tingle and the blood speed faster around her body. She could see why so many chaffs (or people, as she now must call them) liked the vitality it gave. Its effects were far stronger than those of nuts or seaweed, but it was a jittery kind of energy and Ember held up her hand to find that it was shaking.

"Hooked already?" Nick sat down opposite her, not waiting for her to extend an invitation. "Or is it just an excuse to see me again?"

Ember scowled. "I once knew a cockerel like you," she told him. "Crowed all through the day, not just at dawn. Always wanting admiration. Never could be quiet."

Nick smirked. "A cockerel, huh?"

"Until my aunt snapped his neck and boiled him in a pot."

Ember was pleased to see Nick's smile fade.

"Now, that's not a nice thing to say. Not after I've been roaming the streets looking for you." Ember's eyes darted upward and met his. She felt the blush rise from her chest to her cheeks. "You left in a hurry the other evening."

"I'm sorry," she said genuinely.

"Where'd you go?" he asked, and Ember caught something more than curiosity in his voice and lowered her head. "Okay, you're right. None of my business. I just want to get to know you, that's all." Still Ember didn't feel like looking at him. "Okay, wait there."

When he came back, he brought with him two sandwiches and some juice.

"What's this?" she asked.

"Lunch. I'm having lunch. With you. And you don't have to talk. You can sit there in silence if you like. I just want to hang out with you. I'll talk and you can just nod or something. How about that?"

Ember couldn't help but smile. She ate her sandwich, glad to be rid of the coffee taste, and nodded when he pulled out the newspaper to show her his name in print above the article he'd written.

"You're not easy to impress," he said.

"Oh, but I am," she told him. "I'm just trying not to be."

Then he leaned over and kissed her and afterward carried on eating his sandwich as though nothing had happened. Ember wondered if it was normal to kiss girls over lunch when you hardly knew them. She looked around the café to check, but no one else was even touching.

"I have to get back to work," he announced when he'd finished his food, even though Ember still had a last corner to eat.

She left the remains of her lunch on the table and followed him outside. There, against the glass, Nick kissed her goodbye, this time harder and for longer. Ember was able to think as he kissed her. She preferred it this way. She was aware of her body responding. She could feel her lips opening and she could analyze quite rationally the smell of his skin and the taste of his mouth mixing with hers. When he stopped, she was disappointed, but not overwhelmingly so.

"Can I see you this evening?" he said into her ear. Ember nodded. "Here at eight," he told her, and she nodded again. "Later," he said, "you're going to tell me everything."

Ember spent the afternoon in the garden collecting herbs and flowers for her soap and trying not to think about eight o'clock and what might happen then. Melanie watched her from the kitchen and waved when Ember beckoned her outside. But she wouldn't come out, saying the air was too chilly, even though it was perfectly warm. Ember picked her mother some sprigs of sweet cicely and took them to her at the door.

"Smell," she told her, and Melanie lifted them to her nose, closed her eyes as she inhaled.

"Heaven," Melanie said. "Like you."

But still she wouldn't come outside.

"I'm sorry I disappeared the last couple of days. You must have been worried," Ember said.

"I can't worry anymore. There's no worry left in me," Melanie explained.

"That's good," Ember replied, not sure if it was or it wasn't.

"I gave up thinking I could control anything a long time ago. I just take life as it comes," Melanie said, stepping back from the doorway.

Ember sensed it was good advice but knew it would be hard for her to follow. She headed back into the garden and lost herself in the sweet fragrance of the bluebells that grew around the alder tree and the clusters of catchfly that bloomed along the beds. Their scents mingled with the aniseed of the fennel and the pine-spindle of the rosemary. She thought of blends for her soap and was feeling very serene and settled with life when Charlock arrived.

Immediately, Ember looked around for Leo.

"I have come alone," Charlock told her.

Ember met her mother's eyes. "To say goodbye, I suppose," she said sharply, her tranquility wilting like the bluebell flowers she'd picked that now lay in drooping bunches at her feet.

"To say thank you. For your help," Charlock corrected.

"It's all worked out now, has it? Leo with his mother, Poppy with you, Poppy and Leo together."

Ember felt tears form, but her eyes stung with anger, not sorrow. Charlock took her hand.

"Poppy is on her way back to us. All is as it was meant to be."

Ember snatched her hand back. *And what is meant for me?* she wanted to shout. Instead, she started gathering the bundles of flowers from the grass.

"You'll go back to the clan now?" she asked, knowing full well the answer.

"They need us. And Poppy will return there soon." Charlock picked up some of the blooms. "Now Leo has gone, it will be easier for you. You will think less of then and more of now. It will be easier to keep our secret, to pretend we don't exist."

Tears pricked like pins at Ember's eyes and Charlock stared at her intently until she nodded her agreement. Then Charlock lowered her face to the buds and breathed deeply. "There is a good life to be had down here," she said softly. "Choose it carefully, my child."

Ember let herself be hugged.

She felt Charlock inhale her hair. "You'll always be my flower," she heard and then she was released and Charlock was gone.

"Your place or mine?" Nick asked with a smirk that confused her.

They were sitting in a wooden cove within the bar, secluded from the throngs that had stood around talking and laughing so loudly all evening.

"I live with my mother," she told him, as though that was answer enough.

She felt a little unsteady on her feet as she got up to grab her bag and go with him. It was the wine, he told her.

"I don't like it." She'd grimaced when she first tasted it. "It's the color of pee."

"I'll get you some red," he had replied and, in truth, she did prefer that color, though she chose not to tell him so.

"I like the glass," she had admitted instead, twirling the thin stem in her fingers, liking the way it caught the light and how the deep cherry liquid swirled around the sides.

She only had one glass to his three, which she drank over the hours, sip by sip. With each sip, she had told a little more of herself. Her story slipped out of her like strands of hair from a ribbon. How she had a friend who meant everything to her but who had run away. How she had a mother who she loved but who wasn't her mother. How she had a boyfriend who she'd wanted but who loved her friend. He always had, she just hadn't wanted to see it. Not that, not any of it. And she'd had a home that she hated but still missed. She missed all of them. Every day.

Nick was a good listener. If the wine hadn't been making Ember's head spin and her tongue feel heavy in her mouth, she would have realized it was his job to listen. He spoke only when necessary, knowing when to prompt and when not to interrupt.

"Forget them," he said, when she finally finished her glass. "Especially the boyfriend," he added, raising an eyebrow.

She liked how easily he dismissed them; the scorn he felt for them on her behalf.

"I want to," she said, and he lifted the bottle to pour her another glass.

Quickly, Ember covered it with her hand, but it was too late and the wine poured through her fingers.

"I don't think I should drink anymore," she told him, staring at the drops falling from her skin like blood.

It was the last sensible thing she said.

❧

She woke up in Nick's house, in his bed. She wanted to slide off
the side of it and slither to the door, so low she felt, so wrong it
was to be there. She sat up quietly so as not to wake him. She
was dressed, thankfully, as was he. She turned to look at his face
and saw that he looked gentle as he slept, almost innocent. Her
mouth felt so dry, like she hadn't drunk water in days. And her
temples throbbed in pain, especially when she tried to search
her memory for the events of last night. It was a blur of reds as
though the whole evening had been tinged with that wine. She
remembered kissing him. Kissing him before they got here and
then again after. Kissing him to make him stop asking questions, to make her stop answering them. She looked around. She
remembered this room, with its bed and seating and kitchen
cupboards all within the single space like her caravan used to
be. She saw bottles of beer on the table, but she couldn't recall
drinking them. She remembered laughing, though, and springing on the bed, jumping high to touch the ceiling. And the
music playing loudly and how she'd put it louder so she couldn't
hear him anymore, only see him with his cloud-white hair and
summer-sky eyes.

"You are my twin—not her," she'd shouted. "Not him!"

And she had pulled him down to the mattress—she!—and
covered his face with kisses and held him like she wouldn't let him
go. She remembered sleeping, too, and Nick trying to wake her.

"You can't crash out on me. Not now!"

But her head was on the pillow and her eyes were closed and
his voice had sounded far, far away.

Maybe it wasn't too bad, Ember thought to herself. She
had embarrassed herself, to be sure, but nothing terrible had

happened. The taste of bile rose in Ember's mouth as if disputing the truth of this and she groaned.

"In the bathroom, above the sink," came Nick's voice, making her temples throb. Ember looked at him, but he hadn't even opened his eyes.

"What?" she asked.

"The aspirin." Ember wrinkled her face in puzzlement. When she didn't move, he swung his legs from the bed and rubbed his face and his hair with his hands. "I'll get them, but only cos I like you so much."

As she watched him drag himself to the bathroom, Ember smiled. He liked her. For a moment, even her headache faded. When Nick came back, he handed her two pills and a dirty cup full of water. She looked at them.

"You haven't taken a painkiller before, have you?"

She shook her head, and he gave an exaggerated gawp of astonishment.

"What was this clan you lived in?"

Ember's headache returned with a sudden force, cracking through her skull like the promise she had broken. The promise to keep the clan's secret. To never, ever tell.

28

BETONY

Betony had been on a train before. She felt sure of that. She remembered the speed; the train shooting through the countryside like a snake, only with a hiss that roared and shook the ground. Betony dug into her memory to reach for what else she could unearth. She had been alone, that was right. And she had been frightened. She tried to imagine herself, to imagine Leo with her, a tiny baby. But there was no baby. Only a piece of paper in her hand. A ticket to the town of Fairwood.

Seventeen years later and she was, at last, making the return journey. This time that missing baby was sitting beside her, taller and stronger than she. Sometimes he took her hand, and her heart swelled to feel his touch. She knew he felt guilty for going against her wishes and following Charlock's requests. He was too trusting, but she would not make that mistake. Looking across at him, she noticed the shadow above his lip and the breadth of his shoulders. *He is a man,* she marveled. *I have produced a man.* At the same time, he was forever her child and in need of her protection. If only he would let her. If only he would follow her and not

Charlock, who had a child of her own to put first, to put above and beyond all else.

Poppy Hawkweed. Betony mouthed the name, and the syllables soured her saliva. Poppy Hawkweed was the reason for their return. Leo had looked into the lake and he had found her, a bird breaking free and flying home. After that, there had been no more discussion. They would travel north, back to the coven, back to wait for her.

"Charlock tells me my mother died when I was a child," Betony said to Leo, while Charlock was sleeping. "Perhaps if she had lived . . . if I'd had her love and her wisdom, I wouldn't have been so reckless with your father. I loved him, just as you love this Poppy, but . . . " Betony faltered, then found the words. "Don't be like me. You have a mother now and she is telling you, it isn't safe."

"But you and my father had no power," he argued. "Poppy is a queen."

Betony had to stop herself from cursing. "Far easier to change a queen than centuries of tradition," she responded too loudly, then lowered her voice again. "Men are forbidden. It is a rule never to be broken. Look how I was punished for daring to give birth to you."

"I don't know why they feel so threatened. I mean, they're witches."

"They are sisters and sisterhood is broken by men. It is only by keeping the world out that they can keep their world in. Ask Charlock and she will tell you the same. We had a bond, the two of us, to each other. And then I met your father."

"Tell me more about him?" he pleaded and, for a moment, the longing in his eyes made it hard for her to think.

"I remember him being happy," she finally said. "Happy and so full of energy." The images raced through her mind—Danny's feet kicking a ball, his legs running after her, his arm waving at her, his head tipping back as he laughed, his face so animated as he talked. And then she felt a deep sadness in her chest and the trickle of tears on her cheeks.

"I'm sorry," Leo whispered.

"He gave me his jacket. I remember that. And he told me not to risk my neck." She had to pause to stop herself from weeping. "The rest—it just won't come."

"It will," he said so confidently. "Now you're going back. You'll see."

Leo was right. Out on the moors, something in the air struck her. The smell of home. The pine. The slight tang of salt. She closed her eyes and an outline of hills against sky formed in her mind. When they reached the top of the ridge, the view matched that outline exactly, like a drawing placed against an original. She heard a kestrel's call—a sound from long ago—and looked up to see a bird hovering above her, its pointed wings beating at the sky. Betony felt a stab of memory and her heart went warm from the wound she felt there. She'd had a kestrel once, a bird who chose her out of all the rest, who was her faithful companion when all else proved fickle. Feathered brown and gray above, and white below with spots of black that she had liked to count. *He must be long dead now,* she thought, and a sudden sense of grief made her fall to her knees. Kee-kee-kee, cried the kestrel high above, as if lamenting with her. She felt a hand upon her shoulder and thought it Leo's, but it was Charlock who looked at her in understanding and helped her to her feet.

From then on, Betony's legs knew the way even though her mind didn't. When Charlock tired, she took the lead and let them follow.

"Perhaps me and my mother should wait here?" Leo suggested to Charlock as they neared the forest. Betony could hear the nerves lurking behind his suggestion. "There's a dell within those trees," he told them, lifting an arm to point.

"It is best we stay together," replied Charlock. "The clan will be shocked to see you both, to be sure, but I will look after you until Poppy arrives." Betony couldn't help make a scoffing noise. Charlock turned to her. "Raven is dead and there is no witch in the clan who will hurt you. Not while you're under my protection. It is safer if we stick close."

Though it galled Betony to hear it, there was merit in Charlock's words. So they walked on through the pathless forest, picking out a route of their own, until they arrived at the outskirts of the camp. Betony stared at the giant gray stones that flanked it. She felt a sudden compulsion to put her hands on one and lay her cheek upon its silky surface. She knew she had done this once before, many years ago, but she could not recall the circumstance or the emotion that accompanied this act, only the familiar feeling of the cool, hard rock against her warm, soft face. The birds were chattering all around them, as though gossiping about their return.

"Shall we?" said Charlock, gesturing to the hidden gap between the stones.

With trepidation, Betony followed Charlock and Leo inside the camp. Unveiled before her was a picture of home. The colored, painted caravans dotted here and there; the large trees with their long, low branches that sheltered the tables and learning circles beneath them; the hens and geese that pecked around the wooden barrels filled with water or scraps for compost; the donkey and the horse, old companions, grazing the long grass in the southern corner; the washing hanging out to dry like shipless sails and, farther off, the smaller, darker animal skins draped over wooden posts to cure. Nothing had changed. Betony felt the memories blossoming in her mind. She remembered playing under that tree. Eating at that table. Sleeping in that caravan. A name unfurled like petals in her mind.

"Aunt Sage?" she asked Charlock, and Charlock shook her head. Betony closed her eyes in sorrow.

"I think I should go." She heard Leo whisper and her eyes blinked open.

All around the camp, witches were turning, staring, stepping out of caravans and huts, their faces full of shock and fury. Many had their arms raised, ready to attack. Betony took Leo's hand and squeezed it.

"Sisters," Charlock called out to them. "I bring good tidings. Our queen. She is coming home to us." The pause that followed felt as ominous as a dark cloud, black with the threat of thunder. The eyes shifted in that silence to one of the caravans, Betony could not recall whose.

"Is Sorrel well?" asked Charlock, her eyes following the other pairs. "Let me go and greet her."

The crowd stiffened, but still not one witch spoke. Betony reached out her other arm to pull Charlock back.

"What is this foolishness?" Charlock exclaimed, brushing off Betony's hold. "She is my niece and I want news of her." And she strode through the midst of them toward the caravan.

Only one young witch responded. "A male!" she stated and then she pointed at Leo. "He is a male."

"He is, Sister Kyra. But he is with me and he has helped our queen and she would want us to give him shelter."

An angry murmur rose from the crowd and Betony felt Leo recoil from it. "What shall I do?" he murmured, but, before she could answer, Charlock turned to him.

"They will not hurt you," she announced. "You are safe here."

"No one is safe because of you." The young witch spoke again. "We were attacked by other clans."

Charlock glared at her. "I sensed the invasion and I am sorry for it. But Poppy will be with us soon and she will protect us."

"Sister Sorrel protected us without your daughter's help," the girl retorted, chin jutting forward, hands defiantly on hips.

Charlock seemed to freeze, but not with fear. Anger brightened her eyes, bleached her skin, and clenched her teeth. "How dare you take that tone? My daughter is your queen and you will refer to her as that."

"I would if she were here!"

"Where is your loyalty, Sister Kyra?" demanded Charlock.

"Sorrel defended us when we were helpless." Another voice cut across the frosty atmosphere. "She saved young Kyra's life. She deserves our loyalty too."

"More so," came another witch's cry.

An old witch was wheeled forward in a barrow fashioned as a seat. Her skirts were long, but Betony could see that no feet emerged from under them. Charlock must have noticed this, too, for Betony heard her gasp.

"Ada!" Charlock called in dismay. "Oh, Ada."

With the name came a flicker of memory in Betony's mind.

"Poppy should not have left us, Sister Charlock," Sister Ada said gently. "She thought only of herself."

"She did not know!" Charlock defended. "She has so much to learn."

"But you know better," continued the old witch, "and you lied to us."

Charlock bowed her head at that. "I did and I am sorry for it. But it was only half a lie. Poppy needed that time and it was the only way I could give it to her." Then Charlock raised her eyes. "I had the best intentions."

"Is that Sister Betony who stands beside you?" Sister Ada asked, peering so intently that Betony could feel the pressure of her stare.

"It is," Charlock replied. "And the boy is her son."

The collective intake of breath was audible as a gust of wind and Betony felt the chill of it.

"We were told they'd died. I suppose that was a half-lie too?" Sister Ada scorned.

Charlock's cheeks were burning now. "Do not judge my daughter by my actions!" she cried. "She is our queen. Mine and every witch's. Even yours, Sister Ada. She proved this out on the cliffs. Don't you remember what she did that day? What power and courage she showed? Surely you cannot forget that?"

There was a long silence and then came the sound of a door opening. All turned to the caravan, where out stepped a girl with a long scar down one cheek that was still raised and pink and not yet fully healed. This was not the only damage that Betony noted. This Sorrel's eyes were wild, her hair knotted, and her hands twisting together with fingers that were red and chafed and arms that were raw with scratches.

"Aunt Charlock," the girl said in a voice that rose and fell erratically as though out of her control. "Who have you brought with you?"

This time Betony answered for herself. "I am Betony. You were very young when I last saw you. I was once a part of this clan. And this is my son, Leo."

The girl's eyes darted across to him and Betony caught a look of recognition on her face. "A male. A male—a chaff—a witch—all combined. So many of our rules broken in one being."

"Sorrel, they seek our sanctuary," said Charlock calmly, but Betony could sense her confusion. "Poppy will want them here, I assure you."

The girl wrung her hands and shook her head. "And yet Poppy is not here to greet them."

"She is coming," Charlock stated as her eyes searched for some clue to explain Sorrel's strange state.

"So you tell us," replied Sorrel, her eyes blinking repeatedly as she looked around at the other sisters. They nodded their support. "So we will wait to hear it from her. Until then, they are not welcome here."

"Child, what is wrong with you?" said Charlock. "You are not yourself. They are staying."

The girl blinked again and her mouth twitched and muttered words that none could hear. Her eyes closed tight and when they opened they glared red, like fire.

"Go. All three of you, go. Return only with your queen." She pointed a finger toward the exit and, as she did so, a line of fire sprang from the grass like an arrow pointing their way.

Charlock's usually mild expression changed to one of shock at this display of power. She looked to the other witches for support, but none was offered.

"Ada?" she called, the desperation now audible in her voice. "Morgan, Ivy, Martha, Wynne?"

Not one of them answered.

"Shame on you!" Charlock cried. "Look to the stone and see whose name is writ upon it." None stirred to do her bidding. Charlock raised her arm in attack, but Betony grabbed it down.

"There are too many of them," she whispered loudly, pulling her childhood friend away.

"Traitors, all of you!" Charlock shouted at them as she went.

"Leo," Betony urged her son, who was still standing there, mouth open as though unable to comprehend what he had seen. "Move. Now!"

As the sun set, they made their way to town, to a meadow Leo knew beyond a church. As soon as Betony's foot hit the path between the headstones, she felt a shiver. When they reached an ivy-clad wall, a memory formed.

"There's a door," she said as she moved to a spot and felt between the leaves. Her hand found the handle just as somehow she knew it would.

"You've been here before?" Leo asked in surprise.

"I must have." The door opened with a creak and she stepped into the meadow.

"Charlock, have you been here too?" she heard Leo question.

"Never," came the answer.

Betony let her eyes soak in the dusky setting, searching for clues in the pale night that might aid her memory. Leo came to stand beside her.

"Did you come here with my father?" he whispered reverently.

"I don't know," she murmured. "I feel it so."

She walked toward the grass to reach the stream. They all drank thirstily from it and then ate from Charlock's supplies. Betony noticed a tiny grave close by. This she did not recognize.

"What lies there?"

"A cat," Leo told her.

"Poppy's?" asked Betony and, on hearing her daughter's name, Charlock looked up at him.

Leo nodded a little nervously. Since they'd left the coven, Charlock's spirits had sunk into a pit that oozed with anger and anguish. She hadn't wanted to leave the forest, convinced that Poppy would return directly to the coven.

"Is that why you think she'll come here?" she challenged, staring at the mound of earth. "For a cat!"

"For me," he told her plainly.

"She will go home." Charlock shook her head. "We should have stayed closer to the coven."

Leo jumped angrily to his feet. "When are you going to get it through your head? That's not her home." He threw the crust of his bread high and far into the stream, then walked toward the end of the field.

Without a word to Charlock, Betony got up and followed. She couldn't help feeling pleased that Leo's respect for Charlock had at last diminished. They were nobody's puppets and she would not have them used as such. Next, he must be distanced from the girl. This Poppy had such a grip on him, but it could be weakened. Betony felt sure of it. She was his mother, after all. He was a part of her.

That night, she lay down close by Leo and listened to his breathing. The sound was so comforting that her body became heavy and her eyes fell shut.

"Have you remembered any more?" came his voice through the darkness.

"Fragments," she admitted. "Not enough to make a whole."

"If you remember more about my father, will you tell me?"

This was the way, she realized. The way to keep Leo close. He had questions and the past held the answers. If only she could tell it to him. But there were seventeen long years to cross and the bridge that lay before her seemed impassable, full of missing planks with a deep crevasse of ignorance beneath it.

"Maybe tonight I'll find him in my dreams," she said.

She let herself drift off to sleep and soon a voice whispered in her head. "Did you miss me?" Danny asked.

"Always," she sighed as she was carried away, back through those seventeen years, back into his arms.

29

Young Betony

To Betony, summer seemed to begin for her and Danny's pleasure. Fields filled themselves with flowers to greet them, grasses grew waist-high for them to lie and hide in, nights were balmy for them to meet in. But the warmth of the season had done little to thaw relations between her and Charlock. Two months had passed and Charlock hadn't spoken to her since their words about Raven and the prophecy. Betony had tried to make amends, but, after a few rebuttals, her sadness sparked to anger. She had done nothing wrong and if Charlock could not see that, then Charlock was not the friend she thought. At least that's what Betony told herself most of the time. Occasionally, though, she could see how wounded Charlock felt—by her, by her sister who no longer favored her with attention, by the two pregnancies of Sister Mildred and Sister Speedwell—and she felt a pang of pity for her friend.

Charlock had been holding a pail of water when Sister Speedwell announced her news and Betony had seen how Charlock's eyes had closed and how the water had slopped over the brim as her hand began shaking. Putting down the pail, Charlock had hurried to Raven for sympathy only to be brushed away like an irritating fly. Seeing her friend standing there alone, looking so lost, Betony had picked up the water and taken it to her.

"Please forgive me, Charlock," she whispered.

Charlock took the pail but wouldn't look at her. "Are you still meeting with that chaff boy?"

Betony stiffened. "Why?" she asked defensively.

Charlock looked her in the eye. "You are dancing with danger and I want no turn in it."

Betony pulled Charlock toward her so their words were shielded from prying ears. "You are supposed to be my friend . . . my sister."

Charlock tugged her arm free. "Then behave like one. Sacrifice as I have. Put our clan first and not yourself."

Betony rubbed the tears away from her eyes with the backs of her hands. "You are not the Charlock I love. You have let your sister poison you against me. You have let what happened to you turn you sour."

"I am doing what is expected of me," Charlock whispered angrily. "You should try and do the same."

"And end up as miserable as you?" Betony cried loudly, unable to help herself.

Charlock stared at her, the hurt slowly registering on her face so that Betony wished she could retract her words. Before she could apologize, Charlock picked up the pail and threw the water over her. Never, in all the years Betony had known Charlock, had she seen such aggression from her. The violence must have shocked Charlock too, for she was trembling and her hand was at her chest as though she were struggling to breathe.

"I've kept your secret because of the love we once shared," she said in a voice choked with fury, "but I want no more to do with you. You hear me? No more!"

The water dripped off Betony's lashes, disguising her tears, and ran down to her chin and on to her sodden clothes. As she watched Charlock stride away, she noticed the other sisters staring at her in goggle-eyed amazement and she gave a comical shrug, trying to mask her turmoil with good humor. None were fooled though.

Long into the evening, Betony caught them glancing in her direction and whispering behind their palms. Unable to stand it, Betony took her food and ate alone behind her caravan. Her kestrel landed on her arm without her calling for him. She rubbed his bluish beak with her finger and he tilted his head to survey her with black beady eyes. Without Charlock, she had no one but this bird. The other young sisters would show her no allegiance. Charlock was Raven's sister after all and her mother was a prominent elder. It was only Betony's friendship with Charlock that had given her a position within their circle. Without it, she felt like an outsider from her own clan. Her only consolation was Danny. Over the next weeks, the love she felt for Charlock, she gave to him, until he had every last bit of it.

It was hard to find a way to see him now that the yoking season was over. Escaping the camp required every bit of stealth and cunning that Betony possessed. She had used every excuse possible—that she was sick, that she had found a skulk of foxes to watch, that she wanted to stargaze or forage farther afield, that she was waking early to study. This last deceit her Aunt Sage had accepted with a mixture of pleasure and pride that made Betony squirm with guilt.

Having run out of alibis, Betony had started sneaking out at night while the camp was sleeping. With no lie to cover her, this was risky, but it seemed to her as though she had no choice. She had to be with him. If more than a few days passed without their meeting, she felt like a flower cut at the stem, squeezed between pages, drying until she was as flat and thin as the paper that bound her. One touch and she might crumble. Then, when she saw him, it was as though she was replenished, absorbing his touch . . . his words . . . him . . . like he was water that made her bloom once more.

He would meet her in the barn at the bottom of the valley. Often he'd be waiting for her, his bicycle propped against the wooden wall, his head bent over his schoolbooks, his face illuminated by the glow of his flashlight. Sometimes he'd be asleep and she would have to wake him and he'd always grab her down and pull her to him and they'd hardly speak for the kissing and the loving until it was time for her to leave again.

"You look so tired," he told her, putting his fingertips to the circles beneath her eyes.

"That's not very gentlemanly," she said, for she had learned the word from the dictionary he had brought her.

He had seemed embarrassed about giving it to her, apologizing, not wanting her to think him rude. "I just thought you might like it," he said. And she had. She had pored over it every spare moment. Inside was a world for her to explore, some of it like her own, but so much uncharted territory.

"I've figured it out, you see," Danny had explained when she first flicked through the pages. "Your secret," he'd said, and she'd stopped breathing. "I don't mind, though. It's nothing to be ashamed of. Being a gypsy."

Betony had exhaled with relief. "A gypsy," she repeated. Why hadn't she thought of that? "I should have told you."

Danny was looking tired, too. She could see the shadows beneath his eyes and she tried to kiss them away. He was in the middle of his exams, which were important. She had found this word—exam—in the dictionary also and afterward suggested they shouldn't meet until he had finished. But he had looked so aghast and that made her so happy she didn't mention the idea again.

"Did you miss me?" he asked, as he always did.

She gave the same answer every time. "Always," she said, as she buried her face in his neck, wishing she could cast a spell to stop the sun from rising, even for just a few more hours.

She felt him yawn. "You sleep. I'll wake you when it's time."

"You sure?" he asked.

"Sshh," she whispered and he lay down, his head in her lap, and she stroked his hair, soft and silky on her fingers, long after he'd fallen asleep.

He looked so innocent and fragile as he slept that she couldn't help but question why the witches feared men so. She knew the covens had their reasons. Her love for Danny had hindered her sisterhood with Charlock. This she could not deny. "Friends first," they had sworn, but she wondered if she would keep this promise now; whether, if forced to choose, Charlock would take precedence over Danny. She loved Charlock despite their arguments, but it was Danny who was her partner, her mate, like the swans, in their lifelong pairs, gliding down the river. Yet there were so many more examples of creatures who lived life without a partner, females mothering alone. She knew not what was right, only what she longed for. And that was him.

It was because of this—because she could not bear to wake him—that she got delayed. She wanted to give him every extra second of sleep she could, so it was only when the charcoal sky became tinged with mauve that she touched his cheek and his eyes opened.

"You'll be late," he said immediately.

"I'll be fine," she told him, but he was right. She would have to run and even then she might not make it before the first of the witches stepped out of their caravans.

The sky was as red as Betony's cheeks by the time she arrived at the camp. Slipping through the boulders, she splashed water on her face from one of the barrels and tried to look nonchalant as she made her way around the back of the caravans, hoping to pass by undetected. There were sisters about. Not many, but she needed to reach home before her aunt awoke. Her caravan was only steps away when she heard the high warning call of her kestrel. A second later and a voice followed, even louder and more piercing.

"Betony Swift?" If Aunt Sage wasn't awake already, she would be now. "Where have you been?"

It had to be Raven, out of all the sisters. Though she was young, she had always acted far older than her years, and her authority was that of one of the elders. Betony turned to face her.

"I have been to the river to wash." Betony pointed at her wet face and hair.

"You have not," declared Raven. By now other sisters were gathering, some opening their doors to hear. "Why do you lie, Sister Betony?"

"I do not," Betony denied.

Raven pursed her thin lips. "I was the first to wake this morning. I would have seen you leave."

"I left before you," Betony uttered defiantly.

"You went to the river and yet your skirts and boots have meadow grass upon them?"

Betony looked down and saw the evidence of her guilt. "This was from yesterday."

"You were not in the meadows yesterday. And that skirt was newly washed," croaked her Aunt Sage.

Betony reeled around and saw her aunt on their caravan steps, still in her nightgown, her huge nose twitching. Betony took a step back and hoped for a westerly breeze.

"Are you my keepers?" she cried to the sisters now surrounding her. "Is this my dungeon?" It was the wrong thing to say, as all started shaking their heads and tutting. The elders grouped together and Betony cast her eyes on them. "I did not go to town. Only for that do I need to seek permission."

"Then why the lies?" demanded Raven.

"For me," came Charlock's voice, soft but sure.

The sisters parted as Charlock stepped through them to stand by Betony's side. Betony stared at her, but Charlock kept her eyes on the rest of her audience.

"And why is that?" interrogated Raven in obvious disbelief.

"Because . . . ," said Charlock, faltering. Then she took Betony's hand. "Because I dared her to."

One of the young sisters laughed and Raven's eyes narrowed angrily. "You dared her?" Charlock nodded. "You dared her to leave her bed in the middle of the night and run through the hills to the meadows?"

"I did, Sister Raven."

"For what purpose?"

"To punish her." Betony felt Charlock squeeze her hand before she turned to the elders and addressed them directly. "It is no secret that Sister Betony and I have been adversaries these last weeks. She came to me wanting to atone for the hurt she'd caused me and I told her that if she wanted my friendship, she had to earn it." Charlock spoke so sincerely and looked so guileless that Betony wondered how any might doubt her. "It is my fault, you see," she continued. "Sister Betony ran to the meadow and back and risked your anger to prove herself to me. I am to blame, not she."

The elders seemed sympathetic to the story, but Raven's face contorted with suspicion and disappointment as she struggled to think how to respond. Thankfully, Sister Sage beat her to it. "Well, there we have it. I hope there'll be no more of this nonsense, girls?"

Betony and Charlock nodded and kept their heads bowed as though in shame.

"Sister Raven," Charlock called to her sister. "I hope you will forgive me."

These last words, Betony could tell, were genuine, but Raven only scowled and walked away without reply.

"I'm sorry," Betony whispered in Charlock's ear.

Charlock pressed her thumb on the scar on Betony's palm and it almost stung with the sudden memory of the knife cutting there. What two different girls they had been then, not so long ago. Certain. Optimistic.

"I've missed you," Betony murmured. "So much."

And, with that, her heart seemed to expand as her love for her friend lay beside her love for Danny. It didn't have to be one or the other, she realized. It could be both and more.

30

Young Charlock

They sat high up in a tree, lost in the leaves, their whispers hidden in the whistles and warbles of the wrens and wood pigeons, the robins and redstarts and the rustlings of a breeze through the branches.

"Do not tell me any more," Charlock interrupted when Betony paused for breath. Seeing her friend's face fall, she quickly explained herself. "It is not that I am angry or that a part of me doesn't long to hear it all. I just think it best. For they may ask me . . . if you go."

There was a question in her words that she dared not ask directly.

"You are right," Betony said, and Charlock had her answer.

"When?" was all she could say, the hurt sticking in her throat.

"We have talked of summer's end. When he will leave for college."

Charlock tried to guess at what this was, but Betony provided the meaning. "It is a school for adults where the chaffs go to study. It is west from here, he hopes."

"And you will go with him to this school?" Betony nodded, and Charlock suddenly wanted to cry, she felt so angry and sad at the same time. "What will you do there?"

"I will be with him," Betony said so naively that Charlock wanted to shake her. She shifted her position on the branch so that Betony had to grip the bark to stop herself from falling.

"Careful," Betony cried.

"Exactly," Charlock whispered churlishly, "what is it that you imagine, Bet? That you can pack your bags and say goodbye? That the sisters will just wish you well? That they won't come after you?!"

Betony did not speak for a moment and Charlock realized her friend's plans were mere dreams from which she could easily be woken.

"I will find a way," said Betony so pathetically that Charlock's temper lost all its force.

"You must think this through, Bet, and consider all the consequences. You know what they will do to you if you leave. They will wipe your memory clean. And his, too," she said softly. "If you are penitent, then it will only be these last few months that you will lose. But you could lose everything. Your home. Yourself. It is worse than death, I believe."

"I will risk it!" Betony replied, without due thought or care.

"And what about him?" Charlock countered. "Will you explain to this boy what dangers he faces and let him choose or will you just jeopardize his life as if it were your own?" Betony bit her lip and Charlock could see she was struggling not to cry. "I say this as your friend," she reminded her. "Because I love you."

"Oh, Charlock," said Betony, the tears now rolling down her cheeks. "I would sooner throw myself down from this tree and break my back than put him in harm's way."

"So you will stop seeing him? For both your sakes," Charlock insisted. Betony gave a sob. "Promise me, Bet. It must be done."

Having convinced Betony she must end things with Danny, Charlock tried to persuade her not to visit him again.

"The sisters will be watching you," she warned. In truth, her greatest concern was not the risk of detection but of a change of heart if Betony saw him. She could tell her friend was teetering on the edge of her decision and one word, even one look, might topple her. "Your absence will say it all," she reasoned to Betony, who looked sick with grief. "He will work matters out for himself without need of any explanation."

But this, Betony refused completely. "I have to tell him, Charlock. I cannot just leave him there, waiting, night after night, not knowing why, not knowing whether I am dead or alive."

Charlock thought to argue but sensed that, on this subject, her friend would not be converted. So one evening, when Raven and some of the elders were away at a meeting of the clans, Charlock helped Betony make her exit. As Betony ran through the forest, heading for the hills, Charlock entertained the supper table with the story of how a hog had trampled the fresh laundry, trailing it through the trees, and how poor Betony had returned to the river to wash it once again. She imitated Betony's furious expression and acted out a performance of how she'd run and tripped in her attempts to catch the offending beast. The table laughed at her rendition and Charlock was surprised at her success. Only Sister Sage looked serious and stood up to go and assist her niece. Immediately, Charlock assured the old witch she'd promised to take a plate of food and help Betony herself.

Out at the river, as night robbed the water of its color, Charlock sat and waited, nibbling nervously on Betony's meal, feeding pieces of the meat to the kestrel that had followed her there. The laundry was neatly folded in the baskets where she and Betony had hidden them earlier. Finally, when the moon was high above the treetops, her friend appeared. The kestrel opened his wings and took off to an overhead branch to get a better view. Other birds followed, swooping around Betony, like a dark cloud above her head. Charlock began to run toward her friend to comfort her.

"Charlock," Betony gasped as they met. Her face was so contorted with pain that Charlock looked to check she wasn't injured. "It was truly awful. He did not believe me. He refused to. He wanted to come up here and face my family. He said he knew it was their doing and not my decision."

"What did you say?" Charlock asked, now concerned for Danny also. It seemed he might not be as terrible as she'd expected.

"What you told me," replied Betony, closing her eyes and swaying so that Charlock held out an arm to keep her up. "I said there was no future for us. That I didn't want the life he offered. That he should go to college without me." Charlock felt Betony's fingers digging into her skin, gripping her arm as if her life depended on it. "But he was so angry," she continued. "He said he'd never forgive me if I walked away. He was shouting so loudly that my ears rang and I had to use my magic to calm him."

Charlock put her other arm around her friend's shoulders. "Hush, now. It is done. Let us return home and put all this behind us."

Betony nodded, her hair flickering like a fire that could, at any moment, consume her, her freckles like scorch marks from its sparks. Charlock fetched the baskets and Betony took one in her arms.

"Can you manage it?" Charlock asked her friend, who was usually the tougher of the two of them.

Betony nodded, but she only took a few steps before her legs gave way and she fainted to the forest floor. To her shame, it was the basket that Charlock's arms went to catch first; the basket with the linen so white and neatly folded. Next minute though, she was crouched beside her friend, cradling her head in her hands.

"All will be well," she told Betony as her eyes slowly opened. "The worst is over, I promise you."

Charlock thought of those words over the following days, kicking herself for her stupidity. Nothing was well. Indeed, the worst was yet to come.

Betony was late for breakfast and Charlock found her in the lavatories, retching. A notion flew at her suddenly, striking her in the heart like an arrow.

"Betony," she said urgently. "Betony, look at me," she commanded. "When was your last monthly bleed?"

"I . . . I . . . ," Betony stuttered. "I'm not sure. A few weeks past."

"How many weeks, Bet? Think!"

Betony's body heaved again and she gagged, but all that came was spit. She wiped her mouth and turned her head back to Charlock. "It's not that. It is the strain of yesterday. I am wounded, Charlock," she groaned, "and I do not know if I can recover."

Charlock reached out and put a hand on Betony's belly, feeling for any sense of life within.

"It's not, I tell you," cried Betony. "I would have felt it. I would know!"

"You have done it, though." Betony looked away. "How many times?" Charlock demanded.

"I have lost count," Betony whimpered.

"Oh, Bet. All this yoking—did you not think of where it might lead?"

"I did not think at all," she moaned.

That evening, when all were taking to their beds, the two girls sneaked into the storeroom and pushed a table across the door to block it.

"Do you have it?" Betony asked.

Charlock reached for the ring she'd taken from her mother's chest. Snapping a thread pulled from her shirt with her teeth, she tied one end around it.

"Lie down," she told Betony. "We must be quick."

Betony did as she was told and lifted up her shirt. Charlock's heart was battering against her ribs and she willed her hand to stop its shaking. Betony's stomach was so flat, concave now that she lay prostrate on the ground, it seemed inconceivable that a baby grew within her.

"I'm sorry," Betony said, alerting Charlock to her task. "To make you do this so soon after . . . "

"Just hope. Hope for a girl," she said as she held the ring above Betony's womb.

Betony closed her eyes and Charlock said a charm and waited for the ring to begin turning.

"What's happening?" Betony whispered after a few moments.

But Charlock couldn't answer. She did not know how . . . and then she didn't have to. Her silence was enough. Betony's hands went to her face and then her body curled up on her side like she was the baby, not that tiny heartbeat of a boy within her.

31

LEO

Leo could feel Poppy getting closer, her magic powering her along. Charlock must have felt it too, for one day she went into town and returned with a bag of clothes. She set to work on them with a pair of tiny scissors and a needle and thread. When they were ready, she asked him where to hang them so that Poppy might find them easily.

"There," Leo told her, pointing to the willow that he slept beneath each night. It was where he and Poppy had first kissed, where they had been happy for one night, before everything had changed.

When the clothes were hung, they looked a perfect fit for Poppy, and Leo could close his eyes and imagine her in them.

"Do you think she'll like them?" Charlock asked. "I found them in a row of black bags behind a store. So many clothes, all stuffed together." Leo nodded, wishing he could feel as light and hopeful as Charlock sounded. "Every day I cast spells to give her speed and send winds to glide her closer. It won't be long now," she told him. "Can you feel it?"

But Leo felt nothing but nerves. He looked up to the sky, but it was clear, without a cloud, without a bird. Still, he felt his heartbeat pick up tempo. He wished he hadn't left the dogs down south. They might be a reminder that he had magic in him.

At the moment, he felt helpless with all this waiting. Poppy was only coming back because he was part witch and yet that part of him was erratic and disobedient, appearing not on command but when he least desired it. His mother had told him to keep his magic hidden away. She didn't seem to understand that it was not within his control. It was like when his voice had broken, one minute a boy's, the next a man's, the tone beyond his choosing.

Poppy was a queen and he was a novice. They were no match. What if she flew all those hundreds of miles only to be disappointed? Leo could hardly stomach thinking of it.

She didn't arrive that day. Or the next. Charlock looked skyward for birds so often that Leo could tell her neck was beginning to hurt her. She stretched it constantly, rubbing at her shoulders to ease the pain. Betony would watch, saying nothing, but looking irritated. When she caught Leo's eye, she would roll her own, but he felt only pity for Poppy's mother. He would be looking upward, too, if he wasn't such a coward.

In the end, it wasn't birds that alerted Leo but spiders. One night, while Charlock and Betony slept, he saw them emerge from the grass and gather at the willow where he lay. There, they crawled up the tree's trunk and took their many positions before starting to spin their cobwebs. Leo watched them closely.

All different kinds. Some fatter and squatter, others as delicate as their lace. Long into the night, they kept weaving, creating a curtain in the branches between himself and the clothes for Poppy. The sky was clear, a midnight blue, with a half moon that shone a perfect white. The webbed circles sparkled like the finest filigree. The temptation to reach out and touch them was great, but knowing he might break them, Leo resisted.

For a long while, it was easy to stay awake. Then, as the hours dragged by, his eyes began to loll shut. He would snap them open as soon as he realized he was drifting, but, after a while, he lost track of time. The next occasion he remembered to open his eyes, Leo heard a noise, as faint as breath, but enough to make him raise his head and stare.

Through the layered latticework the spiders had created, he saw a shape. Skin gleaming under the moonlight, hair loose around the shoulders, thin limbs reaching to the branches, long back bending, soft curves being covered by the clothes, her face turning toward him.

"Leo," came the whisper.

The breath caught in his chest. He couldn't speak, but his hand reached toward her as if guided by some power other than his own. He touched the cobwebs and they shattered as though made of frost that tinkled and shimmered as they hit the ground.

"You are magic," she said, dispelling all his fears.

He looked up at the face he'd dreamed of for so long, seeking every detail of it, checking she was flesh and blood and not a mere illusion.

"You're home," he said. She stepped toward him and his arms wrapped around her and his head bent to her hair. "You're real," he murmured, and she laughed.

"The change. It doesn't hurt," she uttered in amazement. "It doesn't hurt because of you."

She bent down and reached for something at her ankle. Her eyes met his as she tied the heart stone around her neck. As each second ticked by, the harder it became to move their eyes away or break the silence. In the darkness, Leo became aware of the fluttering of the moths, the perfume of the night-scented flowers, the rustling of the willow leaves, the running of the water in the river. But, most of all, he was aware of her—the pulse in her throat, the quickness of her breath, the smell of her skin.

As though choreographed to music, their heads moved slowly toward each other, tilting, lips touching for a kiss. Leo had kissed Poppy before and he knew he would kiss her again, but this was like the first and the last combined, with all the passion of both the beginning and the end. As their mouths met and their bodies responded, he felt every nerve ending in his body stir.

"Look," she said, breaking away breathlessly.

She held out her arm and he saw that it was sparkling, like the magic inside her had been illuminated. She took his hand and held it up for him to see. His skin was shining too. They placed each palm flat against the other and felt the sparks burst like tiny fireworks. He heard her gasp.

"Are you scared?" he asked. He could feel the electricity travel through his veins into his heart. She shook her head and closed her eyes, and the glitter sparkled on her lids. "Is it too much?"

Her fingers curled around his hands, holding them tight. "Never," she whispered.

❧

They awoke with the sun glinting down on them from a blue sky and Charlock watching them from across the green grass.

"I didn't want to wake you," Charlock said shyly, as they emerged from the willow.

Leo could feel Poppy's body tense. He put a hand on her shoulder and she reached across and held it.

"Hello, Charlock," she said in a voice husky with sleep.

"Will you walk with me?" her mother asked.

Poppy glanced at Leo and he gave the slightest nod of reassurance.

As she strolled beside Charlock around the hedgerow, he kept his eyes fixed on her, even when Betony came and joined him.

"She looks little like her mother," he heard his mother comment.

"We have that in common then," he said with a smile.

"Happy to see her?" she asked, even though she must have known the answer.

He put his arm around Betony's shoulders. "I love Poppy. I love the woman who looked after me, Jocelyn. And I love you. You three. No one else."

"What about that poor girl, Ember? She seemed to care a great deal for your happiness."

Leo felt a sudden stab of guilt. Ember hadn't crossed his mind in days and, now that she did, his heart went out to her. "You're right. She's family too."

"Clan," his mother corrected. "We two are family. The rest are clan."

Poppy and Charlock were circling back to them.

"What do you think they're talking about?" he asked Betony.

"You, of course."

He watched Poppy's and Charlock's mouths moving and tried to listen. Slowly, even the smallest sounds faded and he heard his name being spoken. Poppy looked up at him and smiled and he waved back.

"Love . . . hate," said Betony. "They exist on either end of what we feel. But edges are dangerous places. One slip . . . " She took his hand, which lay on her shoulder, and squeezed it, just as Poppy had done earlier. "Tread carefully, my son," she said and then she turned his hand and kissed the palm of it. He heard her words and felt her kiss, but his eyes, they were on Poppy and he couldn't drag them away if he tried.

He gave Poppy breakfast—fruit and a packet of biscuits—and she devoured it all with a hunger that made him smile.

"Sorry," she said between ravenous bites. "I'm starving!"

"I can go into town. Get you more."

"No," she said quickly. "Stay with me." He looked out across the water and let himself feel loved.

"Where were you?" he asked, and she told him of her travels, of a witch called Mma and her great-grandson Teko, and all they had taught her. She said little about her capture and he didn't want anything to touch their happiness, so he didn't push her to say more. Instead, he told her about his mother. How Charlock had found Betony and brought her to him. How his magic had been flicked on suddenly, like a switch. And how relieved he felt to learn that he wasn't unwanted or abandoned. Poppy's eyes filled with tears.

"Hey, don't cry," he said. "It's all right. Everything's all right now."

She gave a wonky smile and he pulled her over to his lap and kissed her. Soon they fell back on the grass, their limbs entwined, not wanting the tiniest of gaps between them after so great a separation.

"Our mothers," she reminded as his hands reached underneath her shirt.

"Mine's gone to get supplies," he said, trying to pull her back to him.

She looked around for Charlock. "Well, mine hasn't." She grinned and got to her feet, holding out a hand to haul him up. "Come on," she said, wrinkling her nose. "I need a wash."

"Turn your back," she told him as she started to undress.

He smiled. "Really? After last night?"

She reached out and slapped his arm. "Turn around," she said. "It's daytime now." She suddenly looked shy and awkward. "And I'm new to this. I've never had a boyfriend before, okay?" She steered him around and he let her.

"Not even in Africa?" he asked, hearing the clothes fall from her skin.

She came up and pressed her body behind him. It took all his strength and willpower not to move.

"I'm yours," she said softly. And then she was gone and he heard the splashing of the water as she stepped into the river.

Later when she was dry and dressed, they walked along the stream where the waters ran shallow. He rolled up his jeans and she hitched up her skirt and the water rippled cool around their ankles.

"How's Ember?" she said, sounding casual, but not meeting his eye.

"It didn't work," he answered. "Your plan for me and her."

"I'm sorry," she said. "I thought you'd be better off without me. Honestly, I did. I saw you and Ember before I left, and you looked so right together. Like you were meant to be."

"How could you ever think that?" he asked, and feelings of hurt and anger that he'd suppressed for so long rose to the surface like bubbles of exhaled air.

"I don't know," she whispered. "I was confused. I saw you two in a vision, before I even met you. I thought . . . ," she tailed off, unable to finish.

"Well, visions can be wrong then," he said and she looked so reassured that he felt all those bubbles pop and disappear as though they'd never been inside him.

"I kept trying not to think of Ember when I was away," Poppy admitted. "Because of you—you and her. But I missed her." She looked so bereft that he put his arms around her.

"We'll go and see her," he promised and her body relaxed. "She'll want to take you to Paris," he warned.

He could feel Poppy smile into his shoulder. "Ember loves that place. But you'll have to come, too," she told him.

"If you both will have me?"

The expression on Poppy's face changed. "She might hate me now," she said in a small voice.

"She loves you." And when he said it, he knew how true it was and he felt a pang for Ember that he had Poppy with him when she was all alone.

"And my mother? I mean, Melanie?" The self-correction broke his heart.

"She can come, too," he told her. "It'll do her the world of good."

As a reward, she reached up and kissed him and his hands went to her hair. He felt the tingle in his feet as she did. They both looked down and saw the water rippling in circles around them.

"Is it you? Because you're queen?"

She blinked at that and he caught a glimpse of apprehension in her face. "I didn't come back to be queen. I came to be with you." Then she smiled. "Anyway," she said, looking down at the water, "this isn't me. It's us." She turned her face back to his. "Will you show me?" she asked. "Your magic?" He screwed up his face to show his reluctance. "Please."

He sighed. "I don't know what I'm doing," he admitted.

"I remember that," she said. "Stuff just happens and you don't even know if it's because of you." He nodded, comforted that she understood. "It gets easier," she told him. "But you have to study. And practice."

"I think Betony would disagree with that." Poppy looked confused. "Seems there aren't too many like me. Male witches. I'm like some freak."

Poppy shook her head. "You don't understand—you being a witch means we can be together. Apparently, if I love some normal guy, I kill them. Literally, their heart breaks. I'm the freak here."

Leo couldn't help grinning. "You mean I'm, like, the only man for you. The only one in the whole world."

She rolled her eyes. "I guess that depends if there are any other male witches out there."

"None," he said, trying to act serious. "I'm the only one."

She grinned. "Let's see it then. Your magical powers."

"Okay," he said, "but don't expect much."

He closed his eyes and tried to still his thoughts. He wondered what he should attempt, but all he could think of were the magic shows he'd seen as a kid—coins out of ears, rabbits out of hats, doves out of handkerchiefs.

"Oh, that's not bad," said Poppy, startling him. "Romantic, too."

He opened his eyes. Across the river were two white doves, just like the ones he'd been imagining, but cooing gently at each other while they fluttered in the air. They flew toward Poppy and circled around her head before settling on a branch of the willow tree.

Poppy clapped with delight, then stopped and stared into the distance. "Your mother's back."

Betony was walking toward them with a dead rabbit in one hand and a bunch of carrots in the other. Before Leo had a chance to stop her, Poppy had splashed out of the water to greet her. He saw her saying something, then holding out a hand. Betony looked at it and Leo turned his face away, unable to watch in case his mother was rude, or worse. But when he looked back, they were talking pleasantly and Charlock had joined them.

"Get over here," his mother called as though nothing at all out of the ordinary was happening. "You have a rabbit to skin."

He must have looked aghast because all three of them laughed.

In the days to come, he would look back on that image—three women in the meadow together, their long skirts swishing in the tall grass, their eyes bright and smiles wide—and he would mourn the loss of it.

The rabbit tasted better than he ever thought possible.

"Where'd you get it?" he asked his mother.

"From a garden. The creature had its own little house, with these carrots laid out for its lunch." Poppy's hand flew to her mouth. "What?" Betony snapped at her.

"That's some kid's pet," Leo explained, thankful now that he had refused to skin it and, instead, put up with his mother's teasing.

"Not anymore," Betony mumbled through her next mouthful.

Poppy looked at him with horrified amusement. Then her mother spoke and her features straightened.

"Poppy," Charlock said. "There is something we must discuss."

The atmosphere around them changed. All went quiet, even the birds and the bees.

"I don't want to be queen. And I don't want to live out there," she declared at once, pointing to the hills, "in the forest with them. I want to help people, ordinary people. Be a healer. And I want to be with Leo." She took his hand and squeezed it.

Charlock waited until she was sure Poppy was finished before answering. "The clan was attacked."

"I know. I felt it and I'm sorry, but I can't be who they want me to be." She sounded so sure and confident that Leo had to stop himself from grinning.

Charlock sighed. "It's your cousin. Sorrel."

All the bluster in Poppy dropped away and Leo felt her hand go limp. "Oh no."

"Something is very wrong with her," Charlock went on. "She threw us out of the camp and there was so much anger and violence in her. After you revived her, Poppy, she was so mild and cheerful. She used to have a mean streak, it's true—but this . . . this was far worse."

"She's taken your place is what she's done," said Betony sharply.

Charlock shot her friend a critical look before turning back to Poppy. "I am afraid she must have discovered the harm I caused her."

"Oh, now we have it. Another one of your victims. What did you do to her, Charlock?" Betony responded. Leo put a hand on his mother's arm, but she pulled it free. "Don't hush me, boy. This one has guilt running through her very veins."

Poppy was looking from Betony to Charlock.

"My mother has a lot to answer for, I'm sure," she said, not noticing how Charlock's eyes widened in pleasure at the word "mother." "But she's not the cause of Sorrel's behavior. That'll be Raven. I'm certain of it."

"Raven," echoed Betony, her eyes turning sharply to Charlock. "You said she was dead."

"She is," said Charlock flatly. "She died this winter on the battlefield."

"That's true," answered Poppy. "But it is her ghost we're dealing with."

Charlock's hands went to her cheeks, which had flushed a sudden scarlet. Then she stumbled to her feet and ran back to the stream, where she bent low and was sick. Poppy got up to go after her, but Betony reached out an arm and stopped her.

"Let me," she said and, despite all her tough talk, Leo knew then that his mother still loved her friend.

"Poor Sorrel," murmured Poppy once they were alone.

"She didn't look poor to me," muttered Leo. He knew where this was leading. Poppy would go. He would stay and he would be left waiting once more. As if in apology for this, Poppy took his hand again.

"I have to help her. I can't just stand by and do nothing."

"Because you're queen? Is that it? You just said you didn't want that." He had to stop himself from saying more.

"Because she is my friend," she corrected.

And family, thought Leo. *And clan. But what,* he wondered, *am I?*

32

POPPY

Whenever she and Leo touched, Poppy was aware of their magic meeting, drawing them together like magnets, making it an effort to pull apart. She could feel the tug of it as she walked farther away from him, toward the door in the garden wall.

"Poppy!" he yelled as she reached it.

She felt like running back, jumping into his arms again, and wrapping herself around him.

"See you soon," was all he said, but she knew the meaning that was hidden in those words, just like the door that was hidden in the ivy, the door that she made herself open, made herself step through.

As she walked down the road toward the hills, she reminded herself why she was leaving him. The great witch. The aunt who had cast her out as a newborn, coveting the throne for her own daughter, Sorrel. A ghost come back to haunt them. But for what? *If it was the throne Raven wanted, then she could have it,* Poppy thought. Then she trembled. Charlock reached for her hand and Poppy was glad to take it. She stretched out her other hand for Betony. Together they would find a way to banish Raven for good.

When the three women entered the darkness of the forest, Poppy's heart sank further. Now that she neared the witches' camp, a sense of responsibility spread like moss inside her mind. In Africa, the coven had felt a million miles away, but now that she was back in their woodland, she felt their suffering with every tree she passed. She refused to regret Africa, though. If she hadn't gone, she would be a queen, but a brokenhearted one. She would have no purpose. Despite how it had ended with Mma and Teko, they had given her that. And she wouldn't have Leo, only an ambitious mother who cared more about the throne than her daughter's happiness. But Poppy's absence seemed to have changed Charlock too. That morning, when they had walked the length and breadth of the meadow, Charlock had admitted how wrong she'd been about Leo.

"I should never have tried to separate you. He crosses two worlds . . . but so do you."

"What about being queen?" Poppy asked warily.

"You think this is a choice, a decision for you to make, but it is not. You are queen, whether you like it or not. It is only for others to choose whether they accept this."

"What are you saying?"

Her mother had sighed at that and rubbed at her forehead with her hand, but when she spoke she sounded certain. "I am saying that I have lived too long without you and I just want you close—whatever path you take and whomever you take it with."

Poppy should have hugged her mother then. She knew she should have. The seconds had stretched as though stalling for her, but she was paralyzed. Charlock's words had been good to hear, but Poppy wanted more than words, something that would prove her mother's sincerity once and for all.

As they approached the camp, the cats appeared. They slunk through ferns and leapt from branches to come up behind Poppy, fanning out behind her skirt like a glorious train of fur. She smiled with the pleasure at seeing them again, faces new and old. Suddenly, she felt regal and she raised her head and pulled back her shoulders, readying herself to face Raven. The cats slipped through the stones before her so when she entered she stepped into the circle that they'd formed. Looking up, she gave a shiver and it occurred to her that the air was colder here than in the rest of the forest. Then she noticed that the light was different, too, bleak and gray as winter. Clouds lay low above the camp, blocking any sun. The painted caravans looked drab; the leaves seemed withered on the trees, and the grass, dry and pale. It was as though all color had seeped away, like the camp was sickening.

The witches too seemed drained of life. They moved slowly toward her with haggard faces and sallow skin.

"Do you see this?" Poppy whispered to her mother, who had reached her side. "Is this my fault?"

Charlock's mouth was an oval opened wide, as though in a silent scream. "This is my sister's doing," she replied, but Poppy still felt sick with guilt. Raven's grip had only taken hold because she had not been there to weaken it. She had been selfish, she saw that now, putting her needs first and causing their suffering because of it. She wondered what she could say or do to show how sorry she felt.

The other witches were murmuring to one another, making a droning noise that became louder and louder.

"Say something," urged Charlock, but Poppy closed her eyes and held her tongue until finally there was quiet and the silence became so uncomfortable that all would be thankful for the breaking of it.

She felt the absence of one of the elders immediately.

"Sister Morgan?" she asked. These were her first words, and the witches all bent their heads in recognition of it. "Take me to her."

Without any anger or retribution, the witches made way for her and led her to the holly tree where Sister Morgan's ashes had been scattered. The cats followed and sat while Poppy knelt there, whispering words of gratitude and apology. Then she spread her arms and fluttered her fingers, gliding them through the air—together, then apart, from low to high. With them rose the tiniest specks to form a shadow in the air. Poppy lifted her arms above her head and the shadow grew tall and took the shape of Sister Morgan. The witches gasped and a few cried out in distress. Then Poppy closed her fists and opened them and the ashes flicked up high and fell back down, disappearing between the blades of grass.

"Rest in peace," Poppy whispered.

Next she went to Sister Ada. The cats rose to follow her, but she shook her head and they stopped and waited. The old witch, usually as tough as wire, was stooped and ailing in her chair.

"May I?" Poppy asked. When Sister Ada nodded, Poppy put her hands on the empty space below the stumps where the old witch's legs used to extend. "It's painful?" Poppy said.

"It is," Sister Ada confirmed, sounding surprised at Poppy's question. "Though I cannot understand why. 'Tis only air, not flesh."

Poppy said the African charm that Mma had taught her, and Sister Ada nodded her thanks. But Poppy was not finished yet. "Where are the limbs?"

"Buried," Sister Ada told her.

Poppy went to the spot and scooped a bit of earth from the ground and tied it in a piece of sackcloth, which she put in her pocket. "I carry your pain now," she said. "Not you."

Sister Ada nodded and Poppy could see the tension in the old woman's jaw release and her mouth soften. A second later, Poppy felt the hurt invade her own legs and it took all her strength to force it to retreat into that little bag of earth in her pocket.

"Now where is Sorrel?" she asked once she'd recovered. The sisters glanced at each other, but none gave an answer.

Poppy looked to Sorrel's caravan. It had been painted black or so it seemed. For when she peered closer, Poppy saw that the paint was moving, just a fraction, as though it were alive. She blinked and stared again. Flies! The caravan was covered with them, every inch of it, vibrating, buzzing. Poppy glanced at Charlock and Betony and saw the horror on their faces as the realization hit them too. The other sisters hung their heads as though the shame was theirs.

"Where is she?" Poppy gasped. "Answer me!" She looked to the sister she knew best. "Kyra, will you tell me?"

Kyra stepped forward. "She's not here."

Charlock started walking to Sorrel's caravan to check. "It's true," Kyra called after her.

Charlock stopped. "Where is she then? In the woods? By the river? Someone go and fetch her," she ordered.

Kyra looked to the elders and Sister Ada nodded her assent. "We can't. She has gone yoking."

Poppy saw her mother blanch. "Alone?" Charlock asked.

Sister Ada answered this time. "She insisted. And there was no persuading her otherwise."

Sister Martha was nodding. "She has not been herself. Not since . . . "

"Not since the other clans attacked," Poppy finished.

A weight fell on Poppy's shoulders and she felt any light that remained from her reunion with Leo being pressed down and out of her.

"What did Sorrel say before she left?"

"Just that she must have a daughter. That it was the only way," Kyra answered.

"The only way for what?" Poppy asked, and Kyra shrugged.

"None of us could understand this burning need of hers. She seemed quite desperate," Sister Martha explained.

The weight on Poppy made her want to slump and sit, but she pushed up against it, standing even straighter. She looked at Charlock, whose eyes cautioned her not to speak of Raven.

"Sister Sorrel needs our help," Poppy told them all instead. "I think you know this."

Kyra shook her head, now visibly upset. "She has been so strong," she said. "She saved us when you were gone."

"She is my cousin and I care for her, too," Poppy replied gently.

"You just want the throne!" Kyra cried. The cats sprang to their feet, bared their teeth, and hissed. Poppy raised a finger to silence them.

"I don't. I never did. But that doesn't seem to make any difference." Poppy looked around at the witches, who looked both appalled and distressed by her words. She felt the crystal grow warm against her skin. "Bring me the stone," she said instinctively, without understanding why. "The stone with my name."

A young sister walked to fetch it. When she returned, she was running. She held it up above her head and, before she even reached them, they could see the letters glowing, just like the crystal that hung around Poppy's neck glowed.

POPPY HAWKWEED.

Poppy found that she was shaking. Before she left, she had been told of the queen's stone, but she had never seen it. And now her name was written on it, shining out for all to see. She was a queen. Charlock was right—there was no escaping it. The letters on the stone felt more than just her name, more even than a signature. It felt like proof of life, just as letters on a gravestone were proof of death.

Poppy took a deep breath and addressed the sisters again. "I ran away from this and you were hurt because of it. Sorrel, too. And others. And I am truly sorry for that. I'd like to make it right, but only if you'll let me."

"What will you tell Sorrel?" whispered Kyra.

Poppy thought about her mother's words that morning and found she was able to make sense of them. "I'll tell her exactly what I'm telling you," she said. "That I can come back and try to live up to what's written on that stone. But I will not come alone. I bring my mother with me." She glanced at Charlock, who bowed her head. "And Sister Betony, who was once one of you." Poppy could feel the beams of disapproval, not helped by Betony, who was staring back at them so aggressively. Quickly, before the sisters had time to object, Poppy spoke again. "And with her, I bring her son—Leo."

The shock blew through the camp like a breeze, rustling leaves, ruffling skirts, and rattling objects.

"A male?" came the question from several mouths. "The male who came before?"

"He is a witch. A witch like you and me," Poppy answered.

"This cannot be," called Sister Martha.

"This has never been," added Sister Ivy.

"It is forbidden," bellowed Sister Wynne.

"By whom?" Poppy enquired calmly. As she guessed, none could answer this. "By the queen?" she asked.

"It is our way and it exists for good reason," stated Sister Ada loudly, and there were mutterings of agreement.

"I accept that. I do. And I would never force this on you. I don't like rules. I never follow them and I'm not going to make them. It is for you all to decide."

"So we take you with those three or not at all?" cried Kyra.

Poppy nodded. "That's the deal."

"But that's no choice," Kyra complained.

"How can you be queen when you have so little respect or understanding of our customs?" asked Sister Wynne, and the others were agreeing and nodding their support.

"I don't know," Poppy said honestly.

There was a cry of surprise and everyone looked to see the stone fall from the hands of the young witch and onto the ground.

"I did not drop it. I did not!" she swore, holding up her empty hands in bewilderment.

The stone was rocking very slowly on its end, as if struggling to find the energy. Back and forth it went, before toppling over and beginning to roll. The cats scattered to make way for it and the letters on it became a blur as it picked up speed, even though there was no slope to aid it. It stopped abruptly before Sister Ada and the other elders, and Poppy's name was clear once more.

"Pick it up," Poppy told them. "And keep it safe."

Suddenly she wanted to go. She'd said all she could. She'd set out her terms. Now she wanted to be back with Leo in their garden, under their willow tree, and in his arms. Sensing it was time to leave, the cats congregated behind her once more.

"Tell Sorrel I am here for her," Poppy said. "Whatever you choose, I want to help."

To prove it, she looked up at the misty clouds above and closed her eyes. Summoning all her power to a single pinpoint in her mind, slowly she breathed in, then out. Even with her eyes closed, she felt the clouds lifting and parting, letting the light back in. When she opened her eyes, she saw the color returning like a tide of dye to the grass, the leaves, the flowers, and even to the witches' cheeks. Only Sorrel's caravan remained untouched, darkly dying and decaying, swarming with flies.

33

SORREL

S orrel couldn't wait for the cover of darkness. She didn't care if she aroused suspicion. She needed to get this done now and not a moment later. Her mother was inside her, clawing at her heart, nibbling at her innards, pecking at her brain. If she didn't act, she would be consumed. Day by day, it was becoming harder to distinguish which parts of her were hers alone and which her mother had laid claim to. She hardly had a thought or a voice that she could call her own. Even this mission she'd embarked on, to yoke, to have a daughter—was it her idea or Raven's? She couldn't remember. She just knew it was the only way to make her mother leave.

She had tried spells and charms, starving her mother out, pleading with her, threatening her. But she only ever got one response and it was always the same. Granddaughter. Before her death, her mother had forbidden Sorrel to take part in any of the yoking ceremonies each spring. Ever the dutiful daughter, Sorrel had listened to her mother and followed her instructions. She had watched her friends go out in their groups and waited anxiously for them to return, not sure whether to hope for their success or failure.

She had listened to their tales of fear and triumph, trying to prevent the pricks of jealousy and isolation from piercing her friendships. She was above the others, her mother told her. She was the future queen. And Sorrel had tried to believe it, but those words were a cold and empty substitute for the warmth of shared experience.

Now, here she was, yoking all alone. No ceremony to send her off. No advice from her elders. No friends to support her, and no one to listen to her story on her return. Only her mother's ghost swirling in her lungs, making it hard for her to breathe.

There were males everywhere Sorrel looked. She was surrounded by them on every street and at every turn, but this seemed only to make the choice harder. Just as she was about to despair, a voice called down to her from above, low and gruff. She didn't catch what this male had said to her and she looked up to see his face. There were several of them standing on planks of wood held up by poles that ran along the front of a house.

"What did you say to me?" she asked guardedly.

There was a pause before one of them answered. "I said you look lost and d'you need a hand?"

This wasn't what he had said. Sorrel was sure of it and the raucous laughter from the others proved it.

"Why don't you come down here and tell me what you really said?" she challenged with a smile.

The male's demeanor changed instantly. He went from bull to mouse, all that boldness shrinking to a startled timidity.

"Go on, Gav," jeered a voice from the rooftop. "Get down there."

Sorrel felt her glimmer of opportunity waning. "Don't be scared," she called up to him.

There were more gibes and jests from his fellow workers, but the man shook his head.

"I'm a married man," he told her. "Got my missus to think of."

Sorrel tutted with annoyance. "Are any of you without a 'missus'?" she asked.

Now all of them were cowering creatures, sniggering to try to hide their fear. Despite their goading of one another, she knew that none of them would leave the safety of their frame.

"Pathetic," Sorrel muttered.

She hurried away, ignoring their heckling and thinking instead of how best to find a boy of her own age. After a few minutes, she spotted one alone, sitting on a bench outside some stores. He was a tall, lanky, pimpled youth with hair greased up so it stuck on end above his face. He looked both bored and cross. *He would do,* thought Sorrel. It was forbidden to use magic on these yoking rituals, in fact on any chaff, unless one had true need, but she didn't have time to spare. She felt her mother's ghostly hand squeezing at her throat. The spell sprung from Sorrel's lips as she held the boy's eyes. She could feel him trying to tear his gaze away, but he had not the strength. As the spell took hold, the panic faded and he turned tame and tranquil.

"Follow me," she instructed.

She set off down the street, looking for somewhere hidden where they could do the act. There was a park, she remembered from one of her past forays into town. She would lead him there.

"Jamie?" came the shriek that made the boy blink and turn. "Where the hell do you think you're going?" Behind them was an older lady, laden with bags. "You said you were going to help me carry this stuff!"

With every word she spoke, the spell's power perished and Sorrel couldn't revive it. The boy was looking around him, startled, trying to think who she was and how he'd gotten there. Then he darted back to his mother, who handed over some of the shopping. Sorrel could still hear the woman berating him as they disappeared into the crowd.

Sorrel felt Raven's grip move to her heart. She looked around her wildly. Males of all sizes and in all manner of clothing were touching distance away, but how was she supposed to reach out and grab one? It had been a mistake to come in daylight. Sorrel realized that now. If only there was one she knew here. And then a thought seared across her mind.

"No," she cried. "I can't." The name sizzled on her brain and she clutched her head in pain. "I won't," she wept. "He's Poppy's."

"All the better," came the voice in her head.

In spite of all her efforts to resist, Sorrel found herself in the park, seeking out the ingredients for a potion. She was aware of her surroundings and of why she was there, but her body was moving of its own accord, without her direction or permission. Her foot crushed the plants, grinding them with the heel of her boot. Her hands scooped the tiny mush into a leaf, folding it carefully. The words to the charm sprang into her mind and leapt out of her mouth.

Then she hurried to the churchyard, running through the gravestones to the garden wall. Try as she might, it was impossible to slow her legs or halt her arm as it opened the door to the meadow. A part of Sorrel's mind, the tiny part that was still her own, remembered once watching Leo as he read a letter in this place. His dark despair had matched the weather that day, the rain hammering down from black clouds as though sent in anger. Today, only two slim curls of cloud smudged the sky, cushioning the sun. The light was soft and the air was mild and sweet. And Leo was there, just as before, but he was peaceful and Sorrel could feel his good temper from across the grass.

"Please," she whispered to Raven. "Leave him be. I will find another. I promise you."

She lurched forward as though pushed from behind and staggered in Leo's direction. He didn't back away when he saw her. He didn't look scared when she spoke. Instead, he moved to greet her.

"You're Poppy's cousin," he said kindly. "She's gone to see you."

She opened her mouth and tried to speak. *Go,* she wanted to warn. *Go!* But the words wouldn't come. Instead her lips began to move and her mother's voice sounded.

"I have been out," she told him. "But it has not gone well. Could I rest here a while?"

"Sure," he said. "Do you want some water? I have food as well, if you'd like?" He sounded concerned for her well-being.

"I'll have some if you join me," she said, willing him to disagree.

"Why not?" he replied, then walked over to a willow tree and disappeared beneath the branches.

Against her will, her hand moved to her pocket for the leaf.

When Leo returned, he brought with him some bread and cheese. "I'll just get the water. It's from the stream, if that's okay?"

"Of course," she answered, and then, when his back was turned, she watched as her treacherous hand broke off a piece of bread and put a small smear of potion upon it, before covering it with cheese. When she took the cup of water from him, she handed him the bread. "For you," she told him.

"Cheers," he said.

How could he not sense the danger? How could he be so trusting? Sorrel wished she could reach out and shake him. But as he bit into the bread, she felt her mouth being stretched into a smile that stayed upon her face, although inside she felt like screaming. Leo chewed and her cheeks began to ache as she waited in dread.

"You're not eating," he said after he swallowed.

Her stomach turned as her hands picked up a piece of cheese and brought it to her lips.

Leo took another bite and then another. Only then did he suddenly stop and put the bread down.

He bowed his head, then raised it. His eyes were blurred. "What have you done to me?" he asked in confusion.

Sorrel wanted to beg his forgiveness, but the explanation came to her mouth with no apology. "It is a love potion. You've heard of those?"

"Poppy," he slurred.

"Not Poppy. Not for now."

"Poppy," he said again, and Sorrel realized he was trying to call for her.

"She cannot hear you. But look at me. It is me you love. Just for this short while."

Sorrel winced at the words, wishing she could turn and run far, far away. Instead, she had to sit and watch as Leo's eyes glazed and then refocused.

"Sorrel?" he said in a tone she'd never heard before.

She left Leo sleeping off the effects of the potion and hurried back to the forest. Tears were pouring down her face so thick and fast that she couldn't see clearly and often stumbled over the uneven ground and lost her footing in the heather. At least now she had control of her limbs and could direct them to the waterfall where she could wash.

The water poured fast from its rocky spout, a torrent of white against the mossy green. It clattered on the stone below, drowning out Sorrel's thoughts of what had happened. It seeped through her hair, hammering her body, washing away her tears. Raven, though, would not be dislodged.

"Why are you still here?" she screamed. "I did what you wanted. Now go. Leave me!"

Sorrel waited for a moment to see if her mother would heed her words, but she felt no change. Raven was a parasite and Sorrel was giving her life. She could see this now. There was only one thing to be done. Splashing through the shallows to where her clothes lay, she reached for the knife that she kept in her skirt pocket. It was only for peeling, but it would serve her needs. Holding it, point down, above her chest, she spoke in lowered, gritted tones.

"If you don't go, I'll make you." Sorrel felt a slight shift within her. "No daughter. No granddaughter," she threatened. "I will not live like this and neither will my child."

She raised the knife, ready for it to plunge.

"You wouldn't dare," came the words, so scathingly dismissive.

"Wouldn't I?" Sorrel shrieked. Her arm was shaking, but she gripped the knife tighter. "You are evil and you have made me evil too. And I would rather die than be like you."

"What you call evil, I call power," came the retort.

"And I want none of it," Sorrel sobbed.

"Do you deny your own mother?" she heard.

"I do," she said simply.

"We could have been magnificent together. We could have raised a queen."

"There is no *we*," Sorrel cried, her fingers stretching before wrapping around the knife, about to strike.

She felt a sudden rush of air. Her mouth opened and out spewed the black ash that had once entered her.

34

EMBER

Ember saw the swallows arrive, their long tails streaming through the air as they glided farther inland. She heard them too, their familiar trills and twitters as they found their nesting spots under the eaves of old barns and in the nooks and crannies of sheds and garages. Immediately, she thought of Poppy and her arrival. Where would she stop? Whom would she see first? Ember pictured Poppy's reunion with Leo, with Charlock, and with all the clan. But not with her.

As the days passed, it became clear that her friend had flown straight to the north, without interruption, despite all Ember's wishing for it. Poppy had not sought her out and hugged her and told her how much she missed her and begged to know her news. There had been no message, not a word. And every day Ember didn't hear from Poppy, she felt her heart harden against her. The tears she kept inside froze to ice, while her sorrow fired to anger.

Nick seemed puzzled by these swings in mood, but not deterred. He pursued her every day, even coming to her home and introducing himself to her mother. When Melanie saw him, she hurried off to put the kettle on, and when she returned, her hair was tied back and her pale lashes were dark with mascara. The television got switched off and afterward she seemed quite energized, even agreeing to eat out with Ember that evening if it was just the two of them and not too far from home.

"You and Nick look quite the couple," she told Ember as they sat in the nearby restaurant.

This irritated Ember. "Not like with Leo, then?"

Melanie paused to choose her words. "He wasn't the one for you."

"You think?" This sarcasm tasted tart on Ember's tongue, the expression not her own but one she'd learned from Nick.

"Have you heard from him?" asked Melanie.

It was the first time her mother had asked about Leo since he'd left. Ember shook her head. Suddenly, she felt like weeping. "He'll be with Poppy now," she replied.

Melanie sat up. "She's back?"

"Don't hold your breath," Ember muttered, employing yet another phrase of Nick's, this one feeling better, tougher. "I doubt she even remembers us."

"Oh, Ember, she must be busy. Give her time."

"What do you care anyway? You didn't want her," Ember muttered, immediately regretting her words when she saw Melanie flinch.

"She was a baby and I loved her as best I could. She just wasn't my baby."

"Well, she doesn't care about us. When I met her, it was just the two of us. No one else. We saved each other. But now she has everything—Leo, Charlock, the clan—and I'm not needed any more."

"You have me," said Melanie quietly.

Ember's temper fizzled out, but, without it, she felt helpless. "I know that," she replied, trying hard not to let the tears fall. "I just want my friend, too."

Later that night, she went to Nick's and rang the bell repeatedly, waking him from his slumber. He raised his eyebrows when he saw her.

"Well, this is a surprise," he said with a smile of satisfaction that almost made Ember want to leave. "Come on then," he told her, opening the door for her to enter.

She kissed him fiercely, not wanting to be put off any longer, and he kicked the door shut and pulled her to the sofa without breaking their mouths apart. It was a few minutes before he took her face in his hands and pulled back so he could look at her.

"What is it?" he asked.

"It doesn't matter," she said huskily, trying to kiss him again.

"What's got into you?" he said.

Ember leaned back on the sofa in defeat.

"I can't tell you," she claimed, her voice cracking and the tears seeping forth.

"Let me help you," he urged, more earnest and sincere than she'd ever heard him before.

"I just want to see her," she sobbed.

"Who?" Nick questioned.

"My friend," Ember told him through ragged breaths.

"Your friend Poppy?" Nick asked.

Ember's tears stopped for a sudden second. "How did you know?" she whispered.

"You told me. Poppy. The witch."

Ember's head fell and her hands rose so they met somewhere mid-journey.

Since that night she had spent in Nick's flat, worries had been sprouting in her mind like weeds, but she had been tugging them up by the roots and tossing them aside. Surely, if she'd said too much, Nick would have been more shocked? He would have said something. Wouldn't he? But now she knew the truth. She had flouted the clan's most sacred rule, to keep its existence secret. The coven had feared she would do this. They had wanted to wipe her mind so she could never betray them, even unwittingly. But Poppy had refused. She had vouched for her, promising that she could be trusted.

Ember gave a groan. "What have I done?" she wept as she rocked back and forth.

"What are you getting so upset about? I'm not going to tell anyone," Nick reassured her.

"You won't?" Ember peered up at him through her fingers.

"I promised, didn't I?" Ember didn't recall this either, but she was glad of it. "Besides," he went on, "everyone would think I'd gone mad."

"Is that what you think I am, then? Mad?" Ember tried to smile, not minding if he did, such was her relief at his reaction.

"Not you. Them. You got out. You're the sane one. The rest of them must be brainwashed. I'm just sorry they ever got their hands on you." Ember rubbed the tears from her cheeks. "Come here, you," Nick said affectionately, pulling her into his arms so her head lay on his chest. Then he kissed her forehead and stroked her hair like she was a young child that needed soothing. "I tell you what," he murmured softly in her ear. "You sleep here tonight, have the bed to yourself—I swear it. And if you still want to go and see this friend of yours in the morning, I'll take you."

Ember blinked, unsure of what to make of it. "You will?" she asked into his T-shirt, which was damp from her tears.

"Yeah. Someone's got to take care of you, right?"

She felt so warm and safe in his strong arms, his heartbeat firm and constant in her ear, that she agreed to stay the night. There would be no trip up north, Ember told herself. Poppy could have Leo and Charlock and the rest of them. She had Nick and Melanie and that would be enough.

When she awoke, Nick's bag was packed and a car that he'd borrowed from a colleague was waiting downstairs.

"We'll stop at your mom's," he said, "so you can grab your things."

Ember sat up in bed, trying to take it all in.

"My things?" she echoed.

"We better get going. It's a long drive," he told her.

"We don't need to go," she said. "I feel better today."

"It's all set," he announced. "Be good for you anyway. Get some closure."

Ember wasn't sure what that was, but it didn't sound good. Nonetheless, she did as she was bidden and before long she found herself in the car, with her bag in the back, heading northward.

She watched Nick's hands on the wheel, so firm and able. In the rearview mirror, she saw the land she now called home disappearing behind her. Gradually, a feeling of excitement tingled inside of her. This trip seemed like a chance to show Poppy all that she had done and all that she had become. She had her own business. She had money in her pockets. And she had Nick beside her. As the car sped along the road and the music thumped through the speakers, Ember couldn't help but smile. *The witches might have magic, but she had this,* she thought with pride. All she needed was for them to see it. Then she would feel complete. Then she might feel this closure.

35

Young Betony

As Betony approached the school, a sudden siren split the air. She felt like covering her ears to shield them. Quickly, she glanced around, half expecting chaffs to rush out and imprison her, torture her, and burn her at the stake. For this was what all witches had been taught happened in the past; it was why they must live separately and never mingle. Betony clutched her bag around her middle in pointless protection. It contained all her worldly possessions. Some clothes, a blanket, a few herbs, some food; not much, but heavy enough to make her arms ache from carrying it so long.

A few moments later the chaffs did appear, but none were interested in her. They poured out the school doors and gates, a flowing tide of youngsters, short and tall, some still children, others full grown like she. Betony kept her eyes wide and searched for Danny. When she spotted him, he was with the others from the playing fields that night. It made her sad to think of Charlock so far away without her, while Danny's friends were in the thick of their pack and full of such hilarity.

Danny was smiling, too, and talking animatedly. *You are meant to be heartbroken*, Betony thought. Then he was putting his arm around another and pulling her into view. It was the girl, Emmy, and she was gazing up at him as devoted as a pup. Betony would have turned and run, but her feet were stuck in a bog of despair and she couldn't pull them free. She bowed her head and waited for the crowds to pass. When she felt it was over and all had gone, she looked up. Only one of them was left there. It was Danny, standing in the spot where she'd last seen him and staring at her with an expression of angry disbelief.

He seemed as stuck as she was and voiceless too.

"I'm done," he said after several long moments. His voice sounded strange, like it belonged to a different boy and not the one she knew and loved. "Today was the last exam."

"I am happy for you," she croaked.

"I thought . . . ," he started but then couldn't seem to finish. She waited, not wanting to speak and ruin the small and fragile hope she held. "I thought I wouldn't see you again."

"Can we talk?" she asked.

He looked away before answering and she knew then he'd make it hard for her. She couldn't complain. It was only fair.

"I'm supposed to be with the others," he replied. "Celebrating."

"I can wait," she told him.

"No," he said sharply. "You come with me."

Betony felt a shiver of apprehension. To be with his friends would only serve to alienate her further. She wouldn't fit in. She would not feel comfortable. He would see that and want to get rid of her. Betony felt certain of it.

"I can't. It's not a good idea. You celebrate like you deserve and I will wait for you," she entreated.

He shook his head. "You don't get to choose this time."

They had pizzas from large brown boxes, with cheese that stretched and pulled like sticky string. Danny didn't speak to her again, just passed her a slice and then licked his finger where the cheese had got caught. Betony ate, surprised to find she was hungry, and listened. She heard stories of exam disasters, each one more drastic and dramatic than the last. Danny shared his experiences, but he didn't smile and laugh like the others. He didn't look at her either and, after a while, Betony wondered whether he would notice if she slipped away and left. She stayed, though. If this was her punishment—to be ignored, to see how full his life was without her—then she would willingly endure it.

The girl, Emmy, was the only one who deigned to speak to her. "Cut the tension with a knife," she remarked, plopping herself down on a large cushion on the floor next to Betony.

Betony looked at her in confusion. "A knife?" she echoed anxiously.

"You and Danny," she whispered, leaning over conspiratorially. "You had a fight?"

"Of sorts," Betony replied. "But not with a knife."

Emmy giggled. "Funny," she said. Then she leaned farther in, closer to Betony's ear. "He's really into you. You do know that, don't you?"

Betony looked across into Emmy's deep blue eyes. Suddenly, she saw the attraction Emmy held and marveled that Danny had chosen her instead. She had no one else, only him. But he . . . he had Emmy and all the other girls in this room and in that school and in the town to pick from. For the first time that day, Betony felt encouraged, just a little bit, but enough for her to pluck up her courage and do what she had come for.

"Thank you, Emmy," she said sincerely. "And sorry for last time," she added, leaving Emmy looking puzzled.

Stepping in between the boxes that littered the floor, Betony made her way over to Danny. She stood tall in front of him, looking down on his slouched form as he lay back on the sofa. He glanced at her, but then his eyes turned away.

Betony swallowed her hurt and spoke. "It's time for us to talk," she said firmly. And then she left.

It took less than a couple of minutes for him to catch up with her on the street.

"Let's go someplace," he said, before she could start on the speech that she had been preparing all day.

They walked for some time and it felt good to be by his side, in daylight, an ordinary couple if it wasn't for her clothes and their lack of contact and conversation.

"I hope you passed your exams," she said, breaking the silence that had layered them like leaves.

"Yeah. So do I." He didn't sound confident.

"I hope I did not spoil things for you," she added with concern.

He looked at her with raised eyebrows, then turned into the grounds of a church, walking quickly along a path through a graveyard and she almost had to run to keep up with him.

"Where are we going?" She had deliberately not asked before, but now her curiosity got the better of her.

"Somewhere we can be alone," he told her.

Then he left the path and trod between the headstones until he reached a wall. He put his hand into the sprawl of ivy and, after a few seconds, a door swung open. Just like magic. Pulling the tendrils of ivy aside, he made a space for her to crouch through. On the other side of the door was a meadow full of wildflowers and brambles. A stream ran through it, beside it a weeping willow tree that bowed to the water below.

"It's beautiful," she said.

"I've often thought of bringing you here," he confessed. "And then, when you ended things, I thought I'd missed my chance."

"Do you want to sit?" she asked, thinking it might feel less intimidating if he did.

Of course he said no, so she had to stand on shaky legs as she told him.

"I have run away," she announced. His eyes flickered in surprise. "I can never go back."

"Why?" he said. "I mean, good. But why? You sounded so sure when you dumped me. You said you could never leave, that you would never want to leave."

"I said that, I know, but . . . "

"So, you've changed your mind?"

"Listen to me. Please!"

He stepped toward her. "I did listen to you. I listened to every word about how you couldn't be with me and how it was for the best and how sorry you were."

"I was sorry!" she shouted, and then she stuffed her fist into her mouth and bit on it so both were stopped and she couldn't say more and she couldn't strike him, either. It was time for truth. Some of it, at least. She had so many secrets that she could spill, but one of them would have to do. She let her hand drop and took a breath. "I am with child," she told him.

It was like diving off a cliff, jumping from a tree, retrieving honeycomb from a hive, pulling out a thorn. It had to be done fast before the thinking made her fearful.

Danny blinked as his brain broke the sentence into bits. "You're pregnant?" he questioned slowly, as though he didn't quite understand what he was asking.

"I am. And it is a boy. And I cannot stay there or we will not survive, neither him nor I."

"But . . . but you told me . . . you told me it was okay," he stuttered.

"What do you mean?" she asked. Shock, she had expected, but not this. Not blame.

"You said you had protection."

Betony blinked as her memory cast back to fish for the word, the scene, the meaning.

"Don't you remember?" he accused.

"I didn't understand. I'm sorry," she cried.

He didn't soften at her sadness. He didn't hold her or tell her that he loved her or that he would take care of her and their son. His arms stayed by his side and his mouth stayed shut; his jaw jutted and his eyes glowered. Thoughts, desperate and dreadful, thundered through Betony's mind. *What would she do? Where would she go? What about the baby? How would they live?*

What had she done?

36

YOUNG BETONY

Dear Aunt

Please forgive me, but I cannot go on any longer. This is both my goodbye and my apology–for hurting you and shaming you. It was never my intention and I wish there was another way.

There is no place for me in this world, no place that I can reach.

I have a baby inside me, only a speck, but a boy. And if he must die, I will die with him. It is my wish–the only one that can come true.

Forgive me and then forget me. That is all I ask. I will not be alone. I go to join my mother. Two mothers together, for I will have my son. So, though I fear death, I embrace it too.

Your loving niece,
Betony

37

Young Charlock

It took Charlock several hours to compose the letter. Many words were crossed out. Many drafts were crumpled and burned. All the while, Betony fretted about seeing Danny again. She worried aloud about how he would respond to her, to her apology, to her news about the baby.

"You are worrying too much. He loves you, does he not?" Charlock told her.

Betony nodded, but still she looked anxious. Charlock handed her the letter with a set of instructions.

"Read it and think on it. Whatever your reservations, wait until you have read it once more. Remember who will read it. Remember why."

Betony took the letter and read it quickly, then reached for the quill and dipped it in the ink, writing it out in her own hand, word for word, without a single murmur.

"Will it do?" she whispered once she'd signed her name.

"It better do," Charlock told her.

Betony glanced over the letter once more. "Is this how you felt? About your boy?" she asked.

Charlock sighed. "I did. For a brief time."

"But no longer?"

"I want my life here. With my clan, my family. With you, I had hoped."

"I'm sorry," Betony said softly.

"No. It is I who should apologize. I cut you adrift and left you alone. If only I had stayed close to you, I could have stopped you being carried away by the waves. I could have warned you how deep the waters were that you were swimming in and how far from shore you'd floated. Instead, I turned my back and walked away and left you to drown."

"Nonsense," Betony told her. "Nothing could have stopped me or the waves or the drowning. Nothing. Not even you."

It gave them the idea of where to leave the note, at least. Down where the rocks met the sea, on top of Betony's clothes. The waves crashed and frothed before this little offering as though demanding more. Charlock shivered. The water seemed cruelly cold and she wondered at the other souls whose lives it had dragged under and never released.

"They won't even search for your body this way," Charlock murmured.

Betony blinked and Charlock could tell she was playing out their lie in her imagination—removing her cloak and skirt and folding them neatly; untying her boots and slipping them from her feet; flinching at the icy sea against her toes; stepping deeper in, then slipping on the rocks and swimming out into the ocean; battling against the waves until she finally succumbed; being sucked under and gasping for breath, wanting to die but needing to live; water entering her mouth, her nose, her lungs until all air had left her and bubbled to the surface as she sank and breathed no more.

Charlock inhaled deeply. Betony looked so pale beneath her freckles that Charlock covered her friend's cheeks with her hands, trying to restore the warmth there.

"It feels like I am dying," Betony confessed, and her words were swept away by the sea air and snapped up by a soaring gull.

Charlock shook her head, although she felt it, too. A kind of ending, a kind of suicide. "Rebirth," she said. "Let's call it that."

Late into the night, Charlock led her friend out of the camp to the edge of the forest. Betony hesitated only once by the giant stones that surrounded the coven.

"Hurry," Charlock mouthed, not even risking a whisper.

Betony put her hands upon the stones as though making a wish and then she laid her face there, her cheek against the stone in silent goodbye. Charlock half expected some response, as if the stones themselves might shift, but there was nothing, no animal cry, no rustling from the wind.

The rest of the way, Betony hurried, placing her feet carefully where Charlock trod, making sure her clothes did not catch on any thorn or bramble. She carried with her a bag that Charlock had packed, with some clothes and other odds and ends that they'd collected from around the camp. They had been careful to cover their tracks so it would appear that Betony's belongings had not been touched. She even wore a pair of old boots they'd found in a storeroom and quickly mended for her journey.

They stopped at the last tree, the first grass. This was to be their parting place. Betony was crying already and she didn't bother to wipe the tears as more kept coming.

"Think of Danny," Charlock tried. "He will be so pleased to see you. Think how happy he will be to hear that you can be with him." Betony sniffed, then sobbed, so Charlock continued. "And the baby—when Danny learns he will be a father, he will jump for joy. I am sure of it."

"I don't know," mumbled Betony, at last wiping her face dry.

"Don't be so silly!" exclaimed Charlock. "Of course he will. All his dreams will come true in an instant." Betony tried to smile and Charlock felt spurred on. "You will be the first witch to leave and find another life, without fear of being found, without worry of any reprisal. We've done it, Bet. You're free!"

Betony looked up to see her kestrel flying high above. She whistled and he came to her and landed on her outstretched arm.

"He cannot go with you, though," warned Charlock.

"I know," Betony told her, stroking the bird's head with a finger, whispering to him so quietly that Charlock couldn't hear.

Then the bird stretched his wings and took off to the skies, disappearing without a backward glance. Betony gasped in pain and clutched her ribs as though she had been wounded.

"I will look after him," Charlock assured her.

"And my aunt?" Betony asked.

"I will comfort her," Charlock promised.

"And who will comfort you?" Charlock bit down on her lip and squeezed shut her eyes. She would not cry; this she had sworn to herself. Then she felt herself being pulled into a hug. "What will I do without you?" Betony cried.

"You will do wonderfully," Charlock croaked in reply. Over her shoulder, she could see the distant lights of the town bobbing and blinking in the blackness. "Be careful out there," she whispered.

"You too." Betony clutched her tight, then let her go, and Charlock was half-surprised not to hear a sound at this sudden split, for it felt a painful tear, a rip, deep down inside her.

Without a word, Betony picked up her bag and started to walk away from the darkness, toward the light. Charlock stood and watched her, though it hurt to do so. She couldn't make the gap any wider by turning to the woods. Not yet. Then Betony turned and ran back and hugged her again.

"I didn't say thank you."

"You did."

"I didn't say I love you."

"You did."

"I didn't say friends first."

"Friends first," Charlock said.

The next day, there were questions. There was searching. There was panic. Then, late that afternoon, the clothes and the note were found, and there was shock. No witch had ever taken her own life before. The news rippled round the camp, then silenced it. The tears, from both young and old, followed quickly. Charlock's were the first to fall. She had been holding them in until now, so they fell thick and fast as she wept for all the past she had shared and all the future she had lost.

"Come with me," Betony had pleaded when Charlock had first hatched the plan.

"The both of us dying together?" Charlock rejected.

"Why not? They would believe it too."

But Charlock had refused. Despite the events of this spring, she loved her life within the coven and could not imagine another, better one. She just hadn't imagined how big a hole Betony would leave. Every few steps, she nearly tripped and fell into it. For everywhere she looked, she saw the shadow of her friend—on the caravan steps, in the orchard and the vegetable patch, in the learning circle and at the dining table, in Sister Sage's caravan and in her own. Whom would she laugh with, if not her childhood friend? Whom would she tell her secrets to, if not her only confidante? Charlock heard a bird's call and peered up at the sky to see the kestrel circling there. She wondered if he saw the shadows too.

At Betony's funeral, they burned the clothes in the absence of her body. Aunt Sage was stricken with sorrow and Charlock wished she could tell Betony how much the old woman loved her after all. In the days to come, this became a familiar sensation— wishing she could run to Betony with some titbit or other. Each time, the disappointment scraped at her insides. It took months for the scabs to harden and fall away and, even then, she still felt raw.

At first, there was much talk, some kind and regretful, the rest slanderous gossip. Much was made of the contents of the letter, especially about the baby. None would admit that they could understand the sentiments, even those who had carried boys themselves. It was as though the world would end if such ideas were spoken, that if these thoughts became word, they would pollute the very air that carried them and poison all who heard them.

Sister Sage wished to keep Betony's letter, but the elders decided it must be burned, and so it joined the funeral pyre.

"It's best she's gone," Charlock overheard one of the sisters whisper as they dined that night.

"She was not worthy to be a witch," said another.

"I'm only grateful her mother was not here to see this," remarked an elder. And at this, Charlock pushed herself up from the bench and ran from the table.

Her mother and her sister followed her to the caravan where she lay weeping on her bed.

"I am sorry, Charlock," soothed her mother as she stroked her hair. "You must miss her very much."

"She told you nothing of her plans?" grilled her sister.

"Raven!" scolded Sister Starling.

"I knew she was sad," wept Charlock, just as she'd rehearsed. "But I never knew how much."

"I am surprised," said Raven.

"We all are," said Sister Starling.

"I am surprised she would make this choice. I had not thought it in her," explained Raven thoughtfully.

Charlock felt her sister's eyes upon her and dared not meet them. Instead, she buried her face in the blanket and hid away and let herself languish in the loss—the loss of her friend and the loss of her mission. The adventure that she had set out on had come to an end. For a short while, it had felt like her own escape that she'd been planning, her own journey that she'd embarked on. She had felt so light and heady with excitement, so buoyed up by pride. Her plan had worked just as she'd intended. But now it was over. The last traces of it were in the glowing embers of the fire and in the smoke that rose to meet the stars.

38

POPPY

As soon as Poppy stepped out of the camp and into the forest, she thought of Leo. The need to see him hit her so hard that she felt winded.

"I have to get back," she told Charlock and Betony, ignoring their calls as she began to run.

Through the trees she raced, ignoring the brambles that tore at her skirt and the stitch that burned in her side. Betony hadn't wanted Leo anywhere near Raven, but Poppy wished now that they had brought him with them because this yearning for him felt wild and desperate. She didn't stop running. Not for a second. Not until she reached the moors. Not until she heard the caw. It was an ugly, hellish sound and it halted her in her tracks. Looking up, she saw a dark cloud sweeping through the sky toward her. Not a cloud, she realized, but the shadow of a bird with enormous wings, flapping down to engulf her. Before she could react, traces of the bird entered her mouth and began to choke her. Her throat closed, her mouth, too, as she held her breath. If she wanted air, she'd have to let Raven in.

Poppy's mind grappled with what to do, searching for a spell that might save her. But without air, she couldn't think, or act. As her body weakened, her knees buckled to the grass. She was suffocating, but still she wouldn't surrender and take a breath. Last time she'd faced Raven, Charlock was beside her. Poppy had held on to her mother's hand and watched as Raven had been killed. She recalled the sound of Raven's skull cracking and the silence of her body sinking into snow. *Raven is dead,* she thought, and with that fact, her neck relaxed.

"You're dead," she said out loud. "You are nothing."

The bird hung before her face, its wings hunched and curved around her. Poppy coughed and bits of ash dislodged from her lungs and flew from her mouth. The bird gave another cry, but this one was not as fierce. It echoed softly across the hills, then faded into silence.

Poppy got to her feet to face her enemy head-on. "Raven Hawkweed, I hereby banish you from this world. You will return to the dead where you belong and you will not visit us again."

"My work is done," Raven screeched.

Poppy blinked as she felt these words bore into her confidence. It took all her strength to block them. "You only have power if I let you. And I don't let you. Time to go, Aunt."

Poppy opened her mouth and took a deep breath in. The bird flapped its wings in dismay as Poppy exhaled gently, as though blowing out a candle on a cake. As soon as her breath touched the bird, its ash scattered through the sky. Poppy watched as the wind dispersed it in all directions and the last traces disappeared from sight. Raven had gone. It felt more final even than death, only there was no one who would mourn it.

The garden door swung behind Poppy with a whine as if protesting her force. Then she ran toward the willow tree, pushing past its branches to find Leo. He was curled up on the ground.

"Are you sleeping?" she said softly as she bent down to see his face.

Her hand stroked his head, but he kept his eyes closed.

"I was so scared. But I did it, Leo. I banished Raven." Leo's eyes shot open. Without waiting for his reaction, or lack of it, she put her arms around him and held him close. For a second, he felt limp, but then he gripped her so tight that her ribs hurt. "Everything's going to be all right now," she whispered, and his arms relaxed. "I just know it is." Her lips touched the pulse of his neck. "I'm never going to leave you again," she promised. "It's going to be the two of us—together. Okay?"

"Okay," he said into her hair.

She pulled back to look at him and smiled widely. "Come on then," she said.

"Where to?"

"To celebrate. Me and you. It can be like a date. Our first date."

"We've been on a date before."

"Yeah? Like when? In my house when the electric went out? Or in the dell with Ember?" Just saying Ember's name made Poppy long to see her. She wished her friend were there. Refusing to be sad on this day of victory, she took Leo's hand in hers. "What date were you remembering, then?"

"Right here, in this very spot. That night last winter," he said. A breeze gently shook the leaves so they seemed to chime with his words.

Poppy felt herself blush. "I meant going out . . . you know, like . . . like bowling."

"Bowling?" he repeated with a smile.

"You know what I mean. Like a meal."

"In a restaurant?"

"Yeah, in a restaurant."

"You got any money?" He felt inside his pockets and brought out some change. "Coffee?" he suggested wryly.

"Wait," she said. She felt inside her own jacket pockets. There was a hole right through the lining. Her fingers stretched along the seam until she reached it. Two crumpled-up twenties. She held them up triumphantly and smiled. "Just like magic."

Leo took her to a small café that he knew. It had a glass counter along one wall covering a landscape of cheese, with hills of shining olives and promontories of ham.

"What's good?" Poppy asked as they sat at a small table. She picked up a menu.

"I've never eaten here," he admitted. "Just used to look in the windows, wishing that I could."

Poppy looked up at him. "I'm sorry. I should have known that."

"Hey, we're here now, aren't we?" he said with a smile, though Poppy knew it was for her benefit and still felt bad. "The spaghetti always looked good," he added. "But I was pretty hungry."

Poppy put down her menu. "Then that's what we'll have."

After that, Leo went quiet. He ate the food and listened, but she had to carry the conversation. It felt weird, like she wasn't herself but some other chatty, lighthearted, quick-witted girl with a whole lot to say about nothing. She wondered if he was angry that she'd left that morning. She reached across the table for his hand. Their skin sparked with electricity and both of them flinched. Immediately, he took his hand away, lifting his glass to drink. She stared at him, trying to read his thoughts but finding no way in.

"You haven't asked me about my visit to the coven," she said, hoping he would open up to her.

He picked up his fork and twirled the spaghetti around it. "How'd it go?" he asked flatly.

"They're in a terrible state. And I'm responsible."

He closed his eyes for a moment. When he opened them, they seemed even blacker than she remembered. "We should go," he said. "We should get the hell away from here."

He held her gaze, making it hard for her to answer. "I can't leave them again," she blurted. "One of them died. One lost her legs. They need me."

"I need you," he said gruffly.

"I told them I'd only go back if you came with me."

He looked startled and leaned back in his chair. "What?"

"They need some time to get used to the idea, but they'll come around."

"Me, live there? With all of them?"

He looked appalled. Poppy kept her voice calm. "They're not that bad, you know. And you'd have your mom and I'd have mine and my cousin too."

Leo pushed his chair back, creating an even bigger space between them. "I thought you didn't want to be queen. I thought it would be me and you now."

"It will be."

He shook his head. "Not with them."

"Why are you being like this?" she asked. "Talk to me. Tell me what's wrong." He put his hands over his face. "Leo?" she said, worried now. "We love each other, don't we?"

When he looked at her, there were tears in his eyes. Poppy's heart suddenly felt heavy in her chest. She felt a prickle of fear and the hairs on her body bristled.

"Well, well. The happy couple." She recognized the voice immediately.

"Ember!" gasped Poppy. She sprang up from her seat and threw her arms around her friend. It was only after a few seconds that Poppy processed how rigid Ember felt and how snide her tone had sounded. Poppy pulled back and looked at Ember's pained expression.

"You're angry with me," she said.

Ember didn't answer her but looked at Leo instead.

"She's angry with me," he said quietly. "And she's right to be."

Suddenly Poppy felt exhausted. She had thought that by banishing Raven she was helping put the world to rights, but everyone seemed more unhappy than before.

"Actually," Ember said flatly. "I want to introduce you both to someone."

She looked over to a guy standing at the doorway and beckoned him. His hair was even whiter and his eyes even bluer than Ember's. When he stood next to Leo, the difference between them was startling, and Poppy knew why Ember had chosen him. He held out his hand and Poppy took it.

"This is Nick," Ember was saying, but the words blurred in Poppy's ears because a pain had traveled up her arm and landed in her head.

"So you're Poppy, the long-lost friend." It was only when he let go of her hand that the pain receded and Poppy could answer.

"Not so long or lost," she replied.

Nick turned to Leo. "And you must be the ex."

"Nick," muttered Ember, her cheeks flushing.

"I've got to go." Leo grabbed his coat from the chair.

"Leo!" Poppy exclaimed, and they stared at each other for a long moment as she willed him to say sorry. But no apology came. Instead, she felt a storm gathering inside him. The plates and cutlery on the table began to rattle. Poppy saw Nick's eyes dart to them and she made the tremors stop. "Go, then," she said to Leo quietly before the storm broke out in front of everyone.

He didn't hesitate and walked away, between the tables and out the door.

"He's good at that," Ember said in a bitter tone that Poppy hadn't heard from her before. "Leaving."

"I'm sorry," Poppy said. "You turned up at a bad moment, that's all." Ember looked wounded and Poppy quickly tried to make amends. "I'm so glad to see you."

"You are?" Ember asked in a small voice.

"Of course, I am. Can I see you properly?" she asked. "To-morrow?" She didn't like the way Ember turned to Nick, as if seeking permission. "Just you and me. At our place." Ember slowly nodded, and Poppy hugged her again, squeezing her tight until finally she squeezed her back. "Come alone," she whispered in Ember's ear.

Poppy's eyes scoured the streets for Leo. Suddenly an arm reached out and grabbed her and she was in his arms and he was kissing her like he'd never stop. There was anger as well as love in that kiss and it felt charged with so much passion that Poppy could feel it crackling up and down the length of them. His hands were in her hair, on her scalp, and they stayed there, pressing into her mind as he spoke.

"I can't lose you again," he mumbled.

"You won't," she promised, and he kissed her again.

When they reached the meadow, they went straight to the willow and fell against the tree and then the ground. At last, sheltered by the curtain of leaves, they could do more. Poppy felt the desperation building and building between them. Their kisses were wild, their breaths ragged, their hands rough and urgent.

Then, without warning, Leo froze and everything stopped.

"I can't," he mumbled.

Poppy's heart was galloping in her chest. "Because we had the fight?" she cried, the tears rising rebelliously in her eyes.

"No, no. It's not that."

"Then what is it?" She rolled away from him, vanquishing the tears, hoping he hadn't seen them. "Because of what I said about the clan?"

He lay back in defeat and sighed heavily. "I just can't . . . " His voice cracked. "Not today." They lay there in silence for a while and the heat and the longing slowly left Poppy until her body felt her own again. "Please don't cry," he whispered.

"I'm not," she retorted sharply, blinking back the tears.

She turned away from him, lying on her side, and closed her eyes. All she could hear was his breathing. All she could feel was his heart beating. At least this way she couldn't see him too.

"I'm sorry," he said, the words low and weighted with regret.

"I don't understand," she muttered, wondering how a queen as powerful as she could be so helpless when it came to her own heart. A spell came to mind that would make him talk to her. Immediately, she rejected it, knowing how she'd hate him for trying such a tactic on her. Tomorrow they would talk of their own free will.

"Tomorrow," she vowed.

But tomorrow he was gone.

Ember was at the dell before her. When Poppy spied her from the top of the steep slope, it felt like the months melted away and it was last autumn once more. Ember's fair head turned to greet her. Poppy was smiling as she hurried down to reach her. They had been seeking the truth, believing it would free them. They hadn't expected it to have teeth, to hold them captive in its jaws.

Ember looked up at Poppy, but she didn't wave. It wasn't last autumn. It was late spring and the leaves weren't golden but newly green and the flowers weren't fading but freshly in bud. So much had changed. Especially them.

When Poppy reached the bottom of the dell, she stretched out a hand, waiting for Ember to take it. Ember observed it for a while, her face blank and unchanging, and then she held out her own and they touched. Poppy felt the depth of Ember's disappointment and glimpsed why.

"He's left me, too," she told her.

Ember's face softened with surprise. "He'll come back to you. He'll never leave you."

Poppy tried to hide the desperation she felt at her words. She wanted to tell Ember her worries, all her pain and confusion about why Leo had gone, but she stopped herself. "I'm so sorry," she said instead.

Ember shook her head. "He was never mine. I just borrowed him for a bit, but we never really fit. He was just the first boy I ever saw and I wanted so badly for him to love me."

"I should have come to you first." Poppy felt like weeping. "When I got back. It should be friends first."

At that, Ember's face crumpled, releasing all the tension lingering there, and she flung her arms around Poppy and hugged her close.

"I don't understand," she said. "I thought things would get better once I found out who I was, but I feel so alone."

"I missed you. Every day. I swear it. But I thought you were happy. I wanted you to be happy."

Ember stepped back to look at her. "You know, sometimes I wish I could turn back time, to when we met, right here in this spot. Before Leo."

"And Charlock," Poppy said. "And Raven and Sorrel."

"And Melanie." Ember smiled.

"How is Melanie?"

"She's . . . she's stuck. She doesn't go out. It's as though she only feels safe at home, shutting out the world."

Poppy looked up at the sky, so perfectly blue. "What about this guy, Nick?" She lowered her eyes to Ember's. Ember moved from one foot to the other, defensively. "Do you trust him?"

"He's been good to me," she replied, but Poppy caught the edge to her voice.

"Do you trust him?" Poppy asked again.

Ember blinked. "Yes."

But Poppy knew it was a lie.

39

BETONY

etony woke when the moon was high and the bats were still feeding. She caught a flash of a fox's eyes and heard the shuffle of a hedgehog. Her head turned to the willow tree. Something was wrong. She could feel it. It was as though the tree itself were under some kind of strain, as though there was a tension running through its sap, making the twigs taut and the leaves tough. She longed to rush over there, push the leafy curtain apart, and see her son. *He and Poppy must have quarreled,* she thought. She guessed it must be about the coven. The girl thought they could all live happily ever after in the camp. Leo would have known this was a fairy tale.

Betony couldn't get back to sleep. As the night sky lightened, her mind brightened with it and she could see her memories scattered in her head like pieces of material, each a different color and a different pattern waiting to be stitched together into something whole. A bird, a boy, a baby. A forest, a town, a city. A ring, a bee, a bear. If only she could find the thread and start to sew, then she could make this quilt to wrap around her son. But the thread wouldn't pass through the eye of the needle however hard she tried.

Just as her brain was giving way to tiredness and her eyelids were drooping, the tree softened. Out slipped Leo like a shadow, through the silken leaves. Betony waited for a moment for the girl to follow, but she made no appearance. He was sneaking away, Betony realized. He was dissolving into the dawn, leaving no word or clue to his departure. Betony got to her feet, taking care not to wake Charlock or Poppy as she moved. Her legs were stiff, but she made them hurry. Through the graveyard he went, heading out of town, into the hills, toward the forest. *Oh no*, thought Betony, *please no. Not there.*

Leo had slipped away so furtively, but now his steps were long and loud. He strode across the bracken so fast that he didn't notice her following him. Often, she had to run just to keep him in her sights. Only when he entered the forest and she was sure it was the coven he sought did she allow herself to close the distance between them. He was lost, she realized. Walking in circles, covering the same tracks twice. Betony rolled her eyes, despairing of her child. As she did so, her foot hit a twig. The snap resounded through the trees. Leo stopped and listened. Betony waited. An owl hooted and there was a rustle from the undergrowth. Leo didn't move. The atmosphere became charged. He was alert, his magic bristling, changing him from chaff to witch. Betony could feel it, just as she felt the hairs rise upon her arm.

"Poppy?" he called.

Betony stepped forward. "It is I."

He squinted, searching for her through the trees. "Betony?" he whispered. "My mother?"

She took another step. "Why have you come here?" she asked directly with no preamble. His mouth opened, but he didn't answer. "You'll never find them," she told him. "The Northern clan have kept themselves hidden here for centuries."

"I'll use my magic," he said, and, without meaning to, she made a scoffing noise that angered him. "Go back to the others," he barked.

"Does she know you're here? This love of yours? Perhaps I should inform her."

"Leave Poppy out of it."

"I wish I could. But she is in it, isn't she? Deep up to her neck in it. You're here, putting yourself in danger, because of her." He couldn't deny it. His head bowed as if in shame. "What did she do?" He gave the slightest shake of his head, a tiny gesture of surrender Betony only glimpsed through the forest gloom because a ray of morning light had caught him in its beam. "What?"

"Not her," he admitted.

"Then who?" she asked. He didn't answer. "Leo . . . my son . . . look at me." And he obeyed. "Who?" she asked again.

"Her cousin."

The words were piercing. It wasn't the thought of Charlock's niece that hurt her. It was Raven. Betony's memory was still a fog, but Raven—she was a silhouette, bold and black, sharp and pointed, with edges that cut into her brain like thorns.

"What did she do?" Betony murmured.

The tears fell from Leo's eyes and she felt her own eyes sting in response.

"What did she do?" she screamed.

"I can't tell you," he howled, and then Betony whimpered as the understanding hit her like a blow.

He must have seen the shock cross her face as he cried out with the shame of it and the tears began running down his face so fast that they were dropping to the ground. On landing, they sizzled, singeing the greenery brown.

Betony stepped toward him. "Sorrel is possessed by her mother's ghost. It is Raven who has done this to you."

The shock stilled him, but only for a second. Then he gave a savage yell and raised his arm, releasing a bolt of fire from his hand so fast it felled a tree. The serrated stump smoked from the heat. Leo stared at his hand in disbelief.

Betony looked around her. "Don't," she told him.

She couldn't protect him. Not against Raven. No one could. But another ball of flames was flickering from Leo's palm.

"Sorrel," he said. "Where is she?"

"I can't tell you that," she argued.

He passed the flames from one hand to the other like a conjuror. He wasn't crying now. His features were lifted, hard and set with resolve. "I have to talk to her. Poppy can't find out what happened. She can't," he declared, and then he fired another shot against another tree.

"Stop!" Betony cried. "It's not safe."

"I got this from you," he told her. "This magic. So don't pretend it's not a part of me."

Betony could feel the danger circling, ready to pounce, and she braced herself.

"Be careful," she croaked.

"What is it you're so afraid of?" he cried.

And then it was upon them.

These witches were like none Betony had seen before. It was as if they'd emerged from the earth itself, their bodies sinewy and coiled like ropes, or from the bottoms of ponds, slimy and scaled like reptiles. Leo fought with fire, blasting away the roots they sent to trip and tie them. Betony tried hard to find the fire within her, but her mind could only find portions of its power and sections of spells. Never had she mourned the loss of her memory more than now—her son in danger and she powerless to save him. Instead, it was he who protected her, shielding her with his body, his back to her front, his shoulders wide, his arms outstretched, turning to block every attack. But then another clan arrived with faces like snow and hair of frost, snuffing out his flames with their ice.

"Who are they?" he cried to her.

"What do you want with him?" Betony called to the witches.

But then a pain seared through her side and she was falling and Leo was catching her, holding her. She tried to shake her head. She tried to tell him, *Save yourself!* But she couldn't move. She couldn't make a sound, not even as his arms were pulled away from her and she could see the roots around his legs, his middle, his throat. She tried to scream as he was dragged away, his heels digging so hard into the earth that they gouged two tracks.

"Mother!" he was shouting, and she tried to keep her eyes open, to see his face before he was gone, but then the world turned dark and she was tumbling back, through the years, into her long-lost memory. She was in freefall and, in her mind, she reached for anything to stop her descent. Then there it was—the thread, the needle, the eye. And the patches of her past, at last in position, waiting for her to stitch them together.

40

Young Betony

She wasn't Betony anymore. Betony was lying at the bottom of the ocean with seaweed in her hair and fish nibbling at her toes. She was Bee now. Bee wasn't magic. She was just a regular girl who wore pants and T-shirts and sneakers bought from charity stores. She lived in a big city, miles and miles from the forest by the sea. Her boyfriend had begged her to move there with him, so they could be together, be a family. He studied at the university, while she read books and watched movies. Bee ate cereal and pasta and baked beans. She had money—not much—but it lived in a purse that she loved to clip and unclip with a snap. She rode a bicycle. Danny had taken her to an empty parking lot at night and he had taught her how. He held on to the handlebars as she pedaled, then her waist, then his hands were gone and he was shouting, "You're doing it . . . you're doing it," and "Be careful!" as she wobbled precariously before mastering the handlebars once more. It felt like flying, like Bee could go anywhere and do anything. This was Bee's magic.

Bee owned jewelry—a silver chain that hung around her neck and a ring with an oval stone of amber that sat on her finger, secretly reminding her of the eyes of a faraway friend. Danny had put it on her left hand, on what he called her "ring" finger.

"That's a promise," he'd said as the cool metal slid along her skin.

She had stretched her hand out before her in newfound admiration of this part of her body.

"A promise of what?" she'd asked.

"That I'll take care of you. That we'll get married one day."

Bee was engaged. She didn't think of the past, only the present and the future. Her belly was rounded now and the baby moved inside her. She and Danny would lie on their bed with a duvet, in a room three stories up, with walls made of brick and a lock on the door, and they'd marvel at the life that was growing inside her. He would lay his hands on either side of the bump until one day they no longer met in the middle. The next day, Bee found that she couldn't fit into her clothes and had to wear a dress that flowed to her thighs, revealing arms and legs so out of proportion with her middle, like a spider or a beetle.

She didn't go to a doctor, despite Danny's attempts to persuade her. She told him that she couldn't give her name, for fear of discovery by her family.

"So what?" he said. "They can't force you to do anything."

"You don't know them," she muttered. Then she told him that all gypsies knew about babies and none of them ever went to a hospital. They all gave birth at home.

"Here?" Danny gasped, his eyes scanning the room with his books and papers in piles on the floor.

Bee giggled. "Yes, here."

"You're crazy," he told her. "What if something goes wrong?"

She wanted to tell him she was a witch, that it would go well because she would make sure of it. But Bee wouldn't say that. She simply smiled and said, "Nothing will go wrong because I have you. You'll be holding my hand and that is all I need." He still looked pale, so she took his hand and squeezed it. "It's just blood and slime and gore," she told him seriously, and then his mouth turned upward and she grinned and kissed him.

They didn't give their son a name—Bee still had some of Betony's old superstitions. But she did allow the teddy bear that Danny brought back home and that now sat in the corner, waiting as the days ticked by for its purpose to begin. Bee made soups and cleaned, not just her room but the shared bathroom and communal living area. The students who regarded her so warily slowly warmed to her and thanked her and lent her books and magazines and gave her chocolate and made her cups of tea. They told her she was really brave, that her bump was gorgeous, that she and Danny were the coolest couple. They slept late and woke late and soon Bee did the same and the sun's rise and fall became of little significance to her.

The place was so empty when they all went to class, leaving her alone. And then so noisy when they returned. There was nothing in between. Danny would come back full of news and he would ask her about her day and she would give him her report— not much to say, then a little less, then hardly anything at all. She could tell he was concerned and she would kiss his worries away and join him and his friends in the bar downstairs and smile and laugh, even though she wanted to have him to herself, just for a while, before another day began. She relished the nights, when it was just the two of them, when she had the whole of him—his eyes, his brain, his hands on her. But all too soon, he was gone again and she was left behind.

Then one day on one of her long walks around the city, Bee entered the zoo. There were animals that she'd never seen before, only read about. Some bigger than she ever thought possible—elephants and giraffes and gorillas. And cats of enormous size with teeth like daggers. It was the monkeys who noticed her first. They swung on ropes and branches to look at her through the glass, jumping and grunting and chattering in excitement. Then the birds in the aviary swooped down to perch upon her so that the other visitors gasped and started taking photographs. By the time she reached the penguins, the zoo staff had been alerted and some of them came to watch. The penguins slowly left their pool and waddled their way across their patch of ice toward her. She leaned over the barrier and stroked their glistening heads.

"They seem to like you all right," came a friendly voice. Bee looked up to see a man with a body stout and solid, much like the penguins, smiling at her. "D'you work with animals?"

She thought back to her work in the coven, milking the goats, feeding the chickens, skinning the rabbits, and nodded. "I used to."

"I can tell," he said. "You're a natural. A whisperer." She must have looked confused because he elaborated. "You can talk to them, can't you?"

She didn't want to lie. "In a way."

It seemed to satisfy him because he gave her a job. She started with the worst tasks—clearing up the never-ending elephant dung, scrubbing slurry off the cement floors, heaving hay bales.

But when her belly grew too big and her back started aching, she moved to less physical work like cooking and blowing snow into the penguin enclosure. Then one afternoon, a zoo keeper asked her to look at a chimp who wouldn't come down from his tree, not for any food they offered him. His mate had died and Bee could feel his pain through the glass. They wouldn't let her inside, no matter how much she begged, but she started to feed him and watch him, placing her forehead and hands on the glass, trying to send him messages of condolence. It took over a week, but finally the chimp came down. After that, Bee was called in when a tiger chewed all the hair off its tail and when a bear kept ramming the glass of his enclosure and a zebra wouldn't stop licking the walls.

"They shouldn't be in here," she told the staff.

"They live longer here than in the wild," came the reply.

A long life or a free life? Bee knew which she would choose. But she took the money gratefully each week and tried to help the animals as best she could. They couldn't go back home. Even if they could, they wouldn't know how to live there anymore. This place had changed them. This place was home now. She told it to them—and to herself—until they all started to believe it.

When Danny told his parents about the baby, they got in the car immediately and drove to see him. Bee cleaned herself up, put on her best clothes, and made her best soup. They didn't stay to try it. Danny's father wouldn't even look at her, his face drawn into a frown of disappointment. And Danny's mother began to cry as soon as she laid eyes on them. They were not tears of joy.

"You can't be a father," she told her son.

"Why not?" he asked.

"You're just a child yourself."

"I'm eighteen," he said.

"You have no idea."

"I'll learn."

"You're supposed to be studying . . . not . . . not parenting."

Bee spoke then, wanting to make things better somehow. "He is studying, Mrs. Marchetti. Really hard."

"Do you have family, Betony? Whom you can go to when the baby comes?"

"She's staying here, Mom. With me." Danny took Betony's hand, but she wished that he'd let go and not upset them further.

"Here? With a baby?" his mother exclaimed.

"And you expect me to pay for it?" Danny's father spoke for the first time.

Betony felt Danny flinch. "We'll manage," he retorted.

His mother started sobbing then, and Bee wanted to put an arm around her, sit her down, offer her some food. But Danny's father was ushering her out of the room.

"You're ruining your lives," he muttered.

"It's your grandchild you're talking about!" Danny yelled after them before slamming the door.

"I'm sorry," Bee said right away and, to her relief, he hugged her.

"We can't be sorry," he whispered into her hair. "Not about this."

It was as though Danny's parents took Bee with them—the girl with the bright future, the chaff who fit in. In her place, up floated Betony, cold and bedraggled and missing Charlock with a keenness that stung like a stitch in her side, making it hard for her to breathe. These other students were not her friends—they only knew Bee, not Betony. They were Danny's friends and he studied with them, drank coffee with them, and went to gigs with them. She tried to join in, but she was tired after work and her legs hurt and she couldn't pretend to be like them anymore. All she really wanted to do was to lie down and wait, like the teddy bear in the corner, for her purpose to begin.

41

Young Charlock

With every plum and every apple that Charlock picked, she mourned a little more. With every berry that stained her fingers and every barrow full of leaves she gathered, she missed her friend. She thought her grief would cool with the passing of the seasons, but winter had chilled the last of the warmth and still her sadness smoldered within her.

She tried to think of Betony alive out there and thriving, but her mind balked at that, like a horse refusing a jump. Instead, Charlock told herself that Betony had been swept out to sea that sunny day and now swam as a mermaid underwater, shells around her neck, red hair to her waist, beautiful and free. It was a softer image and a safer one too. For Charlock could tell her sister's suspicions had not dulled. Raven still watched her with a curious look that made Charlock fret that she could read her thoughts or creep into her dreams and see the truth hidden there. So Charlock rehearsed the story of the mermaid until it began to convince her. Sometimes she'd even catch herself looking out to sea, hoping for a glimpse of silver tail or flash of auburn hair.

Her mother told her that time would be her healer, but time was no match for lies. Charlock's bereavement became an infection that, untreated, only worsened as the months went by. After a while, others began to worry about her condition. Her skin had paled and her weight had dropped. Raven was awarded the task of caring for her. Charlock trembled when she was told this news. If anyone could see through her deceit, it would be her sister. Trying to keep the panic from her voice, Charlock argued that she just needed rest.

"Besides," she told the elders, "Raven is busy with Sorrel. She shouldn't have to bother herself with me."

Raven cocked her head as she surveyed her. "Nonsense," she announced. "Who else but I, your sister?"

"She is right," agreed their mother. "Raven has already been preparing various remedies for your symptoms."

Fear whirled through Charlock like a gale, leaving her swaying on her feet. She could not faint. She must not. "Truly, Mother. I am determined to be well," she proclaimed. "I have wallowed too long in my misery, I realize that. But I can get better by myself. I know I can."

The elders looked at one another and gave a mutual shake of their heads. "You have fallen into a deep hole, my child," said Charlock's mother. "And it may take magic to lift you out. Let us do what we do best."

"I will get to the bottom of it," declared Raven with a relish that made Charlock want to cower. "Just leave my sister to me."

The first of Raven's tonics was for her sleep. That night, Charlock slept the deepest and longest she'd done in months. She closed her eyes at seven and didn't awake until well past eleven the next morning. She told Raven she felt better, hoping that might be the end of it, but Raven insisted she open her mouth so three drops could fall from a vial onto her tongue.

"For ease of mind," Raven told her.

There was a fillip for her appetite, a restorative for her anxiety, and a potion for her heart. Then came the spells—charms whispered in her ear, amulets hung around her neck, herbs placed in her pockets. Raven pulled a hair from her head, made her spit in a jar and pee in a pot. Charlock protested as best she could, but Raven would not be deterred.

"Don't you want to get better?" she scolded.

After another month had passed, Raven's patience had dwindled. Although she was sleeping better, Charlock still found it hard to eat and swallow. Her stomach had shrunk over the last months and she felt it small and hard, like a walnut shell inside her. Just one nut was enough to fill it.

"Is this starvation for her? For Betony?" At the sound of that name, tears sprang to Charlock's eyes. She hadn't heard it in so long. No one spoke of Betony anymore and, on the rare occasion they did, it was never by name. "She was weak," Raven berated. "A disgrace, to her aunt, to our coven. You forget about her—you hear me."

"I can't," cried Charlock, the tears falling now.

Raven grabbed Charlock's arm and dragged her out of the camp, through the snow until they reached the river. Charlock was crying and wailing, but her sister only yanked harder, making her trip and graze her knees. When they reached the river's edge, Raven pulled up Charlock's top and tore down her skirt.

"Look at yourself," she ordered. "Look!"

Charlock peered into the river and blinked at what she saw. It was another's body, not hers; more mythical in appearance than human. The ribs jutted from her sides, threatening to burst through skin that seemed so thin it was translucent. The hip bones were sharp, the stomach concave, and the legs like branches, ready to snap at any moment. Could they possibly belong to her?

"Betony is gone," said Raven. "She will never be back. Will she?"

Charlock kept staring at the hollow cheeks of the face in the river. Reflected on the water's surface she saw Raven's hands reaching to take hold of her chin before she actually felt them. The fingers pressed into her skin and turned her head so that Charlock was looking into her sister's eyes.

"Will she?" Raven said again, this time as a question demanding an answer. "She will never be back. Will she?"

Charlock thought her eyes would bulge from their sockets, so long and hard she had to stare. Her mouth was dry with fear, glued shut with panic. She couldn't breathe. She had to swallow, she had to.

As soon as she did so, Raven's eyes lit up. "I knew it!" she cried in elation. Her hands fell from Charlock's face as though she couldn't bear to touch her any longer. Charlock dropped to the riverbank and scooped the water into her mouth and drank.

"I saw it on the whiteness of your tongue and in the smell of your piss. Oh, the lies you have told. And for her. As if the brat would end her life like that. She—the joker with the quick retort and the mischief making. She—who thought she was above us all."

"That's not true," Charlock couldn't help replying.

"Do not speak to me of truth, little sister. Where is she?"

"She is in the ocean."

Raven rolled her eyes and tossed her head. "Don't make this any more difficult, Charlock. You know what I can do to you."

"Mother wouldn't let you," Charlock whispered.

"Mother wouldn't know. She'd be too ashamed to look you in the eye. She'd be too busy wondering what she'd done to deserve a daughter such as you."

Charlock hung her head between her legs. "You can't prove it," she muttered.

"You think Sister Ada won't interrogate you? Sister Martha, Sister Morgan, Sister Wynne? You think they won't stick their hands down your throat and pull the truth out from your guts?" Charlock stared at the ground, wishing she could dissolve and disappear into it. "Where is she?"

Charlock looked up, summoning the last of her defiance. "I don't know!" she shouted.

In among the guilt and the self-loathing, it felt a relief to tell the truth. It was cleansing both to mind and body, all the deception washed away. And as soon as Charlock told the coven about Danny, she felt hungry. She ate and ate and each bite was seasoned with the salt of her tears. Her mother's face looked ashen when she heard the news, but the blood returned to her face when Raven reported that Charlock had come forward of her own accord.

"At least," Raven stated, "she has corrected her mistake."

The rest of the clan were not quite so forgiving, but again Raven became Charlock's advocate.

"My sister is committed to righting her wrongs. She will assist me in my search every step of the way."

Charlock's eyes darted across to her sister. *Not that*, she begged with her eyes. *Don't make me help you.* But Raven was merciless. She took Charlock aside and demanded every detail of the boy—his hair, his eyes, his height, his weight, every location that she'd seen him, every word she'd heard him speak.

"Can't you just leave them be?" Charlock begged.

"Tell me."

"She'll never betray us..I know she won't."

"Tell me."

"I beg you, Raven. You have known Betony all her life. She is a sister to you."

"She is no sister of mine. Now tell me, Charlock, or I tell the elders where your loyalty lies."

Charlock closed her eyes. When she opened them, she was resolved. "I'll tell you, but on one condition. You do not hurt her—not body, nor mind. You bring her back here, as you found her, and she can face her punishment within these stones." Raven's face puckered to a point. "Agreed. But the boy and the baby must be dealt with."

The thought of this made Charlock shudder, but she nodded her accord. "Swear you won't hurt her," she said. "Swear it on the moon, on the sun, on the earth."

"I swear it."

There was only one more thing that Charlock could try to save her friend. After Raven had gleaned every kernel from her and at last she was alone, Charlock looked up to the trees. The kestrel was there, as she sensed he would be, perched on a branch, his curved head and beak looking down on her with large, expectant eyes, knowing already what was needed of him.

42

YOUNG BETONY

Betony was walking down the street when she heard the kestrel's cry. She looked up and saw him in the cold sky, hovering high above her head. The bags of shopping she was carrying dropped from her hands without her realizing, the eggs cracking and the fruit bruising. Until this moment, she had never understood that joy could hurt, but the happiness at seeing her bird again hit her hard, right in the chest, and left her winded and blinking back tears. Weakly, she lifted her arm and down the bird swooped to land on it.

Her hand trembled as it touched his head; her fingers tingled as they stroked his feathers. Countless, thoughtless times before, she had done this act, but now the very familiarity of it felt extraordinary—the silky smoothness, the delicate bone, the quivering of life beneath her fingertips, reminding her of who she was, reminding her of home. The kestrel nodded and unfurled his wings, and that's when she noticed the tiny scroll of paper tied to his leg. She knew it was bad news. She knew by the way her stomach dropped to her kidneys and her hands refused to move to untie the string. She hardly need read Charlock's note. She knew what was written there. They had been discovered. This new life she had made for herself—it was over.

Betony ran through the streets, unaware of the people she knocked into or the cars that blared their horns at her as she stepped across their path. Her hand gripped the note so tightly that her nails cut into her palm. Over the rooftops the kestrel flew, calling to her his jagged cry, urging her on. At last, she pushed open the door and bounded up the stairs, two, three, four at a time, ignoring the sharp, jabbing pains in her belly as the baby jolted within her. She knew it was dangerous to race like this, but a worse danger was closing in on them and she needed every second to escape it.

She wrestled with the key to get it into the lock and turn. She wanted to scream and breathe out the fire of her desperation like a dragon. Instead, she let her head fall onto the door and her breathing cool before trying her hand once more. On the next try, the key slid into position as though denying it had ever been stuck in the first place and the door opened effortlessly. Betony grabbed two bags and started to pack.

They know.—that's what Charlock had written. *Run.* Only three words, but the first two would have sufficed. Betony could tell from the slant and scrawl of the letters that Charlock had no time for more, not even to sign her name or add any words of affection or encouragement. Betony imagined her hidden behind a caravan or hunched behind a tree, tearing the scrap of paper, balancing it on her knee as she wrote, tying it to the kestrel's leg. "Thank you," Betony whispered quickly under her breath, wishing her friend could hear her. She could only hope that Charlock was not in too much trouble. She dreaded to think how the sisters had extracted the truth. She knew that Raven must be the instigator, and though this made Betony quake with fear, she felt relieved for Charlock's sake. It might mean that Charlock would be spared the worst of the clan's sanctions. Raven might show her sister mercy, but Betony knew there would be none for her.

She was zipping the bag shut when Danny walked in, muddy soccer cleats swinging on their laces from his hand, his thick socks muffling his tread. He stopped when he saw the room so disheveled, with the open drawers and cupboard doors and clothes tossed around like a storm had hit. Then his eyes alighted on her face.

"What's happened?" he asked, noticing the bags, stuffed with their belongings.

Betony opened her mouth to speak, to tell him everything, but a pain stabbed into her side and she gasped. He came over and sat her down on the edge of the bed.

"Bee—you're scaring me." She took his hand and placed it on her tummy. "Please talk to me."

"We . . . " Her voice was breathy as a sigh. She tried again. "We have to . . . " She sucked in the air once more. " . . . Have to go."

"Go where?"

"They're coming."

"Who? Your family? Is that who?"

Betony nodded. She tried to look him in the eyes, but his face was blurred and the dizziness made her feel sick, so she looked down at her bump instead.

"Now," she said. "We have to go now."

"No way," he responded, his voice ringing so loudly in her ears. "I have to meet them sooner or later."

Betony was shaking her head and her brains were rattling against her skull. "You don't understand," she whispered.

"What's the worst they can do? A bunch of gypsy women. Curse me? Hit me over the head with sprigs of lavender? It'll be okay," he promised her.

"They're not gypsies." It came out so fast, before she had time to prepare what she'd say next. She turned to look at him. She owed him that much. "They're witches." Danny stared at her and then his mouth twitched. He was smiling. "They will hurt you and there'll be nothing you can do to stop it," she told him. The smile faded but only into an expression of sympathy and concern.

"Bee," he murmured.

She held up her hand. "Betony, not Bee. And you have to listen to me. They will kill him. Our baby boy. They'll kill him. And we won't be able to protect him."

"How are they going to do that?" he said skeptically.

She stood up abruptly. "They're witches!"

Now Danny was shaking his head. Betony grabbed the bags and thrust his at him. "We have to go. There's no time for this."

"You want me to up and leave because you think your family are witches?"

She hated him then, the condescending tone, the arrogant disbelief as he chucked the bag back down on the bed without a care for why she'd packed it.

"I don't think it," she told him. "They are." He raised his eyebrows, making it easier for her. "I am."

There. It was out. The truth had been told. Danny looked at her with eyelids stretched wide, and then he laughed.

The laughter bubbled and frothed inside her head like a potion in a cauldron. Suddenly, without her summoning a spell, the wardrobe door slammed shut. Danny blinked and the laughter stopped as abruptly as it had started. Betony turned her eyes to the chest of drawers. One by one, they closed with a bang. Danny's mouth dropped open. She cast her gaze across the room and, as she did so, all the cupboard doors flapped back and forth like they were wings, fluttering and pulsing with energy.

Betony felt her spirits soar as the magic gushed through her veins and made her heart pump faster, so much stronger than the sugar or the coffee or the beer that Danny and his friends consumed. This power had lain dormant within her for so many months and now that it had awoken, its energy felt boundless. For a few moments, she didn't care that Danny looked agitated, that he was backing away, that he was shouting.

"Stop! Stop!" he was ordering—no—begging her.

But the wood was clattering and booming so loudly, building to a crescendo, and only when it reached its peak could it then fall back to silence. The last thud was so limp and soft, it hardly seemed magical at all.

Betony's heartbeat slowed and now she focused only on Danny again. There was an expression in his eyes she'd never seen before. His hand reached slowly for the door as if she were a wild beast and he must be careful not to startle her.

"Don't go," she gasped. He swallowed, then gave a tiny shake of his head. "I'm sorry," she choked. "I couldn't help it. I just . . . I just needed you to believe me." Danny's fingers clasped the door knob and turned it. "Please . . . you have to come with me. They will find you here." He looked at her like she was a stranger, and she realized that the expression in his eyes was fear. Her stomach flipped and she wanted to be sick. "Danny," she pleaded.

"Stay away from me," he whispered, and those were the last words he ever said to her. For then the door was opening and he was gone.

Betony stood there, motionless, in the silence. The quiet seemed more striking and significant than all the commotion she had made. Suddenly, she felt a fool. Of all the wondrous magic in the world, she had chosen to slam doors, like a petulant, angry child. She sank down on the edge of the bed. Someone stared at her with shocked concern through the open door but, catching her eye, he hurried on his way. She tried to make the door close to conceal herself, but it wouldn't move, not an inch. The power had left her, just as Danny had. She didn't have the energy to get to her feet, let alone to get away. She could only sit and wait for Raven to arrive. Raven, who could send a bolt of lightning to smite her down, or a hurricane to tear her limb from limb, against a girl who couldn't even move a door a few inches.

Betony closed her eyes and, in the glimmer, she was three years old again, staring down at her mother's lifeless body, knowing for the first time what it was to be alone, running on little legs through long grass, running to get help, though knowing there was none to be had. Then the light blurred and she was lying on the cool, damp earth, her body long and lean, looking up at the wooden boards of the caravan above, hearing the footsteps, hearing her aunt call her name, hearing the calls fade until there was only the sound of her breathing and the deep, tangy smell of the soil. She was used to solitude. She had lived alone and she would die so. Then she felt it—a jab, small but sharp in the top of her belly, bringing her back to the here and now. A knee or elbow, she couldn't tell, but it was enough to remind her. She would never be alone again, whether this be the beginning or the end.

Betony took the ring from her finger and placed it on the bed cover next to Danny's bag. She picked up her own bag and pushed the teddy bear down inside it. Then, standing up on wavering legs, she made her way through the open door and out onto the street, finding her way and making her escape, one more time.

The next train was going south. Betony looked at the long list of names on the timetable, cities she'd never heard of and could never conceive of.

"I want somewhere smaller," she told the ticket lady, who looked her up and down suspiciously. "More remote."

"You'll need to change," the woman warned.

"That's fine."

In the end, she settled on Fairwood because it sounded like a smaller and friendlier version of her forest home. Making a wish that this place would live up to its name, she purchased the ticket, then walked to the very end of the platform and stood at the small precipice there. Below were the iron tracks that would take her away, stretching into the distance and beyond. As her eyes looked forward, her thoughts went into reverse, back to Danny, back to his departure, and she felt a sob rise in her throat.

Now that she was out of that room, out of that moment, his reaction seemed so reasonable. She had tried to scare him into trusting her. If only she had touched him, kissed him, shown more love, more understanding, then he might be here, standing beside her, holding her hand. Instead, her attempts to keep him safe had endangered him further. And her efforts to keep him close had driven him away. Now he was as vulnerable as a mouse on sun-scorched land and Raven would swoop in with pointed talons and pierce his mind.

The train's silver head stretched toward her, its lights shining like yellow eyes. There was no time to turn back and try to find him. She heard the click-clack of the wheels, like a metal heart-beat, getting closer and louder. There was no time to persuade him to come with her. The body of the train could be seen now, long and slim as a snake. In a few moments, she would be gone.

Could it really be she'd never see Danny's face again? That he would never meet his child? That their son would never know his father? Betony gripped the ticket in her hand, a piece of paper only, but her baby's life depended on it. The train was hissing to a halt and its doors were opening. Only a few more steps and she'd be on board, carried off to safety. She must move. She must hurry. But her legs were rebelling, remaining planted in their spot. Passengers were climbing the steps, taking their seats, opening their bags.

Betony looked down at the ticket she was holding. Fairwood. Suddenly, it no longer sounded fair, only frighteningly far. She would come back, she told herself, once the baby was safe. But Danny wouldn't even know her then. Raven would wash his memory clean and any crumb of thought he had for her would be wiped away, forgotten forever. It would be like she had never existed. Like they had never met. And he would meet another girl. And he would have another son. She must go. For the baby, she must go.

Betony leapt toward the train door, reaching out her arm to open it, but, in that stride, there was a burst within her and a warmth came seeping down her legs. She didn't mean to stop. She just had to. Just for a second, for the shock. But then a whistle sliced the air and a pain pierced her belly. The train shuddered to life and slithered on its way, slowly at first, sliding down those metal tracks, then picking up speed and leaving her far behind.

43

POPPY

Let him go and I am yours. This was Poppy's thought as Betony came stumbling toward her, clutching the gash in her hip.

"They have him!" Betony was calling. "They've taken my boy."

I'll be your queen. I'll give you every bit of me. Just let him go. This was what she would say to the witches. She only prayed it would be enough. Betony was recounting Leo's capture, but Poppy could hardly bear to listen. She'd been so hurt to wake and discover him gone that she had run straight to Ember and found her comfort there. She should have gone after him. She should have protected him.

Let him go and I am yours.

"It's you they want," Betony accused, the blood spreading through her clothes.

"Then they can have me," Poppy promised.

She knew where they'd be, back on that battleground beside the cliffs. Last time she faced them, she had fought. This time she would surrender.

They were waiting for her in their hundreds, numerous clans, all distinctive in appearance. There were more than she remembered, but perhaps that was because she was alone, without her mother or her aunt or her clan. Some of them were women, just like her, whom no one would ever guess to be witches. Others seemed more animal or plant than human. Her eyes scanned their legions for some sight of him.

"Where is he?" she demanded.

"Show her," announced a witch all in white like winter—dress, hair, skin—with a voice as cold as frost that chilled the air with every word she spoke.

On her command, the crowds parted and there was Leo tied to a stake, thorny branches around his feet that magically grew and grew until he was at the top of a tower of firewood. Leo was squirming, trying to call to her, straining to break free, but his limbs and mouth were bound tight by roots that pulsed and tensed against him.

Poppy forced herself to look away, then made her muscles still like stone. "You have my attention," she told the clans. "Release him and we can talk."

"He is an abomination," cried a voice from the crowd.

"He must die!" screeched another.

Poppy refused to let her eyelids blink. "So you would burn him?" she challenged. "Like a witch?"

"Like his kind did to ours!" exclaimed the winter witch, who stepped toward her.

Poppy stared into the witch's eyes. Even her irises were white, the pupil a bolt of black within, but Poppy held the witch's gaze. "If you kill him," she uttered, "I will never be your queen. I will go and I will never return. This, I swear to you."

The witch threw back her head and laughed, her breath so cold that tiny snowflakes floated from it. "We have another Hawkweed to take your place. What do we need with you?" replied the witch.

"You had the ghost of my aunt Raven and now she is gone."

Murmurs of consternation rushed and then roared through the crowd like an avalanche.

"You lie," accused the winter witch.

"You know I speak the truth. Now set him free." She turned to the army before her. "Let him go and I am yours," she told them, just as she had planned.

Leo's eyes widened and he twisted against the ropes that only tightened around him.

"He has witch blood," called a voice.

"He must die. He should never have been born," cried another.

"He is no threat to you," Poppy reasoned. "He'll do you no harm. There must be others like him. There must be. And they have not hurt you."

"We are sisters. There are no brothers amongst us. The sisterhood must be protected."

"Kill him! Kill him!" came the chorus.

Poppy raised her hand to stop their chanting, waiting until all were silent. "So be it," she stated and she walked toward the waiting bonfire.

"You cannot save him," warned the winter witch.

Poppy grabbed a branch high in the heap and pulled. It wouldn't budge. The magic held it firm. Keeping her grip, she hoisted herself upward, climbing, from wood to wood, until she reached Leo's side. There, she pulled at the root that gagged him and it slipped down to his neck.

"Poppy," he gasped, and she threw her arms around him. She felt tears on her face but couldn't tell if they were his or her own.

She looked out on the throng of witches. "Let him go," she offered, "and I will be your queen. Just like it is written on the stone. Just like the prophecy has always told."

"No!" Leo cried, but she kissed his lips to hush him.

"It's the only way," she whispered in his ear. "Trust me?" she asked, and he nodded. Then she turned back to the crowd and addressed them once more. "If he is to die, I die with him."

Leo squeezed her hand, but there was no other movement. Not from a single witch from a single clan, not from a bird in the sky or a beetle on the land. Poppy waited and waited for them to succumb, but no one said a word. Finally, she closed her eyes and said the spell. The words were spoken slowly, but the flames came fast, their warmth rising far sooner than she would have predicted.

Leo gripped her hand so tightly, she thought her bones might break, but the pain was somehow comforting as the smoke began to sting her eyes and the temperature rose, degree by degree, hotter and hotter. Leo writhed and twisted at the ties that bound them, trying to lift his feet from the heat that was eating at the wood below. She could hear his heart beating fast, his gasps and groans, as he struggled to free himself. But then the crackle of the flames grew louder until it became a roar.

Poppy felt the panic fire inside her brain. She had miscalculated. They would burn to death on this bonfire that she had climbed, that she had lit. They were going to die.

Then it came. The reprieve. A resounding "No!" from a multitude of voices blasted like a hose of water across the air.

The winter witch lifted her hand and within seconds the branches had iced over and the flames were extinguished with a sizzle.

"He may live," spoke the witch. "But you will rule as queen, without him."

Poppy bowed her head in acquiescence. "I will."

"Poppy," came Leo's voice, but they were falling to the ground as the firewood gave way beneath them. They landed in a scattered pile of charred sticks and he spoke again. "Poppy, you can't."

She could make out Leo's words. She could hear his urgency. But both sounded distant in her ears because her body had gone cold. She got to her feet and looked down in confusion. Her clothes had turned white and her hands icy. She closed her eyes and tried to summon some control, but the sensations were overpowering her. Now her bones felt dry like twigs and her skin looked rough and dark like wood. From bark, her body parched further and switched to scales. Then she aged, then grew, then shrank, her clothes and hair turning from black to red to purple until she had paid tribute to them all. She was their queen. She could feel it now. They were a part of her and she a part of them.

"What's happening?" Leo was shouting. "What are you doing to her?"

He was taking hold of her and trying to gather her in his arms as though his touch might stop the magic.

"Go," she tried to whisper to him.

"I won't. I won't ever go," he told her.

She tried to shake her head. "You have to."

Then she looked to the winter witch. "Take him. Please," she begged. "Take him to safety."

"No!" yelled Leo, and she could feel the magic stirring uncontrollably within him. "Let go of me." She couldn't look. "Poppy!" he shouted. "Don't do this." She couldn't listen. "You should have let me die." The words echoed in her mind until they faded.

When Poppy finally looked up, she was alone. There was no sign of the witches, no trace of Leo. The clearing seemed undisturbed. Even the sticks had gone and the grass stood tall and untrampled, swaying in the clifftop wind. There was no scent of magic on the breeze, only something unfamiliar. A stranger.

Then she heard it. A click. The click of a camera. Poppy turned her head and looked toward the trees. It was only a flash of clothing, there one second, gone the next. But immediately Poppy knew who had trespassed there and her heart, already low, sank further for what she must do next.

44

EMBER

His fingers were dancing feverishly across the keyboard, the tiny black letters reeling in long rows across the screen. He had come back and sat straight down at the table, without a hello, without taking off his coat.

"Nick," she'd asked. "What happened?" He hadn't seemed to hear her, hunched as he was over his laptop, ears shut, eyes focused, fingertips tapping. She had tried another simpler question. "Where have you been?" But again, no answer.

That was half an hour ago and still he hadn't looked up or acknowledged her presence, just kept on typing at the same frenetic pace. Then, suddenly, without any intimation that he was nearing the end, he stopped and looked at her.

"It's absolutely insane." His eyes were red, the veins burst and running like rivulets within them.

"What is?"

"You were right. You were freaking right." He thumped the table with his fist.

Ember felt her insides shake and shudder. "Right about what?" she questioned, fearing she knew his answer.

"They're witches. My boss is never going to believe it when he reads this!" He gave a sharp, high laugh that made Ember wince. "Proper, fairytale, nasty, magic witches. Only weirder. No hats. No brooms. But they were witches all right. And your friend, that Poppy girl, she's like right in the middle of them, doing all kinds of crazy crap."

Ember was half listening, half just trying to breathe. Her chest was working hard, but the air wasn't coming in, wasn't reaching her lungs. She took more breaths, then tried to slow them but found she was still wheezing.

"What have you done?" she gasped.

"Are you all right?" he asked, sounding more confounded than caring.

Ember sucked down a lungful of air and was rewarded with a voice that sounded more like her own.

"Have you sent it?" she demanded. He looked at her petulantly. "Have you sent it?" she repeated, louder.

He shut his laptop, then laid his hands upon it as though to guard it from her. "I've got to read it over first, polish it up. This'll make the nationals, I know it. It's the photo—they'll have to believe it."

Suddenly, Ember hated him—his soft, pale hair and baby blue eyes disguising the dark dregs within him. "I'm nothing like you," she said, the thought popping into her mind like a cork from a bottle.

"Calm down," he told her, lifting his laptop to his chest.

She wanted to slap the self-satisfaction from his face and tear the stolen words from his hands. "Is that why you brought me back here? For this? So you could spy on people and profit from them?"

"I'm a journalist, Ember. And they're not people."

"They are more than us, not less."

"The world can be the judge of that—when they hear the truth."

"Truth—from you?" she scoffed. "A good-for-nothing liar. The clan will come after you and I swear you'll wish you'd never met me."

"Yeah, well that box is ticked already." He grabbed his bag, then looked at her. For the first time, Ember saw a hint of hurt in his eyes. "I don't know why you're taking their side. You said they'd forgotten all about you, that they didn't care a whit about you. You're so sure they'll come after me? I'd worry about yourself if I were you." And then he left, just as he'd entered, without a goodbye, or even a glance in her direction.

It was only when Nick's footsteps had disappeared that Ember thought about what he'd said. So many of his words were soft and silky with deceit, but this was edged with truth. She had brought him here. She had broken the coven's trust, spilled their secret. They would hunt down Nick . . . but she would be their prey, too.

Ember jumped to her feet and ran. Outside, the car was reversing out of its parking space and turning. She slammed her hands on the hood and Nick slammed his foot on the brake. She dashed to the window and, just to aggravate her, he made her wait before he opened it.

"Yeah?" he asked smugly.

She felt like kicking a dent in the car's shiny side and watching his expression change to one of horror. Instead she said what was needed. "Take me with you," then added for politeness, "please."

The locks clicked and he leaned over and opened the door. "Get in."

It was dusk. They had left the town behind and were on the road home. She was almost feeling safe when Nick swore and swerved. As the car spun, she caught a glimpse of a figure in the headlights. Flung forward, as the car skidded off the road, her neck whipped back and her head landed with a thud on the headrest. Then the car was still and Nick was shouting, "Did you see her? She came out of nowhere!"

Not nowhere, Ember thought, as she waited for Poppy to reach them.

"Rob's going to kill me," he yelled, undoing his seatbelt and jumping out of the car to inspect the damage.

Not Rob, she wanted to say. Then it occurred to her to tell Nick to stay inside, to lock the doors, but she felt too tired to speak when any effort now was futile. The music kept playing on the radio, through the suddenness and the shock, a sweet, soothing song meant for more sentimental moments.

The car door opened.

"I'm sorry," Ember said, before she even looked up.

When she did, she saw that Poppy's face looked sad. It was worse than anger. It was as though Poppy was already grieving.

"You better get out," Poppy told her.

Ember put up no objection. She followed Poppy to where Nick sat against the tire. Next to him were his laptop, camera, and phone.

"It's my fault. I should never have told him about my past. I was angry and I'd drunk wine. I didn't know what I was saying. I'm so sorry." Ember started to cry and felt pathetic for it. Nick, meanwhile, didn't speak or move at all.

"He can't," explained Poppy, though Ember hadn't asked. "I didn't want to have to chase him."

"Please," she pleaded.

"Is it you or him you're asking for?"

Ember looked at Nick, so helpless and vulnerable, the cock-sure expression on his face now replaced with one of naked fear.

"For both of us."

"You told another chaff about the coven."

"I know," Ember whispered. "But you're the queen. You can do anything." Poppy closed her eyes and her face slipped further into sorrow. "Poppy!" Ember sobbed.

"There are consequences. I have others to protect. So many others."

Ember thought of the clan and all the sisters there, and all the other clans, with women young and old, and their way of life that they'd tried so hard and for so long to protect. Then she thought of what might happen if the newspaper printed Nick's article, if people saw that photo. There would be no witches living peace-fully in the woods. Instead, there would be war. She should be the casualty, not them, not others.

"I understand," she said, and her head dropped, accepting the blow that was to come.

She heard Poppy chant the words—words that she herself had been taught as a child along with all the other spells the witches had to learn, repeating them over and over, only in her case never being able to put them into practice. And now they were being said to her . . .

> *Memories vanish, memories fade*
> *Like the mist across the glade*
> *Memories weaken, memories die*
> *Leave the body like a sigh*
> *Forget, forget the days that passed*
> *No memories keep, no memories last*

As Poppy continued, Ember readied herself for the outcome, for her thoughts to evaporate and her brain to empty. She cast her thoughts back to her earliest recollections—the smell of Charlock's bread, the sound of bees around the hive, the sight of her first shooting star, the coolness of the river water on her skin, the softness of a rabbit's fur, the pain of a wasp's sting, Poppy's eyes, Leo's touch, Charlock's warmth, Melanie's tears. Brighter and faster, these remembrances came, from long ago and only yesterday. None were evaporating and her mind felt fuller, not emptier.

> *Forget, forget, this time, this spell*
> *And when you rise and go, live well.*

Tentatively, Ember opened her eyes and squinted at Poppy. She was still there by her side.

"It had to be done," Poppy said sadly. "For the clan." Ember glanced at Nick. His head had flopped onto his chest. She gasped and Poppy put a hand on her shoulder. "He's sleeping. When he wakes he will remember nothing, not of you or me or anything of these last months."

Ember felt a pang of regret that she had not said goodbye. For a short while, he'd stood at the center of her world and now he was on the periphery, about to disappear forever.

Poppy handed her a small booklet.

"What is it?" Ember asked.

"It's my passport. I packed it when I left my dad's last winter. Like I needed it." She gave a half smile. "Anyway, it's your passport now."

Ember opened it and looked at the name printed there. "Poppy Hooper," she whispered. "It's got my picture. You did this?"

Poppy shrugged and handed her another slip of paper. "Your boarding pass." Ember looked at her blankly. "For the plane."

"A plane?" She thought of the silver ships she'd seen flying high above, leaving tracks of cloud in their wake, streaking the sky behind them.

"You can't stay here, Ember. Not after this."

"You're sending me away?" she whispered, unable to contemplate all that it meant.

"You will remember us. And that's what matters most, isn't it?" Ember looked at Nick, so limp and lifeless like a withered tree, as though his memories were the sap that kept him nourished and without them he couldn't stand tall. She imagined herself in such a sorry state and took the paper from Poppy.

Banished but still strong, she thought. *Still me.*

45

LEO

The witch's hand was cold on his shoulder, making his muscles shiver and his teeth chatter, as though it were deepest winter and not the middle of spring. He tried to summon the fire that had come to him so readily before, but there was not even a spark to warm himself by. They were in a wooden boat, gliding down the river, leaving patches of ice bobbing behind them as they passed. A second, older witch stood at the front holding a long pole she used to steer. He wasn't sure why the younger witch kept her hand on him. He suspected her touch froze not just his body but any magic he might have within it. He tried to think of Poppy but could only picture her returning to that coven in the forest, the trees like guards, the boulders like a fortress, shutting her in for a lifetime, shutting him out. *A queen,* he told himself. He'd only really comprehended what that meant today when he'd seen her embody all the different clans. It was only then that he knew he'd truly lost her.

He hated the forest now that it had her. He hated the witches, too. No wonder his mother had broken free to seek another, better life. It was as though he was a disease they must rid themselves of before they became infected. Now Poppy would stand at the head of them. She would learn to live like them and think like them. For a wild moment, he wished he'd died on that bonfire rather than have her despise him. Then he thought of his mother and immediately felt ashamed at his self-pity. He remembered the blood soaking through her clothes as she held on to him, her desperate cries as he was torn from her hands. And then the cries had stopped. Leo closed his eyes.

"Your mother is alive," said the young witch seated beside him. Leo glanced around in surprise. "The wound—it was not fatal." He looked at her gratefully, but she kept her eyes set ahead, her hand heavy on his shoulder. "I have never met one like you," she confessed.

Leo wasn't sure if he was supposed to answer. "You mean a boy?" he said.

"I mean a boy witch."

Without Poppy this felt meaningless. It was a fact, but not one he understood. He had been waiting for his mother to provide the answers to his questions, but, until the rest of her memory returned, she could not help him. He had tried asking Charlock, but she had refused.

"It is Betony's story to tell," she'd said.

It had been easy to be patient when Poppy was flying back to him. But now that she was gone, it felt like he had nothing. No past. No future.

The boat rounded a bend and immediately Leo got his bearings. They were approaching the meadow beyond the graveyard. He sat up eagerly in his seat, his eyes scouring the field for signs of his mother and Charlock.

"Wait," the young witch said, and they drifted a little farther before turning into the reeds and reaching the riverbank.

As she released her hand from his shoulder, Leo felt an energy rush through him. He got to his feet and the boat rocked beneath them.

"You owe the queen your life," she added, holding out her hand to help him step from boat to bank. It took Leo a moment to work out that she was referring to Poppy. His Poppy.

"Not yours," she said, delving into his mind again. "Not anymore."

The cold of her hand burned straight to his heart, more painful than the flames from the bonfire. When she released him, he stepped quickly onto firm ground and examined his palm. Already a blister had formed there. And then he heard his mother's calls and he looked up to see the elation on her face. When he glanced back, the boat was already gone, the frosted water lilies the only evidence of its departure, sparkling like rhinestones on a roll of river blue.

"You have to go to her and stop her. You can't let her do this. She's giving up her life for me." He never talked this much, but the words were rushing out of him and he could not slow them. He had run from the boat to tell them about Poppy, to urge them to help. It had never occurred to him that they might not be willing. "Someone's got to save her," he begged. He felt like falling to his knees before Charlock and tugging on the hem of her skirt.

Charlock's hands were clasped, her face shut just as tightly. "Poppy is the queen. She does not need saving," she replied, her mouth moving, but everything else remaining still.

"Charlock is right," Betony declared, with a frustrated sweep of her arm. Then her finger started pointing. "It is we that need to be rescued. We need to go. We need to get away from here. From her."

But to Leo, his mother's words were just noise, buzzing in his ear, and he brushed them aside and kept his focus on Charlock.

"It's what you wanted from the start, isn't it?" he accused. "What you planned for all those years? Poppy on the throne. Well, how does it feel? Are you happy now? To know what she has sacrificed?" He hadn't meant to shout, and already he regretted it. With every sentence, he could feel Charlock recoiling further from him until she turned away and he had to reach out and pull her back. She looked at his hand in such surprise that instantly he let it drop. Then she stepped close and spoke softly in his ear.

"If she gives up the throne, your life will be in danger. Tell me, is that what she'd want?"

"I don't care!" he told her. "Just get her out of there."

"She would never forgive me," Charlock uttered, and Leo knew it was true.

"That's all you care about, isn't it? Forgiveness. From your daughter, from my mother, your niece, your sister. From me! So you feel better. But what good does it do us?"

"I have been trying to make amends, to make good my wrongs," Charlock cried, her face creasing. "I have been trying all I can, but the more I do . . . " Her hands flew to her mouth and she couldn't finish. Leo had never seen her so overcome.

"Enough," said Betony, having listened too long, her patience at an end. "Leo—it is time to do your mother's bidding."

Leo dragged his eyes from Charlock to Betony and, for the first time since his return, he really saw her. Her hand was cradling her wounded side and the pain was twisting her, body and face, yet still she seemed so strong. The spirit in her eyes flickered far more brightly than in either his or Charlock's. He had been so wrapped up in saving Poppy that he hadn't appreciated her joy as she first spied him on the boat, as though he had been brought back from the dead and the winter witch was Charon returning him from Hades. Or her relief as she'd limped toward him, calling his name, touching his cheeks, his eyes, his hair, his arms, his chest—as though to check that he really was alive. And how she'd squeezed him so tightly that her wound had bled and Charlock had needed to redo the bandage.

He took her hand and kissed it. And then he told her, not asking this time, but demanding. "I need to know," he said. "I need to know what happened to my father."

His mother's eyes flicked to Charlock's before she answered him.

"I can tell you all I have remembered," she replied. "But Charlock must tell us both the end."

He looked at Charlock intently. "You have to give me that," he said.

Charlock didn't move, but Leo felt something in her cower. *She's scared,* he thought, and he braced himself for the story to come.

46

Young Charlock

Neither Charlock nor Raven had been inside a chaff house before. For once, Raven was as ignorant as she, not knowing for how long to shake the proffered hand, or where to sit, or whether they took milk or sugar in their tea. Inside this place of softness—so carpeted and cushioned—she and Raven seemed rough and hard. Charlock's boots had left a trail of dried mud along the hallway and she longed to hurry back there and sweep it up into her hand and throw it out the door. They perched, the two of them, like birds on the edge of the biggest chair she'd ever seen. It felt more like a bed and, in truth, was wide enough for her to lie along. Danny's father had told them to "make themselves comfortable" and they had sat, but Charlock could tell that Raven felt as uncomfortable as she.

This was not because of Mr. Marchetti's welcome. They had expected a door to be slammed in their face and Raven had been prepared to use her magic to extract the information needed. Instead, he had only eyed them with surprise before ushering them inside.

"You must be Betony's relatives," he had declared after taking in their appearance. "Are you her sisters?" Raven had nodded. "You better come in," he continued. "We have a great deal to discuss."

Raven had glanced at Charlock with raised eyebrows, amazed at their good fortune.

"I'm afraid my wife is out," Mr. Marchetti said as they stepped inside this home of shining floors and sumptuous fabric. "Though perhaps that's for the best. It's been a very trying time for her. Danny even refused to come home for Christmas."

The tea was sweet and soothing to Charlock's nerves. Raven didn't touch hers, just left it on the tiny glass table beside her.

"You know about the baby, I presume?" Mr. Marchetti was saying, and Raven was nodding. "A terrible mistake for such young people, I'm sure you'll agree."

Charlock nearly choked at that and Raven put a threatening hand on her thigh. However, she could tell that her sister was as surprised as she at such misgivings. They had both presumed the chaffs would feel differently about the baby, and Charlock wondered why Danny's father was so displeased.

"It was a terrible shock, to be true," Raven murmured.

"I don't know how they think they're going to raise it. He's a student, for God's sake," Mr. Marchetti lamented. "My wife and I are prepared to help, of course, as I'm sure are your family."

He stared first at Raven, then at Charlock, daring them to contradict him.

"We want Betony to come home," Charlock blurted, buckling under the weight of expectation.

Raven stiffened beside her, but Mr. Marchetti was leaning forward, eyes focused. "Well, that is a relief. Danny is a very bright boy. He's got a great future ahead of him."

After that, it became all business. Mr. Marchetti wrote the address on a piece of paper, then showed them on a map, and even ordered them a taxi, which he paid for.

"I insist," he told them. "The sooner it's done, the better. Danny needs to get on with his life. Be young. Be a student. He's a good boy, our Danny. Too good."

Charlock had to look away. She felt like gagging, the guilt like rotten meat festering in her gut. She climbed inside the car and it trembled and rumbled beneath her, making her stomach churn even more. Mr. Marchetti started thanking them and Charlock tried to shut her ears. The truth was heaving inside of her, rising up her throat and threatening to spew from her mouth. *Can't you see?* frothed the words. *We mean to cause your family harm. Don't trust us. Don't thank us.* Raven clasped Charlock's hand, digging in her nails in warning, and Charlock bit her lip to stop the thoughts escaping.

Only when the car set off and Mr. Marchetti disappeared from view did Charlock's sickness settle. Speeding through new stretches of wintry hill and vale, so like home, and yet so different in detail, Charlock thought of the kestrel passing over this same land. He had a full day's start on them, but he had no address like they did. She could only hope with every essence of her being that the bird had found his mark and that Betony had read her message and was gone.

"What are you thinking so hard about, sister?" came Raven's voice.

"Nothing," Charlock replied too quickly.

She tried to relax her jaw and shoulders, realizing they were set tight.

"This is for the clan," whispered Raven.

And Charlock nodded and tried to sound convincing as she echoed her agreement. "For the clan."

It was night when they arrived. The taxi dropped them outside the door of a large, red-brick building and Raven and Charlock loitered there for a few minutes, waiting for the door to be opened by one of the residents. It didn't take long. A girl with a stripe of pink in her hair and earrings up both ears held the door open for them. She even smiled as she passed. *It's too easy,* Charlock thought. *It's as though this were meant to be.* It felt comforting—the idea that some hidden forces in the world were approving of her actions, conspiring with her to alleviate any obstacles. As she climbed the stairs and walked the narrow, bright-lit corridor, Charlock tried to picture her friend treading these same steps, taking this same route. Soon they came to a door with the number seventeen marked on it. It was ajar and a sense of commotion was palpable even before they nudged it wide and saw the mess that lay within. Inside, drawers and cupboards were half open like they were intoxicated and couldn't straighten, the clothes and contents belching from them.

"She's gone," said Raven, handing Charlock a ring that lay alone on the center of the bed.

It had a large amber stone and Charlock felt Betony's connection to it as soon as she touched it. Betony had got her warning.

And she had acted on it. The relief relaxed the muscles in Charlock's face so that she could meet her sister's eye without betraying her true feelings. More than ever, she had to keep calm and choose her words carefully.

"I sense they had a quarrel—Betony and the boy. Perhaps she is coming home to us?" she suggested.

Raven's face twisted with her thoughts. "A quarrel, yes. But she is running from us, not to us. She cannot be far, though."

Raven turned to the door and Charlock felt the panic prickle at her skin.

"The boy," she said quickly, to give Betony more time. "Since we're here, shouldn't we deal with him first?"

Raven's lip curled in irritation. "Let's be quick about it then."

It didn't take long to find him—a few questions and a short walk to the college bar. Raven sent Charlock in to fetch him.

"He's met you. He'll trust you," she said. A rancid taste oozed from Charlock's throat onto her tongue. "Go on," Raven commanded with a shove.

Charlock squeezed and slid between the bodies to reach him. She never thought so many could fit into a single space. Danny, of course, was on the far side of the room, giving her time to dread their meeting even more. He spotted her before she reached him and immediately pushed his way toward her. The crowds parted, such was the force of his approach. When he neared her, he reached out long arms and grabbed her.

"Where is she?" he said. "Is she okay?"

His pupils were large in his eyes and his breath smelled of whatever alcohol he'd been drinking.

Charlock swallowed. "She is out back. Waiting for you."

His eyes lit up and he didn't hesitate. Charlock closed her eyes, unable to watch him go. After a few moments, she followed him outside.

He had Raven up against the wall, one large hand around her throat. Charlock's feet froze and she blinked in disbelief.

"What have you done with her?" he was shouting.

Raven didn't move, or speak. *Use your magic,* Charlock willed. She couldn't understand why Raven wasn't fighting back. It would be so easy for her. And then it struck Charlock. Her sister was actually scared. It wasn't the force or the attack, it was him—a male—touching her.

"If you've hurt her," Danny was threatening, "I'll kill you. I swear it. Where is she?"

Raven's eyes were staring at her, desperate, pleading. Charlock tried to grab Danny's arm, but he pushed her off easily.

"Let her go," she begged.

"I know what you are," he said, his voice raw and ragged. "She said you'd hurt us. That you'd kill our baby. And I won't let you. I won't."

His hand was tightening around Raven's throat. Charlock looked around her wildly, not knowing what to do. Spells flew into her head, but all jumbled and none of use. Then she saw the bottle lying there, as if waiting to come to her aid. Her body seemed to move without her brain's instruction. Her fingers clasped the glass. Her arm swung up. Then down. The bottle broke on impact and the pieces flew in all directions. Danny stilled and then his arms let go and his eyes glazed.

Later, Charlock would wonder why she had come to her sister's rescue. She would wish that she had turned away and let Danny carry out his threat. But in the midst of it that thought simply hadn't occurred to her. Not even for a second. Before she could comprehend it, Raven's mouth was moving as the magic surged within her and her arm was rising and her vengeance was wrought as the power shot from her hand. Then Danny was falling, his head knocking on the ground with a sickening thud. And all was completely quiet.

47

Young Betony

There were people around her, touching her, sitting her down, talking at her, talking at one another.

"Is anyone a doctor?" they were saying.

"Just breathe."

"Call an ambulance!" At that, Betony responded, pulling herself away from their hands, mumbling, "No, no, no."

She lurched forward a few paces, then held onto the wall as the pain rolled back through her. Once it had subsided, she waddled out onto the pavement, looking around, trying to figure out where to go, what to do. She remembered the cats in the camp, taking themselves off somewhere safe and secluded to give birth alone. She could do that. She just needed a quiet place to crouch down and let the baby come.

She had only made it a few hundred yards when the colors caught her eye. In a small shop window hung crystals and gems that shone and sparkled in the light. The blues of lapis lazuli, peridot, and turquoise; the greens of malachite and jade; the reds of coral and garnet and jasper—a luminous rainbow drawing her forward, through the door, to the sweet spice smell of incense within. Sinking to her knees, she clutched a wooden chest covered with scented candles as another wave of pain hit and crashed over her. She closed her eyes and let it sweep her away until she floated back to shore. When she opened them, a birdlike lady with glasses and a spiky red crest of hair was standing over her.

"Hold this," she said, and into Betony's palm she put a stone, cool and pink and soothing. "Rose quartz," she explained. "Unconditional love for your baby."

Betony nodded. "Can I stay here?" she asked. "I can't . . . I can't go back out there."

The lady's eyes flicked to the window and then back again. Then she hurried to the door and hung the closed sign upon it and shut the blinds. Bending down toward Betony, she put a hand on her back. "Would you like me to call someone?" she asked. Betony shook her head. "The father?" Betony shook her head again. "Well, it's going to be me and you then," she said. "How far apart are the contractions?" Betony looked confused. "The pains?" she added.

"I don't know," Betony admitted.

"That's okay. We can time them."

She took off her watch and held it in her hand, checking the minutes as she fetched towels and water.

"Why are you helping me?" Betony wondered. "I mean . . . you're very kind, but you don't even know me."

"I saw it in the cards," the lady admitted. "The baby."

"The cards?"

"You might be skeptical, but I have lots of people wanting readings," she said kindly.

"I'm not skeptical. I'm just grateful," Betony told her. "You're saving our lives and I don't know how to thank you. I don't even know your name."

"I'm Jocelyn," the lady told her with a smile.

And then another swell of pain rose within Betony and she cried out. In her hand, she felt the stone turn from cool to warm. When she looked, it was glowing and her fear waned in its brightness and the cramps ebbed away, so all that was left was her and her baby and his arrival into the world.

Late that night, he was born. He lay along her chest, his dark hair slick across his tiny head, his black eyes peering at her sleepily. *My boy,* thought Betony, as she kissed his wrinkled head. *My perfect, beautiful boy.* Jocelyn cut the cord, but Betony didn't notice. He was a part of her, attached forevermore.

Through night and day, he slept and slept, but she could not. Despite her need for rest, she could not let her eyelids drop and mask the sight of him. With his little fingers curled around just one of hers, gripping her with such surprising strength, she let her eyes absorb every bit of him. Jocelyn went out and came back with supplies.

"He must look like his dad," she commented as she bent over to admire him.

Betony blinked and looked afresh. It was so cloudlessly clear, she wondered how she could not have seen it before. It was Danny's familiar face, only in miniature, that lay in the crook of her arm. A pang ploughed through her, churning up old pains, leaving them exposed. The tears rained down and she lifted the baby up to kiss him—one from his mother, one from his father, over and over, until she had to wipe the drying salt from the softness of his skin. Still, the kisses didn't feel enough. Danny should be here with them, just as they had planned. He was but walking distance away. Half an hour only and they could be together. But the journey was a perilous one. Dare she go to him when Raven might be watching for her? Would Danny even know her if she tried? Betony looked down at her child, the same dark hair and lashes as his father, the same wide mouth and dimpled chin, the same long fingers. Suddenly her decision seemed a simple one.

Jocelyn needed no persuading. She was happy to help find Danny and discover what he still remembered. Promising to take great care, she set off in search of him. While she was gone, Betony packed up her belongings, filling a second bag for the baby. She took the ticket for the train and put it in her pocket. Perhaps Fairwood might become home after all. As she waited, she paced with the baby in her arms. Up and down. Back and forth. Every step was a second closer to finding out if Danny would still know her.

When Jocelyn came through the door, Betony felt her worst fears confirmed. Her friend's face was white and drawn, her hands were twisting around each other in agitation. She tried to speak and couldn't and then she tried again. Betony got to her feet and was about to shake her when Jocelyn finally spoke.

"Please, you must sit."

"I don't need to sit. I know what has happened. He didn't remember us, did he? What did he say? Perhaps if I go to him . . . if I explain . . . if I show him his son? . . .

"You can't," Jocelyn whispered.

"He won't believe me at first but maybe the others, his friends . . . "

"You can't," Jocelyn cried.

Betony moved to the door, but Jocelyn hurried after her and took her hand and led her to the chair, and Betony let herself be moved, like a sheep into a pen, unable to think for herself any longer.

"Danny is dead," she heard, but the words were warped, as though she was submerged underwater. "Did you hear me?" came Jocelyn's voice from far away. "He's gone. I'm so sorry. He was killed last night. At . . . at the same time as your son was born."

With a surge, Betony surfaced and her ears popped and she gasped for air. And then she howled and Jocelyn was taking the baby from her and she was hitting the walls and throwing open the door and running into the street. She knocked into people, bikes, cars. She tripped and fell. But none of it hurt because her grief was a monster so immense that it consumed all other feeling—pain, fear, responsibility, self-preservation—all gobbled up to fuel the anguish of her loss. She knew neither her route nor her destination. She couldn't think clearly enough for that. She just let her legs carry her, let the magic rush from brain to heart to feet. With every step and at every turn, her eyes scoured her surroundings. She could hear her kestrel screeching to her from on high, a desperate, keening call, but she couldn't look up. She was too busy searching.

She found them at the zoo. They had tracked her that far. They both looked shocked to see her there, striding toward them, shouting out their names. If Raven's surprise was one of pleasure,

Charlock's was of utter horror. Her hand flew to her mouth and her head was shaking from side to side and her body was rocking with distress.

"Murderers!" Betony screamed, her finger stabbing the air as it pointed. "Murderers!"

The monkeys were climbing onto the cage of their enclosure, rattling the bars. On the other side of them, the zebras were gathered by the fence, pawing at the ground and baring their teeth. Raven and Charlock were glancing anxiously from the animals to the people, who were stopping and staring.

"They killed my love," Betony announced to the small crowd. "They killed him."

Not one of them moved; only Raven, walking toward her with a look of fake concern upon her face.

"Don't come any closer," cautioned Betony, suddenly regretting her haste and wishing she'd thought to bring a knife. For Raven ignored her warning and continued forward and then she even dared to put an arm around her. "Don't touch me. Don't you lay a hand on me!" Betony shouted, lashing out with her arms, hitting and pushing Raven away. But it was too late. She could feel the spell on her, crawling over her like bugs, burrowing under her skin, sucking at her blood.

"You promised," called Charlock, breaking into a run, taking hold of Raven's arm, trying to drag her back. "You promised me."

Raven looked to the observers who were gawping at them, their eyes and mouths wide with astonishment.

"Please, give us space. She is not well," Raven asked.

Betony knew when she heard the tone of Raven's voice that they would obey. It wasn't even magic, just the power born of confidence and control.

"No!" Betony cried out to the crowd. They were her shield—Raven couldn't hurt her in front of them. If they went, she'd be defenseless. "Don't go," she begged. "Call the police. Please . . . one of you . . . somebody . . . "

But her voice was fading, despite her attempts to keep it strong. And the people were turning their heads in embarrassment and hurrying away. Raven put a hand on Betony's shoulder and Betony felt herself sink beneath its weight, unable to resist, until her knees were on the path. The gale of anger that had swept her here was subsiding now and all that was left was fear. She heard her kestrel cry and looked up to see him soaring downward, talons outstretched, ready to attack. Betony's eyes brightened with hope, but Raven must have spied him for she turned and raised her hand, just in time, and suddenly the bird seemed caught by an invisible force that made him spin and tumble past his target until he crashed into the ground.

"No!" screamed Betony, trying to lift herself up but unable to move.

Charlock started in the kestrel's direction, but Raven would not allow it.

"Leave it," she commanded, and Charlock stopped, her frightened eyes sending messages of apology to Betony. Raven gave a sigh of satisfaction. "That's better," she declared. "Now, Sister Betony. We've cleaned up one mess on your behalf. Where is the other?" Betony felt her mouth open to reply, but she clenched her jaw and ground her teeth together. "The baby, Betony. Where is he?" Betony shook her head, refusing to let her lips part company. Raven bent to Betony's ear. "She helped me kill him, you know. Sweet, simple Charlock, your dearest friend. It was she who struck the first blow."

Betony's eyes shot to Charlock and instantly she knew it was true. She gave a deep, guttural groan, but still she would not speak.

"I didn't mean to," Charlock cried. "Betony, I swear to you."

Betony lowered her eyes to the ground and focused there—the dirt, the ant, the bottle top, the elastic band. She breathed long and hard through her nostrils.

"Where is he, Betony?" Raven commanded.

The spell was wriggling through Betony's veins like worms, slithering through her brain, making her want to scratch at her head, to say anything to stop the torturous itch.

Her mouth opened. She couldn't stop it. She had to speak.

"I'd rather die!" she spat.

Raven's hand sprang away as if the truth had burned her.

"Leave the baby," Charlock begged her sister. "It does not matter. He will never know. No one will ever know." Then she crouched down next to Betony and took her hands. "Bet, come with us now. Let us put this all behind us. Let us take you home."

Betony raised her eyes to Charlock's and looked deep into them. Wet with tears and shining amber gold; the color was startling even after all these years, the color of the ring that Danny had given her when he promised they'd always be together.

"I'll never forgive you," Betony whispered, and she watched how Charlock flinched, her fingers freezing before falling away. "Never," she repeated, and Charlock closed those jeweled eyes of hers and Betony reveled in her pain.

"My dimwit of a sister made me promise not to harm you," hissed Raven. "And I might have kept my word if you had given up your brat. But you never did know how to be one of us. You were always on the outside of the circle."

"Raven," Charlock sobbed. "You can't."

"Do it." Betony tilted her chin upward in defiance. "I'll be happy to forget I ever knew a single one of you."

It was a lie. She knew it was. For into her mind came the image of her baby boy—his dark hair and lashes, his wide mouth and dimpled chin, his soft skin, his sweet smell, his strong grip, his fierce cry, his . . . his . . . his . . .

The monkeys shrieked. The cats roared. The elephants trumpeted. The apes beat their chests. But Betony no longer knew the reason why.

48

BETONY

Forgetting was a painless process. A thin and airy vanishing, like twilight. But remembering—that was the end of a long eclipse. The brightness of it was blinding, blurring, baffling. Baffling that she could have been so young and stupid, that she could have ever left her two boys alone, especially him, her newborn baby. She wanted to take her seventeen-year-old self and shake some sense into her. If only, all those years ago, she had stopped for a second to think, to let her passion pass, to let reason rule. This benefit of hindsight made her ache so hard with regret that she wasn't sure for how long she could bear it. Her life was now laid out behind her like a peacock's tail and she could see the pattern in the colors there. In among the love and the danger, there had been choices. And she had chosen badly.

"I have to think," she told Leo and Charlock after her story had ended. She had taken over the telling of it as the memories came to her, one by one, linked like beads on a bracelet that had long ago been broken and had scattered, lost under chairs and beds and beneath floorboards, gathering dust, but were now polished and rejoined.

Charlock hadn't interrupted. She hadn't tried to defend her actions. Only at the end, she added that she had found the train ticket falling from Betony's pocket and had placed it in her friend's hand before Raven had ordered that they leave.

"I wasn't sure you would go there, but I hoped that's where I'd find you one day. You see, I struck a deal with Raven. That she would never seek out your son if I never sought you. We told the coven you had both perished that day. The lie had to be preserved." Charlock lowered her eyes in shame. "I told myself that you had forgotten me and I should try and do the same. But I couldn't. Not even the name of the place you'd picked to take your baby. Fairwood." Charlock looked up and her eyes sparkled with tears. "I cannot undo the damage done, Bet. But I am so sorry for it."

Leo and Charlock both were crying. But not she. They were holding hands, but she was walking away.

"Please," she said as they called her back. "I need to be alone. Just for a while," she added softly to her son, who was looking so forlorn.

She went back to the forest where her life had begun, back to the trees that were her elders and that would outlive them all. And there she sat and remembered it all again and tried to make some sense of what had happened. When anger rose, she dampened it down. When misery moved in, she sent it packing. This time she would make a plan. She would think of the future and act to secure it. She would not let history repeat itself. Not for her. And not for her son.

Poppy was happy to see her. She took her hands and then pulled her close, and Betony found herself hugging this girl that she so feared.

"How is he?" Poppy whispered and Betony could hear the yearning in her voice.

Putting a hand to her heart as if to shield it, Betony answered truthfully. "Missing you."

Poppy's eyes darted up and over Betony's shoulder. "He isn't here, is he? He mustn't come."

"He doesn't even know that I am here."

"I can't see him," Poppy told her in a quiet voice. "It's the only way to keep him safe."

She meant well, but Betony was all too used to that. It would take far more to keep her son from meeting his father's fate.

"Can I talk with you? Away from this place."

Poppy nodded and followed her out into the woods.

"Does he understand?" she asked tremulously. "Why I had to send him away?"

"He doesn't want to understand, but he knows why."

Poppy suddenly stopped and Betony turned back to look at her. "I love him," the girl said, "but I never got to tell him properly."

Betony felt her heart contract as she resisted the tugs on its strings. She continued walking, distancing herself in body and mind.

"He loves you too," she admitted, for the girl deserved a bit of happiness given what was to come. "He would do anything for you. Anything," she added, if only to remind herself how fraught with danger this love was.

"I know." Poppy, caught up with her. "And I for him."

Their eyes met and Betony believed her. *Best intentions,* she thought. She knew how perilous they could be. Holding out her hand, she pulled Poppy up the small but steep slope that faced them. Above, the ground was awash with bluebells and their color seemed to dazzle the girl, for she seemed fixed to the spot.

"More wonderful than any magic," commented Betony.

Poppy took a couple of steps, her hand trailing over the bright petals.

"I remember this," she murmured dreamily. "I've seen it in my mind." Then she turned slowly and peered at Betony, still dazed as if in some kind of trance. "You're going to kill me, aren't you?"

Betony's mouth dropped and all her muscles slackened as the energy sped to her mind, thoughts racing this way and that, deciding what to say . . . judging what to do.

"Why?" Poppy asked. "I have left him. I will not let them hurt him."

"I know," said Betony sadly.

"Then why?"

"Because he will never rest until you are together. He will never stop fighting for you and he will die because of it."

Poppy tilted her head to the tops of the trees. "So I die instead. What then?" When she looked back at Betony, her face was no longer dreamy but wide awake and fully animated. "What do you think he'll say to you?" she challenged. "How do you think he'll feel?"

"He will be safe!" cried Betony, the fervor that she'd fastened down flying from her.

"And that is all. That's all he would be," Poppy remonstrated. Betony shook her head. She couldn't falter now. She couldn't change course. And then it came to her.

Poppy was still talking. "Do you really think I'll let you do it? I am far, far stronger than you can even imagine."

For the first time to Betony's ears, the girl sounded like a queen. But Betony had the words stored up and ready to release, like arrows in a quiver.

"Your cousin, Sorrel. He yoked with her." Poppy's face creased with confusion. "She will have his baby."

She had thought the last a lie until she said it, until she saw it hit its target and pierce the heart in front of her. For Poppy clutched her breast at the truth of it, then doubled over in pain. It seemed so simple then for Betony to take the knife from her boot and stab it up and under her. The skin split softly, like fruit. And it felt merciful, like she was putting an injured creature out of its misery.

She didn't run. She knew the others would come quickly, so she waited, holding the girl's hand, watching her blink and bleed and gurgle and die.

"I'm sorry, Poppy," Betony whispered. "Leo, Danny, Charlock. I am sorry."

49

CHARLOCK

Leo got there first. He swept Poppy into his arms and, for a moment, Charlock thought that might be enough—to bring her
back to life, to bring the light back into her eyes and the color to her
cheeks. But no tears or kisses, not from either of them, could revive
her. Her head lolled and her limbs were loose and Charlock knew
she was gone. Charlock looked at Betony sitting there so placidly in
the blue beside the violent stains of red. She wanted to berate her
and beat her and break her into bits, for she knew without asking
who was to blame. Leo knew it too, as he kept asking the same
question, half-shouting, half-weeping, over and over again.

"What have you done? . . . What have you done? . . . What
have you done?" he cried, out loud and then muffled into Poppy's
body.

His words reverberated through the trees, rustling the leaves,
ruffling the peace, rattling the birds, but Betony didn't answer.
When Leo turned to leave, Charlock followed him. She was Poppy's mother. She should take the lead. A part of her mind realized
that, but the other part lagged behind. It was as though there was

a gap between events and her reaction to them that she couldn't seem to close; not since they had felt the danger and bounded through the forest, trampling over twigs and bracken, whipping through the pine needles; not since they had seen Poppy's body sprawled out on the ground, the blood pouring from her side. So Charlock hurried after Leo, trying as she might to catch up.

As soon as they approached the camp, the coven came swarming around them and the crying and wailing began. *Not that,* thought Charlock. *Not for my child.* Then suddenly time sped up and Charlock was in the present and the feeling, the terrible tsunami of feeling, flooded through her. She pushed past the crowds and went to Leo and took Poppy from his embrace into her own. Then she laid her daughter down on the grass and kept stroking her hair and her arm and her hand and then she started rubbing them as she felt the cruel coldness enter. Leo was kneeling on the other side, but he had his head lowered, his face buried in Poppy's shoulder. He was so still it seemed as though he too had died. Charlock wanted him to sit up, to do something, to help keep Poppy warm, but then there was a cry and all but Leo turned.

"Look . . . look at the stone . . . the queen stone!" came the voices.

The crowd parted as Sister Frey hurried over, holding out the stone in her hands like an offering to the dead. On it, the letters of Poppy's name were slowly fading, then vanishing. They all watched in stunned amazement as the P disappeared and then, after it, the O started to dissolve.

"Does this always happen?" Charlock croaked. "When a queen dies?"

Sister Ada answered as the eldest of the clan. "I have never heard of such a thing. I understood that one name vanished just before a new one appeared."

"What does it mean?" asked Sister Wynne.

"It means there is time," Charlock realized.

Sister Ada shook her head. "Poppy has departed. There is no time left for her."

"Get me the nightshade!" Charlock shouted. Everyone stared at her in horror, none of them moving. "Someone get it for me. Now!"

Sister Ada nodded at Kyra, who sprinted away. Then the old witch looked back at Charlock with concern. "This is the grief making you act this way. You must be strong."

But Charlock didn't look at her. Her eyes were on the stone, on the letters. The O had gone now, too, and the next P was following fast.

"Hurry," Charlock muttered to herself. "I must hurry."

And then Kyra was back and Charlock grabbed the tiny vial and popped the cork and lifted it to her mouth before a single one of them had time to stop her.

Immediately she was gagging and choking, grabbing her throat to try to squeeze the vile poison out of her, spitting what she could onto the ground. But it was slipping to her stomach, burning all the way. Then she was screaming as the agony spread like wildfire, making her body twitch and her eyes bulge from the heat of it until every vein and every sinew and every organ turned to ash and only charred stumps of them remained.

When she awoke, the pain had gone. Everything had gone. The ground, the sky, the grass—all life had disappeared, replaced by a tasteless, scentless, colorless fog. As Charlock floated through it, she saw other wandering spirits crossing a plain that was bleached of pigmentation. She looked at the other ghostly figures, but none acknowledged her. Her eyes looked past them, searching for a glimpse of Poppy.

"Poppy? . . . Poppy?" she called. Her voice seemed to fade as soon as it left her mouth as though sound as well as color were sucked from this place. "Poppy?" she sighed.

Over the dusty ground she moved, past the barren, withered trees, their branches raised like arms that reached in dying protest at their fate. The earth beneath her feet was dry and flat, but not solid like stone, more thin and brittle, like parchment. It seemed impossible to believe that joy, with all its fullness, could be found in this forsaken place. Refusing to despair, Charlock kept on calling for her daughter, her eyes searching the shadows, until, suddenly, there she was, waiting for her, as if she knew that she would come. Poppy's face, with those features that she so loved, was before her. The eyes were both gray, without their usual brilliance and contrast, but they were looking into hers. "I'm Poppy," came the voice that she had so longed to hear.

But no sooner had she heard it than a second voice answered with the same face and eyes and words. "I'm Poppy."

"I'm Poppy," said a third.

Charlock spun around. There was her daughter, so many of her, all so insistent, all seeming so real.

"Poppy!" Charlock cried in desperation, searching for a sign that might distinguish her child from the rest.

"Pick me," the first girl pleaded.

"Pick me, pick me," the others echoed.

Putting her hands over her ears, Charlock shook her head to rid herself of this torment.

"Mother . . . Mother . . . Mother," the girls lamented, and their cries tore at Charlock's heart.

It was so hard to push through and leave them behind. They were a figment born of her doubt. She knew that but still she faltered, wondering if she should turn back and talk to them, just to be certain her child wasn't among them. But she couldn't look back as that way madness lay. She must walk on, wherever that might lead.

There was no sun nor moon to give a measure of the time. Charlock couldn't tell if minutes or hours had passed. She only knew her sense of purpose was shriveling like the shrubs beneath her feet. Up ahead was a lake of lifeless water that stretched out as far as the eye could see. From it pointed blackened twigs that stabbed the air like spikes. Charlock peered at the shore. There was a shape upon it, bent like a rock. She blinked, then looked again and hurried forward.

"Poppy?" she called. It was a figure, curled on its side. "Poppy!" she called again, hardly daring to trust in what she saw in case it was a mirage like the rest. This girl didn't turn. She didn't answer or plead like all the others. Charlock's heart swelled with hope.

"Poppy," she said. "It's me." The girl turned her head slowly and gazed up, but there was no recognition in her eyes. "Do you know who you are?" Charlock asked.

The girl laid her head back down. "I'm so tired," she said. "So very tired."

"You are Poppy and I am your mother." A flicker of memory crossed Poppy's face and Charlock knew then that her words were true. "Leo is waiting for you. Leo and Ember—you remember them. They need you." Poppy didn't stir, but Charlock could tell she'd heard her. "They love you. You must go back to them."

"Am I dead?" Poppy whispered.

"You are," answered Charlock. "We both are."

Poppy looked up at her and slowly shook her head. "You shouldn't have followed me here."

"I love you," Charlock told her. She said it now knowing she would never have the chance again. "It's time for you to go back. You have to live." Poppy sat up and then stopped as though the effort were too much. "That's it. Stand up." Still she didn't move. "Do it, Poppy. Get up. Now!" Charlock ordered.

Slowly Poppy lifted herself to her feet. "What is this place?"

"It is the land of lost souls."

"Is that what we are?"

"We are not ready to let go."

Poppy looked all around her. "Then I will stay with you," she announced in a voice more her own. For a second Charlock let herself imagine it—an eternity with her child. They had never been together. She hadn't held her as a baby, or nursed her, or comforted or taught her, or scolded her. She hadn't even been loved by her. How could she let her go without feeling that just once? "I won't leave you here alone," Poppy insisted surely. And there it was. The love.

"I have come," Charlock explained, "so you may return. A whole life is waiting for you." Poppy closed her eyes and Charlock could feel the strain of the decision pulling at her. "Let me be your mother. Let me make up for all the years lost," she said. "Please—for me."

Poppy's eyes flicked open. "Come with me."

Charlock tried to smile. "I've come to take your place. It is the only way. Please, you must be quick."

"But I can't leave you here." Her voice broke as she spoke and Charlock's will almost cracked with it.

"For me, Poppy," Charlock insisted. "If you love me."

As soon as she uttered those words, Poppy's skin began to sparkle. The ghostly gray was becoming shimmering particles of light, incandescent in their beauty. They glowed until they burst. Until there was only air in place of them.

Instantly Charlock felt the emptiness and she knew nothing would ever fill it. She looked around her at the other ghosts that drifted by with their hidden, aching scars. She dreaded staying here with them and wondered when she might move on and finally rest in peace. She had done right by her child, but still she couldn't cease. Not yet. Not when there was one last guilt to atone for.

Her eyes searched through the dimness, out across the land and over the water.

"Sister," she called. "My sister!"

She looked out across the lake to where the faintest line of a horizon formed. She stared and stared until her eyes spotted a shape, only tiny, but growing bigger as it flew toward her. The raven swept down and scratched the surface of the water with its talons. In the ripples, a picture formed. There was a girl lying on the earth, her skin white, her clothes red with blood. A boy was crouching over her. Suddenly, he put his head to the girl's chest. A second passed. Then another. His mouth opened with amazement and he glanced up at the girl's face. Her lashes fluttered, almost imperceptibly. And then they opened. One eye green. The other blue. A dot above the pupil.

Charlock looked up at the bird. "Thank you."

The bird cawed. Charlock held out her arm and the bird flew down as if to perch there. Instead, its shape changed and lengthened until her sister was standing beside her, just as she had done countless times before. Charlock looked into Raven's eyes, the eyes she'd known for all her life and now in death. And then she felt it. Forgiveness.

50

LEO

A wisteria grew unfettered along the front of the house, its purple blooms crowding the brick, pressing on the glass, tickling Leo's hand as he reached for the doorbell. *Ding dong*—the sound rang in his ears and in his heart. Behind this door were his grandparents. Behind these walls, his father had once lived. Betony had told him where to come and what to expect, her parting gift to him. But still he had not been prepared for such a proper home as this; with such tall windows to either side and in a row above; with a driveway and a garage; with not just one chimney but two; and trees even in the front yard. He wondered whether he was right to have come, he with his shabby clothes and lack of money and learning. Suddenly he felt like running from this door, from his grandparents, from his past. And then he thought of Poppy. How he'd heard her heart move, one beat, then another. How he'd felt the warmth enter her body and emanate from her skin. How he'd watched the color come back to her cheeks and her eyes flicker open and her lips try to smile when she saw him. How he'd kissed her before shouting out to all the others. These thoughts made him stay and lift his head in courage. This was where he needed to be, what he needed to do. Poppy had told him so and he trusted her completely.

After they were sure that Poppy lived and breathed again, the clan switched their thoughts to Betony. They wanted to go after her and make her suffer for her treason. Leo felt his heart race with panic, though in his head there was a part of him too that wanted to see his mother punished.

Poppy raised her arm. "There will be no vengeance."

No one complained. They all backed away, compliant, and it was left to him to question her. "My mother did something terrible. I nearly lost you because of her."

"She loves you." She looked at him with serene simplicity. "And how is it going to help me or you or her to cause more pain?"

"She killed you!"

"She set me free."

"Come on. You know that wasn't her intention."

She put her hand on his chest and he knew what she'd say before she said it. "Her intention was to keep you safe. And she had good reason, didn't she?"

He took her hand and kissed it, and she pressed it to his cheek. "I've lost my mother," she spoke sadly. "Don't lose yours too."

Over his shoulder he saw a group of witches tentatively approaching.

"Sister Poppy? Can we show you?"

They were carrying the stone that held the queen's name. Poppy turned and beckoned them forward. Without a word, she took the stone from their nervous hands and studied it. There was no POPPY now, only HAWKWEED. Her name had been erased.

When she looked up at Leo, her eyes shone with relief. "I told you, didn't I? Betony set us free."

For a moment it felt like they'd been blessed, like the curse of the throne had been lifted and they could be together. The happiness soared within him, lifting his spirits to dizzying heights, but then in the distance he glimpsed Sorrel and caught the way her hands covered her belly like a shield. The knowledge felled him like an axe. Sorrel was pregnant with his child. Poppy's hand touched his arm, but he wasn't able to look at her.

"You know?" he asked. And he felt her nod. "I wasn't strong enough," he mumbled, trying to choke back the rebellious tears that were threatening to spill. "Not to stop Raven, or the other witches, or my mother from hurting you. I have no power at all—not when it matters." Poppy put her arms around him. "How can you touch me?" He squirmed in shame.

"Come with me," she whispered.

They sat on the old tattered sofa in the dell and somehow it felt like home. The air was sweet and warm and full of birdsong.

"Show me," she said, holding on to his hands.

He didn't think he knew what she meant until his mind opened of its own accord. It was hard to replay the events that had hurt him so. But this time he was not alone. He had Poppy's hands to grip onto and her strength to aid him. He felt her flinch as he ate the bread Sorrel offered. Then again at Raven's words. He felt Poppy's fingers grip him back as the rest of that brief time unfolded, but she never let go, not even after it ended.

"I'm so sorry." He closed his eyes.

"It's not your fault," she whispered. "I love you."

Leo let the words linger. He meant to reply with "I love you, too" but when he spoke, a stronger truth came out instead. "You shouldn't."

Still she kept hold of his hands. And when she spoke it was in a language he couldn't understand, but the words carried a magic within them, for he felt the memories of that encounter with Sorrel and Raven lighten. Slowly those memories lifted inside his mind until he could move them himself and decide where to let them settle.

"Was that a spell?" he asked once she'd finished.

"Mma called it a charm. She and her grandson, Teko, taught it to me. It's for healing."

"Weren't they the ones who trapped you?"

She shrugged and gave a smile. "Best intentions, remember. They were trying to protect me just as Betony was trying to protect you."

And in that moment, Leo realized he'd be able to forgive his mother and the relief of this rushed through him.

"We have to forgive Sorrel too," Poppy said, sensing his thoughts.

"What about Raven?" He felt her stiffen. "Could she come back?"

"She got what she wanted." Suddenly Leo understood she meant the baby. His baby. "And my mother will keep Raven with her."

He took Poppy's hands again and felt the electricity tingle there. "Nothing will change this. Ever."

She smiled and leaned forward, and he sealed this promise with a kiss.

I love you too, came the thought. This time he said it out loud and the words came strong and sure.

So here he was, standing before the door of his father's house, waiting to meet his relatives. Poppy too had somewhere she needed to be. Her "purpose," she called it.

He had put his arms around her, smelled her skin, felt her body pressing against his, and wondered how he'd ever walk away.

"It'll be fine," she'd said, releasing him with her words, but not her arms. Not yet. "It's just my turn to wait for you, that's all."

Ding dong. A figure moved along the hallway toward the door. The breath caught in Leo's throat as he circled so fast from past to present and his mind centered on this one moment in time. The door began to open. He felt himself tremble with fear . . . then hope. There before him stood a man with eyes and mouth and skin like his, only older and more lined. The man opened his mouth to greet him, but no sound came. He just stared and blinked and then his hands flew to his face and tears sprang to his eyes.

"Danny?" he whispered. "My boy?"

51

POPPY

After Leo had gone, the witches started collecting branches for a funeral pyre. Poppy made them stop. She wouldn't have her mother burned, her ashes scattered to the wind. It would feel like losing her again. After a childhood full of mystery, she wanted something permanent, somewhere that she could visit Charlock, someplace that felt like home. She headed back into the forest.

Betony hadn't moved. She sat like a sculpture, striking a defeated pose, the orange of her hair clashing with the bluebells. *My executioner,* thought Poppy, though she seemed too small and slight for such an act. Too beautiful. But Poppy felt the scar just beneath her ribs where the knife had struck and remembered Betony's arm swinging back, then forward, driving the blade in. It hadn't hurt, not as much as she'd have imagined. The pain of Betony's words had been far worse.

Betony seemed neither surprised nor scared to see her victim standing there alive and well.

"You lived," she uttered.

"My mother saved me."

Betony looked down at her palm and rubbed it. "We thought it was friends first. But that was before we were mothers."

"The scar," Poppy realized. "My mother had one too."

"Had?" echoed Betony.

"It was the only way she could bring me back."

At that, Betony's face thawed and her features seemed to melt with the falling tears. "Charlock," she cried softly. "Oh, Charlock." Then she looked at Poppy. "If you've come for revenge, I am ready to die."

Again Poppy could feel the knife slipping in, the life slipping out. She waited for the anger and fear to arrive, but only sadness entered. "I haven't come to kill you. I've come for you to bury her.

"Come on." She knelt down and took Betony's hand. "It's what Charlock would have wanted."

They had the sisters bring Charlock's body to them. Then alone they dug a grave among the silver birches, in the very spot where as girls Betony and Charlock used to play. It was there, Betony told Poppy, they'd made their pledge before their first yoking day, where they'd cut their skin and pressed their palms together.

"I wish I could forget it all again. It is too painful," Betony choked.

"Do you?" asked Poppy.

Betony lowered her head, then gave it the slightest of shakes. "Remembering is an agony but of the sweetest kind. Charlock was my only friend. I'll keep hold of any part of her I can."

Tenderly, Betony washed the blood from Charlock's eyes and the spit from her chin. She combed her hair and changed her stained clothes, then she sat and held her hand for a while. Finally, she looked up at Poppy.

"I hope one day your daughter has her eyes."

And Poppy began to weep then, sobbing as they lifted her mother's body and lowered her into the ground, crying as they pushed the earth upon her. At last their work was done. Their arms and backs ached, their hands dark with earth, their knees sore.

"Forgive me," Betony whispered to the grave.

As they walked away, she took Poppy's hand and Poppy felt a comfort from it that only hours before she could never have imagined.

When Poppy left the next day, she took Betony with her. Leo might be ready to forgive his mother, but the clan was not. Betony resisted the idea at first, wanting to stay close to where Leo was.

"He will come to us," Poppy told her. "I promise."

At her neck, the heart stone glowed and Poppy felt its warmth on her skin and inside her chest. Betony's eyes widened as she saw it and she nodded her agreement to the plan.

"You're not leaving?" came a voice from behind them. Sorrel was looking scared and full of grief. "It is not because of me, I hope. Because I am so sorry." Her voice cracked as she began to cry. "I am so very sorry."

"It's not your fault." As Poppy said it, she felt it change from fact to truth.

"It was Raven," Sorrel sniveled, nose and eyes running with remorse.

"We know." Poppy nodded.

"I wasn't myself."

"We know."

"What can I do to make amends?" The scar along Sorrel's cheek was a livid red reminder of past pain.

"Nothing," Poppy replied. "It stops here. We can mend ourselves."

But Sorrel reached for Poppy's hands and bent her head to them in supplication. "Please," she whispered. "Let me do something to make things better."

She needed a task, a mission, just as Charlock had, so Poppy gave her one. It was the one that Sorrel was raised for. "You are a Hawkweed. It is your time to take the throne and keep it safe."

Sorrel's head shot up. "I can't. I'm not strong enough. Not without my mother."

"Not your mother this time. Me. I will help you."

"You will?" Sorrel stared at her in disbelief.

"I won't be here. But I will always be ready to help. You and them." Poppy looked around at the other sisters. "And others too. I think helping people to heal is my purpose."

Sorrel took Poppy's hand and pulled her to the caravan steps where they couldn't be heard by anyone.

"My mother said the baby will be a girl," she whispered. "I am worried she is Raven's child, not mine."

Fear flapped inside Poppy. She squeezed Sorrel's hand. "You are her mother. Only you. But take care—this baby will be powerful, with magic on both sides. Perhaps more powerful than any of us."

It only took a second for Poppy to regret her words. Already Sorrel's hands had drifted to her belly as if placing an unseen crown on an unborn head.

"It's true," she murmured. "My mother said so too."

Poppy closed her eyes for a moment. She was almost able to see it—the tiny sprout of ambition poking through the earth of Sorrel's mind. Even then she knew she should have cautioned her against it. She should have said a charm or cast a spell. But, to her shame, she couldn't dwell on that baby any longer.

"The stone," she said instead. "It's time."

Kyra brought it to them, her usual feistiness replaced with a new humility. "I'm sorry I ever doubted you."

"Call and I will hear you," promised Poppy, and Kyra nodded. Then Poppy turned to Sorrel. "Shall we?"

Together they walked to the tree trunk and placed the stone at the center of its rings. And before their eyes, new twigs appeared with new shoots bursting from them, rising up and around the stone like a throne.

Poppy and Betony made their way between the trees. The air was full of pine and bark and forest flowers. To Poppy, it smelled of Ember.

"It must be hard to leave this place again," she said to Betony.

Betony turned and took one last look at the camp. "It stopped being my home a long time ago."

"There's one more I must collect on our way. She's spent too many years alone, without a home. You understand?"

Betony nodded and they began to walk, through the forest, over the hills. Southward.

Melanie didn't look surprised to see them. She seemed relieved, letting Poppy take her hands and listening to the charm.

There was a second's fear when Poppy told her they were leaving and that she was coming with them. Then she went upstairs and packed her bag. She didn't question where they were going or ask to return home. Not even when they arrived in another country, a city with cobbled streets and old buildings with yellowed stone and dark slate roofs, a place where old and new, ugly and beautiful, all had style. Not even when they passed the busy shops and noisy cafés and the river crossed with bridges. She walked quietly beside Betony, following Poppy's lead. When they saw the Eiffel Tower carved into the Paris sky, she beamed. And when she saw Ember cutting through the crowds, running so fast toward them, she cried.

Poppy felt Ember's arms around her, encircling her with love. Melanie's too. She reached out a hand and pulled Betony into the embrace. Not outsiders anymore, none of them, but belonging, all. Only one was missing, but he would come. He'd be with them soon. For now, she let herself feel cherished.

My coven, Poppy thought. *My clan.*

ACKNOWLEDGMENTS

This is a story about sisterhood and clans, and I am so lucky to have so many of both to thank . . .

First of all, the clan at Hachette Books who turned this story into such a fine looking book. I thank you all. At Orchard Books, my wonderful publishers in the UK. At Felicity Bryan Associates, Inkwell Management, and Andrew Nurnberg Associates.

Cindy Eagan for all the superb edits and refinements, and for her generosity of spirit. Your emails are like a hug reaching out to me across the Atlantic. Sarah Leonard, my brilliant UK editor, for all her many spot-on suggestions. Catherine Clarke and Catherine Drayton for their support and sage advice.

My friends, Michelle Coulter who read all these pages on a laptop on her holiday and is always there for me; Norma Kelly who learned how to make a website, how to set up twitter, and where the hashtag key was just to help me out; Debra King who proofread for me despite having a million other things on her plate; Kirstin Stewart for all the info on Africa; and all my inspirational Write Club clan, Kathryn Stokes Arbour, Vicky Zimmerman, Courtney Clelland, Tash Bell, and Jess Kimmel.

My own clan, here and in Greece, especially my mum, Voula Tavoulari-Brignull, my biggest fan; my dad, Tony Brignull, for making me want to write in the first place; my forever pals—my sister, Rosie, and brother, Harry; my long-time partner in all, Billy, proof that "insta-love" can last and even get better; and my children, my best bits, Theo, Athina, and Phoenix.